Cyrus Cobb

The Veteran of the Grand Army

Cyrus Cobb

The Veteran of the Grand Army

ISBN/EAN: 9783337064990

Printed in Europe, USA, Canada, Australia, Japan

Cover: Foto ©Andreas Hilbeck / pixelio.de

More available books at **www.hansebooks.com**

THE

VETERAN OF THE GRAND ARMY.

A NOVEL.

BY THE BROTHERS COBB.

IN EIGHT PARTS.

BOSTON:
CYRUS AND DARIUS COBB,
228 Washington Street.
1870.

University Press: Welch, Bigelow, & Co.,
Cambridge.

TO

The Grand Army of the Republic,

WHOSE SUBLIME PURPOSE IS TO BIND THE DEFENDERS OF THE
UNION IN ONE GREAT BROTHERHOOD; TO GUARD AND
PROTECT THE FAMILIES OF THEIR FALLEN COM-
RADES, DEAD, AND OF THEIR DISABLED
COMRADES, LIVING; TO TEND THE
EVERLASTING FIRES ON
THE SACRED ALTAR
OF LIBERTY,

THIS WORK IS FRATERNALLY DEDICATED

BY

CYRUS AND DARIUS COBB,

Post 30, *Dep't Mass.*

THE VETERAN OF THE GRAND ARMY.

CHAPTER I.

NIGHT was settling over the city of New York. It was in the fall of 1866. Wall Street had been through one of its fiercest campaigns of that year; but now, as the darkened sky looked down on this field of many battles, it gazed upon a field of silence. The bulls had retired triumphant, the bears discomfited. In other words, one set of speculators had gone home to count up their increased fortunes; the other to contemplate their ruin.

About eight o'clock a man issued from a broker's office near the Treasury Building, and looking upwards, around, and then downwards, as if he were uncertain whether he trod on solid earth or not, he turned and wended his way with an unsteady step to his store; for this man was not a professional speculator, but a dry-goods merchant, who had caught the fever of speculation.

As he passed through the store to his counting-room, the few clerks who remained for special duty looked after him, and exchanged significant glances.

Closing the door of the counting-room, he fell into a chair and buried his face in his hands.

As the gas-light strikes down upon him while he thus sits, a picture of despair, his thin, yellowish hair matted with perspiration, and his long, bony fingers clutched and quivering in the midst of these scanty locks, one cannot withhold from him a profound sympathy.

At length he uncovers his face, and rising, he paces up and down the office. Presently he stops, and resting one hand on the desk, he fixes his eye on a photograph which hangs on the partition that separates the counting-room from the store, and mutters to himself.

The name of this merchant who suffers so much is Jonas Cringar.

As he stands before us, he appears to be a little over fifty years of age. He is tall, and his shoulders are somewhat bent. His thin hair, and rather bristly beard, which he wears full and of moderate length, are mixed sandy and yellow. His eyes are blue, and have a cast in them; and while they indicate a kindness of disposition, they also convey an impression of obliquity in his character. His nose is nearly straight.

His mouth has a peculiar expression. It is somewhat long and well compressed, as it appears under the trimmed mustache; but mingled with this compression, which to the casual eye would convey an idea of great firmness, is an expression of weakness, not unlike that which is seen in the mouths of certain inebriates.

The whole face, in moments of excitement, is drawn down and elongated.

As he gazed on the photograph, which was the likeness of a man dressed in the uniform of a captain of infantry, his muttering gave place to a silent look of intense mental anguish, his face being drawn down to an extraordinary degree.

Suddenly he started, looked at his watch, and with an effort at self-control, stepped to the door, and told the remaining clerks they could leave and he would lock up.

Cringar stood looking at the clerks as they retired. One seemed to delay.

"Will you leave?" cried the merchant in an abrupt, harsh voice.

The clerk turned at the sound of this voice; but if he was intending to speak, he was silenced by the haggard expression of his employer's face, and quietly turning to the door, he was about to open it, when a man entered from the street.

"Garvin!" muttered the clerk as he passed him; "he's doing Cringar no good. Any one can see that with half an eye."

As this man entered, Jonas Cringar trembled, and drew back into the counting-room.

The new-comer walked through the store, while his boots seemed to vindictively grind the dust of the floor at every step; and as he crossed the threshold of the counting-room, he extended his hand to the merchant, and exclaimed in a harsh, metallic voice:—

"How are you?"

Cringar instinctively drew back. But as his eye met the glance of his visitor, he stepped forward and took the proffered hand, allowing his to remain till the other saw fit to drop it; which doing, the latter seated himself, not removing his eyes from the merchant.

It is plain that he is a man of power. As he removes his hat, which is still done without taking his eyes from Cringar, the light brings his head and features out in bold relief, affording a striking contrast to the appearance of the merchant.

His head and face are broad, the complexion dark. That which first strikes the beholder is the eye and mouth. The iris is of a greenish-gray hue, which usually is rather dark, and not remarkably brilliant. But when the mind and will seem actively at work, as at the present time, there appears a light ring, which expands and contracts, sometimes almost filling the space around the pupil, and again forming simply a narrow band, giving the iris an appearance of varied colors, and an expression as cruel as in the eye of the beast of prey.

There is, however, with their fixedness of look, a certain restlessness in these eyes, scarcely to be called a motion, as if they were ever on the watch at a post of danger. The mouth unites in this restlessness.

The upper lip, though firm and biting, has a continual tendency to show the white upper teeth, as if it were in constant expectation of these fangs leaping out to fasten themselves on a victim.

The upper lip and chin are shaven, the whiskers starting from the corners of the mouth, and extending in a downward angle back of the jaw.

His forehead is capacious, and rounds into thin, dark hair, which is sprinkled (as are the whiskers) with gray, and fast giving way to baldness, with also a peculiar dryness, as if the heat of an incessantly plotting brain were gradually withering it away.

Such was the man who now sat with his eye fixed on the haggard merchant. His name was Daniel Garvin; his business a Wall Street broker.

"You don't look well to-night, Cringar," he said, after a quick glance to the photograph and back again.

"No, I'm not feeling well to-night."

"The battle's been too much for you, eh?" And Garvin laid his hat on a chair near him, and slowly rubbed the palms of his hands.

The only answer Cringar gave was an inward groan.

"You went with the bears, eh?"

"I understood from you —"

"Pshaw, man! — well, what? you understood what?"

"I understood that we should be sure to win." And Jonas Cringar again groaned.

"This is your reward."

"My reward?"

"For not putting faith in *me*."

"You always bear the market."

"Not always. For instance, to-day a man with eyes half open could n't have failed to see how the thing was going to turn. There are times when a man must doff his claws and don his horns."

Garvin gave vent to a rapid guttural laugh as he uttered this witticism, but Cringar looked as if this mirth would be as appropriate over a new-made grave. Rising from his chair, he walked to the door, turning his back to his tormentor.

The broker contemplated him a moment, while the rings in his eyes seemed to gleam with a phosphorescent light. Suddenly he spoke with his abrupt, harsh voice: —

"Cringar!"

The merchant turned as if he had received a shock from a galvanic battery. As he met the deadly eyes of the broker, he blanched, for he saw there was a struggle coming, and to enter into a struggle with this man was to engage with a relentless foe.

"Cringar, you 're not playing true with me."

The merchant was stung.

"Playing true with you, sir!" he exclaimed, in a voice which indicated a courage of which he was capable at times. "Do you have the face to fling that at me?"

The broker's eye gleamed with a grim smile, and his upper lip begun to play, revealing his fangs.

"What am I to-night, sir?" continued Cringar, "and who has brought me to it?"

"Well, what are you?" rejoined Garvin, in a sarcastic voice, exquisitely cutting.

"A ruined man!"

"Not so fast, not so fast, Mr. Cringar. You're not ruined yet."

"Ay, a ruined man!"

The merchant's countenance assumed an aspect of profound desperation.

"Pshaw, man!" said Garvin, who now changed his voice to a tone in which consolation and contempt vied for the mastery; "so long as a man *is* a man he should n't despair. Now I think I can get you out of the bog, and set you on your pins all right."

Jonas Cringar turned on the broker fiercely.

"Despair! Set me on my pins all right! Be done with these lies!"

Daniel Garvin sprang to his feet. But this time his eyes met the eyes of a man who, not lacking in a certain degree of strength, was now roused to desperation. The merchant waved his hand for the broker to be seated, and his rounded shoulders straightened into something like majesty.

"I say, be done, Daniel Garvin, and hear me! You have deceived me from beginning to end! Professing to take me into your confidence, that you might get mine, you have made me your dupe, and the victim of your machinations! You it is who have tempted me from my legitimate business into speculation, and the crimes which this damnable curse gives birth to! I am a defaulter, and, with no power left to help myself, I am ruined. To-day's business has finished me! I am gone!"

With these last words the merchant sank into his chair, and covered his face with his hand.

Garvin's eye seemed for a moment to be disturbed by a sentiment of pity. But if so, it was only for a moment; for it instantly settled into a cruel, triumphant look, as he contemplated his victim.

"You speak like a madman, Cringar," he at length said.

The merchant's only response was a tighter clasping of his forehead in his bony fingers.

"You speak like a boy who, thinking he can swim, follows another who goes into deep water, and because he finds he can't swim, he splutters out that the other has drowned him."

The merchant did not move.

"You are pleased to say that you are a defaulter through my machinations, as you call it. This is nonsense. Because you take money of a company in which you have a strong interest, and, as treasurer, deem it wise to invest it for a short time for the benefit of the company, is that a crime? If you did n't succeed, it was your misfortune, but no crime."

Cringar raised his head, and viewed this utterer of plausible sophistries with gloomy eyes.

"Your sentiments, sir," he said, "are destroying scores of men who have stood as I once stood. It's of no use. I 'm a defaulter, and the world has got to know it."

"Why has it? You 're not a dead beat."

"I *am* a dead beat. I have lost forty thousand dollars of the company's money, and curse the day I ever touched it; and to-day I have given notes that cover all my available property, including every cent I have in this store."

He now rose, and, turning, gazed in gloomy despair through the counting-room window into the store.

The broker also rose. Unobserved by the merchant he stood before the photograph, and bent upon it a dark, malevolent gaze. Then he placed his hand on Cringar's shoulder.

CHAPTER II.

"NOW, Cringar," said Garvin in a voice which he knew well how to use, "I can get you out of all this difficulty. Perhaps my method of doing business is n't the method for you to adopt. Now that you have come out so unfortunately, I 'm inclined to think it is so. If I made a mistake in judgment in this respect, it is unfair to make me guilty of much that is worse. I have meant you well, as I call my conscience to witness. I don't mean to say that my methods of doing business are perfect, when viewed by the standard of the old style. Speculation may be a dangerous thing, and may lead to acts as risky as war does, and to strategic deception, as war does; but war is necessary at times, and so is speculation."

His auditor did not move, so he continued.

"Now that you are dead beat, and say it 's of no use for you to try to keep your head up any longer, — in short *ruined*, as you put it, — what harm can there be in giving me a fair chance of bringing you out? I can do it."

These last words were spoken with strong emphasis, and caused the merchant to turn.

Garvin smiled in his face.

"Cringar," he said, showing his white teeth, while his ring-gleaming eyes restlessly passed and repassed from one eye of the merchant to the other, — "Cringar, if you really consider yourself dead, what harm in letting me try a little surgery, with the guaranty that I will make you live ?"

Jonas Cringar's mouth began to work, and his face to elongate in a manner which the broker understood.

He knew he had conquered.

He took the merchant's unresisting hand.

"Now, Cringar," he said, "let us be friends; at least," he added with a smile, "until we have you out of this terrible fix."

Cringar was not convinced of Garvin's sincerity. But it was life or death with him, and he now listened with the resignation of despair to anything he might propose.

When he told Garvin that he had made him a victim of his machinations, he told the truth.

But he was not the chief object of these machinations.

He was simply the tool.

The original of the photograph which we have seen the merchant contemplate with such emotion, and the broker with such malignity, is the man on whom the latter's evil eye is ultimately fixed.

The name of this man is Allen Paige, half-brother to Garvin, and partner to Cringar.

A merchant in uniform is but one of the many sublime anomalies of the Rebellion.

From the opening of this mighty struggle for the destruction of freedom on the one hand, and the maintenance of it on the other, Allen Paige yearned to join the conflict.

For over three years it was impossible.

In the fall of 1864 he would endure it no longer. He determined it should no longer be impossible. Leaving the business in charge of his partner, he went to the front with the rank of Captain.

He fought in the Army of the Potomac, and rapidly mounted to the rank of Lieutenant-Colonel.

At the battle of Petersburg he was wounded for the first time. A ball from a Rebel sharpshooter struck him in the right breast as he was bending forward, and penetrated to the lower part of the spine. It was a frightful wound; but no vital was hit, and he was not killed. He commenced to die from that time, however, and had been slowly but surely wasting away.

Though younger than Cringar, he was the senior partner, the style of the firm being PAIGE & CRINGAR, for his superior tact and energy had been mainly instrumental in building up the business.

But though shrewd and energetic in his business, he was free and open-hearted, to a fault. Quick to trust those whom he called his friends, and slow to suspect them.

Up to the time of his return, wounded and disabled, from the war, and for several months afterwards, nothing was done by Jonas Cringar in violation of good faith with his partner.

But within the past two or three months a change had taken place. A serpent had commenced to wind about Jonas Cringar. This serpent was Daniel Garvin.

The half-brothers took their characters, each from his father. Daniel's father, the mother's first husband, was a dark, scheming, tyrannical man, who made his wife miserable. Allen's father, the second husband, was a noble, open, generous man, who made his wife the happiest of women.

After his mother's second marriage, and the birth of Allen, Daniel felt himself outlawed. He heard much of his dark father and his resemblance to him.

He hated his half-brother, but his natural craftiness warned him to hate in secret. He concealed it by a general moodiness, under cover of which he would, in boyhood, dart out and make his unsuspecting brother feel the weight of his pent-up vengeance.

It thus occurred that while he, with more or less frequency, gave open expression to his hatred, it was not attributed to hatred, but to the ungovernable display of a bad and moody temper.

The mother and second husband were now dead; and Daniel's secret hatred was not diminished by the manner in which the property had been bequeathed. The bulk of it went to the detested half-brother.

Avarice is not the least of the dark passions that govern a nature like Daniel's. When he found himself comparitively disinherited, his hatred was resolved into implacable vengeance, and his avarice devoured him with an unquenchable thirst for his brother's riches.

But the stronger his internal passions, the more solicitously he concealed them.

When Allen Paige returned with his terrible wound, Daniel Garvin made pretence of sympathy. He called at the house, and his countenance assumed an expression of the profoundest pity as the wound was unbound and exposed to sight. He declared, with well-simulated impulsive candor, that he had up to the moment he first beheld this fearful wound entertained toward Allen a feeling of bitterness; but to look upon him now would turn a heart of stone. He clasped him by the hand, and helped dress his wound: and who so tender as one of these men when his schemes demand it?

But the only sincere emotion that found a place in his bosom, as he now often stood by the side of his suffering half-brother, was the secret but intense satisfaction with which he saw that he was gradually and surely dying!

We will return to Jonas Cringar.

Through this man of complicated strength and weakness, Garvin commenced active operations.

A short time before Paige's enlistment an agreement had been signed between the partners, that neither should engage in any outside speculations.

This was a barrier. If once broken, it would place him between these two partners, enabling him to take the enemy in detail.

With his varied arts he labored to entangle Cringar in the interdicted outside speculations. He was successful. Fire brought in contact with wood is not more certain of kindling a flame than was the flaming temptation of speculation — rampant in those days, and spreading like some vast conflagration — of starting into a blaze the lust for wealth of Jonas Cringar, when once the broker's arts had been brought to bear upon him.

Once entangled, and the victim could only struggle. The history of scores who have been held up to notoriety in these past few years is his history.

The demon of speculation first devoured all his own immediately available means; then into its maw went forty thousand dollars, held by him as treasurer of a Nevada silver mining company; and now, on the day which opens this tale, he has given notes, with collateral security, which cover all property he had remaining.

Through it all his evil genius was leading him on with false hopes and pictures of chimerical fortunes. For once, as we have seen, he had in his desperation been able to tear himself from Daniel Garvin, and trust his fortunes in another broker's hands.

In his downward course, beside his criminal use of the funds intrusted to him as treasurer, he had committed acts which, as he thought of them, made him tremble.

* * * * *

At length Garvin had his struggling victim in his power. He now prepared to push forward his ultimate design.

A few days previous to their introduction to the reader, he had dropped into Cringar's ear a dark and diabolical hint.

This hint revealed, as in a twilight, an atrocious plot.

This plot was the robbery of the widow and orphan children of the patriot half-brother.

By means of his subtle arts, he had been appointed, with Cringar, executor of his step-brother's will. As executors, they would accomplish the work.

Jonas Cringar had entertained a sincere affection for his partner, and had been received into his home as one of the family. But he possessed not the character for a long fight against the powers of darkness, for the sake either of affection or principle.

On this day that had decided his fate in Wall Street, he had, as has been before stated, ventured to make an effort for freedom, by engaging the services of another broker. He had got wind of a certain great combination of the bears, and having possession of what he believed to be valuable points, he put up a margin on a large amount of the beared stock; and as the tide, to the dismay of all bears, unexpectedly set in against them, "more margin" was called for, and again "more margin," each time with a yet more frantic voice, and at each call the merchant covering with yet increasing desperation, till the crash came, and blasted his last hope.

We have seen him stagger to his store, and have witnessed his anguish, alone, and his desperation in the presence of Daniel Garvin.

We left him passively awaiting a proposition from the broker.

"I will tell you what I will do," said Garvin. "I will give you the advantage of knowledge which I possess of the operations of a certain ring, that I am not permitted to speak of now to any one outside of it. Suffice it that you have seen me win, and I tell you I shall win again."

"My margin," uttered the merchant in a gloomy voice.

"That is what I am coming to. There is no difficulty about it at all. I will give you acknowledgment of margin without cash down. I recognize that you have n't always been fortunate in your ventures with me, but now I am master of secrets that will insure success, *taurine* or *ursine*. You can repay me afterwards."

A gleam of hope lit up the gloom of the merchant.

"Mr. Garvin," he said, "give me a start that will enable me to pay that money back in the treasury of the Bald-Eagle Silver Mining Company, and I'll bless you with prayers."

"It shall be done!" exclaimed the broker decisively, bringing his hand with a familiar slap on Cringar's knee.

Then fixing his malevolent eye on the wavering orb of the merchant, he said in a low, ominous voice, —

"But, Cringar, the night is going by, and I have important business to propose, which cannot be longer delayed."

Cringar's eyes suddenly became fixed in a frightened stare, but he remained silent.

"First take that away," said the broker in a voice in

which command and guilt mingled; and he pointed to the photograph of his half-brother.

Cringar hesitated, but starting spasmodically from his chair, he took down the photograph and set it on the floor outside the counting-room, face to against the wall.

When he had again seated himself, the broker proceeded to disclose his plot against the original of this unendurable photograph.

As Daniel Garvin commenced to unfold his diabolical scheme, the perspiration which had disappeared from the merchant's forehead began again to make its appearance; and it increased as the broker proceeded, until, no longer able to endure the terrible eye that was fixed upon him, he dropped his head into his hands, and soon he formed a repetition of the picture which he presented just after entering the counting-room from the street. His hair again became matted, and his long bony fingers again quiveringly clutched his head under the scanty locks.

The broker marked the effect he was producing with Satanic triumph. Each separate matted lock, and each long, quivering finger, seemed to cry out to him, —

"*Master, behold your slave!*"

At length he finished, and then sat contemplating the suffering merchant, who seemed too stunned to move.

Jonas Cringar finally raised his head, and as his face met the light it seemed to have grown, in the last five minutes, twenty years older. It was drawn to an unwonted length, and his chest heaved as if some heavy weight were pressing upon it.

He rose from his seat, and with an unsteady, and sort of tottering stride, he passed and repassed between the door and chair, clutching the back of the latter each time he approached it, as if for support.

At last he stopped with his hand clasping the back of the chair, and turned to Garvin.

At this instant the store door was thrown open and a man hastened to the counting-room and exclaimed, —

"Mr. Paige is dying!"

CHAPTER III.

THE chamber in which Allen Paige had been confined an invalid for so long a time was located in the L of the house, which was situated on West Twenty-seventh Street. It received the sun throughout the greater part of the day, and this fact, together with its seclusion from the noise of passing vehicles, had rendered it peculiarly favorable as a room for an invalid unusually sensitive to chill and noise. Here, with his wife and daughter to attend him, he spent month after month of uncomplaining illness, rather inspiring those around him with buoyant spirits, than seeming to need such inspiration himself.

As we have said, his nature was free and generous, and his desire to cause no trouble on his account, combined with a natural elasticity of spirits, had filled this sick-chamber with an almost perpetual sunshine, even when the clouds hid the sun in the sky. I say almost perpetual, for times there were when even his elastic courage was unable to conquer the pain which would occasionally come on in an unexpected moment, and seizing him in its grip, compel a groan of agony.

Such moments served, however, to reveal in stronger light the fortitude of this patient sufferer; and not unfrequently the affectionate mother or daughter, touched too deeply by this display of suffering, and by the thought of much more suffering which was endured in silence, being unable to control their emotions would hastily quit the room and weep.

But he was not often deceived. The reddened eye would tell the tale, and then he would put on so playful and sportive an air that she who but a short time before was weeping would now find herself smiling and laughing as if all were enjoyment.

It was rare that these devoted nurses permitted any one to take their place; and often as the wounded soldier lay and gazed upon them in the midst of their tender labors, he would silently call down upon them the benedictions of Heaven.

Isabel, the wife of Allen Paige, was one of those women of whom many are found to redeem the sex from the obloquy, which is often unjustly attached to it through that class whose houses are the dry-good stores, and whose firesides are the opera.

Her appearance prepossesses the beholder at once. Of medium height, her countenance especially impresses one with its goodness. She possesses beauty to a high degree; but her air is so marked of one who devotes herself to the duties of life, to the entire exclusion of all vanity, that the beholder instinctively shrinks from gazing upon her countenance with any thought of this beauty only as it expresses her virtues. Her form is noble, and a grace pervades it, which advancing years cannot remove.

Emma, the eldest daughter, is nineteen years of age, and rarely does the eye find such pleasure as in the contemplation of this charming girl.

She is not so tall as her mother, but equally well proportioned, her form impressing one with an exquisite combination of lightness, grace, and maidenly dignity. Her eye is of a dark hazel; her nose just enough relieved from the straight to give life and character; her mouth full and finely formed, with a certain action, as the lips meet in the middle, which I have observed to be accompanied with purity; her face is a full oval, with an expression, as the cheek descends in a rich curve from the ear to the chin, which implies great force of character with a remarkably affectionate disposition; her hair is of a rich brown, and is slightly brushed away in a waving roll from a classic forehead, which, with its purely feminine air of thought, affords a fit crown for all the other beauties of the face.

Besides Emma, there are three other children of this family: Alice, a charming and faithful young girl of thirteen years, who proves herself of great aid in the attendance on her father; Albert, a thoughtful boy, two years younger, who, even at this early age, is at the head of the first class of the public school; and Little Dorrit, as they call her, her name being Dora, who is seven years old, and the pet of the whole family.

On the day previous to the one which has opened our story, Allen Paige had begun to sink rapidly, and as this succeeding day dragged its painful hours, it was evident that the moment of dissolution was near at hand.

He seemed insensible most of the day, but as evening approached he indicated returning consciousness.

It was about six o'clock. He had in his wanderings been giving orders to his men, whom he fancied marching with him into battle.

"By the right flank! — Steady, men! — Halt! — Ready — aim — fire! — Steady! — Fire at will! — First Company deploy as skirmishers!" were incoherently uttered at intervals, as he might imagine himself a line or field officer.

There was something inexpressibly touching in the manner of the mother and eldest daughter, as they listened to this raving re-enactment of these terrible scenes of battle.

While grief took possession of their countenances, there was yet mingled with it an expression of tender pride, as they seemed to witness in his unconscious pictures those acts of bravery which had won him distinction in the field. They saw their husband and father marching to his duty as a patriot who loved his country and was ready to die for it; and, in their sorrow, their souls seemed pervaded by the lofty sentiment that, though spared to them for so many months, now were they ready to yield him a sacrifice on the altar of his country.

A soldier's family, — his widow, his orphan children; they who gave their protector and support to their country, strengthening him with their love, encouragement, and blessing, and thanking God that they could give one to fight for Liberty; — what objects more worthy the protection of a preserved nation?

Such thoughts cannot fail to inspire the breast of him who beholds the scene around the dying bed of this patriot soldier.

As the dying man was in the midst of an order to storm the breastworks of the enemy, he awoke to consciousness.

At this instant the rays of the setting sun were cast in golden light across his face.

The wife made a movement to close the curtain, but by a look he detained her.

"Let it rest upon me," he faintly uttered. "I would fain let this messenger from the skies baptize me before I go hence. Ah! how near heaven seems to me now!"

By a beautiful coincidence, as he uttered these words, a soft strain of music floated through the air, and seemed to mingle its harmonies with these baptizing rays of the golden sun.

This music, so enchanting and so opportune, was produced by a quartette of male and female voices, who were rehearsing that beautiful chant, "THY WILL BE DONE," in tones of exquisite harmony and sentiment.

As the closing words of each verse, "THY WILL BE DONE," floated into the chamber, and reached the ears of the dying patriot, his countenance kindled with adoration, and his dimming eyes turned to heaven, while his lips moved as if he were joining in the chant with invisible angels.

It was not sorrow; it was not grief; but tears rolled down the cheeks of the mother and daughter, and they knelt by the bedside, and with clasped hands silently united in this inspired prayer to Heaven, while Alice and her brother Albert stood in reverent awe, their youthful souls penetrated by the touching sacredness of this scene.

As the third verse was bearing these adoring souls upward to God, the door was silently opened by the servant, and a young man crossed the threshold.

The scene before him caused him to pause, and he stood immovable as he contemplated this profoundly impressive picture.

The sun's rays had passed the face of the soldier, and now with even a yet more glorious light, appeared to encircle his head with the sacred nimbus, while the music, filling the room from an unseen source, seemed in combination with this light to come from the unseen world.

This young man was of a nature rendering him unusually impressible to such a scene; and as he stood by the threshold without moving, a trembling seized him, and his eyes were suffused with tears. His effeminate face, slightly touched with a downy beard, his full blue eyes, and fine, light, wavy hair, at once indicate this sensitive nature, combined as they are with a slight and delicate form.

His soul is evidently kindred with the soul of the family before him, for his emotions seem not merely quickened by the outward picture, but from a deep sympathy of spirit.

The last tones of the chant now hover through the room, and as they die away, the golden light, lingering a moment afterwards, like some sweet refrain, passes away with them, leaving silence and the shades of evening in their place.

Allen Paige now turned his head, and the wife and daughter rose. Looking toward the door he smiled, and Mrs. Paige, turning, discovered the visitor.

He was now greeted as if he were one of the family, and he came forward and spoke to his uncle; for, strange as was the anomaly, this light, delicate, and ethereal young man was the son of Daniel Garvin.

And yet not so strange, for he was a complete transcript of his mother, whose delicate organization, with her uncontrollable sensitiveness, had yielded to the harsh contact of the father's unfeeling and aggressive nature, and found that peace in death which she never found after her marriage in life.

William, for this was his name, now offered to act as nurse for a while; and with the promise that he would call them at the first indication of a change, the family, yielding to the desires of the now somewhat reviving patient, left the room for a brief respite from the cares of the sick-chamber, and to attend to necessary household duties.

Soon after they had retired, the soldier fell into a quiet sleep.

He slept thus for about two hours. When he awoke it was evident the end was approaching. There was a marked change, which the doctor, who came in a few moments afterwards, pronounced the change of death.

The family were now called to the bedside, and the

dying man, having expressed a desire that his brother and partner should be present before he passed away, William Garvin volunteered to seek them.

It was he who entered the store so suddenly, and gave the announcement as recorded at the close of the second chapter.

On the utterance of this announcement, the broker took his hat, and, with a meaning glance at the merchant, went out of the counting-room in silence.

Jonas Cringar followed, also in silence.

Both were startled; but while Daniel Garvin recovered himself immediately, the merchant shivered perceptibly as he followed the former out of the store, and his long hands clenched and unclenched themselves incessantly, indicating a terrible conflict.

As they entered the chamber, Allen Paige greeted them with a look which long afterwards haunted Jonas Cringar, and then turned his eyes with an imploring glance on his family.

They approached the bed, but, as the dying soldier attempted to speak, his tongue refused its office, and with another of those looks, which were destined to disturb the future sleep of the merchant, he relapsed into unconsciousness.

Had the invisible beings, whom the dying so often contemplate, warned this devoted husband and father of the diabolical plot of which his loved ones were the intended victims?

None here can tell; but such a thought penetrated to the guilty conscience of Jonas Cringar, and he trembled as the devils tremble who believe that there is one God.

The soldier now commenced re-enacting the martial scenes of his military life.

At length he began talking in tones of the profoundest affection of a comrade, whom he spoke of only as Prescott.

"Who is this Prescott?" asked Daniel Garvin, who seemed slightly ill at ease.

"He was a dear friend of Mr. Paige. He was a lieutenant of cavalry. His name is Prescott Marland," replied Mrs. Paige.

"Father seems to have loved him as a son, and has often wished that we were acquainted with him," added Emma.

As Emma said this, William Garvin turned suddenly toward her, and his delicate features were disturbed by an expression which caused a slight blush to suffuse her face. In another instant he seemed to realize where he was, and the solemnity of the event in which he was then to a degree an actor, and with a frown of self-reproach he turned his gaze to the dying.

The patriot's utterances now grew fainter and more and more incoherent.

At length he lay still and silent, and it seemed as if the spirit had finally departed.

But suddenly he started from his pillow with that apparently supermundane strength which the dying so often reveal, and, waving his arm, he shouted: "Forward, men! To-day you conquer! Remember your country!"

Then sinking back, he gave signs of the last moments. His eye began to glaze, and his breath to labor.

At this instant the door opened, and a tall man of majestic, military bearing silently entered the room, and, reverentially approaching the bed, gazed on the expiring patriot with an expression of profound solemnity.

With one exception he was unobserved by those around

the bed, who watched with all-absorbing attention the last signs of life in the form before them.

The broker was the only one who observed this new-comer, and as he fixed his sinister eye upon him he felt a nameless foreboding.

The eye of the stranger, as if drawn by the power of magnetism, turned for a moment from the dying soldier, and met the eye that was fixed upon him. Unconsciously, probably, to himself, his own assumed a look of iron sternness, and it seemed to the inwardly quailing broker as if it penetrated his most secret thoughts. Turning his gaze again on the patriot, his countenance reassumed its expression of tender solemnity.

Presently the face of Allen Paige was lit up by a divine smile. His eye seemed for an instant to break through the glaze that was rapidly covering it, and look into heaven, and his lips moved as if he were speaking to the awaiting angels; and then the spirit of the brave soldier passed to its home, to be greeted by the patriots of all the past ages, while the mortal face lay white and still, with that last divine smile to relieve the coldness of death.

As the family now gathered with weeping eyes around the motionless form of him who had loved them so much, the stranger silently withdrew, followed by the now furtive glance of Daniel Garvin.

CHAPTER IV.

AFTER a few words of formal consolation, Daniel Garvin and Jonas Cringar took their departure, glad to escape that chamber, where their consciences seemed to hear the solemn denunciations of the dead.

When they had arrived in the street, Cringar turned towards the broker, and opened his lips to speak; but there was a look about the latter which, for the present, at least, compelled him to remain silent.

The arch-schemer had not been so absorbed by the impressive scene through which they had just passed as to fail to take exact note of every change of expression which in turn agitated the countenance of the merchant. As we have seen, it was a face calculated to reveal in a strong manner the character of the soul's emotions, and the broker easily read the fierce but suppressed struggle that was going on within him.

The reader can readily imagine the nature of this internal conflict. The effect of the look which Allen Paige cast upon him when he entered the room, together with subsequent influences of that death-bed scene of one whom he had learned to love, and who had never failed to trust him, brought into action the strongest elements of virtue he possessed. As he contemplated the family of this dying friend, and thought of the diabolical nature of the plot which the broker had opened to him just as he received the announcement that called him to this scene, his heart had nearly rent his bosom; and his haggard face was contorted in such a manner, that, while the casual observer would mistake it for the struggle of grief, Garvin well knew that a crisis was approaching in the soul of this wretched man.

The broker understood the situation, and prepared himself to meet the decisions of a perturbed conscience with the force of an unyielding will. Accordingly, when the merchant turned to speak to him in the street, he silenced him with his look, well apprehending the nature of the intended speech.

But Cringar had been too profoundly affected by the mental conflict through which he had passed to be silenced for any length of time.

After passing into Fifth Avenue, and by some half-dozen blocks, he suddenly stopped, and turning fiercely upon his tempter, he poured forth a storm of invective; and in the midst of it declared his determination to be done with both him and his diabolical schemes, let come what might.

During this harangue the face of Daniel Garvin became more agitated than we have yet seen it. His eyes burned with lurid fires, and his upper lip seemed to both turn and shrink back, to reveal in all their glistening array the white fangs beneath it, while the entire expression seemed formed of a devilish grin.

"You are grateful," he said, in a voice harsh and hissing, but low, after the merchant had come to a stop from exhaustion. "In the first place, you talk too loud, and in the next place you talk like an idiot!"

"None of your damnable thrusts and cuts! I'll have none of them!" exclaimed Cringar with desperate courage.

"Cuts! so you have decided to cut me, have you?"

"Cut you, yes! and may the devils incarnate quarter you too! If you dare push this thing, may the dead curse you!"

The broker quietly approached a lamp-post that was near by, and taking out a large wallet, opened it and drew forth a piece of paper. He then motioned for the merchant to approach.

Cringar obeyed, and Garvin held the paper under his eyes, so that the light of the street lamp should fall directly upon it.

At sight of this paper the merchant paled, and, staggering back, uttered a groan.

A patrolman who had heard Jonas Cringar's harangue, and drawn near, now apprehended some foul play, and advanced to the spot.

"It is nothing," said Garvin; "my friend has n't been rightly used above here, and his excitement has made him unwell."

"Yes, it is nothing," said the merchant in a faint, broken voice,—"nothing, I assure you."

The watchman withdrew.

"Well, what do you say now?" said the broker, as he carefully folded the paper, and replaced it in his pocket-book.

Cringar remained stunned and silent.

Garvin said no more, but, taking the unresisting arm of the other, he led him away as one would draw a rudderless craft along the shore.

That night was a terrific one for Jonas Cringar.

After parting with Garvin, he went to his store, for he could not go home, and there throughout the long, gloomy hours he could have been seen, now pacing the floor with staggering steps, and now fallen in a chair, the picture of hopeless despair.

"A forger," he muttered to himself. "Branded as a forger! — no, no! — ah, my God!"

This paper, which we have seen to produce so powerful an effect on the astounded merchant was a note made to the order of one Samuel Townsend, whose name was written across the back as indorser.

This name was a forgery.

The forger was Jonas Cringar.

Speculation the cause.

And this same speculation has led many another of its votaries to the commission of crime equally heinous.

But they have not been detected.

It is the nature of speculation to pervert the channels of business, and corrupt financial character. Men who would repel with abhorrence the temptation to certain acts, before plunging into the Stygian stream of speculation, would, after this plunge, take to them as kindly as the lamb to salt.

So with Jonas Cringar, who, it will be borne in mind, was continually led on by the Satanic influence of Daniel Garvin. "Kiting," "shoving," and the like, with all their attendant slips, lies, and mortifications, became the order of the day; until, in an evil hour, the merchant, when pressed to desperation through the secret machinations of Garvin, made out a note, and with only a few moments left to save himself at the bank, forged the name of an opulent friend, which name was gold in the market, and "shoved it through," intending to take care of it the next day, "no one being the wiser," said he to himself, "and much good done, and no harm."

As vain as the sophistry with which one instalment after another of the funds of the Bald Eagle Silver Mining Company had been cast into the abyss!

An eye was on this desperate merchant.

Early the following day, Daniel Garvin despatched a

trusty messenger to take up this note. It was in the hands of a private banker; and Cringar had requested him to hold it, and keep the transaction strictly private on account of peculiar circumstances which he could not make known; he to take it up within six days, paying two per cent a day.

The messenger professed to come from Jonas Cringar, and laying down good money for it, the banker delivered it, nothing showing that it was not all right.

Four days' time had elapsed, and during these four days the merchant had this note constantly in mind; for now that he had done the act, — done it, it is true, without intending crime, — he began to realize the consequences if he should be brought face to face with it before the public eye; and it was the thought of this forged paper, which he supposed still in the hands of the banker, whom in his distracted efforts to save himself he had not seen since negotiating the note, that seized his soul in a yet more relentless grip when he contemplated his utter ruin, as previously described.

"A forger! Branded as a forger!" exclaimed this victim of another's wiles and his own cupidity; and he wrung his hands in despair.

The Devil triumphed. Before the streaks of dawn began to appear in the eastern horizon, he was the slave of Daniel Garvin.

The broker did not hurry down to see Jonas Cringar. He felt too sure of his prey to do this, but instead he occupied his time in laying out the diabolical work, which had for its object the robbery of everything from the widow and orphan children of his patriot brother.

Among other things he did not fail to call to see the corpse, and offer some words of consolation to the living, and of admiration of the dead. That he was able to do so without exciting suspicion was proof of his mastery of hypocritical arts; for while he uttered these words, his heart beat with an exultation which few could conceal, and his mind was busy with malevolent purposes.

In due course of time the will was read and entered for probate.

Through Garvin's influence, Allen Paige, with his accustomed generosity and lack of suspicion, had declared his executors exempt from giving bonds, thus providing one important step for the ruin of his own family.

Where legal or strict business transactions are concerned, let it be remembered that generosity may so act as to turn the edge of the sword from those who deserve it to those who are innocent, and whom it would be the last to intentionally injure.

The operations of the schemer now commenced.

First there came whisperings of complications, and of the revelations of transactions which threatened to change the entire aspect of the affairs of the estate. Isabel Paige would not believe these things; but in times when the reputation for judgment of no merchant seemed to be proof against his dabbling in speculation, when it was no uncommon thing for a man to die reputed to be rich, while really his estate would be found inadequate to meet the liabilities, it was by no means a difficult task for the executors of her late husband's will to impress the public mind with the truth of whatever they might be pleased to assert.

Although Mrs. Paige paid but little heed to these whisperings, feeling sure, from a knowledge of much of her husband's business (for like a wise man he secured a good wife, and then confided in her), that they had no good foundation, yet erelong she began to practically feel the effects of these pretended revelations.

As executors of Allen Paige's will, it was the duty of Daniel Garvin and his abject slave, Jonas Cringar, to retain all property, real or personal, belonging to the estate, including moneys, until its liabilities should have been fully ascertained. Under these conditions, it is not difficult to conceive of the position into which Mrs. Paige found herself thrown. For a while she was enabled to get along without serious inconvenience, by means of available funds left her by her husband, but erelong she began to feel the band as it was being drawn around her.

CHAPTER V.

A FEW weeks after the death of Allen Paige, Mrs. Paige and Emma were seated in the library, the one sewing and the other embroidering. At first, after the loved form had been consigned to the grave, no place seemed so utterly lonesome to them as did this library. Here Allen Paige had spent much of his home life, among the books which lined the walls; and the room seemed peculiarly a part of him, the everlasting absence of whom caused the very footfalls to echo through the house.

But, as day succeeded day, the feeling began to change, and in this room of all others, except, perhaps, the chamber in which he had been so long confined, they came to feel as if he were near unto them. Here, therefore, they would now often come and sit.

Each seemed busy with her own thoughts.

"Mother," said Emma at length, "I can't help thinking of the Deering family."

Mrs. Paige looked up with an air of anxious interest.

"Do you think they are in trouble?" she asked.

"I cannot keep them off my mind."

"You know Mrs. Deering sent word by Alice that Joseph had a place, and they should n't need any more assistance."

Emma said "yes," but did not seem satisfied. She continued awhile embroidering and thinking. At length she again spoke: —

"Mother, I feel anxious about them, and I cannot help it."

"But, my child, they would send word."

Emma slowly shook her head.

"You know, mother, Mr. Stanfield recently died, and it is said he left his business in a bad state."

"I have heard so."

As Mrs. Paige uttered this, her countenance assumed an expression of anxiety, as if she were thinking of the reports about her late husband's estate, which Daniel Garvin was so insidiously circulating.

"And," continued Emma, "supposing they had to discharge employees from the store, and Joseph were one of these, how would they be situated?"

"Would not Mrs. Deering let us know?"

"I fear not. You must consider, mother, her pride. She is a soldier's widow; and though she has been compelled, through the forgetfulness of the people her husband fought for, to depend much on charity as if she were a beggar —"

"Too true!"

"— it has been hard for her spirit, as we well know. And I believe she would have starved rather than be treated as a beggar, if we had not found her out, and made her feel that she could accept bounty from us, because we were also a soldier's family."

Emma's cheeks glowed as she spoke.

"And do you think she will now hesitate to call?" asked Mrs. Paige.

"I fear it. She sent so decided a message that they could get along comfortably for a good while to come. And you know even with us she has felt much humiliation."

"She has shown a good spirit, however."

"Yes, and I know she has felt sincerely grateful. But she has also felt under too great obligations. O, how I do wish there would be a society formed to look after soldiers' families, like the Masons and Odd Fellows, and societies of that kind!"

"By whom would you have it formed?"

"By SOLDIERS and SAILORS! those noble men who fought on land and sea for their country!" exclaimed Emma, her eyes beaming with a light as if inspired by her father's presence.

At this instant William Garvin entered.

At sight of his beautiful cousin, with her countenance flushed, and her eye beaming with the noble sentiments that moved her, he trembled.

"Ah!" cried Emma, "here's Cousin William, and he shall be my escort!"

"Where are you going?" asked Mrs. Paige.

"To look after the Deerings," answered Emma; "and William must go with me."

"With the greatest pleasure," responded William, his face flushing with happiness.

As the reader has probably inferred, this delicate young man, with a temperament of the most exquisite sensibility, loved his beautiful cousin.

Though they had been together as cousins from early childhood, William Garvin had scarcely entered his teens before he began to look up to Emma as an object of adoration. He secretly worshipped her, and at any time he would have laid down his life for her, as an enthusiast will for his religion. But this love he had never made known. Nothing he dreaded more. It was not associated with ideas of possession; she seemed too far above him for that. But he contemplated her with a sort of rapture, as a being whom he could not conceive of as the wife of any mortal man. When she would speak of her shoemaker or dentist, he wondered how these men could dare profane her by their commonplace touch. He looked upon the brush that brushed her hair, and the combs, and all other articles of her toilet, as favored far beyond such articles used by other women. He was, in truth, jealous of them.

He had become an artist by profession, and the influence of this profession tended to enhance the sentiments of adoration which held such an all-powerful sway in his soul.

Emma's desire, therefore, that he should accompany her to look up the Deerings made him the happiest of men.

"You must n't be gone long," said Mrs. Paige, "for it is now late. And if you are out after dark in that part of the city, I shall feel anxious, for you know several acts of violence have been recently committed there, almost in broad daylight."

"Do not fear," answered Emma, "I have William for a protector."

On uttering this last remark she smiled on her cousin, and went out, he following with a throbbing heart.

The Deering family had lived in a tenement situated in a court running from Third Avenue, and thither Emma, accompanied by her cousin, directed her steps.

She found them gone.

She inquired of women and children about the place where they had moved to; but they did not seem to know.

At length an old woman of haggish appearance came to the door next to the one in which the Deerings had lived.

"Git out! away wid ye!" she cried, brushing the dirty children right and left; and then, adjusting her crimped cotton cap, which flared up broadly in front, she called out to the cousins,—

"Is 't the sowldhier's family ye 're looking for?"

"Yes, their name is Deering," answered Emma, eagerly, at the same time approaching the hag.

"Yis, by the name of Deering. You 're come to help thim, I suppose?"

"Yes, we fear they are in want; and if you can direct us where to find them, we shall be much obliged to you."

"Yis, yis, I know ye would, sure. Well, by me sowl! I pithy that poor sowldhier's family, and Margarit Roone is the woman that 'll dirict ye to thim without any thanks at all, sure. Holy Mither, protect us! but meself is the woman that would be sthruck dead with pithy for sich as thim, and espishally the little cripple,—Jasus protect her!"

"If you will tell us," interrupted Emma, getting a little impatient with the old woman's volubility.

"Ah, throth! an' it 's meself that 'll do that same. Ye 'll be goin' down to the Avenoo below this, and—"

"Second Avenue?"

"Sicond Avenoo is it? Yis, the Sicond Avenoo, so it is. Well, ye 'll be going down to the Sicond Avenoo, an' thin ye 'll be afther kaping your way along up till yez pass Fortieth Strate and along beyond that till yez get up to Forty-sivinth Strate; an' it 's down that same strate; it 's Margarit Roone that 's sure indade. Thin it 's meself that must think —" Here the hag commenced rubbing her mottled forehead. "Well, thin, ye 'll find an open space, that ye 'll be after knowing on account of the large excarvations, an' there ye 'll find a small bit of a house, which is afther being not the one ye 'd be wanting; but the next house is a high, slim buildin', wid archways for the winders — ye 'll sure an' know it."

"And is that the house?" asked Emma, now beginning to fear that the sun would go down before the old woman's tongue would stop its wagging.

"The same, bless your swate pretty coontenance, me lady! I 've talked much, but it 's Margarit Roone that would talk much more for the sake of the sowldhier's family."

William Garvin, who had remained silent up to this time, was vastly pleased with the old woman's compliment of his cousin's face, and from an impulsive desire to increase this admiration he exclaimed, —

"And this lady is a soldier's daughter?"

"Holy Mary bless her!" returned the hag, with a grimace, "and thin Margarit Roone is sivenfold rajoiced to send yez on your way."

On the utterance of this benediction, the cousins departed, and the hag withdrew her frilled cap into the door, at the same time muttering through her broken teeth, —

"Bad luck to thim! if they hunt till they find the house meself has given thim, it 's the widow of Patrick Roone — pace to his blessed sowl! — that hopes much good it may do thim! May purgatory take the sowls of the whole brood of thim!"

This hag was the widow of one of the rioters of July, 1863, who was killed by the military. The very name of soldier made her gnash her teeth with rage; but she was cunning and did not always show it. In the present instance she gnashed her teeth in secret, and sent her inquirers on a fruitless errand.

The cousins rode up to Forty-seventh Street as the hag had directed, and then proceeded to search for the house she had described. There being no such house, their search was of course in vain. They went up and down, and up and down, from one street to another, for Emma was of pertinacious temper when aroused, and William was only too happy to have the time extended to the last moment that thus enabled him to act as her protector.

Relying on the old woman's direction, Emma had not stopped to make inquiries at the court about the condition of the Deering family, or why they had left their former lodgings; but now as she was seeking them in vain, the words of the hag in reference to them, and her own fears, served to impel her on to find them if it were a possible thing, her excited fancy picturing them turned out of the old quarters, and now dying of starvation.

So, though night was coming on, she still persevered, while her cousin, absorbed in the delight of acting as her protector, forgot the dangers which were likely to attend this delay, in a part of the city where violence was of almost daily occurrence.

In the mean time let us return to the old hag.

After retiring into her den, she continued to mutter and gnash her broken teeth, cursing soldiers and Abraham Lincoln, — "*the nagur*," as she called him, — and wishing that his soul might be in purgatory.

At length, in the height of her solitary fury, she suddenly gnashed her fangs with such vehemence that one of them broke, and she spit it out with a sound between a hiss and a growl; and bounding from her chair, with her back rounded over, as if projected by a spring, she brandished her bony fist, and with a horrible grin that completely overspread her repulsive visage, she exclaimed, —

"The fine sowldhier's daughter! its Mammy Roone that 'll furnish yez with the night's lodgings where your marvillous beauty will be appraciated! and where they love the mimory of the sowldhier!"

Then taking down an old hood and shawl from a nail driven in the wooden partition, she put them on; and with her dried and shrunken lips drawn back from her broken teeth, and her bloodshot eyes glittering with diabolical passion, she opened the door and passed out.

CHAPTER VI.

A HALF-HOUR had elapsed after the departure of the old woman, when a stranger entered the court and looked intently about. The women held their gossip, and the children ceased their noisy play, and, drawing back, gazed up at him with open mouths and wondering eyes, overcome with childish awe.

The appearance of this man is remarkable.

His stature is lofty and martial in its bearing. It rises considerably above six feet, and is so finely proportioned that only by comparison is his full height realized.

His head is large. His face is wide, and at the same time projects forward with aggressive energy. The nose aquiline; the cheek-bone high; the jaw long and massive, extending the chin downwards without detracting from its executive strength; the lips somewhat thick, but closely compressed.

The eyes are gray; and, combined with a sternness that indicates long habit of command, is a contemplative fixedness, giving an effect of profundity to the expression of an iron will.

This is enhanced by a remarkable scar, that deeply and widely indents his left cheek-bone.

His hair is dark and thick, and appears in clustering locks under his small felt hat, which, though of civilian form, has the military bend to it. His beard has the cavalry cut, the mustache and imperial only being worn.

Imperiousness, severity, high temper, quick passions, magnanimity, and humor can be traced through his physiognomy to his nature; which in earlier years have evidently held independent sway, but have been by a tremendous experience compelled to harmonious action.

In his massive head, which rounds out from his small hat, with its wide and capacious front, is seen an intellect corresponding with his physical power.

The forehead is a forehead of plans and strategy, and it is evident that he cannot be easily circumvented. His age is difficult to judge, but he appears to be about fifty.

All were so busy staring at this man that no one thought of speaking to him, though he had asked twice if the Deerings lived there.

At length a washwoman, who was evidently American born, came forward, and, looking about on the gaping people, cried out, —

"Are you all deaf? Do you keep the gentleman standing there with no answer for him? And what is it, sir?" she added, addressing the stranger.

"I have been told that a family by the name of Deering lives here."

"The soldier's family."

"The same."

"They 've gone."

The stranger looked disappointed.

"Can you tell me where they have moved to?" he asked.

The woman shook her head.

A little girl now ventured to come forward.

"Please, sir, I think I can tell you."

The stranger bent upon her a look which encouraged her.

"I heard Mammy Roone tell a gentleman and lady this afternoon that they had moved to a tall, slim house, next to a short one, next to an open place, on Forty-seventh Street."

"Thank you, my child," said the stranger, taking out a coin and giving her. "And who were the gentleman and lady that came here?"

"I don't know their names, sir. But the gentleman was small and slim," — here the child's eyes wandered up and down the gigantic form before her, — "and the lady was very handsome, and I heard the gentleman say the lady was a soldier's daughter."

The grave countenance of the stranger lit up with interest.

"A soldier's daughter?"

"Yes, sir. I heard him say so to Mammy Roone."

The stranger now turned to go. But just as he had left the court he felt a hand placed on his arm, and a voice said, —

"I would spake wid ye, sir."

On looking around he beheld a little Irishwoman, who had a face which, though pitted with the small-pox, was kind.

There was so much solicitude in her countenance that he bent his head at once.

"Mammy Roone does n't mane well by thim that was here this same afthernoon."

This was uttered in a sort of hoarse whisper.

The stranger's brow darkened.

"What mean you?"

"This sure, sir, an' it's not Mary Connelly that would tell ye an unthruth. It's riskisome, sir, to be tellin' ye what I have on me tongue, but I could n't slape in peace if I did not tell ye."

"Well, my good woman, what is it?"

"Well, thin, I'm nixt neighbor to Mammy Roone, an' afther she had sent the beautiful young soldhier's daughter an' the fine young gintleman away wid a diriction that I don't believe is thrue at all, she carried on in her room like the wicked Satan himself; an' I heard her spittin' fire, an' cry out with a horrible laugh, that she'd secure lodgings for the young lady, where them that knows could appraciate her beauty."

The expression that took possession of the stranger's features so startled the little woman that her tongue seemed suddenly frozen in her mouth.

"Well!" he exclaimed, under his breath, "what more?"

The poor woman now began to tremble before the aspect of this man; but a reassuring look which appeared in the midst of his frown gave her courage again.

"And thin, you honor, she went away with a slam, an' she's no friend of the soldhier nor the soldhier's family, sir, for it was her old man, Patrick Roone, that was killed in the murdhering riot. An' sure she made the family you'd be afther feel her wicked spite, and a betther family lives not in this blessed city."

The stranger's military mind grasped the whole plot.

Placing his hand on the little woman's shoulder, "If it

is as we fear," he said, "you shall neither come to harm for informing me, nor go unrewarded!" and then hastened away for that part of the city to which the hag had directed the cousins.

The little woman gazed after him, at the same time talking to herself.

"He's a wondherful man," she uttered. "It's meself can tell by his eye. An' he's a soldhier too, if Mary Connelly knows ought of mankind. It was an awful cut he got on his powerful face, sure!"

She now watched him awhile in silence, her face lit up with a gleam of profound satisfaction.

Presently she again spoke to herself: —

"Now, look well to yourselves, ye mane-spirited hirelings of Mammy Roone! If ye dare do harm to her who is the soldhier's daughter, I pithy ye! I pithy ye!"

And with this she went back into the court.

It was now dusk.

* * * * *

The sun had disappeared behind the house-tops of the great city, when Emma found herself weary and discouraged, after her long and unavailing search.

"William," she said at length, "I fear we must give up our search, and leave this poor family, Heaven only knows in what a state of destitution!"

William was about to answer, when Emma uttered an exclamation, and pointed down the street.

"It is the old woman," cried William.

William was not mistaken. Rapidly approaching them with a halting gait was the old hag, who had suddenly appeared in view from an intersecting street.

When near enough to be heard, she cried out between gasping breaths, —

"The blissed Virgin be praised! Mammy Roone has found ye at last! It 's been a hard thramp for me aged bones; but it 's your dear silves that 's found, any way! Me sowl was throubled for all of yez; for afther ye had gone from me sight, it 's meself that feared I had been wrong in the diriction, an' Margarit Roone was n't the woman to set back in her aizy-chair, an' think of yez not finding the sowldhier's family, — the family it 's Mam Roone that can swear on the blissed Book she 'd cut off this poor bit of a shrivelled hand for! An' ye 're a sowldhier's daughther yourself, me swate young lady — "

"We have not been able to find the house you directed us to," interrupted Emma, impatiently.

"Ah, but the blissed Virgin only knows how Mammy Roone, — you see they call me Mammy ginerally," — here the old woman showed some of her broken teeth, — "an' it 's afther sounding a sort of social like — but let me see — as I was about to tell yez, the blissed Virgin only knows how Mammy Roone can rattle with her tongue, — but her heart is right, as the hiven of hivens knows, so hilp me God! — an' I 'll prove it to yez same, for hav' n't I hobbled up the long distance to make it certain that ye 'd find the poor unfortunates, Hivin bless thim! for — "

The hag here wiped her eyes with her dirty shawl, and then exclaimed, —

"But the good Lord protict us, me sweet lady! it 's gettin' dark, an' it 's no place for sich as you to be out afther this hour. Come with me, an' it 's meself that 'll prisintly show ye the house; for I need not the name of the strate to find it."

Having spent so much time hunting in vain, Emma could not think of returning home without finally seeing the family, whose sufferings were continually pictured in her excited mind, and whom she now felt certain of meeting in a short time, under the guidance of this old woman, whose worst trait she thought was her volubility

As for William Garvin, he was but too happy in yielding to the will of his cousin.

The hag now led them from street to street, shaking her head as she went, and saying, —

"It's not near. Ye've wandered far. But it's meself that'll lead ye straight to the house."

But it now began to grow dark, and the old woman assumed a plaintive voice.

"Me poor eyes! me poor eyes!—the darkness throubles thim; but niver mind."

So from street to street she led her victims, every now and then turning away her head, that they might not see the drawing back of her shrivelled lips.

Objects were rapidly growing indistinct.

The hag had now led the cousins to a district which, even in that part of the city, was marked as God-forsaken and solitary.

Emma's heart began to be troubled with an oppressive dread.

Her cousin's face indicated that he also was not free from oppressive fears.

They now came to a spot where the very houses seemed more like dens of robbers than abodes of honest people.

As they entered this precinct, the form of a young man of bold free step appeared from a cross-street several rods behind them.

He paused in surprise as he beheld the group in the dusk before him, and intently observed them.

Presently he turned, and looking down the street from which he had just emerged, he whistled softly, and then beckoned with his hand.

CHAPTER VII.

ABOUT the time the stranger was parting from the little woman with the pitted face, two young men left Central Park by one of the eastern gates, and wended their way to East River.

One of them instantly strikes the attention by his fine athletic form and noble countenance. His full and handsome oval face, with its dark eye, open forehead, freely chiselled nose and mouth, and dimpled chin, captivates even the masculine beholder. There is an air of freedom and boldness about him, which indicates that he has, even at his early age, seen much of the world.

This bold and handsome young man's name is Prescott Marland. He it was who occupied the wandering thoughts of Allen Paige in his last moments, and the speaking of whom by Emma caused the glance from her enamored cousin.

He has just come from the West, and is sauntering over the city of New York, with which he has made himself pretty thoroughly acquainted in former years. His present companion is a clerk, who has been for some time in the employ of Jonas Cringar, and who has got off early this afternoon to take a stroll with him through the Park.

The sun had just set when they arrived at the river; and as the last rays disappeared, the moon, as if by some aerial signal, rose full and clear above the eastern horizon.

Soon its white rays passed over Long Island, and descended with glistening beauty on the river; the long slim form of Blackwell's Island lying in the midst like some sleeping denizen of the deep.

Prescott Marland contemplated the beautiful scene before him for a while in silence.

Presently he exclaimed, as if to himself, —

"OLD THORBOLT!"

His companion looked at him in surprise.

Marland laughed.

"This moon brings Thorbolt before me," he said.

"Thorbolt?"

"Yes, Thorbolt, or Old Thorbolt, as we used to sometimes call him."

"Who 's he?" asked the puzzled clerk.

"As strong and brave a man as ever wielded sabre."

"A soldier, then."

"Yes, a soldier and a VETERAN!" exclaimed Marland, with admiring energy.

"Come, now, there 's a story. Tell it."

"With all my heart. You see Thorbolt's name was really General Hammond, — General Julius Hammond. He 's had a tremendous experience in his day He went into the war with Mexico when he was sixteen, and gunpowder and steel have been his food ever since. But I tell you what it is, he 's no adventurer by any means. He has a mind equal to his body; if he had n't have had he never would have lived to see this day, in spite of his gigantic strength and heroic courage. He 's great for strategy."

"Well, how did he get his name of Thorbolt?"

"That 's what I 'm coming to. In the first place, you must understand that few men could match him either for size or strength. If you were to be cut in two, and your upper half put on top of me, your head would be about on a level with his."

"A pleasing picture."

"To be sure," rejoined Marland, laughing. "A sort of half-and-half picture. Well, that gives you an idea of his height. But there 's his breadth."

"Which could be suggested, I suppose, by putting me under a trip-hammer."

"Exactly."

"And then roll me up to get an idea of his thickness."

"Capital. The long roll. That long roll never was able to get more than half through before Old Thorbolt would come striding out of his tent, armed and equipped for the fight."

"OLD THORBOLT. Now will you please tell me about that, without any more joking?"

"Certainly. As I was saying, Colonel Hammond — he was colonel then — was a man of gigantic stature, and with a strength which would inevitably break some of our bones, if he should hit us with his clenched fist. The long roll came one night, and pretty soon we had it. The moon was up in the east as full and bright as it is there across the river. Hammond was the first into it. Our column was ordered to his support. It was a grand sight, that fight! The Rebs had advanced up a sort of valley, and when we came in view, there was the Colonel at the head of his column, slashing into them as if they were so many corn-stalks. The moon was shining right down the valley, so we could see everything almost as plain as by daylight. It seemed to make Hammond stand out like some avenging god. A Norwegian — a Major, who had just joined our regiment — was riding by my side; and after watching the Colonel a moment, he asked, —

"'Who is he?'

"'Colonel Hammond,' said I.

"He misunderstood.

"'Hammer!' he exclaimed, 'Hammer! He is Thor's Hammer!'

"Then, as the Colonel's sabre threw off the gleams of the moonlight, a Rebel seeming to go down at every sweep, he cried out again, —

"'Thor's Hammer! No, 't is the BOLT of Thor!'

"'Yes, *Thorbolt!*' cried another officer. 'That 's the name for him! Thunder and lightning! the old Scandinavian God himself could n't do better!'

"That 's the way he got the name. Sometimes we used to put the '*Old*' on, because he was one of that kind. He looks and acts fifty, but he is n't more than forty to-day. I tell you what it is, those kind of men have iron wills, — the kind that get '*Old*' stuck on to them early."

"So that 's the way he got his *soubriquet?*" said the clerk.

"Yes, and I never see a moonlight like this, that it does n't remind me of it."

They now turned, and sauntered down the river.

"This is as good as a romance," said the clerk, as they walked along. "Tell me more about him."

"Ah! you ought to see him! It 's a tremendous scar he 's got on his cheek!"

"How did that come?"

"In a fight with a Rebel infantry-man."

"What, swords?"

"No. In a charge on Rebel infantry his horse was shot under him. A Rebel private rushed forward to transfix him. But Old Thorbolt was ready for the fellow. He leaped to his feet, and at it they went, sabre and bayonet. Those that saw the duel said it was fine. You see the Rebel was a herculean fellow, and they made the sparks fly like a blacksmith's hammer on red-hot iron. Presently they both fell at the same instant, the Rebel with Thorbolt's sabre through his body, and the Colonel with the Rebel's bayonet driven through his cheek-bone into his mouth."

"Ugh!" ejaculated the clerk, with a grimace.

"It was a terrible wound, that 's a fact," said Marland, smiling at his companion's contorted face. "But he was more fortunate at another time."

"I should hope so."

"He was dismounted, and lay wounded on the ground, when two or three Rebels attacked him at once with the bayonet. But he warded off every one of their dastardly thrusts, until they were finally put to flight by reinforcements."

"I should think he would keep that sword."

"He does. It is hanging in his library, with other mementos and trophies, with gaps that you can almost put your finger in, made by his powerful blows against the edges of the bayonets."

"You speak of his library. Is he a book-man as well as a warrior?"

"Yes. You know I told you his mind was equal to his body. He has an extensive library, which he uses to as much purpose as he did his halting-grounds."

"His halting-grounds? What do you mean by that?"

"Simply this. Whenever the column in which he held command came to a halt, it was his custom, instead of laying back with his eyes shut, to scrutinize the surrounding country, and then start a discussion with other officers as to where a surprise might be attempted by the enemy, and what should be done in case of one. In this way he made himself master of the situation."

"Good! He must have been as able an officer as he was terrible as a fighter."

"He 's one of the first cavalry leaders of the age."

They now struck an avenue, through which they continued their way.

Both walked on awhile, thinking.

"I am greatly interested in this Veteran of yours," at length said the clerk. "It seems to me he must feel a good deal safer in this part of the city at midnight than I should."

As he said this he began to look about him with suspicious glances.

Perhaps the sight of the Penitentiary on Blackwell's Island, from which he had just turned, did not inspire him with the calmest of thoughts.

"Yes," responded Prescott, laughing, and looking around with a mind evidently untouched by solicitude, or such fancies as the nervous are apt to indulge in lonely places, "a man who has been through with what he has is n't much disturbed by such places as these. His California experience, when he was a mere boy, was enough to inure him to New York dangers."

"Did he see much of life there?"

"A good deal of it. He was scarcely twenty when he was made sheriff, and any one who lived in California sixteen or eighteen years ago knows what that means."

"It means a good deal of danger, I suppose," said the clerk, looking about him again.

"It means pistol-muzzles lining the walls of his hut, like the cells of a hornet's nest, in the daytime, and knives hanging by hairs from the roof, like the stalactites in the Mammoth Cave, in the night-time."

The clerk laughed aloud, and then, glancing around, lowered his tone, and said, —

"It must be an enjoyable life."

"It really was to one of his make. I'll give you one little incident before we part," he added, as they now approached the street where they were to separate. "You will bear in mind that this was in his youth. Yet with all his wildness then, one can see the same traits, only in a crude state, in the reckless sheriff of California which afterwards appeared in such grand form in the Rebellion. In both cases he was always studying his ground, and his mind was restlessly engaged in mastering probable strategic points. But we are nearing the corner, and so for the incident, which is only one of many. You see, while he was sheriff there was a desperado at the mines who had defied all other sheriffs, having killed one of them and wounded another. Julius promised to arrest him. He found him in front of a liquor-shanty. 'I have come to arrest you,' said he. 'All right,' returned the desperado; 'but let's come in and take a drink.' 'Very well.' They went in. The liquor was poured out, and each raised his glass. Julius stood leaning against the counter, with his glass in his left hand and his right hand thrust in his side coat-pocket. Now, you see, this pocket was lined with leather, and so formed as to receive a pistol like a leathern case, directing the muzzle to the front of the coat. There was a pistol all loaded and cocked in this pocket, and Julius held it grasped in his hand so that it covered the desperado's body. The desperado, who also held his glass in his left hand, lowered it for an instant, looked at it, and then raised it again. At the same time he made a movement of his right hand. Julius kept on sipping. The desperado took another look at his glass, and commenced scratching his face close to the ear. But Julius kept on sipping. Suddenly the desperado left off scratching, and, as quick as you can wink, drew a bowie-knife from behind his neck.

But while the knife was in the air the pistol in Julius's pocket exploded, and the desperado fell to the ground a dead man."

The clerk shuddered as Marland finished this short but graphic tale; and as he parted from him the dusk of evening seemed loaded with dismal gloom, while the moonlight that touched the house-tops had something ghastly about it.

CHAPTER VIII.

THE nervous and hastening step of the clerk was rapidly bearing him away from a spot which exerted so dismal an influence upon him, when his progress was arrested by the sound of a low whistle. He turned, and saw Marland beckoning to him.

The reader has already seen this action of Prescott Marland, for he was the young man with the bold free step who appeared as Emma Paige and William Garvin, accompanied by the old hag, entered the forbidding precinct which seemed so fitted for the dens of crime.

Prescott's manner did not serve to allay the apprehensions which had disturbed the breast of the clerk; but his pride would not permit him to do otherwise than respond to his companion's signal. As he approached Marland, the latter placed his hand to his mouth to enjoin silence, and pointed to the group which had so fixed his attention.

"Who are they?" asked the clerk.

"It's more than I can tell you," said Marland. "But if something is n't in the wind, then I 'm no judge, that 's all."

At this moment the objects of their scrutiny stopped, and then they heard the voice of the hag, which was raised on a louder key than heretofore, expostulating with her victims, and assuring them that they were near the house they sought.

"Let 's come around on their flank," whispered Prescott, "and find out what all this means."

"Pshaw!" exclaimed the clerk, in a whisper. "What 's the use? We 'll only get ourselves into a scrape."

"Use or no use, I 'm bound to see what it all means."

"Leave that to the police."

"Come now, Billings (Marland thus addressed the clerk), there 's a young lady, who I 'll swear, even in this light, is beautiful; and a young fellow with her that Old Thorbolt might use for a cane, if his backbone were stiff enough; and if ever a hag meant mischief, I believe that one does. I 'm in for it."

On the utterance of these last words Marland started off to come around on the group by a side street. The clerk, seeing there was no help for it, followed.

Let us return to the cousins and Mammy Roone.

The dread, which the former began to experience before reaching the spot in which Prescott Marland discovered them, now increased to such a degree that they halted, as we have seen; and Emma, casting on the old woman a look of strong suspicion, refused to go any farther in the direction she was leading them.

As we have also observed, the hag now pitched her voice to a high key.

"Oche! and is it meself you suspict, me darling? Nay! nay! ye would n't be for thinking so evil of poor Mammy Roone!"

"I certainly do not like the way you are leading us about," returned Emma, with some severity.

"It does n't look right to me, I must confess," joined in William Garvin.

"O me honies!" cried the hag in a plaintive voice, "to think that meself, with the good name that I 've earned, and labored hard to kape, should come undher such a look as ye jist now cast upon me! Meself, that 's hobbled away down to the place we 're treading this blessed moment, to be of assistance to ye! Arrah, me swate lady, and me fine young gentleman! ye 'll never suspicion Mammy Roone more when once ye 've turned into yonder strate; for now, bless the name of Jasus! it 's meself that recognizes the spot at last that we 're seeking."

As she was uttering the last portion of this characteristic speech, the old woman had suddenly taken a step, and extended her body forward, while her face lit up with an expression of joyful intelligence.

"Come! come!" she exclaimed, seizing Emma by the sleeve. "Ye 'll be glad to see the sowldhier's family at last!"

The cousins now moved reluctantly forward.

On their right was a dark, lonesome-looking alley. As they passed this alley William Garvin held his breath; for he observed the dim forms of three men, and he was sure these men were watching them.

Catching his cousin by the opposite sleeve to that which the old woman had grasped, he whispered, —

"Let us go back, in Heaven's name! This old woman is leading us —"

He was interrupted by a movement of Emma, who, on turning as he began whispering to her, started back, and uttered a slight cry.

William followed the direction of her frightened glance, and also started back; for he now beheld the three dim forms issuing from the alley, and approaching them with a sinister air of mischief.

The old woman did not appear at first to observe them. When Emma started back and uttered the cry, she broke forth with, —

"Arrah, me darlint! but your nerves are not sthrong. Indade it is that as old as is Mammy Roone, she 's not to be frightened by the dark looks of the strate —"

Her eyes now fell on the three figures that were approaching. Stretching her head forward, she placed her hand above her eyes, and peered through the dusk upon them.

"Me sight is dim," she uttered in a hoarse whisper, "but I like not the looks of thim that 's coming this way."

Then, suddenly retreating, she gave vent to a suppressed shriek, and with the cry, "The Holy One be wid us!" she hobbled off, moaning and ejaculating in the most dismal tones of fear and alarm.

As for Emma, she stood trembling, not knowing which way to move; while William Garvin, who might have hastened away under other circumstances, now placed himself between his cousin and the three sinister-looking men, whose intentions could not be mistaken.

As the slight form of this devoted lover stands erect and defiant, the spirit inspired with a courage which knows nothing but that the beloved object is in danger, one instinctively longs to see it expand into the proportions of a giant that shall be commensurate to this courage.

As it is, however, a laugh issues from one of the three ruffians, and he exclaims, —

"Stand where you are a minnit, my fine chick, an' I 'll pen a description of ye for the newspapers."

The other ruffians responded to this speech with a hoarse laugh.

William Garvin's face changed from pale to red, and then grew pale again. He was in a desperate situation. The scoundrels whom he confronted were evidently accustomed to rough business. The one who addressed him was a burly, powerful fellow, who seemed strong enough to break his delicate form across his knee; while his companions, though not his equals in strength, had an aspect quite as ferocious; and either seemed strong enough to fling this delicate, yet devoted protector with a single hand from one side of the street to the other.

When within a pace or two of the cousins these three ruffians stopped for a moment, and contemplated them with a leer.

"Now, my Hercules, what 's the use of making a disturbance in this 'ere peaceable neighborhood?"

"Ha! ha! ha!" hoarsely again responded the other two.

"We 're peaceable citizens, we are; and seein' this 'ere female being carried off by such a ruffian as you be, an' no mistake (another hoarse laugh), we 're bound to do our duty, an' rescue the same."

With these words he advanced.

Emma had now recovered herself, and her native spirit came to her aid.

Stepping forward, she confronted this leading ruffian with a look such as compelled him to halt in his tracks.

"Villain!" she exclaimed, "leave us and go your way!"

There was silence for a moment.

Then one of the rear scoundrels cried out, —

"O blinkers! ain't she a pictur, though!"

"Ha, ha, ha! Dick 's afeared of her!" responded the other. "I say, On to the rescue! save her from the young reprobate!"

With this the last speaker pushed forward, and grasped Emma by the arm.

William, who up to this moment could not entirely realize that any living man, however degraded, would dare profane the object of his adoration with the hand of violence, was by this act wrought to the pitch of frenzy. With a loud cry he sprang upon the wretch who had grasped his cousin.

The attack was so sudden and unexpected that the object of it fell back in momentary confusion. But the leader, whom they called Dick, catching the frenzied assailant in his powerful arms, threw him violently upon the ground, where he lay stunned and immovable; then crying out, "No more tomfoolery! let us be off!" he seized Emma around the waist.

Emma uttered a shriek that penetrated far into the approaching night.

Prescott Marland and the clerk were just entering the street below when they heard this shriek.

They hastened forward and beheld Emma struggling in the arms of the leading ruffian, while the others were making an effort to gag her.

"By Heavens!" exclaimed Prescott, "we are just in time for that crowd!" and he bounded up the street.

The clerk was for a moment staggered; but though his former fancies had been generated by the gloom through a nervous organization, and in an imaginative mind, yet now that the reality was before him, his naturally courageous nature quickly prepared itself to meet the conflict. Closing his lips, and clenching his hands, he followed his companion with nerves drawn taut like so many springs.

As he sped on his way he caught a glimpse of an old woman, whom he judged to be the one he had seen with the cousins, peering around the opposite corner upon the struggling group.

"By Jove!" exclaimed the clerk to himself, as the athletic form of Prescott Marland went bounding on before him; "if he don't give 'em a taste of his gymnastics then I 'll give in!"

In the mean time Marland rapidly approached the scene of outrage with long leaps; and it seemed as if several yards yet intervened, when with one tremendous bound he planted a blow on the side of the head of the ruffian Dick that caused him to drop his intended victim, and stagger half stunned against a doorway, near which the struggle was taking place. Then, drawing Emma back, he extended his clenched hand which had just struck so powerful a blow, and cried out, —

"Scoundrels! take yourselves off, or I 'll teach you a lesson that 'll make you behave yourselves in future!"

With a curse the stricken ruffian, who had now recovered himself, sprang forward, and, foaming with rage, yelled in a hoarse voice, —

"Who dares strike Dick Smasher? D—n him! I 'll see to his life insurance!"

With this he aimed a fearful blow at the head of the young athlete.

But though encumbered as he was by Emma, whom he supported on his left arm, Prescott skilfully caught the blow, and at the same time, by a dexterous stroke of his foot, sent his burly but too impetuous assailant sprawling on the ground.

The other two ruffians, who had shrunk back from Prescott's first onset, now, from both shame and rage, made a rush towards him.

But the clerk had now arrived. As we have said, his

nerves, as he followed his companion, were toughened like so many springs. When, therefore, he reached the scene of conflict, just as these two scoundrels were about attacking Prescott, his body was launched upon one of them as if shot from an engine, and in the next instant the fellow was staggering to and fro with the clerk's hand tightly clasped about his windpipe.

The third ruffian succeeded in planting a blow on Marland's cheek, and, having a ring on his finger, he brought blood. Then, standing back, he drew a knife.

Stung by this blow, and perceiving that the moment had come for the use of all his resources, Prescott relaxed his hold of Emma, and, throwing all his power into his left arm, he delivered such a blow under the ear of his new assailant that he was knocked clean from his feet, and fell far backward across the body of William Garvin, as insensible as he on whom he had fallen, while his knife, which he had had no time to use, rattled upon the opposite sidewalk.

As he now turned on the again-recovered Dick Smasher,— as this herculean shoulder-hitter grimly called himself,— the staggering ruffian, whose windpipe was compressed under the tightening fingers of the brave and nervous clerk, fell gasping beneath his assailant, who still continued to tighten his grasp.

On seeing his two accomplices down, the leader backed a few paces, and looked anxiously around.

"Curse it!" he muttered. "This fellow 's seen the elephant, and no mistake. Hang me if I would n't like the Doctor's lancet!"

On the utterance of this sanguinary wish, he glanced at the insensible form of the man whom Prescott's left arm had just laid out, and whose *soubriquet* was evidently "The Doctor."

But in the next moment he seemed ashamed of his cowardly wish; for, with a sound half-way between a *pshaw* and a hiss, he advanced to meet Marland's attack.

The latter delivered a tremendous blow; but the object of it had been taught by his former experience that, if he had any pugilistic skill, he must use it. Making his best effort, therefore, he succeeded in partially parrying the blow, and at the same time attempted a counter. This fell with some effect on his opponent; but, in return, he received a stroke that sent him once more staggering back in confusion.

At the same moment, the ruffian, under the unrelaxing clutch of the clerk, sank into insensibility.

CHAPTER IX.

EMMA had witnessed the scene — which had been enacted quicker than I have been able to write it — in a sort of stupor. The appearance of the ruffians, the cruel treatment of her devoted cousin, the seizure of herself, the arrival of Prescott Marland and the clerk, and the subsequent struggle, — all had rushed into these few moments in such a manner as to stupefy her without causing her to faint. But now, as she beheld the huge form of Dick Smasher again fall back before the power of Prescott's arm, and then saw the clerk rise from the immovable ruffian whom he had throttled, she experienced a reaction, and clasped her hands with an emotion of hopeful gratitude; and as Prescott advanced to follow up his last blow, she instinctively started forward also, as if she would lend to her preserver the assistance of her own brave spirit.

At this instant she heard a yell, and on looking down the street she beheld two more burly figures rapidly approaching the spot. She started back, and for the first time gave utterance to a moan.

"Oh, will not help come?" she murmured.

At the same moment a hooded old head was quickly thrust beyond the corner whence these men had issued, followed by a shrivelled clenched hand, from which fell back the tattered fringe of an old plaid shawl. They remained only for an instant, and then were as quickly withdrawn.

When Prescott discovered the approach of these lawless reinforcements, his attention was diverted. Dick Smasher took advantage of this diversion, and, rushing in, he seized him in his powerful arms, at the same time crying to one of the fresh confederates, —

"Take the girl, and cheese it!"

The other ruffian in the mean time had drawn a pistol, and, levelling it on the clerk, pulled the trigger.

It missed fire, and with a curse he hurled it at the clerk's head, who was just in time to dodge it, and then prepared to close on him.

But the clerk was not prepared to meet him by force, for his encounter with his throttled victim had left his nerves somewhat unstrung by the reaction; so, stepping back and thrusting his hand into his bosom, he exclaimed, —

"Beware!"

The ruffian, who was a coward, feared a deadly weapon and held back.

While this was going on, a fierce struggle was taking place between Dick Smasher and Prescott Marland.

The villain, whom the leader had ordered to seize Emma,

had hastened to obey, and clasped this beautiful girl in his brutal arms.

She now gave vent to loud shrieks, and struggled desperately. But the ruffian held her in a strong grasp, and bore her rapidly down the street, using his best efforts to smother her cries.

As Emma's first shriek pierced the air, William Garvin stirred, as if this shriek from his cousin penetrated ears insensible to all other sounds. Then, as cry succeeded cry, his eyes opened, and he raised his head and the upper portion of his body, and, sustaining himself feebly by his elbow, he looked around.

The first thing that met his gaze was the prostrate form of the ruffian, who had been knocked insensible by Marland, lying across his own body. Then he saw the forms of Prescott and Dick Smasher still engaged in a fierce struggle. But his eyes passed quickly to the receding figure of the ruffian, who bore his cousin in his foul grasp.

As he beheld the one whom he so much adored thus being dragged away to a terrible fate, his orbs threatened to tear themselves from their sockets, his countenance assumed an aspect of ghastly horror, and he gave vent to a loud groan.

"O God! O God!" was all that burst from his lips. His soul was overwhelmed.

But even that short, ejaculatory prayer from a soul so crushed seemed to have been heard; for scarcely had it passed his lips when he saw a tall, gigantic form, which seemed to his distorted vision to loom nearly to the housetops, enter the street just below the spot where, for a moment, the ruffian was compelled to halt by the struggles of his beautiful victim.

He beheld in the dim light this form advance upon the

ruffian with fearful strides, and, seizing him by the arms, unclasp his hold of his cousin, and, lifting him in the air, hurl him sheer beyond the corner whence appeared the head and hand of the hooded hag.

This was followed by a hoarse shriek of alarm, which seemed to issue from an aged female voice, and then all was silent.

William now, with unutterable emotions of joy, saw his beloved cousin taken under the protection of her titanic deliverer.

This man of such terrible strength, who had arrived at a moment so opportune, is recognized by the reader as the stranger who had been sent this way by the little woman with the pitted face.

Having taken Emma under his protection, he advanced toward the scene of a still fierce struggle between Prescott and Smasher.

"I beg you to leave me," William now heard his cousin exclaim, "and hasten to aid that brave young man, who needs you so much!"

Even in the midst of this fearful scene, poor William experienced the pangs of an indefinable jealousy.

The stranger, seeing that Emma was for the present safe, advanced with a long, quick stride, and, laying hold of Dick Smasher with his right hand, he tore him from Marland as a man would tear a weed from the ground, and, shaking him violently, exclaimed,—

"Scoundrel! What means this outrage?"

He was interrupted by the entrance upon the scene of a policeman, who had been attracted to the spot by Emma's shrieks.

The ruffian, whom the clerk had so cunningly kept at bay, now cleared the spot at a bound, and sped away at a rapid pace.

His leader, with a curse, took advantage of a moment's relaxation in the hold of the stranger, who turned toward Emma as the confederate fled past her, and with a desperate effort tore himself free, and followed this confederate, evidently the worse for the severe handling he had received from the athletic Marland.

With the departure of his cowardly assailant, the clerk now had time to look at the colossal stranger, who had so opportunely come to the rescue.

"By Jove!" he exclaimed to himself, as his first glance ran up and down the majestic figure before him; "there 's power enough for a score of these fellows!"

His eye now fell on the scar, and his voice became audible as he again exclaimed,—

"Old Thorbolt — or the ——!"

He was interrupted by Prescott. In his excitement this spirited champion had not entirely withdrawn his eye from his late antagonist; but as his ears were greeted by the audible voice of the clerk, he turned his gaze on the stranger Starting forward, he caught his hand, and cried,—

"By heavens! General Hammond!"

"What! Marland!" responded the stranger.

"Yes, Prescott Marland, and no one else, General.—Well, this *is* a meeting!" exclaimed Prescott, in a tone of delighted astonishment.

They were here interrupted by the patrolman.

"What 's the trouble?" he asked.

"This young lady, with that young gentleman, was led here by a miserable hag, and then attacked by these scoundrels," answered Prescott.

The patrolman gave a signal for aid, and then turned his attention to the two ruffians who had been lying insensible. William Garvin had revived sufficiently to work himself clear of the one that lay across him, who by his movements had been stirred into signs of returning life.

Emma and William were preparing to express their gratitude for the timely succor which had preserved the former from the terrible snare that the old hag had laid for her, when the recognition took place between General Hammond, or "Thorbolt" (we will also call him the Veteran), and Prescott Marland, as we have described.

Their attention had been chiefly drawn to the stranger, whose majestic presence, combined with the marvellous display of power which had appeared in his treatment of strong and desperate ruffians, served to inspire in their breasts a sentiment in which awe mingled with gratitude. But when the name of Prescott Marland was uttered, the eyes of both were turned upon him.

The emotions of these two cousins at this moment it would be difficult to analyze.

Emma's instincts at once told her that the object of her father's friendship and praise and this handsome young man of heroic strength and courage could be none other than one and the same person. The ideal which had gradually and almost unconsciously formed itself in her bosom and the real that now stood before her were one also. A secret delight took possession of her heart, and a crimson blush suffused her rounded cheek.

Her cousin's emotions were more conflicting.

Though insensible during Prescott's heroic display, he apprehended the truth; and that gratitude he was on the point of expressing was at once disturbed by a pang which only such a soul, for so many years absorbed in the adoration of the object of its love, could experience.

He, poor fellow, when he would have protected her, had been thrown to the earth like a child. But this young man had saved her. Humiliation, therefore, mingled with this pang.

Emma was the first to recover herself, and, without waiting for formalities, she advanced and expressed her thanks in such a manner as to thrill the heart of her young preserver with pleasure.

William, whose fate it seemed to be to experience jealous emotions on the utterance of Prescott Marland's name, on occasions when, to his sensitive and morbid conscience, such emotions were not less than criminal, now, internally accusing himself, approached the group, and joined his expressions with those of his cousin. After warm words of gratitude, he said, turning to Prescott,—

"Did I not understand you to say your name was Prescott Marland."

"You did."

Emma again blushed. Her heart beat quickly, for she perceived that her cousin was doing what she herself would like to have done, but could not.

"Were you acquainted with an officer in the army named Allen Paige?"

Prescott's fine countenance lit up with pleasing memory.

"I knew him well. We were in the same hospital, and we came to own everything that was sent us in common. Yes, I knew him well, and learned to love him, too," he added with feeling.

Emma's countenance flushed with pleasure; then the blood receded somewhat from her cheeks, and her eyes became suffused with tears.

Prescott observed her emotion. With an impulse he took her hand, and exclaimed,—

"Can it be possible that this is his daughter, of whom he so loved to speak?"

"It is his daughter Emma," interposed William.

As Prescott looked into her beautiful yet tearful eyes, with an ardor borrowed from his remembrance of one whom he had held in such deep regard, he suddenly experienced a thrill which caused him to drop the hand he had taken, while he felt the blood mantling either cheek.

William, whose whole soul was poured into his eyes, received the impression of this scene, even in that dim light, as the sensitive plate of the photographer receives the impressions of nature.

As Emma was the first to recover herself when both she and William were thrown into confusion by the utterance of Prescott Marland's name, so now she first regained sufficient self-control to break the spell which had been so subtly and unexpectedly cast upon them.

She turned to the Veteran.

Prescott understood her. He inwardly rebuked himself — for what he scarcely knew. At the instant he seized her hand her tears had told him that the fearful wound Colonel Paige had received in the same series of battles in which he had received his own last wound (for he had been wounded more than once) had proved fatal; and yet, in the place of the consolation it was on his lips to utter, he realized that he had been overcome by an emotion which his conscience pronounced selfish.

He did not then know that the tender emotions and sympathies of grief oftentimes act as the swiftest conductors for the subtle magnetism of love.

"General," he said, while he still felt the blood tingling his cheeks, "this is, as you have just now heard, the daughter of my friend, Colonel Paige."

The Veteran took her hand, and gazed down upon her with a grave and benignant air.

"Miss Paige," he said, "aside from the satisfaction it gives me to see you relieved from these lawless men, it is tenfold gratifying to know that we have rendered a service to the child of a patriot and a comrade, — especially the child of one whose patriotic devotion has left her an orphan."

The reader has undoubtedly recognized in the Veteran the stranger who so silently entered and departed from the chamber of the heaven-crowned patriot.

The manner of this man, who had so recently displayed such marvellous power, together with his words which he uttered with profound feeling, brought the tears again to Emma's eyes.

A second patrolman appeared now in response to the signal of the first; and the Veteran, offering his arm to Emma, led the way from the street, followed by Prescott, William, and the clerk.

CHAPTER X.

AS they left the recent scene of lawless violence, the rescuers and rescued became more thoroughly introduced to each other.

"Billings," said Marland, with a half-laugh, "I did n't expect that you would so soon have visual evidence of the truth of what I was telling you a little while ago."

The clerk looked at the Veteran.

"No," he said; and then he muttered to himself, —

"Thorbolt,—Thorbolt,—a very appropriate name, I'm sure. He made them bolt, anyhow."

This, however, was not muttered so low as to escape the quick ear and apprehension of the Veteran, who glanced upon Prescott with a smile.

"Still at it, I see," he said.

"Well, who knows," returned Prescott, "if I had not chanced to have been romancing to my companion here, I might not have seen Miss Paige and her cousin as I did."

He then related how he had seen them in company with the old woman, of his immediate suspicions and consequent action in conjunction with the clerk.

"Who was this old woman?" asked the Veteran. "It must have been her scream I heard when I threw the fellow whom I first took hold of."

"She called herself Margaret Roone," answered Emma.

"And Mammy Roone," interposed William Garvin, "which I think much more appropriate."

The young lover was gratified by the glance of approval from the Veteran, on whose arm he beheld his cousin rest with sentiments of pride.

Emma now proceeded to give an account of their adventures up to the moment that Dick Smasher and his confederates attempted to carry out Mammy Roone's diabolical plot.

"Oh!" she exclaimed, as she finished, "what will become of the poor family whom I have sought so long in vain?" and this noble girl seemed at once to forget all the perils and violence through which she had just passed, as the picture of the destitute family of whom she had been speaking came before her mind.

"General," said Prescott Marland, gravely, "of all places New York is the one for an organization which has been recently formed in the West."

The Veteran gave Prescott a significant look. Then, excusing himself a moment, he relinquished Emma's arm, and taking his friend aside, he conversed with him in a low voice.

Then, returning, he again took Emma's arm, and said:—

"It gratifies me to know that not only is Mr. Marland a comrade, as one of the army who fought for freedom, but he is also a comrade in an association, to which, of all the million soldiers who have returned from the battle-ground of the Rebellion, there is not one of good standing who should not unite himself."

"Ay! his duty to his country and to his brother soldier is not entirely fulfilled until he does!" responded Prescott.

"What is the name of this association?" asked the clerk.

"THE GRAND ARMY OF THE REPUBLIC."

"What!" exclaimed Emma, moved by the impressive tone with which the Veteran uttered this name, "is it possible that a political organization can excite such sentiments?"

"The Veteran and Prescott exchanged glances.

"A political organization?" repeated the former.

"Yes," continued Emma, "I heard a gentleman but a few days since, speaking of an organization, called The Grand Army of the Republic, as a political organization."

Daniel Garvin was this gentleman.

The countenance of the Veteran grew stern, and his eye for an instant seemed to range over the vast Union. Emma beheld this expression, and wondered.

"Did the gentleman fight for the Union?" he at length inquired.

"He did not."

"Did he aid the Union cause in any way?"

"I regret to say he did not."

"Did he not aid the foes of his country?" again asked the Veteran, looking down at Emma with an expression that caused her to shrink.

Emma did not answer for her cousin's sake; she did not wish to give utterance to her suspicions, and what she had heard others say, in his presence.

"I read your answer, Miss Paige. It is not necessary for you to speak. Even as during the war the enemies of our country South and North blasphemed the name of Heaven, and calumniated the name of him whom we now call the Martyred President, so do they now distil their poison, by which they would hope to destroy an organization upon which the sainted Lincoln, if he could now speak to us, would pour the blessings of his great and loving heart! Yes, I will prophesy that, as the Grand Army of the Republic sweeps over the land, those who will scoff at it, who will denounce it as a political organization, who will use all manner of means to oppose it, — these men shall be found to have been openly or secretly engaged in the inexpiable crime of this atrocious Rebellion!"

The Veteran spoke with such vehemence, and in a manner so impressive, that his auditors did not venture to break the silence, when he for a moment ceased.

He continued: —

"My dear young lady, I know well I speak to one who, when this organization shall have become established in your city, will be among the foremost women to aid it with your work and influence. Women — may the God in heaven bless them! — stood by the soldiers through the war, and they will stand by them in their noble work, now that we are in the midst of peace. If you find this Grand Army of the Republic to be devoted to the welfare of the widows and orphans of the patriot dead, and of disabled soldiers and sailors yet living, will you not give it your countenance ?"

"Nothing would make me happier," responded Emma, with tears in her eyes.

"I knew it," uttered the Veteran, while he contemplated this noble girl with grave and tender interest. "No other answer could have come from the daughter of one who in his last moments inspired me with a yet deeper veneration for those heroes who, as civilians, left all and encountered the horrors of war for the sake of the Union."

Emma looked up with questioning wonderment, and William Garvin was equally amazed.

Said the Veteran, gently : —

"I entered the chamber of your sainted father at the moment he was about ascending to the arms of his comrades who had gone before him. I simply came and went. You did not see me."

As he uttered these last words he remembered the forbidding face of Daniel Garvin, that alone had been turned upon him in that chamber, and a look of severity crossed his features. In the next instant this face was associated in his mind with the person who had declared to Emma that the Grand Army of the Republic was a political organization.

Emma, on her part, when she thus heard, for the first time, of the presence of this remarkable man at the deathbed of her father, experienced a profound emotion, in which awe was indefinably mingled, as if, in that solemn hour, Heaven had woven in his future with the future of her own family.

The Veteran returned to the subject of the Grand Army.

"Your answer, I repeat, is worthy of that father. And now know that it is the spirit of this organization to seek out the widow and orphans of the soldier, as you have sought them to-day. This is a sublime duty to which it binds itself, and to which it will never be found recreant."

"Ah!" exclaimed Emma, with joy. "Then was my wish granted before I had uttered it."

"Did you wish for such an association?"

"It was this very afternoon I uttered the wish."

"Then is it granted."

"And then am I happy!" responded Emma. "And so it has nothing to do with politics, after all?"

"Nothing. To dabble in politics would be simply suicidal. There are men who believe we are thus foolish, because they are deceived in regard to our object; but, in the main, this report is the invention of those who, having expressed a hope that every soldier who fought for the Union might find a grave in the Southern swamps, now display the same malignant spirit in their efforts to injure the efficiency of organized effort to relieve the families whose husbands and fathers found that grave."

The clerk, who did not lack in penetration of human character, had listened to the Veteran with profound respect.

"General," he said, "I have myself been prejudiced against this organization by statements to the effect that it was controlled by political demagogues and the like; but you have removed those prejudices. To hear you is to believe."

"I thank you," returned the Veteran, with a grave smile. "But allow me to add," he said, his smile giving way to an expression of deep determination, "that there are serious abuses in the treatment of the men who fought to put down the Rebellion, which demand and will receive our attention."

"General," said the clerk, while a look of apprehension crossed his features, "I would like to ask you one question, if you will permit me."

"Certainly."

"Do you think because a man is a Democrat that he is necessarily wanting in devotion to the soldier, and all that appertains to the objects for which the Grand Army of the Republic was formed?"

"By no means, sir. Some of the most zealous members of our organization West are Democrats. Some of the strongest friends of the soldier that I have known are also Democrats. I recall to mind a Democrat living in my native city, Boston, who is a great favorite of the soldiers. They have no better friend. His purse is open to them at all times. He makes no display of his charity, but widows and orphans of our fallen comrades bless him."

"Pray who is this generous Democrat?" asked Emma.

The Veteran gave utterance to a pleased laugh.

"He might even now hear me, and blush, if I should speak his whole name aloud, so I'll beg you to rest satisfied with the familiar appellation, used by his friends, UNCLE NAT."

"I am gratified by your answer to my question, General," said the clerk. "To tell you the truth, my own father, whom I deeply respect, is a Democrat, and he also is, and always has been, a strong friend of the soldier I asked you the question, because you know many think that if a man is a Democrat he must necessarily be opposed to the soldier."

"Far from it. In the workings of our organization we allow no invidious distinctions. Any man who is a true friend of the Constitution and the Union is sure to be a friend of the soldier, and is so recognized, it matters not by what political creed he is known."

"And how is it with the nationalities?" again asked the clerk.

"The same. No distinctions are for a moment entertained. All worthy soldiers who fought for the Union are welcomed to our ranks as comrades and brothers."

"What do they think of the Irish?"

The clerk uttered this with significant emphasis.

"The Irish?" returned the Veteran, with rather a stern glance on the clerk. "I have studied that nation with attention, and will answer you in my own way. This war saw no braver men. Some of the very best of my own command were Irish. The true Irishman is a natural patriot. The Irishman who abetted the Rebellion was false to his nationality. In the two women with whom we have had to do this afternoon we have examples of the two classes. The old woman who led Miss Emma into such danger because she was a soldier's daughter represents a falsehood; the little woman who warned me of the other's infamous plot represents the truth. The possibilities of a race are seen in its representative men. Ireland has furnished such men in numbers sufficient for a dozen nationalities. The *Wild Irishman* is a negative evidence of the possibilities of his race. The greater the capacity for wildness the greater the capacity for civilization. And it would seem as if the Almighty had reserved the Celtic race as grafting-stock, with its extraordinary capacity, for the complete civilization of the world. The Irish stand among the greatest men in the history of England, and to-day Irish blood runs in the veins of some of the most enlightened and progressive men of America. And it is in view of these things that those who are to influence the future of the Irish of this country should realize their solemn responsibility, and see to it that the peasantry, who compose the great mass of this foreign element, be educated to a proper conception of the genius of our institutions. It is the true Celtic character that the Grand Army of the Republic respect, and would see developed from one end of the Union to the other.

"General!" exclaimed Prescott Marland, with earnestness, "as a member of the Grand Army, I thank you for those words. It is the wish of every man who truly loves his country to see fully developed the innate national character of this vast element of our population."

"Very good!" responded the clerk. "But," he added, with a facetious laugh, "how do you account for the Irish bulls?"

"'T is their mother wit in confusion," said Prescott.

"Their swift imagination, which underlies their wit, trips their unschooled tongue," rejoined the Veteran.

The conversation was here interrupted by an approaching car, which the cousins entered, accompanied by the Veteran and Prescott Marland, the clerk here parting company to return home in another direction.

The Veteran and Prescott parted with the cousins at East 27th Street; the former responding to a warm invitation to visit the home of their departed comrade, Allen Paige, by promising to do so at the earliest opportunity, at the same time also promising Emma that she should hear more of the Grand Army and its beneficent purposes.

CHAPTER XI.

ON the third floor of an old building in the rear of the Bowery, and but little more than a stone's-throw from Cooper Institute, Emma might have found the objects of her anxious search, had she been properly directed. They had been driven hither by the raising of the rent of their former lodgings, which, through the machinations of Mammy Roone, was put exorbitantly high for a place so wretched.

The walls of the apartment into which the reader is introduced are cracked and stained, and the rough worn floor bears signs of equal hard usage and neglect; but it is evident that neatness and order are doing their utmost to relieve the room of its unsightly aspect.

Yet this neatness and order only serve to increase the pity of the beholder; for he realizes that the occupants have seen better times, and that this destitution is in gloomy contrast to former comfort.

Joseph Deering had gone out in the ——th New York, and had never returned. He fell in the terrible Peninsular campaign. Though able to comfortably support his family by his daily labor, yet when his faithful hands could no more aid them, they immediately began to experience the pressure of want.

The condition of Mrs. Deering's health, who had been more or less ill for several years, enhanced the misfortune of her husband's death.

Her family consisted of a boy, Joseph, one girl eight years old, named Mary, and a little crippled one, a girl also, whose name was Etta, six years old. This unfortunate little girl was injured by a horse and chaise, which ran over her the year before.

Joseph, who was fourteen years of age, had managed to do something for the support of the family; but in these times of high prices it seemed but a single drop.

It is on the same afternoon the incidents narrated in the preceding chapters occurred that we look in upon this family of the soldier, doomed to an incessant struggle with privation.

The mother is seated in an old straight-backed rocking-chair, an heirloom of her family, which she can never part with, and contemplates her two little girls with a sorrow she can scarcely control.

The picture which thus awakens her grief is the sight of Mary endeavoring to soothe the little cripple, who is suffering from hunger.

"Joseph will bring you something, my poor little sister," said Mary, with a simple faith that sent a new pang to her mother's heart.

At this moment the door opened and Joseph came in.

Mrs. Deering looked at him, but did not speak.

The boy went up to her, and, kissing her on the forehead, said, —

"I have n't done as well as I expected to, mother, but we won't despair."

"No, no, my son, we 'll not despair."

"It would be ungrateful to God, you know, dear mother."

"Yes, ungrateful to God."

"So, dear mother, we 'll take courage."

As Joseph said this he put his arm around his mother's neck and again kissed her.

She could no longer contain herself, but gave vent to her emotions in tears.

The boy remained silent, while the look of a matured man overspread his features.

At length she grew calmer, and Joseph said, —

"Mother, we ought to go to Mrs. Paige."

Mrs. Deering was silent.

"Because," continued Joseph, "if we trust truly in God, we will be reasonable, and not be proud."

"Yes, Joseph."

As the mother thus responded she experienced contending emotions. Pride, and the thought of rumors that had come to her ears of the lamentable state in which Mr. Paige had left his affairs, impelled her to the one side, and the hunger of her little ones impelled her to the other.

The latter influence at length triumphed, and she said, —

"It is well, my son."

As she uttered these few words she seemed for a moment to forget her sorrows in the contemplation of her devoted son.

And well may she thus contemplate this noble boy. He is worthy to be called the son of the soldier who had leaped to the defence of the old flag when it was first trampled underfoot by Rebels. He is never in despair, but in the darkest hours his spirit seems to rise in a never-failing trust in Heaven.

We have seen him just now sustaining his mother, and uttering sentiments that would seem natural to one twice his years. Thus it always was with him, and the other children had come to look upon him as a protector.

This family is but a type of families throughout the land, — families of soldiers who died for their country;

and they have been left to struggle with want, enduring their sufferings in silence rather than seem to come before the world as beggars.

These families, who had given to the Union their husbands and fathers, were being rapidly buried in the oblivion of public selfishness. The promise made to these patriots when they left for the war, that their wives and children should find protectors in a preserved and grateful people, if they should fall, was passing into the dusty archives of history.

Then appeared a protecting arm, — the arm of the GRAND ARMY OF THE REPUBLIC.

This arm was formed by COMRADES.

The civilian, though individually generous in heart, is apt to forget: the soldier, never.

The soldier reminds: the civilian responds.

The Deerings had found in the Paiges benevolent friends. Mrs. Deering, like many another fallen soldier's widow, had found it hard to meet the position into which the death of her husband had thrown her, — the position which demanded that she make known her need and destitution, and be compelled to come before the world as an object of charity.

For they who could justly command the gratitude of the preserved republic were fast coming to be treated as if, unfortunate victims of misalliances, they had been left to the mercies of a cold world by the death or desertion of criminal husbands.

Thus it happened that soldiers' families starved all over the land for which those soldiers had sacrificed their lives, — starved rather than yield to the demands which they felt to be a violation of the memory of their husbands and fathers.

But Allen Paige's family was a soldier's family, and they knew well how to soften the edge of charitable giving by throwing over it the sentiment of duty which one comrade owed another.

Yet still this kindness Mrs. Deering had felt should not be imposed upon; therefore had she often lived in want, rather than seem to presume; until Allen Paige would, perhaps, in the midst of his own pain, turn to his wife or Emma and say, —

"I fear Mrs. Deering may be suffering. Won't you send down and see?"

Alice, who loved to go on these errands, usually went; and on her reporting the state of the case, the suffering family would instantly be relieved.

For some little time, up to within a few days of the opening of this chapter, Joseph had been in the position of errand-boy in the store of Mr. Stanfield, a kind merchant. He, however, had recently died, and left his business in so confused and dubious a condition, that several employees had to be discharged, and among these was Joseph. While he held this situation they managed to get on quite comfortably; and when, some two weeks before Mr. Paige's death, Alice made her last benevolent call, she was assured by Mrs. Deering that they should probably need no further assistance.

Since the death of Mr. Paige Mrs. Deering's reluctance to trouble them with her wants had, from the combined causes known to the reader, increased to such an extent, that it is doubtful whether she would have appealed to their charity for herself before she had experienced yet far greater destitution; but the sight of her children suffering from hunger caused her to yield to the pleading of her boy.

Having, as we have seen, prevailed with his mother, Joseph received her kiss and blessing, and, putting on his cap, went out.

As soon as he had departed Mary came up to her mother, and laid her head in her lap, while the little one looked up and cried, —

"I'm glad Joseph is going to get something to eat. I'm hungry, dear mamma!"

Joseph hastened on his errand, each step seeming to bring food to the mouths of his mother and little sisters.

Mrs. Paige received him with great kindness. It was more than kindness, for her eyes filled with tears as she contemplated this noble boy, whom her husband thought much of on account of his devotion to his mother.

She questioned him closely about their situation, at the same time telling him of the departure of Emma and William to seek them.

Through all Joseph's efforts to brighten the gloom of their poverty she saw the truth; and it was then that she gave way to an inward dread, as she thought of her executors and her late husband's estate.

Her own inconveniences, the result of Daniel Garvin's schemes, had not sufficed to excite that dread; but the contemplation of this poor family's destitution, who had depended so much on their benevolence, for the first time aroused her mind to a vague conception of her possible future.

She left Joseph alone in the drawing-room while she repaired to the pantry.

As he sat in this room he gazed around on the walls, and thought of the wealth which could buy all these fine paintings and engravings; and then he looked at the bronze and marble groups which adorned the room, then on the carved furniture, and a sigh unconsciously escaped him.

"They are all very happy," he thought. "To be sure, Mr. Paige is dead; but it is n't like father's being dead."

Then he thought of his poor mother and little sisters, and sighed again.

It was very still, with the exception of the rumbling of teams outside; and his imagination, which was naturally active, began to picture the enjoyments of this wealthy family, in whose drawing-room he was now sitting.

"They can buy whatever they want," he ruminated. "They are not cold, for they can buy warm clothes and have fires."

Here he fixed his eyes on the ornamented register, which was already sending out the heat to warm the chilly air of late autumn. "Ah, yes, they can be very happy here"; and Joseph fell to musing on the blessing of riches.

He was interrupted by the entrance of Mrs. Paige, with a basket filled with bread, meat, crackers, and the like, in one hand, and a basket of fruit in the other.

Just then a visitor was announced, and Daniel Garvin was ushered in.

At sight of this man Joseph shrank back. He remembered his face to be the cruel, forbidding face which was in the carriage that ran over his little sister Mary.

Joseph remembered aright. It was the face of the broker that he then saw.

Garvin's horse was high-spirited and given to rearing. This little child was playing in the street, and the horse coming upon her, Garvin shouted to her to get out of the way. She was so intently engaged with her play that she neither saw nor heard. The horse reared, and then shied to one side, but not far enough to save the child from the wheels, which passed over her, and made her a cripple for life.

What Joseph remembered was the harsh and unfeeling expression of Garvin's face, and the way in which he drove on, without stopping to see what harm he had done.

He had never again seen him until this instant; and now as he looked at him he shrank back.

But he also experienced the same feeling of stern indignation with which he looked after him on that day.

The broker beheld the shrinking, yet stern and indignant boy with displeasure, and a frown gathered on his sinister brow.

Mrs. Paige saw this frown, but did not divine its meaning, though she observed the boy's manner.

Neither did Joseph, who had good reason to see it.

The boy thought it was because he, being so ill-dressed, was found in this rich and beautiful drawing-room; for he did not know how he had looked at the broker.

But Daniel Garvin scowled because he had come in to see how his schemes worked, and he had been unexpectedly met by Joseph's stern, indignant gaze, which seemed to pierce his soul.

"Who is this boy?" he said harshly.

Mrs. Paige turned toward the broker with a look of surprise. Her face slightly flushed, and her form was instinctively erected.

Her voice, however, was calm.

"He is the son of a soldier who was killed in the war."

"Ah!"

Now this "ah!" was short, but uttered as it was, and accompanied by a supercilious glance, first at Joseph, then at Mrs. Paige, and then on the baskets, it possessed a deep significance. Mrs. Paige now assumed an air which had its effect; for no man could behave like a boor in Margaret Paige's presence, and not be made to feel her rebuke.

"Yes," he added in a manner considerably modulated, and yet so artfully graduated that it would seem to be the result of his own thoughts, — "yes, yes, the son of a fallen soldier. Well, yes; you're a good boy, I hope?"

Joseph made no answer to this patronizing question; but beginning to feel very awkward in that fine room, with the broker's sinister eyes running up and down his patched clothing, he looked to the floor and blushed painfully.

Mrs. Paige came to his rescue.

"Yes, I can speak for him, Mr. Garvin, as being one of the best of boys."

Saying which she took him kindly by the hand to lead him out.

"By no means," exclaimed the broker, on seeing her movement. "I have only dropped in for an instant, and my time is up."

He looked at his watch, and with the ejaculation, "So late!" he bowed himself out, evidently not desirous of lengthening his visit for that time.

Both Mrs. Paige and the boy breathed more freely when this man had freed them of his ill-boding presence.

Joseph began to stammer out apologies for having intruded himself.

"Do not let your mind be troubled, my dear boy," said his benefactress. "But why did you look at him so when he came in?"

Joseph glanced down on his old clothes at this question.

Mrs. Paige read his thoughts.

"You looked at him as if you had seen him before," she added.

"Never but once," replied Joseph, as his face began to gather the same expression which it assumed when the broker came in.

Mrs. Paige saw there was something to be explained, and she drew from Joseph his story.

Having finished his story, so full of significance to her who had already herself begun to feel the malevolence of this man, she gave him the baskets, and an order on the wood and coal dealer, and sent him home to cheer those who were anxiously awaiting him.

CHAPTER XII.

SEVERAL weeks have passed. Mrs. Paige has been made to feel more and more the cordon that is being drawn around her. For a while after his visit, when he met Joseph in the drawing-room, Daniel Garvin had deemed it advisable to reassume his plausible and hypocritical manner; but as he watched the final development of his plans his fangs again began to show themselves.

At length the time arrived when she felt that her mind must fully prepare itself for whatever might happen.

As a first step she determined to ascertain, if possible, the intentions of her executors. She therefore wrote to Jonas Cringar.

This was the note:—

JONAS CRINGAR, ESQ.

DEAR SIR, — Will you be so kind as to call and see me this evening. I confess to feeling much anxiety regarding the settlement of Mr. Paige's estate. Besides your own expressed fears, I have heard many rumors of a nature calculated to have long ago alarmed me, if I had not been sustained by a very strong confidence in the business character of my dear husband. But even this confidence will not suffice to sustain me without some more definite statement of affairs, as things now appear.

I write you because I have learned to esteem you as Allen's long-trusted partner and friend, and can consult with you with greater freedom than I can with Mr. Garvin.

Trusting you will grant my request, I remain

Yours, very truly,

ISABEL PAIGE.

When Jonas Cringar received this note his face was agitated by conflicting emotions. He read it over two or three times, as if first his eyes read it, then his mind, then his conscience.

Finally he crumpled it in his nervous fingers, resting his hand on his knee, and gazed before him in a sort of stupor.

Presently he heaved a sigh and exclaimed, —

"My God!"

Without saying more, he took his hat and went out, the clerks gazing after him with looks which said, —

"His conscience troubles him."

That evening Mrs. Paige sat in the drawing-room, anxiously awaiting the merchant.

As she sat there she contemplated the paintings, statuary, and carved furniture, which had thrown Joseph into such a deep revery, and sighed.

In the midst of this revery the door-bell rang, and Jonas Cringar was ushered in.

As he entered the door he glanced around the room where he had spent so many hours with his late partner, and his conscience smote him with such violence that for a moment he did not move, and he visibly trembled.

Mrs. Paige observed his emotion; but though she partly

interpreted it, she did not dream of the hidden anguish of this unhappy man, nor of the fearful struggle which was incessantly going on within him.

She advanced to meet him.

"I thank you for coming," she said. "I am now anxious to hear all that you know or think about the condition of the estate."

The merchant continued to hold her hand in his embarrassment, but could not at once find words to answer her. But at length his tongue was loosened a little, and with a halting speech he said, —

"Mrs. Paige, I really thank you for reposing confidence in me. I — really shall be happy to tell you all I know or think."

Poor slave! It was the last thing he intended to do.

He being seated, Mrs. Paige at once entered into the business for which she had sent for him.

"Mr. Cringar, there have been many reports that have come to my ears, as you well know, some of them very injurious to my departed husband's reputation; but these I cannot afford to notice, only as they affect the hearts and feelings of those who hold his memory dear, and who are jealous of his good name. It is to you that I must look for the information that is to govern our future actions."

Cringar, during this speech, had been exerting himself, with all the mental strength he possessed, to acquire the firmness necessary to carry him through the coming ordeal; and Mrs. Paige had not been unobservant of the varying expression of his countenance.

"My dear Mrs. Paige," he said, "you must prepare your mind for the worst."

"I have."

"I am rejoiced to hear it."

"You have the worst to tell me?"

"Yes."

Cringar now hesitated, and looked from the ceiling, where he had cast his eyes when he had begun to speak, down to the floor; for he was not yet able to look the intended victim of his wickedness in the face.

"You will oblige me by at once telling me the whole," uttered Mrs. Paige, with anxious severity.

This compelled the merchant to turn his eyes upon her, but they instantly turned off again.

"You must give up the idea of indulging in acts of benevolence, my dear madam, even toward soldiers' families."

"Mr. Cringar, I have not requested you to come to give me such advice as this. Tell me the truth as regards my husband's business, and I will judge what I can give to others."

Jonas Cringar, now driven to a corner, broke out with desperation, —

"Well, then — *all is lost!*"

Mrs. Paige turned pale, but retained her composure.

"All?"

"Yes! — all! — everything!"

"It is impossible!"

"Ah, madam! I knew you would say so!" exclaimed the merchant, in a voice in which sympathetic distress and remorse were strangely mingled.

"And have I not reason to say so?" asked this wronged woman, who, though inwardly agitated, fixed a penetrating gaze upon the guilty merchant.

He quailed before this gaze.

But now he felt that all his resources must be brought to bear, or he should have to answer for bad work to Daniel Garvin.

That natural obliquity of character, which has been intimated as belonging to him now came into play and gave him what might be called (if we may be allowed a rather uncouth figure) a second mental wind.

Having thus gathered strength, he for the first time was able to look his interlocutor fairly in the face.

"You certainly have reason to *think* so, dear madam; but Mr. Garvin and myself can submit statements to you which will convince you that all I say is true."

"May I ask what those statements are?"

"Certainly; and I will say that they seem to be supported by the most conclusive evidence."

"Well."

"Some of them are claims of a most unexpected nature; while others have to do with transactions which, while I very deeply lamented them at the time, yet I have kept silent about them, hoping something would turn up to mitigate their evils."

"Well."

"Well, then, Mr. Paige, like too many victims of the fever which has prevailed in business circles for the past few years, has, it seems, risked everything in speculation, and in every instance very unfortunately."

Jonas Cringar stopped a moment, but the intended victim of his abominable falsehoods remained silent.

Gathering strength by working either knee in those nervous, bony hands, he continued:—

"You see, my dear Mrs. Paige, this speculative fever seized many a man as honest and upright as my late partner. Character did not come into the question at all. It had no more to do with a man's reputation than typhoid fever, or typhus fever, or any other fever."

The merchant now extended one of his hands, as if

about to deliver a lecture on the morality and immorality of speculation.

Mrs. Paige interrupted him.

"Mr. Cringar," she said, "I do not need that you should defend Mr. Paige's character to me. I will thank you —"

"Well, then, — well, then, — you see there have been very bad complications in our own business on account of it. Drawing from one's legitimate business so incessantly to allay this terrible fever, it brings things to a fearful pass, madam. You see there it was, — his losing so many thousands in his cotton speculation, it was a bad beginning."

"Mr. Cringar," uttered Margaret Paige, in a subdued but steady voice, "you speak to me in riddles."

"I suppose so; it must seem so, my dear madam," returned Cringar, whom the reader will readily perceive to be devoid of all necessary qualifications for such an interview as this which he had undertaken. "It 's a riddle to all of us, — the way in which what seemed an ample fortune has vanished. It seems like a dream, madam, and if I 'm a little incoherent, ascribe it to the difficulty I experience in trying to make known to you facts which I know must astound you and make you miserable."

"This cotton, Mr. Cringar," said the soldier's widow, in whom now a feeling of contempt was mingling with her apprehensions, "I am aware that Mr. Paige once had a transaction in cotton; but he informed me that he had made much money by it, and he was not accustomed to utter an untruth."

"Ah, madam, it is n't for me, who loved him like a brother, to cast any aspersions upon the character of my late partner, or throw doubts on his integrity. But the fact of it is, madam, he undoubtedly supposed when he told you that he had cleared a profit on that cotton, that he had really done so. The market was rising very rapidly, and he was n't the only man who counted on profits before his time. But he was so unfortunate as to hold on too long, though I kept advising him to let it go; and the result was a heavy loss."

"He never told me of this, Mr. Cringar."

"It is one of the unfortunate features of speculation, my dear madam," spoke this abject tool, who was beginning to find his tongue, — "one of the unfortunate features of speculation, that even the noblest and most open-hearted men will be so shamed by their losses, they dare not say anything about them to others, often feeling the most reluctant to make them known to those who really have the greatest claims on their confidence. In fact, now that you speak of it, Mrs. Paige, I recall to mind," continued the merchant, lifting his right hand half-way to his lips, with the long forefinger extended, and at the same time bent like a claw, — "yes, I recall to mind very distinctly his saying to me once, when I was urging him to sell out, even at a small loss rather than suffer a greater one, 'Jonas,' — for he always spoke to me familiarly, — 'Jonas, I have told my wife that I am good for a large profit on this cotton, and I intend to stick,' — excuse me, madam; that 's a phrase sometimes used in speculation, and I wish to quote his exact language, — 'I intend to stick till the market takes another jump.'"

At this moment Emma came in from the street, accompanied by Alice, and opened the door of the drawing-room, when, perceiving her mother and Jonas Cringar alone, and comprehending at a glance somewhat the nature of the business between them, she made a move to retire. But Mrs. Paige requested her to enter.

This action on the part of the mother was the result of a sudden inspiration.

She had not been deceived by the apparent candor of the merchant, clothed though it was by such verbosity as he had displayed. She had by no means a superficial knowledge of human nature; she had closely observed Jonas Cringar while he so desperately labored to acquit himself properly in the business he had undertaken, and apprehended that some powerful influence had been exerted to subdue the natural impulses which she was certain his heart felt toward the family of his late partner. She therefore, on seeing Emma and Alice, instantly formed a resolve to re-enforce these impulses.

"Emma," she said, "will you and Alice please sing that duet which Mr. Cringar loved so much to hear when he came to see your father."

Emma was surprised by this request, for it was the first time her mother had desired them to sing since their father's death.

As for the merchant, he already began to experience those reactionary emotions on which Mrs. Paige had calculated. He was silent, however.

Emma went up to the piano with Alice, and opening it for the first time for many weeks, turned and said, while she looked inquiringly toward the merchant, —

"Mr. Cringar loved to hear more than one duet?."

The merchant said nothing in answer to this remark, but his face betrayed the internal struggle of his soul.

"Your German song, *Stille Nacht*," said Mrs. Paige.

This beautiful trio, sung as a duet by the sisters, so well calculated both to touch and soothe the spirit in its varied moods and to awake in the soul the tenderest reminiscences, began at once to produce a remarkable effect on the already agitated countenance of Jonas Cringar. The German words had formerly been interpreted to him, so that he understood their meaning, while they lent to the song a sweetness which no translation could have done.

Emma and Alice had not sung this song since their father died, and though their tones were firm when they began, thoughts of this beloved father soon caused their voices to tremble, and the exertion they were compelled to make to master their emotions served but to enhance the profoundly touching effect of the music.

This, added to the natural character of the song, seemed to bring the merchant into the very presence of the departed soldier, and with an audible groan he buried his face in his hands.

Mrs. Paige now rose, and, advancing, placed her hand on his shoulder.

At this instant the bell sounded through the house with a loud, harsh ring.

As his ears were greeted by this ominous sound, Jonas Cringar suddenly lifted his head, clasped the arm of the chair with his quivering hand, and gazed at the door with a face so distorted with fear, that Emma and Alice, who had turned when the bell rang, stopped in the last measures of the song, startled and alarmed by his extraordinary aspect; while the mother seemed to divine the cause of this agitation, to which her own heart to a degree responded.

In another moment the thick and ursine form of Daniel Garvin presented itself at the threshold.

"I trust I do not intrude," he said in a rasping voice, at the same time sending a terrific glance at the blanching merchant.

The ladies made no answer, but Jonas Cringar muttered in a scarcely audible voice, —

"You 're entirely welcome."

"I thought so," returned the broker, coming forward and making a formal bow to all in the room at once, while his upper lip drew back so as to expose his threatening teeth.

Then taking a chair he turned to Mrs. Paige and said:—

"I was at Mr. Cringar's store a short time since, and, though I did not find him there, I found your note requesting him to meet you here this evening, on business concerning the estate of your late husband. And notwithstanding you intimated, madam, that it might not be so agreeable a task for me to perform as for him, I at once decided that you should not be left half enlightened from any lack of zeal on my part, and therefore I am here, at your service, madam."

The closing words of this speech, "at you service, madam," were uttered in a tone in which the hidden sarcasm of it culminated, being also accompanied by a slight bow.

Mrs. Paige heard him through with a firm, steady look; while Jonas Cringar, having cast his eyes on the speaker when he commenced, withdrew them and riveted them to the carpet with a look of distress on Garvin's informing the widow of his finding the note. He immediately cursed himself for his carelessness.

The broker waited a moment, while he changed his glance from Mrs. Paige to the daughters, who still remained at the piano, and then to the merchant.

Then he asked in a harsh, cutting voice,—

"Is the business finished? or is this music only serving you as an interlude?"

We have before seen that Cringar was not without spirit; and the overbearing manner of the broker toward this family, for whom he really had so high a regard, and who, through his villanous schemes, were now on the brink of ruin, served to rouse him for an instant from his lethargic fears.

He leaned forward in his chair, and fixed on Garvin a look of indignant rebuke.

"The music," he answered, "was an act of attention to one who has spent many happy hours in this house."

The only answer the broker vouchsafed to this was a gleam of his malevolent eye, and an apparently unconscious movement of his hand to the pocket from which he had taken the damning paper on the night of Allen Paige's death.

The merchant turned pale, and again sank helplessly back.

Mrs. Paige now spoke.

"Mr. Garvin, Mr. Cringar had barely commenced detailing the condition in what he is pleased to affirm my late husband's business was in when he left me. What he has already told me I must say to you as I have said to him, that it is impossible."

"What have you told her?" demanded Garvin, sharply, fixing his ringed orb on the once more cowering eye of the merchant.

"The cotton," was Cringar's simple answer.

"Well, what of it?" returned the broker, while a frown began to darken his features.

"Simply this," said Mrs. Paige, "that what he has told me about Mr. Paige's cotton transaction is entirely contradictory to my husband's own statements, and is to me incredible."

Garvin's features now began to gather that expression which we have beheld at the crises of his interviews with the merchant. On beholding these signs of an approaching scene, Cringar closed his eyes and shuddered.

Having darkened his direful visage with the gloomy clouds of the coming storm, the broker prepared to let loose the thunder.

"Madam!" he exclaimed, in his harshest and most penetrating accents, "we have found our work sufficiently ungrateful, without the addition of your own ingratitude. Your husband, madam, appears to have been a rash and reckless man; and when he appointed his partner and myself as executors of his estate, he seems to have calculated on our friendship to conceal his folly."

Mrs. Paige now made a motion as if she would interrupt; but Garvin extended his right hand, and cried, —

"You must hear me, madam!"

She remained silent.

"Now, madam, I will at once to business. You may believe my statements or not, but let me assure you your belief does n't affect the result. We 've not taken oath to act according to your belief, but according to law. Know then that Mr. Allen Paige's accounts show up a loss of some twenty thousand dollars in cotton, losses amounting to over seventy-five thousand dollars in mining and oil, and thousands with Mr. Cringar himself in cotton goods, and also from complications in their business, resulting from his speculative mania. Is this not so, Mr. Cringar?"

The merchant did not seem to hear this question.

The broker bent his lurid eyes upon him, and repeated it in a voice that would seem to penetrate to the merchant's marrow.

"Jonas Cringar, is this not sc?"

The wretched man looked up like a defenceless animal wounded by a beast of prey, and said in a faint voice, —

"It is all too true! too true!"

"And now, madam," continued Garvin, rising from his chair, "it is my duty to inform you, without further delay, that you can no longer support this costly house, for it is not yours. It must be sold to pay the debts of the estate, and that immediately. And let me tell you, as a sort of guardian," — the broker could not keep entirely back the appearance of a sardonic grin as he said this, — "that you must either live on the charity of others, or seek some means of support with your daughters here," — he turned his satanic visage on Emma and Alice, — "who, I am happy to see, look hearty and strong."

Mrs. Paige had risen at the last of this heartless speech, and stood, overwhelmed with conflicting emotions, supporting herself at the table. She was moved by profound indignation, not unmingled with disgust; but at the same time her soul sickened with the conviction that the man before her held the power to make real all that, in his words, threatened her and her family. She stood gazing on this diabolical destroyer of her peace, while her various emotions displayed themselves on her countenance, but she could find no words.

Daniel Garvin enjoyed for a space the distressed confusion of this unhappy widow of his patriotic half-brother, and then, drawing back his upper lip, he said, —

"Mrs. Paige, I would add — "

Ere he could say more Emma stepped forward to her mother's rescue.

Her beautiful face was flushed, and her clear hazel eyes were lit by an indignation so deep and strong that even Daniel Garvin could not meet their gaze unmoved. As she thus stood before him, with her form erect, and her head thrown back, she recalled to the mind of this unnatural uncle her father, when his generous and impulsive spirit would be stirred by passion. As this recollection thus crossed his mind, he experienced a secret smiting of his conscience, which mingled with emotions of dark and brooding triumph.

"Sir!" exclaimed this noble daughter, in a voice corresponding with her looks, "you have said you came here on business. That business is for the present finished. Whatever of truth or falsehood there may be in your statements, my mother can hear no more. We would be alone."

"Certainly, my dear," returned Garvin; and, taking his hat, he withdrew, followed by Jonas Cringar.

CHAPTER XIII.

A FEW days after the interview between Mrs. Paige and the merchant and broker, Emma sat meditating in her room. She thought of Cringar and her uncle, and a shudder went through her frame. A woful future loomed before her vision. She thought, too, of her mother, who had just risen from an illness brought on by the revelation, in all its fulness, of the atrocious plot which the previous whisperings and rumors had presaged, and her eyes were wet with tears. The events of the past few days had proved too much for even her brave and elastic nature. Her cheeks had paled, and a shade of blue appeared under her hazel eyes, which gave signs of anxiety and weeping.

In her sorrow, however, there were two figures which continually came to her mind; these were the figures of the Veteran and Prescott Marland. The former rose before her as a power which was indefinably mingled with her future. When the image of her father came to her mind, this majestic form ever seemed to accompany it. She could not think of one without recalling the other.

But from the Veteran she invariably passed to another, who was also associated in her mind with her father. This association was, however, of a more tender character. When she thought of him, the blood slightly flushed the pale cheeks, and the saddened eye kindled with the heart's involuntary emotions.

She would continually recall to her mind the look which appeared in his eyes, when he took her by the hand after his brave contest with the ruffians who had assaulted her. The look was only for an instant, but it was none the less to be remembered. It was one of those impressions that pass beyond the retina of the eye, beyond the brain, to be ineffaceably fixed within the heart itself, where it remains forever.

Her own soul had responded to the thrill which was experienced by Prescott when he held her hand, and which was simultaneous with the look so vividly impressed upon her heart. But scarcely would she acknowledge it to herself.

It is a charming feature of virgin love, that the maiden who experiences its first throbs not only shrinks from the thought that it may be perceived by the world, but she will even shut out her own common self from the scrutiny; and while the budding sentiment is nursed in the most secret and the tenderest depths of the heart, she closes the eye of introspection just enough to lend a delicate fascination to what it beholds; like one who, gazing at the dawn, gently closes the lid that its glory may be seen through the lashes, and acquire a dreamlike charm and beauty.

It was from this maidenly by-play, probably, that the Veteran was generally first allowed to assume definite shape in her mind. It would seem as if he was kept in the foreground, that her own mind might rest satisfied that the heart was not playing false; while in reality the object held in the distance was continually drawing the mind away, lit up in an entrancing haze by the rays of the golden sunlight.

As Emma sat in her room on the day we have mentioned, she had, as we have said, been thinking of those things which filled her heart with apprehension and grief.

At length her thoughts began to dwell on the Veteran and Prescott Marland. Neither had as yet responded to her invitation to visit the home of their comrade, her own sainted father. They had promised to do so, and she could not readily believe the promise would be broken.

Yet, after weeks had passed, and one day succeeded another with no word from either, a fear began to steal into her mind that their adieus, made when they parted on the evening they had so strangley met, might, perchance, be the last.

While in the midst of these thoughts she heard a knock at the door.

"Come in," she said.

The maid entered, bearing a card on which was written the name of Prescott Marland.

This name, announcing the presence, below, of one of whom she was at that moment so earnestly thinking, caused the telltale blood to mount to her cheeks.

"Tell him," she said in some confusion, "that I will be down in a few moments."

The maid, who had observed her mistress's confusion, retired, saying to herself, "It is the common lot!" while

Emma hastily prepared herself to meet one who had recently occupied so large a share of her thoughts.

"Mr. Marland," said Emma, as she entered the drawing-room into which Prescott had been ushered, "I welcome you to the home of my dear father and your friend."

"I thank you, Miss Paige; but I would amend your kind welcome."

"You may do so," returned Emma, with a smile.

"You said, 'my dear father and your friend.' I would say, 'my dear father and your dear friend.'"

"Thank you."

An expression of tender sadness mingled with her smile, as Emma uttered this response. At the same time she experienced a sentiment of pride, on hearing such words from one of whom her father had spoken so highly, and whom she herself looked upon as the type of nobleness.

"My father never dreamed of such a first meeting as was ours, when he used to speak so warmly of your friendship," she said.

"Neither did I," returned Prescott, "when he used to speak of you in our conversations at the hospital. And yet, Miss Paige, being of a somewhat romantic turn of mind, I will confess that my knowledge of the father, added to the pictures he drew of his daughter, led me into youthful dreams of saving her from some great peril; and here the dream is fulfilled, — that is, in a measure."

Both blushed. Such youthful dreams are associated with ideal love; and what Prescott intended in the commencement to be a gallant remark was to both, before he had finished, evidently something that went much further than gallantry.

"You say, 'in a measure,'" remarked Emma, after a moment's silence. "Why in a measure?"

"Because others were engaged in the rescue as well as myself," laughingly answered Prescott.

"I am grateful to all," returned Emma; "but if it had not been for your courage and strength, Mr. Marland, I fear I should not now be here to welcome you."

Having discharged himself of his duty, which modesty demanded to others, Prescott was but too happy to hear his praises from lips so charming.

Both now felt more at their ease, and the conversation flowed on with a mutual enjoyment which each secretly wished might be prolonged into hours. That confidence which underlies all true affection began to manifest itself in a manner which a reader of the human heart would at once interpret.

None had greater reason to repose confidence in each other, at this early stage of their acquaintance, than these young people. That noble and affectionate father, whom both loved, one as a parent and the other as a friend, had brought them together in spirit long before they had ever seen each other in the body. As we have seen, their very hearts had reached out toward each other in response to the utterances of the now beatified patriot; and it only remained that the ideal they had each drawn be tested by the presence of the real.

This test, made under circumstances, as formerly narrated, so favorable to the heart's emotions, had confirmed all that the ideal had fondly pictured; and now, as they conversed, they seemed to have been acquainted for years.

Emma had apologized in behalf of her mother, on account of illness, at an early stage of the visit. When she thus apologized, the ill-boding presence of Daniel Garvin came to her mind, as he appeared on the night that he revealed the future he had prepared for them. She shuddered at this recollection, and for a moment seemed to forget even the presence of her visitor.

Prescott observed her agitation, but ascribed it to emotions connected with her mother's illness and father's death.. She had more than once felt impelled to reveal to him the situation of affairs, and the cause of her mother's illness, which would explain also the evidences of sorrow that appeared on her own countenance; for, with woman's intuition, she knew that he not only perceived these evidences, but that his mind was disturbed with conjectures as to their cause.

At length, in the course of this interview, in which minutes seemed to these youthful hearts but seconds, Emma was sent for by her mother. Excusing herself for a few moments, she left Prescott alone.

He now contemplated, as had Joseph on a former occasion, the evidences of affluence which surrounded him. Like Joseph he admired the works of art, though, unlike this poor boy, the richly carved furniture did not so much engross his attention, nor did the warmth which came from the ornamented registers remind him of a cold mother and sisters in a home of want; for though his family were not wealthy, they never lacked for those things essential to comfort, and had, moreover, been able to gratify, to a considerable extent, their naturally fine taste. But, as I have said, Prescott contemplated the works of art about him with admiration.

The paintings had been evidently selected for their true artistic qualities. Harmony, force, and freedom indicated the master, while here and there a small painting, in which crudities mingled with the touches of genius, confirmed the reputation won by Allen Paige, of kindly encouraging the young and struggling artist.

The statuary indicated equally good taste. In the midst of classic copies appeared some of the famous groups by John Rogers, which present in so vivid and instructive a manner the various phases of the Rebellion.

But what fastened the attention of this already ardent lover more than all else was a water-color, in one corner of which, as he approached it, his quick eye had detected the name of Emma Paige. It was much above the standard of the usual artistic performances of young ladies (no imputation is intended; the young women of America are showing a commendable zeal in the direction of art culture, and are worthily improving their opportunities), being characterized by originality, and a freedom from the conventional hardness and stiffness which results from a false idea as to what constitutes finish.

The subject of this sketch was a vista, formed by lofty and graceful elms, through which appeared the western sky in the glory of an autumnal sunset. Walking down this vista, their forms borrowing a slight glory from the distance against which they were boldly painted, were a youth and a maiden hand in hand.

Prescott stood entranced before this picture, forgetting all else; and as the rumbling of the carriages without had combined with the silence within to enhance the abstraction of Joseph's mind, as he profoundly meditated on the vicissitudes of earthly fortunes, so now this rumbling in the street, combined with the silence about him, served to deepen Prescott's contemplations, as he gazed on those two forms against the golden sky.

With the fervor of newly awakened passion his heart read a prophecy in this picture. It seemed as if the lovely artist had painted herself, thus hand in hand with him.

Ah! the egotism of love, and yet its insidious and tormenting fears! The smitten lover absorbs all things to himself, and yet his heart is an unceasing victim of uncertainty and apprehension. Does one who fancies himself in love not experience this?—then he is not in love.

Thus with the young lover who contemplates this picture from the hand of the one he loves. His heart pictures that fair hand giving to each touch a prophetic meaning, and he the object of that prophecy. Then immediately it is oppressed with doubtful thoughts. "Is her love not pledged to another? And even if it is not, what claims have I, Prescott Marland, a rough fellow, a fellow who has been knocking around the world, and got the smell of camp-fires on me.—A hand" (here he eyes his large muscular hand) well enough to knock a rascal down with who insults her, but hardly the hand to clasp her delicate little fingers,—a fellow that needs smoothing down before he can expect to win one like her." Then, in his enamored musings, he pictured this lovely girl as the one of all others to make him the man he wanted to be. Under her potent influence he would become as gentle as a lamb, and his hasty passions only be reserved for her defence. And all the time the distant rumbling of the teams and the surrounding silence lent their aid to the increasing and all-absorbing influence of the picture before him.

While thus standing, rapt in tender contemplation of her sketch, Emma so lightly entered the room that he did not hear her. He so stood that, while his back was mostly turned toward her, a quarter-view of his face was revealed. In this view the profounder manifestations of the soul often appear on the countenance with remarkable effect. In the present instance Prescott's expressive face, though so nearly turned from her, revealed, in combination with his attitude, the nature of the thoughts which agitated his soul with such tender and conflicting emotions.

In an instant this fair girl's cheeks were covered with blushes.

That the reader may understand the cause of this charming confusion, it is necessary for us to remark that she had more than once stood before that same picture, as her visitor now stood before it, and formed into living portraits the figures of the two lovers who were wending their way down the romantic vista.

These portraits were Prescott Marland and herself!

Becoming suddenly aware of her presence, Prescott turned. Thus finding himself surprised in the midst of his enamored thoughts, and perceiving the blushes on the fair face of her who had so engrossed his meditations, this dreaming lover felt himself detected, and blush responded to blush.

A celebrated preacher and lecturer recently informed his audience that he never saw two young people in love that he did n't wish himself one of them. We doubt not that if he could have looked in at the moment Prescott turned, he would have had but little hesitation in deciding that such a wish here would have been legitimate.

They now resumed their seats.

"Miss Paige," said Prescott, impelled by his momentary confusion to utter what first came to his mind, "I have been admiring your art-treasures, for such I must call them. You certainly must be very happy in the possession of so many mementos of your father, to whose taste, judging from his conversations with me at the hospital, these walls are largely indebted. I should think," he continued, seeing that his listener remained silent, "that you would always wish to remain here. To your mother everything must be especially dear—"

Ere he could go on Emma had quickly covered her face with her handkerchief, and then, with one great struggle to control herself, she broke into violent weeping.

CHAPTER XIV.

AS we have remarked, Prescott, in his momentary confusion, uttered that which first came to his mind. He could have said nothing, to one whose soul had already been so deeply agitated, more calculated to affect her in the manner which now threw him into dismay.

He began inwardly to berate himself as a stupid fellow, who thus early gave indubitable evidence of his unfitness for a mind so sensitive and refined.

"Why did I talk to her in that way?" he said to himself. "Could n't I have seen that her grief for her father's death is as keen as ever?"

But Emma did not thus accuse him. Even in the midst of her sobbing she felt drawn still nearer to him.

"Miss Emma," he at length said, at the same time rising and placing his right hand tenderly on her arm, "forgive me for touching a tender chord so roughly."

This was the first time he had called her by her given name.

From an irresistible impulse, Emma raised her own right hand, while the other still covered her face. Prescott saw this movement. He withdrew his from her arm, and in the next instant their two hands were clasped together.

For a moment it seemed as though each heart was pouring all its streams of life into the other, and then the hands unclapsed.

In the common routine of life, months could not have accomplished what was attained in that moment toward establishing relations of confidence between these two souls.

Emma suddenly, as it were, found herself with one to whom she could unbosom all her sorrows.

When their hands were unclasped, Prescott said, —

"Let me be a brother to you."

"Ah yes! an elder brother. Do you know," continued Emma, now wiping away the tears, while she smiled upon him through her glistening lashes, — "do you know that I have longed for an elder brother, in whom to confide, for several weeks past? And my dear mother needs a son. You will be a son to her, will you not?"

"I will," responded Prescott.

The delightful emotion, on hearing himself thus associated with the mother's name as her son was quickly resolved into a profound sentiment of devotion to the widow and orphan children of his comrade.

"I suspect," he continued, "that you have other causes for sorrow beside the death of your father. Is it here that I can help you?"

"Alas! I can hardly tell!" exclaimed Emma, "but you shall know all."

She thereupon gave Prescott a detailed account of all that had occurred; of the appointment of Jonas Cringar and her uncle as executors; and of the whisperings and rumors, followed by the scene which was described in the previous chapter, and in which Garvin declared to them their state of beggary. When she came to her mother's illness the tears again filled her eyes.

Prescott's fine countenance assumed varied expressions as Emma recounted this tale. Sympathy, indignation, and contempt, in turn, displayed themselves. But when he beheld these tears his wrath broke forth.

"Villains!" he exclaimed. "We will see!" At the same time he rested his clenched hand on his knee.

"Poor mother!" continued Emma. "She hardly knows how to act. If my uncle told the truth, then she cannot bear to think that for a day she is living on the property of others; for not only are we left penniless, but the estate is in debt."

"What does your mother propose to do?"

"She has n't been able to think. She was taken ill the night of the interview with Mr. Cringar and my uncle, and any effort to think of this business makes her dizzy."

"Then please tell her not to think at present. I believe there is a base plot under all this, and I know of one who can ferret it out, if such is the case."

Emma looked at Prescott with inquiring interest.

"It is Thorbolt."

"General Hammond?"

"Yes."

"But would General Hammond trouble himself for us?"

"Your father sacrificed his life on the altar of his country. His death leaves his family exposed to what I believe a villanous plot. When I shall have laid all the circumstances before the General, depend on his hearty co-operation with me. He has leisure, which enables him to do much that otherwise he could not do. It will not be the first time. I cannot now tell you of the number of the families of his comrades he has aided in different ways."

"But my father was not a member of your Order, and we cannot be considered as destitute."

"Ah, Miss Emma! here lies one of the noblest characteristics of our organization. We do not confine our benefactions to its members. We reach out to all Union soldiers, or their families, who suffer. Of course one of our prominent duties is to seek out those families of the soldier who are in need, and relieve their wants. Our fund, which is devoted to this purpose, is often called a Charity fund, but it should always be called a Relief fund. When we aided our comrades, who were suffering on the field for want of food or clothing, we did not call our help *charity*, but *relief*. So with those who demand our aid at home. They are not objects of charity, they justly claim relief; and therefore the fund which accomplishes this should be called the Relief fund. Charity presupposes no obligation, in the common acceptation of that term, on the part of the donor, whereas the suffering families of the patriot soldier have claims which no lack of memory can obliterate from the records of a preserved Union."

"True! oh, how true! It is what we always told the Deerings. Father would say, 'Tell Mrs. Deering that if I had been lying a sufferer on the field, and her husband had been at hand, he would have given me all the aid in his power as a comrade; and now that I cannot be of aid to him as a comrade I want to do my duty to his family.'"

"Yes, your father's sentiments are the sentiments of our Order. He did his duty as an individual; the Grand Army is formed that as an organization it may enable the million of returned soldiers to do their duty in the same way, as ONE. But I have not fully answered your former remark. Though the more prominent work, which the Grand Army has laid out for itself, is the relief of soldiers' families who are in want, yet it intends also to fulfil the spirit of the law!"

"The spirit of the law?" repeated Emma, with an inquiring smile.

"It is an expression that came ready to my lips. This is what I mean by it," returned Prescott, to whose ardor in the cause of the Grand Army was added an exquisite happiness in thus being permitted to expound its principles to one in whose presence he so loved to linger, and whom, in the swift pictures that crossed his enamored imagination, he associated with himself in the noble labors he contemplated in connection with the future work of the organization which so engrossed his attention, — "this is what I mean by it: I mean that the Grand Army of the Republic intends to see fulfilled the spirit of all promises made to the soldier when he left his home and went to the field to help put down the Rebellion. When those promises were made, the country was in danger, and the men who went forth to save it departed with "God bless yous!" that filled the whole Northern air. If they should fall their families would be adopted by a grateful people, and know naught else but comfort; and to their memory should be erected monuments to remind future generations of their heroic patriotism and a nation's gratitude. If they should escape the dangers of war and return in safety, then would they in person feel this undying gratitude. Nothing that could be done for them should be left undone. They would be objects of special favor; and, other things being equal, the name of soldier would be the talisman that should open the way to employment at all times. All this, and much more, rang forth as in an anthem, and with a fervor it seemed as if the chill of a hundred winters could not cool."

"You speak only words of truth," uttered Emma, who

had listened to Prescott's words with unutterable emotions. "How well do I remember all that was said when my own father went to the war; but," she added, "do you not think many of these promises have been fulfilled?"

"I do. There are, in every community, men who forget not their obligations. And God bless the loyal press of the country for the sympathy they have displayed toward the soldier! The press is a great power in the land, Miss Emma; and it has done much to keep alive the memory of those obligations, so freely acknowledged by the loyal citizens while war still made them tremble. I would not speak too harshly. Forgetfulness of obligations is a tendency of public bodies; and therefore it is that the soldiers are combining that they may keep alive the public memory, and act as executors of the consequent public will."

"And will this not accomplish what my dear father so often desired? He used to say that none could so value liberty as those who had offered up their lives for it; and he hoped the returned soldiers would so unite that the deep love of the Republic, which service in the field had implanted in their breasts, would be infused into the hearts of the whole nation, and forever kept alive."

"It will, Miss Emma. Your father presaged in his hope one of the great principles of our Order. *So long as the Grand Army of the Republic lives, liberty cannot die!*"

During this conversation on the Grand Army, Emma's soul had been moved by the profoundest emotions; but now her beautiful countenance glowed as by inspiration. Raising her humid eyes to heaven, "O father!" she exclaimed, "ask kind Heaven to look down and bless these noble men! All that you prayed for so earnestly, when you lay on your bed of suffering, they are to accomplish!"

Prescott was in turn profoundly affected as he gazed upon the face of this lovely girl, thus lit up by her exalted emotions, and listened to the words which she uttered with such inspired accent to her sainted father. He, in that moment, realized the holiness to which the sentiment of pure love is akin; for while his soul went out with hers in that touching appeal, his heart went out with it, and he prayed God that a woman, gifted with a nature so elevated, might yet aid him as a companion in the patriotic labors he contemplated for the future.

When Emma lowered her eyes she met Prescott's ardent gaze, in which inspiration and rapture mingled. A slight blush suffused her already glowing countenance; but it was not the blush of shame. It seemed to lend a yet more exalted character to her expression.

"Prescott," she uttered in a voice of surpassing sweetness, as if all further form had been swept away by this holy and lofty communion, "I feel that it is God who is calling into existence this noble unity of the nation's soldiers. You are to fulfil a sacred mission. The blessings of liberty will be yours, and the blessings of the widow and the fatherless!" Her hand, which she had raised in an earnest gesture, now fell to her side, and her eyes were dimmed with tears. "My dear father," she continued, "would have been made very happy if he had met with you before he passed away. Your name was on his lips, while he was unconscious, in his last moments."

Prescott's own eyes glistened with tender sympathy as he said in answer:—

"I cannot express to you the gratification it gives me to hear of the regard in which I was held by your father. He was brave and noble, and when you tell me of his sentiments, which so accord with the spirit and purpose of the

Grand Army, I feel spurred on to work with still greater zeal for an organization I love so much. But, Emma," he added, with a half-affectionate, half-venturesome smile, as the name "Emma" fell from his lips, "I have not even yet fully answered your question, — the question concerning the General's interest in your case, as a member of the Grand Army. Let me assure you that he will sacrifice much in behalf of Allen Paige's family. And if once he is satisfied that there is foul play on the part of the executors, depend upon it he will not leave a stone unturned to confound these men."

"Ah, Prescott!" returned Emma, who having uttered that name when inspired by her exalted emotions, now repeated it with a freedom which the circumstances of that first utterance seemed in a subtle manner to insure for all coming time, — "ah, Prescott! I now feel that we have friends about us, come whatever may."

"Ay, and I trust the day is not far distant, when throughout the land there will not be one family of the soldier who can say there are not watchful friends about them."

With this ardent wish, Prescott took his leave, and Emma, after musing awhile alone, returned to her mother, to whom she recounted that portion of the interview which interested her in so special a manner.

CHAPTER XV.

TWO months have rolled away, and now, on the day this chapter opens, a storm is howling through the streets and byways with wild and savage fury.

Late in the afternoon a man of colossal stature, who wore a military overcoat that effectually protected him from the wind and sleet, turned from Fifth Avenue and entered West Twenty-Seventh Street. It was the Veteran.

Arriving at the house he sought, he mounted the steps and rang the bell.

It would seem as if the noise of the wind prevailed throughout the house, for there was no response.

He again pulled the bell-handle, but more vigorously than before, for the storm followed him up the steps and blew his cape uncomfortably about his head.

This time the ring was answered. A servant opened the door.

"Is Mrs. Paige within?" inquired the Veteran.

"Mrs. Paige?" repeated the servant, wonderingly. "I 've been in this house but since this morning same; but I think no sich woman lives here."

A harsh voice now sounded through the hall.

"Who has that front door open?" it exclaimed. "Shut it instantly!"

At the same moment the dark visage of Daniel Garvin appeared at the farther end of the hall, from an opened door.

A scowl of impatience disturbed his sardonic countenance; and the wind, that whistled through the house, blew his thin dry hair about in such a manner that the first thought of the Veteran, as he beheld him, was of a man touched with the insanity of a demoniac.

The broker, on his part, left an expletive unuttered, as the looming form of the Veteran met his gaze, covered with the driving sleet, the face half concealed by the flying cape.

"Ask the gentleman in, and close the door!" he cried, advancing into the hall.

The Veteran stepped inside, followed by the sleet, and the servant closed the door against the storm.

As these two men now stood face to face, undisturbed by the fury of the elements, they at once recognized each other.

"I seek Mrs. Paige," said the Veteran, at the same time fixing on the broker a look that made him inwardly quail.

"She does not now reside here."

There was in the broker's tone a slight touch of fierceness, as if his own secret trembling somewhat maddened him.

"She has moved then?"

"Yes."

"Will you be so kind as to inform me where?"

"I cannot."

As the broker uttered this sententious reply, in a voice which combined a snarl with a perceptible tone of defiance, the Veteran bent upon him a penetrating gaze, and his countenance assumed its expression of iron sternness, while the object of his gaze cursed himself for his lack of self-command.

"Excuse me for troubling you," he said; and opening the door he passed out, letting in the howling storm again for an instant, which flew through the hall, and once more sported with the broker's dry and scanty locks.

An hour subsequent to this scene Prescott Marland, on

entering his boarding-house, found the Veteran awaiting him.

"General," he exclaimed, clasping both of the Veteran's hands in his own, "I fear all is lost, and the family of our comrade ruined!"

"Let us be calm," said the Veteran, who, at the same time he experienced the deepest sympathy for his friend's distress, could scarcely forbear a smile at this impulsive evidence of his all-absorbing interest in the family of Allen Paige.

"Ah, yes, General!" returned Prescott, "that is the word, 'be calm'; but with me it has been impossible for many a day. Villains that they are!" he cried, releasing the Veteran's hands, and clenching his muscular fists, "I could mash their accursed heads till they could plot no more! Executors! Heaven save the mark, — Executors! *Executioners!* that's the word, and executioners of the innocent! Worse than executioners! Robbers! thieves! the foulest of thieves! and God only knows whether they will not have been murderers in reality!" he added, while the tears started to his eyes.

"Lieutenant," said the Veteran with emotion, "you know how I feel for both them and you; but feeling alone can do but little good. If the family of a comrade is in trouble, depend on my assistance."

"Ah, General! but you may have to do almost everything!"

"Then I will do it."

As the Veteran uttered these words with undemonstrative firmness, Prescott Marland seized his hand, and a single tear hung for a moment on the lashes, and then dampened his cheek.

"God bless you, General!" he exclaimed. "I told her

it would be so!" Then his countenance immediately gave way to an expression of deep dejection. "But," he continued, "I fear that even you can do nothing now. O, why did you not come sooner?"

"I did not get your second letter till four says ago."

"O, these mails! these mails! Do you know, General, that I felt like flying back to the West" (Prescott had just returned from a visit to the West when he called at the house of Mrs. Paige two months before), "and seeking you ahead of that letter. I knew it would be so. It was fate!"

"Do not use that word," said the Veteran, gently. "Say, rather, Providence. He who ascribes the events of life to fate has not the strength to work with which he possesses who ascribes them to Providence. As soon as I received your letter, informing me of the imminent danger to which this family was exposed by the speedy action of the executors, I immediately made my arrangements and started for New York. I arrived here this afternoon, and at once called to see you. Not finding you in, I proceeded to West Twenty-Seventh Street, and there learned sufficient to confirm my worst fears."

"Yes, instead of the happy family of our dead comrade, you found the accursed uncle!"

"I presumed it was Colonel Paige's brother."

"In the name of Heaven! call him the *half*-brother — or the *step*-brother — that 's even better — but don't, don't call this unmitigated scoundrel Allen Paige's brother!"

An almost imperceptible smile flitted across the stern face of the Veteran.

"I presume it was this step-brother I met there. It was the same face I saw in Colonel Paige's chamber."

"That 's the man, — a man with a dark, piratical look, that showed his teeth, and had a bald head, and whiskers cut in this way?" responded Prescott, at the same time putting the thumb and forefinger of each hand to either corner of his mouth, and bringing them down with a quick jerk.

"The same. I judged he lived there."

"Yes, and there is where the refinement of his devilish spirit appears. In my letter I wrote you that this Garvin and a man whom I believe to be only his miserable tool—"

"Jonas Cringar?"

"That's the man!—a man that looks as if the crack of doom was continually sounding in his ears!—a wretched-looking man, who goes about after Garvin as if this black schemer had a rope around his neck! Well, as I was saying in my letter, I told you that these men were preparing to sell off all property of the estate immediately, and, unless they were soon headed off, they would have Mrs. Paige, Emma, and the children turned out of doors."

"Yes; and, Prescott, you cannot imagine my feelings when I read this information in a letter I should have received nearly a month before."

As the Veteran uttered this, he displayed more feeling than had heretofore appeared on his countenance.

"I think I can imagine your feelings, General. Well, you did not appear; they went at it, and have done their damnable work!"

"And you could do nothing?"

"Nothing. That Garvin is too deep for me. Villany is his trade; and commerce, finances, and law are right under his hands,—and such hands!—did you ever notice them?"

"I have only seen him twice, and his hand I did not observe," replied the Veteran, his features again relaxing.

"A hand that looks as if it were made up of five bloated, broken-backed lizards and a flattened toad. Well, everything is under his ugly hands. He, with Cringar, filed the inventories, and got out the license to sell; and the more I tried to look into it the more I was afraid to do it, for fear of tipping over the dish; and as I expected you on every day,—for you know you told me, when you left, you should undoubtedly be back here last month, even without the incentive of my letter,—I held off till it was too late."

"And all is gone?"

"All! everything! Turned out of that home, in which they had lived so many years, and which the memory of Mr. Paige—their husband and father, and our comrade—made so dear to them! And with a devilish refinement of cruelty Garvin bid off the house and all that was in it, affirming, with tears in his crocodile eyes, that he could n't endure to see the house which his lamented brother's taste had made so attractive pass into the hands of a stranger! And there he lives, the sneaking hound!"

"And do you feel certain still that there is fraud in the case?"

"I would be willing to swear to it. Mrs. Paige tells me that her husband trusted her in all things, and that, if such a state of affairs had existed in his business, he never would have concealed it from her. To assert it to be otherwise is to assert that he deceived her in the most cruel manner, and that this noble patriot was guilty of a gross falsehood."

"Are there no friends that would help her,—friends who knew him well, and would credit her statements?"

"None. General, after you have lived in New York a few years you will realize that business men here have no time to attend to other people's affairs. And even if there were, there seems to be no one who is not easily convinced by these cunning executors that Allen Paige followed in the track of scores of merchants, who could lay claim to cooler heads than he was known to possess. I tell you, General, New York has, of late, been one vast caldron of financial whirlpools; and like those rotary gulfs that suddenly spring to the surface of the caldron below Niagara Bridge and suck everything down within their reach, so have these speculative whirlpools ingulfed, one after another, many who have stood among the highest in this city. No, Mrs. Paige can depend on no one here. You must bear in mind that both Garvin and Cringar stand high before the world; and there is not one to be found so unselfish as to venture to unmask them, even if he believed they were rascals; especially as they have had everything all their own way, and have baked up the whole business in such a manner that it is next to impossible to discover a flaw."

"I see how the matter stands," uttered the Veteran, bending his head in deep thought.

"And they are driven from their home!" exclaimed Prescott, with a voice in which the passions of rage and grief were mingled.

The Veteran did not seem to hear this outburst. His eyes still remained fixed to the floor in deep meditation.

Marland, struck by his appearance, remained silent also, and observed him with anxious interest.

In the mean while the storm was whistling and mourning without; and presently the thoughts of the young lover reverted back to the time when he stood before the sketch in Mrs. Paige's drawing-room, thinking of her who then seemed in the midst of opulence, while the silence was only broken by the distant rumbling of the busy city. As his mind returned to the present, with the stern face of the Veteran bent in thought before him in the contemplation of the situation, which involved the picture of this loved one driven like a wanderer from that opulent and happy home, while instead of the soothing sounds of distant vehicles his ears were filled with the shrieks and howls of the driving storm, his heart threatened to give way to its powerful but pent-up emotions.

He again watched the countenance of Thorbolt with anxious attention.

At length he perceived the strong muscles of the Veteran's cheeks — those muscles which seem only to respond to the action of a conquering will — begin to articulate themselves, like some commanding face of the great masters; while on the brow there appeared rather a general air of awakened irresistible power than a frown of emotional resolution.

This look, as Prescott gazed, seemed to grow for a space, until even he, who had seen Thorbolt in some of his grandest moments, thought he never could have conceived of a mortal being displaying in his expression such an air of invincible strength.

Suddenly this remarkable man, whose face now seemed fixed in a cast of iron, rose to his feet; and bending his stern gray eye on the young lieutenant, he spoke in a tone so deep and penetrating that his listener, whose mind was somewhat overwrought, instinctively started back in his chair.

"Prescott," he said, "I see my duty to the end. I am convinced of the foulness of this business. So be that the Lord gives me his assistance, I pledge you I will work till the question of villany or no villany is solved. The comrade who has gone above," he continued, pointing upwards, "shall not, I trust, have reason to complain of lack of effort on the part of comrades left by Heaven to perform that work, which it seems those who went not to the war are scarcely expected to attend to."

Prescott sprang from his chair, and seizing his comrade's hand, pressed it in silence.

The Veteran then took his departure.

CHAPTER XVI.

NEAR an old cobbler's shop in Vandam Street stands a brick house, which, though not in a state of dilapidation, exhibits the weather-beaten signs of age.

The apartments on the third floor of this house have not the unsightly aspect of the room in which the family of the soldier, Joseph Deering, were presented to the reader. The appearance is, however, humble, and indicates a certain degree of want. An evidence there is of a struggle with the inexorable demands and necessities of life.

Here live now the family of the soldier, Allen Paige.

These apartments consist of a kitchen and dining-room combined, two chambers, and a small bedroom.

Driven from their home by the implacable vengeance of the broker, they have fled to this uninviting precinct of the ever-changing city of New York, to struggle with the situation into which they have been precipitated.

Sorrow has succeeded sorrow. Scarcely have they begun to recover from the profound grief into which they were thrown by the sentence of exile pronounced upon them by the unrelenting voice of Daniel Garvin, when bereavement again threatens them through the dangerous illness of their little boy Albert.

His overwrought brain had yielded to the mental anguish which, young as he was, he experienced on account of the treatment his beloved mother had undergone from the heartless and unnatural uncle.

An overwrought brain!

This unfortunate boy's case impels us to a brief digression, which we make with the conviction that the subject glanced at by us concerns, to an important degree, the future welfare of our nation to which the Grand Army of the Republic is so ardently devoted; for that which vitally concerns the intellectual and moral welfare of our children concerns the country in the coming generation.

Albert has fallen a victim to the pernicious system, existing in various forms throughout our schools, of forcing the intellect by means of extraneous incentives. All incentives, involving prizes and the like, and which inevitably result in invidious comparisons, are antagonistic to healthy intellectual and moral development. And while they may seem, in special cases, to spur on the object of their influence to extraordinary efforts, they fail in a very signal manner to accomplish the good it is their professed purpose to attain.

No incentive can be depended upon for the greatest number which is not founded in broad and unselfish principles. A few may be caught up in the whirl of an unhealthily aroused emulation, but the remainder look on, first with juvenile contempt, then with a blighting apathy, which gathers influence over the mind it seizes in proportion as a morbid ambition urges on those other tender minds, whose love of study has become transformed into a feverish desire for the coveted prize. And we regret to say that the teacher does not always escape the insidious influence of these selfish principles of action.

Pure patriotism was the great power that annihilated the Rebellion. The selfish ambition for prizes (in which we include high military position) was the Rebellion's greatest ally — perhaps not excluding even copperheadism — which this pure patriotism had to contend against. It culminated in defeat after defeat, till the strong hand of General Grant brought it into subjection. And to all observing men this important victory of the great commander presaged all future victories. By all means, let the efficient be placed in responsible positions, but not for the purpose of feeding their vanity.

An impressive manifestation, in the late war, of the truth we would enforce was the manner in which the soldier would, on sight of his country's flag, forget all promised honors, and, inspired by the principles of pure patriotism, implanted silently and unconsciously in his breast, and led by that all-potent emblem, rush on into the cannon's mouth to die; while, perchance, the commanding officer of his division gazed on the field from the rear, gnawed by disappointed ambition, and secretly exulting over the dreadful sacrifice offered up before his unquiet eye, because he knew it was hopeless, and likely to defeat the general in command, whom possibly he looked upon as an arrogant upstart, occupying the place with which he himself should have been honored. While the statement may be severe, it yet seems but just, to remark that this malign spirit was but a legitimate outshoot from those motives with which the young are impelled on to unnatural and demoralizing efforts. And we trust that the Grand Army of the Republic, from which we expect so much in behalf of our country's future welfare, will never be compromised in its workings by that selfish ambition which lusts for personal aggrandizement at the expense of the common good.

The hypothesis, that the excitement of selfishness is the great aid to the attainment of lasting good, will undoubtedly be acknowledged a manifest absurdity by all. Such, however, is the basis on which the pernicious system referred to is founded. Forgetfulness of self, and single-minded devotion to duty and truth, are the principles on which this vast nation, with its future conflicting interests, must rest its great hope.

But it is a lamentable truth, that demoralization is not the only result of unnatural incentive in connection with our schools.* Prostration, sickness, and death are of frequent occurrence, bearing from the sight of an expectant world many a bright young intellect, that might, under proper influence, have remained to develop into powerful minds, fitted for the great work of life.

The white and blue ribbons, associated with the prizes that are held up before the children of many schools as the bait is held before cattle to be gathered for the shambles, are symbols, one of the gravestones which mark the last resting-place of many a tender form that has yielded to an over-wrought, undeveloped mind, and the other of the sky, to which the bereaved parents gaze as they contemplate the premature death of their promising children.

As we stated in a former chapter, Albert, who was but eleven years old, was of precocious mind, and even at that early age stood at the head of his school. We spoke of it then in a manner that would seem to indicate pride in the statement. If so, we made a serious mistake. Rather should a sentiment of fear have pervaded that statement. It would have been confirmed by the results. This little boy,

* We congratulate Boston on the final abolishment of the prize system in its grammar schools, due, in a great degree, to the earnest and persistent efforts of the Superintendent.

now rendered doubly precious to a widowed mother, driven in a day from affluence to want, at the same time that her departed husband's good name was covered with obloquy, this precious boy had been brought down to a bed of sickness and impending death by the unnatural tension brought to bear on his brain, through the pernicious practice we have spoken of.

It is due Mrs. Paige to remark that she had admonished this ambitious child against overworking himself; but often, when every other eye in the house was closed in slumber, he could have been seen sitting up in his bed in the old home, studying by the gas-light near him.

It was through this means that the boy had been brought to a condition which prepared the way for the wickedness of his uncle to finally prostrate him on a bed of sickness.

At first, seized by what appeared to be a simple cold, Albert is now threatened with death from brain-fever. Mrs. Paige sits by the side of the bed, nearly worn down with her distress and anxiety, moistening her palm with cooling water, and then passing it gently over her boy's forehead. No one else is in the room. Emma is away, and Alice is preparing supper in the kitchen.

It is the same hour in which the Veteran appeared in his sleet-covered garments at the door of that mansion on which the mother's mind now so often and so sadly dwells. The storm, which has seemed so fit an accompaniment to the scene that occurred between the two remarkable men who represent the two opposing forces of our story, and which had shrieked into the ears of Prescott Marland as he contemplated the silent figure of the absorbed Thorbolt, sweeps past the window of this sick-chamber with wild and dismal sound.

Albert, who had been lying with closed eyes, opened them and cast upon his mother a look which, though laden with the languor of sickness, conveyed an unutterable expression of filial love and gratitude. He then closed them again.

"Do you feel better, my child?" asked Mrs. Paige, bending over him.

Albert did not answer.

She repeated the question, but Albert did not speak.

All at once a scowl came over his forehead, and he began to mutter incoherently.

The mother started from her chair in dismay.

Ah! the difference between the unconsciousness of the father, dying from a wound received in the defence of his country, and this dread symptom of a terrible fever!

She raised her clasped hands to heaven. Her eyes, which were uplifted, yielded to an overwhelming emotion, and the tears of agony poured down her care-worn cheeks.

"O Father in Heaven!" she cried, "spare him! spare my boy!"

Then she again bent over her child, and taking his head tenderly in her arm, she bathed his face with her tears.

"What is it that wets my cheek?" he exclaimed, staring up at this suffering mother. "It rains," he muttered, as his lids began to droop. Suddenly they were again raised, and his face assumed a look of terror, and he cried in a sort of muttered shriek: "Don't turn mother out in such a storm as this, Uncle Garvin! O Uncle, don't!—not my darling mother!"

This was more than the afflicted woman could endure. Her head sank upon the pillow, and, with her arm still around the neck of her boy, she uttered a loud wail of grief.

Alice heard this cry, and hastened from the kitchen in alarm.

When she beheld her mother thus completely overwhelmed with woe, and heard the mutterings of her wandering brother mingled with the utterances of this sorrow, the picture of her dying father rose vividly to her mind. With frantic haste she rushed to the bedside, threw her arms about her mother, and cried, —

"Mother, dear mother! he is n't dying! O mother, no!"

The mother, without raising her head, threw the disengaged arm around the terror-stricken daughter, and pressed her to her bosom; and for a while her convulsive sobs and the wailing storm, as it drove the sleet against the window-panes, was the only answer.

Once there seemed in the midst of the tempest's wail a mocking laugh. We had nigh said it could easily be fancied the laugh of the half-brother; but no, — even Daniel Garvin could not have looked in upon this scene unmoved, and without experiencing an irrepressible pang of remorse.

While this sad group were thus expressing the passions of grief, anguish, and terror, another figure entered the outer room, having just come from the street.

It was Emma, who wore a water-proof which was covered with the sleet.

She had just returned from a visit in answer to an advertisement. This advertisement was for a teacher, who could give instruction both in music and the French language. She had seen it in a paper dating two days back, which had been wrapped around a bundle that was brought to them, and, fearing to delay a moment, she put on her things and went out into the storm to respond to it; but her errand was fruitless, — it had been answered the day before, and an engagement made.

As she entered this outer room her countenance bore evidence of a mental struggle just passed, which had evidently yielded to a determination to be cheerful. Looking out from her water-proof hood was a face bearing testimony to its contact with the storm, but lit by an encouraging smile.

Her attention was first attracted to a cake which was burning in the oven. She at once hastened to take it out, wondering what could have happened to Alice, who usually performed her household duties with so much faithfulness and care.

Then, in the midst of the noise of the elements without, she heard for the first time the sounds of grief in the sick-chamber.

Hastening to the door, she looked in and beheld the mournful group. There lay the mother as she had fallen on the side of the bed, supporting Alice in one arm, and with the other enfolding the neck of her suffering brother. She saw this brother's eyes glazed in unconsciousness, and heard his incoherent mutterings, with which were mingled the mother's deep and convulsive sobs.

As we have seen, Emma's nature was strong, but it had now nearly given way. Her first impulse was to rush to the bedside with a terror-fraught cry, as Alice had done; but with a mighty effort, which seemed to her to be aided by a higher power, she controlled herself.

Advancing to the bedside softly, she gently placed her left hand under her mother's head, and with her right she soothed her temples. Her palm was still cold from contact with the outer air, and this, with the exquisite touch of filial tenderness, together with Emma's gentle and soothing words, began to produce a visible effect on the distracted mother.

Alice also, over whom the mind of Emma had always held a gentle sway, began to experience the quieting influence of her sister's presence.

And it would seem as if the boy himself felt this sister's soothing influence; for after having made a few passes over her mother's forehead, she alternated between hers and his, and in a few moments he sank into a restful sleep.

After Mrs. Paige had sufficiently recovered her composure, she seated herself and conversed with Emma regarding her mission.

"You know, mother," she said, "I did not expect it, but I thought it only my duty to try."

Mrs. Paige contemplated her with an air of grateful affection.

"My dear daughter," she said, "I do not know what we should do if it were not for you."

"Ah, dear mother," returned this devoted daughter and sister, "I would that I could do a hundred times more." Then with an expression of unconscious sadness she said, "I can do but little. I would like to earn money enough to make us all comfortable, but you know I am only a woman, and I cannot get the pay I could if I were a man." And as a mournful smile made more touching her look of sadness, she added, "I do not know but that I should become a Woman's Rights advocate, if by so doing I could help raise the wages of women who have to support those they love, as I now wish to support you."

Mrs. Paige's gaze was now directed to Emma's neck, and with a quick start she exclaimed, —

"Emma, you have lost your pin!"

Emma instantly placed her hand over the spot where her mother had seen the pin before she went out, as if she would conceal it.

"It is gone!" uttered the mother in a voice of deep concern. "I fear you have indeed lost it!"

This pin had been a gift from the father.

Emma now produced a package, and hastily untying it, exposed to view various little dainties so welcome to the sick.

"You know the doctor said Albert needed these, and so I bought them."

Mrs. Paige cast upon Emma a quick glance of pain.

Emma understood it, and again put her hand instinctively to her neck.

"It is n't sold, dear mother. I am to redeem it."

She had pawned it.

The mother rose in silence, and approaching Emma, placed her hand upon her head, and kissed her on her brow. Then with a hastening but feeble step she passed from the chamber into the small bedroom, where little Dorrit had all this time been asleep, the tears starting down her cheeks as she closed the door.

At the same moment a bold rap sounded at the kitchen door.

Alice answered the summons, and Prescott Marland entered.

CHAPTER XVII.

EMMA, who had been profoundly affected by her mother's manner, heard Prescott's voice in greeting, and confusion immediately displayed itself. The pin, which had been the cause of the scene he had so nearly interrupted, seemed at this instant to have left a space at her neck so perceptible, that she felt certain it would be observed by their visitor; and like one excited by the consciousness of guilt, she, poor girl! could not help fancying him at once divining the reason.

It were easy to say she should not feel ashamed, but, on the other hand, should be sustained by a consciousness of duty nobly performed. The necessities consequent on a change of situation from affluence to privation, however, do not always succeed in compelling at once the instinctive and involuntary emotions to meet their inexorable demands. Perhaps this is one of the most touching features of those trials which follow in the wake of misfortune. A strong will and a resigned spirit will sustain the mind and soul under the most adverse circumstances, and the demeanor ordinarily reveal but little of the inward trial; but the involuntary emotions of the heart ever and anon arise to remind the sufferer of what has been in a manner that rends and pierces.

It were vain, also, to say to this abashed girl, with the supposed taint of the pawn-shop still on her skirts: "Prescott Marland is a young man of a high and generous nature, and he will respect you tenfold more when he shall come to know of this thing you have done. He will profoundly appreciate your self-sacrifice and the nobility of your spirit."

All this will be well afterwards, but at just this time her heart experiences a sinking sensation, and her cheeks are tinged with a slight blush of shame.

She casts about for another pin to take its place; but there is no time to carry the desires of her mind into execution, for Prescott, accompanied by Alice, is on the threshold.

It is a face that would carry cheerfulness into the dungeon itself; and with it a form that looks as if its great delight is to be out in such a storm as is raging without, and buffet with the winds.

In an instant Emma's distress on account of the pin was gone. She now only saw this noble specimen of young manhood coming to greet her, — coming with his great heart and courageous nature, to shed, in that chamber of sickness and privation, an atmosphere of health and hope.

O, how strong her impulse to throw herself into his arms, and claim that protection which had been denied by the unnatural uncle!

BROTHER!

SISTER!

Thus they entitled each other, and they did so in full sincerity. But would William Garvin have so announced it, had he flown by on the gale, and looked through the window at the moment Prescott stood upon that threshold? It is not probable.

And yet this spoken relation of brother and sister is the result, not of self-deception, but of the most manly delicacy; for it is evident that if Prescott should press his suit, the "brother" and "sister" would disappear as mist before the sun. But he realizes that, under the peculiar circumstances, much that may be done on his part will, from an accepted brother, do less violence to a natural sensitiveness than if done by an accepted lover.

He has now come from his interview with the Veteran; and a look of hope lights up his handsome features.

His air is contagious, and through Emma's soul there darts an indefinable emotion of kindred hope.

"Emma," he said, advancing and taking her hand, "General Hammond arrived from the West to-day."

He spoke somewhat loudly, and Emma, at the same time that a gleam of a yet more definable hope overspread her features, placed her finger to her lips, and pointed to the now deeply slumbering boy.

Prescott lowered his tone, and for a moment gazed upon Emma's face in silence, as he perceived the traces of the trial to which her spirit had been that day subjected. She understood this gaze, and her eyes were bedewed with tears.

The ardent but high-souled Marland could scarcely refrain from at once embracing her in his strong, protecting arms, and giving vent to the full expression of his all-absorbing love. But he commanded himself, and leading her to a chair with the careful tenderness of a devoted elder brother, he narrated to her the interview which had just occurred between himself and the Veteran.

Emma, on her part, told him of the dangerous turn which Albert's illness had taken.

She was still speaking when Mrs. Paige came from the bedroom, her swollen eyes telling of the anguish through which she had passed. As Prescott rose and greeted her the sick boy began to show signs of restlessness.

The mother looked up at a watch which was hanging by the bed.

This watch was the last gift of her husband, to commemorate the twentieth anniversary of their wedding-day. She had up to the present moment held this gift, with others, as mementos so sacred, that she could entertain no thought of in any way disposing of them; but in that little room she had yielded, after a severe but noble struggle, and she had come forth resolved to follow the example of her devoted daughter, whose precious token of her father was in the hands of the pawnbroker, and devote all gifts, mementos, everything not absolutely essential to the sustenance of life, to the support of that family which should never beg of living man, so long as they possessed one object of the least possible value not absolutely necessary to keep the soul and body together.

But as she now looked at this watch, she started and exclaimed in a suppressed voice, —

"The time has passed when the medicine should be given him!" And hastening to the mantel-piece, she took the medicine and spoon, and approached the bedside.

Prescott extended his hand.

"Don't awake him, I beg of you. It may be his death. No medicine can take the place of sleep, in such a case as this. I once sat up with a little nephew of mine, who had been given over by the doctors. He was suffering from brain-fever, and was unconscious. For several days and nights he seemed to have scarcely slept. As his mother left me with him on this night, which all expected to be his last, she opened a bureau drawer and showed me a plaid piece of goods, and, with tears in her eyes, she repeated those lines, suggested by an old saying, —

'Death often stays his hand
When friends prepare the shroud,
And joy returns to saddened hearts
When life dispels the cloud.'

It was the last resort of despair, — a superstitious little act, as you probably know, which many sorrowing ones indulge in, springing from hearts that would make the last effort in their power to drive back the dreaded messenger. When I was left alone with my charge I at once commenced gently passing my hand down from his knees to the extremities of his feet, which I drew out soothingly as I relinquished them to recommence at the knee. When I began, his head was tossing from side to side in the most painful restlessness; but soon it settled into the pillow, and he began to slumber. When at different times he would show signs of awakening from this slumber, I would assist the manipulations on his feet by a low humming sound like a top or a humblebee."

"And what was the result?" asked Emma, eagerly.

"The result was, I kept him asleep nine hours; and though I ignored the hours I was instructed to give him medicine, the doctors, the next morning, announced a remarkable change for the better."

"And did he wear the plaid?"

"He did; and is now a strong boy who wears sack and waistcoat."

The mother had listened with absorbed attention, while Emma hung on every word, as if this story, from the lips of him whom she secretly idolized and believed capable of accomplishing almost anything in the power of man, was an account of her own brother's redemption from death.

"I will show you," continued Prescott; and approaching the invalid, who now moved restlessly as if about to awake, he placed his hand under the quilt, and stroked his feet as he had described, at the same time producing the humming sound with his lips.

The effect was remarkable. The boy almost instantly settled his heated cheek in the pillow, and commenced breathing deeply. As Prescott continued his labors he breathed more and more easily, and his cheek settled still deeper into the pillow, until with a sigh he went off into a slumber so gentle, and yet so profound, that the mother, reading the prophecy of life, took Prescott's disengaged hand between her own, and said, —

"It seems to me as if you had been sent to us by Heaven! Your friendship and presence ever seem to me a blessing!"

Emma cast upon Prescott a look of inexpressible happiness.

He remained through the evening, and when he left, the boy was still sleeping.

CHAPTER XVIII.

AT the time the incidents narrated in our story occurred, the New York Surrogate's office was situated on Park Row, up one flight of stairs. It was a long room, by no means diminutive in size; but its capacity was far from commensurate with the immense amount of business there transacted. The accumulating posthumous documents of generations, that had come and gone in this great city whose numbers had rolled up like some vast invading army, were overflowing all available space, and demanded more ample accommodation. Since the date of these incidents, therefore, the office has been transferred to its present commodious quarters; and we learn with satisfaction that the newly elected Surrogate is eminently qualified for the arduous and increasing responsibilities devolving upon this office, which requires in such a marked degree that judgment should be tempered by courtesy and consideration.*

* This seems to the authors a fitting opportunity of expressing their obligations to the Hon. Amos G. Hull, who, through his legal ability, courtesy, and honor, rendered them important favors during an experience which has afforded groundwork for a considerable portion of this narrative.

On the third day following the events recorded in the preceding pages, Mr. ——, Surrogate's clerk, was, as usual, buried in the midst of wills, inventories, and clouds of other papers, which only a clerk of the Surrogate's office, or Probate Court, can really appreciate.

Men and women are seated or standing, awaiting their turn to be heard. They are mostly persons who, as executors or administrators, or recipients of some deceased friend's bounty, or, perchance, simply the objects of his remembrance, have come here to subject this clerk, with others, to an endless series of questioning and cross-questioning, most of them without counsel, and therefore the more dogmatic and troublesome.

"I 've been left out of my sister's will!" says a sharp-faced, vinegary looking woman, evidently unmarried, as she hastens to take her turn, "and I 'd like to know whether I 've got the law on my side or not!"

"That 's for your counsel to answer, madam," courteously replies the clerk, turning to the next applicant.

"But don't you give full information here, — all about wills, and who 's got their rights, and who has n't?" persists the incorrigible applicant.

"Let me advise you, madam," says the clerk somewhat testily, "if you have been left out of a will where you ought to have been in it, to apply at once to counsel. We can do nothing for you here."

The questioner stares at the speaker a moment, who prepares to listen to the next in turn, and seeing persistence is no longer of avail, she retires mumbling.

The next applicant, behind whom the clerk observed a man of remarkable height, with a deep scar on his cheek, was evidently a young man with whom Mr. —— was acquainted.

The reader is also acquainted with him, somewhat, for it is Billings, formerly Cringar's dry goods clerk,—now his book-keeper.

"How are you, Billings?" said the clerk. "Any hitch in your business?"

"I don't call it a hitch exactly, but I'm bothered by Tom Greeder, who says he'll come down on me if I don't pay him his part of my brother's legacy at once. It's only a hundred dollars, anyway."

"What did you tell him?"

"I told him I must have a chance, as executor, to turn, and I should n't pay a cent till I had, if I knew what was law."

"Right! The law's on your side. Anything else?"

"I should like to look a moment at the records of the Paige estate."

"Allen Paige?"

"Yes. Cringar, you know, is one of the executors."

"Yes," responded the clerk, as he turned for the records with a grimace. "Do you know much about this affair?" he said in a low voice as he handed them to Billings, at the same time casting a cautious glance around, as if this were an unusual style of questioning for him to indulge in.

The tall stranger heard this question, and slightly inclined his head.

"I know a little about it," answered Billings. "Why, do you know anything?"

The stranger listened attentively.

The Surrogate's clerk cast a quick glance at this man.

"I'm in no hurry," uttered the object of his scrutiny.

Though the book-keeper knew this voice very well, he did not turn.

"If I did, it would n't do for me to say so," replied Mr. ——, with a half-laugh.

"Do you believe it is all right?" said Billings, in an abrupt, cross-questioning tone, loud enough for the stranger to hear.

The clerk did not answer this question, but the penetrating gray eyes of him who was watching read his mind.

Handing the papers to Billings, Mr. —— said, in a manner that indicated a consciousness of having slightly infringed on the proprieties of his office, — "They are open to your inspection," and then turned his attention to the applicant who had been so attentively watching him.

The stranger stepped aside.

"I will give way to my neighbor," he said. "In the mean time, if you and this young gentleman will permit me, I would be pleased to glance at these papers, which, if my ears caught the name aright, concern the estate of Allen Paige, who happened to have been a warm friend of an acquaintance of mine."

"I have no objections to your looking them over whatever," said Billings. "I also have an acquaintance to whom Mr. Paige was a dear friend, and therefore we are well met."

The book-keeper and the stranger, whom the reader has readily recognized, now proceeded to examine the papers put in by Cringar and Garvin as executors of Allen Paige's estate. It is needless to say that they had understood each other from the first.

We will see how this came about.

On the night succeeding his interview with Prescott Marland, the Veteran lay awake, revolving in his mind the whole business to which he had resolved to devote himself, for the sake of the family of a fallen comrade. As we have formerly stated, his mind was of a high strategic order. He could do nothing without taking a survey of all the bearings of the work in hand.

The following morning he waited on Prescott.

"I need a point to start with," he said, after he had obtained all the particulars Prescott could give. "Perhaps you can help me to it."

"What is it?"

"Communication with some one who is able to open Cringar more or less to me."

Prescott thought.

The Veteran continued: —

"Cringar is undoubtedly a tool, as you have before said. Garvin is the scoundrel at heart, and the leader in this business. But it is evident that Garvin works much through Cringar. I would work through Cringar also, — flank the one through the other. If I can confound the merchant, I have the broker in my grasp. If I may judge from what little I have seen and heard, Garvin is a man remarkably astute and wary, and he would have those about him that could not be readily used by others. I therefore must have some one, if possible, who is constantly about Cringar."

"The very man!" exclaimed Prescott, abruptly.

"Who?"

"Billings."

"Billings?"

"The clerk who throttled that fellow the night we met Emma Paige."

"Ah, yes. And a young man of much acuteness, I judge."

"You 're right there. The very man! — the very man! He 's been a clerk in Cringar's store, and is now one of the book-keepers. Only three days ago he told me it was notorious in the whole store, that Cringar was troubled with a bad conscience. He pronounces him the most miserable and God-forsaken looking man he has ever laid his eyes on. The very ghost of a man, he calls him, and an unshrived one at that."

"I am well pleased. Between this book-keeper, hard work, and Cringar's conscience, I have hopes of accomplishing something."

"Do you think you can fix them?" cried Prescott in excitement, as the picture of the family, suffering from sickness and privation, which he visited the day before, came to his mind.

"Be calm," said the Veteran, kindly. "I can promise nothing more than work. The situation in which we now find things has been legally as well as publicly indorsed, and while I promise you that, if nothing unforeseen prevents, I will not cease working till I get to the bottom of the whole business, yet in what state I shall find that business remains to be seen."

"You are right," returned Prescott in a subdued voice, — "perfectly right."

"So let us to the work. I would see this young book-keeper at once."

"You say you do not wish to touch Daniel Garvin at present?"

"Not directly. Why?"

"Because if you did, I think I know of one who would assist you."

"Who?"

"His son, William, whom we met with his cousin Emma that night."

"Why do you think so?"

"Because he thinks everything of the family, especially of Emma."

The Veteran cast a penetrating glance into the countenance of the young lieutenant, but he observed no jealousy there.

"That may be, Prescott," he said; "but he appeared to me to be a young man who would not readily act against his own father. While it is evident that his attachments are strong, it is also evident that his conscience is equally tender."

"You may be correct. But still, General, I 'm confident that you already hold a strong influence over his mind."

"Ah; and how do you know this?"

"From his own talk. He 's just the person, General, for you to hold with magnetic power. He 's an artist, with a woman's organization, and a fanciful imagination that seems to me decidedly morbid. He says that picture of your appearance in the street, when Emma's shrieks awoke him from unconsciousness, and he beheld her in the arms of the abducting scoundrel, is before his eyes continually, by day and by night. If he sits down to think, it 's there. If he sleeps, it 's there. If he reads, or listens to sermon or lecture, it 's there, — always right before him. He affirms it 's a vision that conveys to his mind a realization of Homer's description of Jove in the midst of war. And by this very Jove! I verily believe he looks on you as a sort of god incarnate! I told him how you got your *sobriquet* of Thorbolt, and you would have laughed to see how soberly he took it. He looked as if, to his mind, you ought to have been christened with it."

"Pshaw! Lieutenant!" uttered the Veteran, not over-displeased by this flattering account of a young artist's infatuation. Up to your old camp tricks, I see."

"Not a bit of it, General. That 's the way this young cousin talks. And between that and his infatuation for Emma — "

The Veteran smiled.

"You think I ought to be jealous, I suppose," uttered the Lieutenant, interrupting himself, and speaking with a freedom to the Veteran in which he would have indulged before no other person; "but it does n't take that course. On the contrary, it delights me to see it. You know what I would n't say to any one else but you, that I think her an angel, and I want everybody else to think so. Now that her young cousin's whole soul is absorbed in her, and he looks upon her as a very goddess — "

"In that case (begging Mrs. Hammond's pardon) I ought to be the one to marry her it seems to me," interrupted the Veteran, who could be facetious at times.

"O, because he makes you a god, eh!" rejoined Prescott, relishing Thorbolt's good-natured sally. "Well, what I was going to say is this, that putting his infatuation for you and his infatuation for his cousin together, and knowing as he must somewhat, at least, of his father's character, I have no doubt that he would yield to your influence, if it directed him in work that should be of aid to one I know he idolizes."

Ah! the difference between strength and weakness! Prescott is strong, — William is weak. The one takes pride in the other's love, as flattering evidence of the estimation in which the object of his own love is held. The other looks upon his rival's love as the iconoclast that shatters the divine image of his own fond dreams.

"I trust," said the Veteran, "that I shall never find it necessary to set him at work against his own father; though Heaven only knows, in such an affair as this, what instrumentalities will have to be used before we get through with it."

CHAPTER XIX.

THE result of the interview between General Hammond and Prescott Marland was the immediate introduction of the former to the book-keeper, Billings.

They found in this young man a ready and willing assistant. He had by no means been unobservant of all the external indications of remorse on the part of his employer, Jonas Cringar, and of the satanic influence of this wretched man's destroyer, Daniel Garvin. The broker came often into the store, and the merchant made him an occasional messenger to Garvin's office, so that his opportunities for observation were good; but he had detected nothing beyond what was revealed by the general actions of the two men. When, however, the Veteran cautiously opened his business to him he at once entered into the spirit of the work; for he was convinced of the existence of an unprincipled plot, and his nature, besides leading him into sympathy with the wronged, was calculated to enjoy the labor of ferreting out this evidently dark and wicked scheme.

The first documents the Veteran desired to examine were the records at the Surrogate's office. But it was necessary for him to so accomplish this that wind of his errand should not get to the ears of Daniel Garvin. What relations existed between this deep schemer and the Surrogate's office he had no means of knowing. That a direct visit from a man of his appearance for the purpose of examining the records would excite attention, his past experience had warned him would be inevitable; and yet these records he must see himself, preparatory to the work he had undertaken.

His astute mind had been perplexed by this part of the business, and up to the time of his introduction to the book-keeper he had not been able to see his way clear. He was still turning and revolving it in his mind.

As soon as he was convinced that Billings was enlisted heart and soul in the undertaking, and could be implicitly trusted, he made known his perplexity regarding the records.

"Good!" cried the book-keeper. "I can help you out of that difficulty at once!"

The Veteran bent on him a look of surprised inquiry.

"I 'm acquainted with Mr. ——, recording clerk," said Billings in answer to this look.

"Then we can work it!" exclaimed the Veteran with an air of relief and satisfaction.

"Perfectly."

"This is excellent! We will proceed at once to business."

"I will obtain the items for you, myself, General."

"I thank you, but I prefer to see the records in person."

"Then depend on my hearty assistance here, and anywhere else, where I can be of service."

"Thanks."

The reader has already witnessed the manner in which the book-keeper kept his word, up to the point where we left him with the Veteran at the Surrogate's office, examining the records.

The Veteran was for a moment staggered. There was a boldness and openness in the statements of the inventories that he was hardly prepared for. He could detect no appearance of a trumped-up job. Names, dates, everything necessary for a clear, unequivocal return by the executors of the estate, were here in black and white.

The book-keeper, who understood something of these things, cast a blank look at his staggered companion.

"It 's a hard show," he said.

The Veteran did not answer, but studiously examined the statements.

At length the expression of his face changed from its surprise to a look of deep determination, and he said,—

"This Garvin is either not the rogue we have taken him to be, or he is a marvellous expert in villany. Which horn of the dilemma do you choose?"

The book-keeper thought a moment over this somewhat unexpected question, and then answered,—

"The latter."

"That he is a marvellous villain?"

"Yes."

"I think your choice a good one."

"It is yours?"

"It is. This man is an able tactician. He would have made his mark in the Rebel army."

"But not in ours?"

"No. His mark must be an infamous one."

"What, General! do you think all in the Rebel army who made a mark made an infamous one?"

"No; but it was a place for infamous work."

"I do not understand the connection."

"Good men may be led into infamous business," returned the Veteran, with his grave smile.

"Ah — yes," ejaculated Billings, depressing his brows in thought.

"While very good men were engaged in the Rebellion, very bad men imparted to it its ruling spirit."

"Like this Garvin," responded the book-keeper, the depression of his brows gathering into a scowl.

"Yes. And here is where the absurdity of those men appears, who, because there were some men in the Rebellion that were misled, therefore they are to be placed on an equality, in history, with the vast army of patriots who brought them to their senses. What should we think of a youth, who, having heretofore enjoyed a good character, is enticed into a criminal transaction; and being pardoned, he claims as much credit for his earnest labors in behalf of crime as can he whose loyal efforts defeated both him and his accomplices?"

"Or as though we should succeed in knocking this array of figures, presented by Cringar and Garvin, into a thousand atoms, and put the rascals in jail, and then, forsooth, they cry from their bars, 'We did nobly! Write us down as criminals devoted to our cause, and therefore entitled to glory!' It seems to me, now that I think of it, quite as bad as that."

"In many cases it certainly does," returned the Veteran. "But let us come back to Garvin in earnest. As I remarked, this man is an able tactician, and with the position he now holds in this affair, I am willing to acknowledge that it seems a desperate undertaking to attempt to drive him from his works."

"For my part, General, I confess I should never dare undertake it."

"That would depend, I think," answered the Veteran, closely studying the physiognomy of the book-keeper. Then turning his attention to the records, he requested his companion to cautiously write down such items as he should read off.

Billings took out his memorandum-book, and holding it

so that no one behind could see his movements, proceeded to do so.

In a long list of items, prepared with that sagacity on which the unprincipled learn so much to depend, there were entered one or two statements, which, from their important relation to the development of this story, we will here record for the benefit of the reader.

The first of these was an account of indebtedness to Jonas Cringar for settlement of note for $ 50,000, given by Allen Paige to one Richard Slaycut, in payment for 25,000 shares of stock in the Long Ridge Silver and Copper Mining Company of Montana, at $ 2 per share, said note bearing date October 2, 1864, to run six months, and indorsed by said Jonas Cringar. The second was also indebtedness to Jonas Cringar, for settlement of note for $ 12,000 to Slaycut & Drorblude, in payment for 8,000 shares of stock in the Pulverizing Gold Mining Company of Colorado, at $ 1.50 per share, bearing date October 4, 1864, to run four months, — indorsed by said Jonas Cringar. The third was an account of indebtedness to one Timothy Augoring, by privately protested note for one fifth interest in the Pioneer Oil Well, $ 15,000, said note bearing date October 9, 1864.

Besides these bold and startling statements, there were accounts of indebtedness to the concern of Paige & Cringar, amounting to nearly $ 45,000.

At length the Veteran stopped dictating to the book-keeper, and silently ran his eye up and down the formidable columns.

"Have you done," asked Billings.

"Yes. We have, I think, all I require. I have seen to my satisfaction how the enemy marshals his forces."

"General," said the book-keeper, "I don't pretend to

know much about law; but I 'll tell you how this appears to me."

"Well."

"It appears like a pretty thoroughly locked up safe."

"Very true," responded the Veteran with an air of concern. "But," he continued, while his features assumed that stern aspect on which we have before had reason to remark, "have you known of a safe that has defied the continued efforts of determined men?"

"I must acknowledge I have not, though I am somewhat interested, just now, in a new burglar-proof lock myself. To tell you the truth, I 've come to the conclusion that iron and steel are no proof against brains."

"It is so. Neither is the sagacity of a rascal proof against the determination of circumspect honesty."

"That is true also."

All this time the Veteran had been busy studying the records before him.

"This is a formidable array," he said, in continuance of their conversation, "and I can detect no flaw in it. It is consistent with itself in every part. The flanks are well guarded. The position seems impregnable, the forces invincible; but only by battle can the reality be revealed.

The book-keeper, who had seen much of men in his as yet brief life, contemplated his companion with sentiments of the profoundest admiration. Though he may not have known so much as many others about law, he knew enough to realize that the array of statements and figures put in by the executors of Allen Paige's estate, and there displayed in those records, with such a man as Daniel Garvin behind them, was of so formidable a character that probably no lawyer could be found to attack them, at any price, if he valued a special reputation for success. And yet here stood a man, whose education had been almost entirely in the field, who contemplated the impending battle with this powerful broker, intrenched as he was behind legal works that would seem to defy the power of men to storm, with a calmness of determination such as would characterize but few, even with a fair and easy contest before them.

Finally the Veteran gave the records a slight push toward the book-keeper, and then with the off-hand remark, "A sad piece of work, but very thoroughly done," which he uttered aloud, he turned away, informing the Surrogate's clerk — who was busy with an old German that had come all the way from Chicago to inquire about a will his son Hans had left in New York for him when he died — that he would have to call at a future time.

Billings returned the records to the clerk, and said in a low voice, —

"Mr. ——, for very important reasons, which I will make known to you at another time, will you be so good as to mention this visit of mine, and this gentleman's, also, to no one?"

"By no means, if you so desire. But that is a man I should like to be introduced to, Billings."

"At another time, if you will be so gracious as to wait."

"Certainly," replied the clerk with a slight laugh; and then he turned his attention again to the poor old German, with whose case he really sympathized, while the book-keeper accompanied the Veteran from the office.

As they descended the stairs, the latter said, —

"Billings, there is one piece of business, whereby Mr. Paige is asserted to have lost a great deal of money, which it seems does not enter into the settlement of the estate."

"What is that?"

"His cotton speculation. I understand that that was

given Mrs. Paige as one of the losses which reduced the estate."

"You understood aright. I overheard Cringar and Garvin talking about that myself, not long ago. It seemed to me as though they intended some one to hear, as a blind."

"They have treated it rather as an open matter then?"

"Yes."

The Veteran with a sudden movement placed his hand on the book-keeper's arm.

"Was the cotton bought in New York?"

"I am quite certain it was."

"Is it possible for you to obtain the name of the house he bought it of."

"I will try and make it possible."

"Thank you. You speak like a man of success."

"You think of making an attack there?"

"I will skirmish a little. Their fortress, which seems so impregnable under their masterly engineering, may yet have its weak point."

They now parted at one of the entrances of City Hall Park.

CHAPTER XX.

DANIEL GARVIN'S office was, three years ago, in the basement of a building, on the left side of Wall Street, about midway between William and Pearl Streets. At the left, as one entered the door, was a counter with a desk upon it for the transaction of general business. In the rear was a small room, partitioned off, in which was transacted business of a more confidential nature; and the reader will readily surmise that with Daniel Garvin such a room would find considerable use.

It is evening. Garvin has done a hard day's work, and made money. He has given "points" to men who called him a friend, and thereby put them on the wrong scent, and then taken them in, points and all, through a third party. The victims think he is a fellow-victim; but now, as he is left alone, he sits by the gas-light and reckons up his plunder.

That conscience yet deals with him, in its own way, is made evident by the manner in which he starts and glances at the street door, which is locked, as a sudden and unexpected click of the large latch strikes his ear. He looks through the partition window with a restless scowl, but receding steps indicate that the threatened intruder simply raised the latch to look in as he passed by, or ask direction to some place or person he was seeking.

The broker went on counting up his booty, every now and then casting a look of impatience toward the street.

At length footsteps, slow and shambling, were heard descending from the sidewalk, and then three raps, partaking of the nature of these shambling steps, sounded on the door.

The broker instantly gathered his papers into a drawer, and then advancing to the door with his grinding tread, he turned the key with a quick, abrupt movement, and admitted the visitor.

"Cringar!" he said imperiously, "I have been waiting for you!"

"I am sorry," answered the merchant, meekly; "but I have come as promptly as I could."

Garvin uttered a "humph!" and led the way into the back room.

The strong picture which Prescott Marland had drawn of Jonas Cringar, in his interview with the Veteran the day the latter arrived in New York from the West, was not an exaggerated one. As he now follows the broker into the lighted apartment he presents an object of unutterable misery. His shoulders, which in the opening chapter of this tale we described as somewhat stooping, now round over upon his chest, as if the weight and cares of troublesome years had borne them down. His step is feeble, uncertain, and shuffling.

As he seats himself his countenance comes into full view. It is a pitiable countenance, — haggard, worn, and weary. It looks as if all spirit were gone; as though death were prevented from claiming its own only by the infusion of a will outside this miserable man, — the will of his master, Daniel Garvin, who appears to hold his shattered mind and body together by a species of mental galvanism.

That habit of painfully elongating his facial muscles seems, under the incessant action of remorse, to have settled into absolute fixedness, imparting an impression of terrible internal suffering.

The broker sat for a moment in silence, contemplating with a secret emotion of diabolical triumph this ghastly work of his hands.

Cringar, on his part, once ventured to raise his downcast eyes to his destroyer's, in which the rings began now to display themselves with deadly distinctness; but he could endure this no longer than a passing moment. With a perceptible shudder his gaze again fell to the floor, and he sat like some statue of despair.

Garvin suddenly broke the silence.

"Cringar!" he exclaimed with his penetrating voice, "are you playing me false again?"

"Playing you false!" uttered this broken victim, raising his eyes this time with a look of terror, "playing you false! Before God —"

"What have you to do with God now? You had better take your oath on the Devil!" was the broker's blasphemous interruption.

Garvin was an atheist.

Cringar, who was naturally possessed of strong religious feelings, experienced an emotion of horror at this remark; and for an instant he was impressed with a feeling, as if the being before him was himself the Fiend Incarnate. His eyes, in place of falling as on the former occasion, became riveted to the demoniacal orbs before him by a terrible fascination.

The broker burst into a loud, contemptuous laugh.

"You are losing your senses, man!" he exclaimed.

"I think I am," returned the merchant, whose eyes had been released by this laugh, and now fell again to the floor, while a tremor went through his shattered frame.

The broker's laugh continued for a single moment, and then it closed as abruptly as it had opened; and bending his annihilating eye on his victim, his face darkened, and his brows met.

"Cringar," he said, "some one is playing me false! Have you seen Baling lately?"

As he put this question he bent a scrutinizing gaze on the merchant.

"I've not seen him for two weeks."

"His books have been examined."

The merchant started in affright.

"His books examined!" he cried hoarsely.

"Yes."

"By whom?"

"An enemy."

"An enemy?"

"An enemy."

"Impossible!"

"I lie then?"

"You — lie. I — protest —"

"Bah! I tell you that an enemy has been through Baling's accounts."

"And — and discovered all!"

"Fool!"

"Your pardon!" ejaculated the miserable merchant, shrinking back.

"Do you think I leave business open in that way?"

"My head is not strong, — I did not think."

The broker contemplated the miserable object of his mental by-play with scornful pity.

"Is nothing discovered, then?" at length asked Cringar, tremblingly.

"Nothing, sir. I do not leave my tracks to be followed up by every spy that happens behind me."

"I am aware of it, Mr. Garvin," returned Cringar, reviving a little under a change in Garvin's voice.

The broker grimly smiled.

"I will tell you, sir, and then you can judge," said this scheming egotist, at the same time throwing himself back in his chair, and thrusting the thumb of his left hand into the armhole of his vest. "You have not forgotten, sir, that Mr. Baling, being my very particular friend, changed the date of Mr. Allen Paige's purchase to meet the facts in the case."

"That is, he found a mistake in his entry and rectified it," joined in Jonas Cringar with a sickly smile, his anxiety to hold the good-will of his master, who he perceived had some reason to suspect him of treachery, now beginning to unloosen his tongue.

"You have it. You now talk like a man of sense," responded the broker. "In the meanwhile let me go over this business a little, for circumstances may occur that will require your memory to be clear."

The merchant, encouraged, straightened a little, and prepared respectfully to listen.

The broker, on his part, thrust his thumb still deeper into the armhole of his vest, and expanding his chest by a slow inspiration, prepared with the egotism of plotting villany to rehearse his sagacious performances.

"As you probably recollect, the original entry was dated August 3d. When I called to see him, last November, he acknowledged the error on its being pointed out to him by so particular and trustworthy a friend as myself, and immediately set it right by a proper attendance to the day-book. And by two simple touches the ledger was made properly to accord with it."

"By inserting the figure 2," again uttered the abject merchant, "and changing 8 into 9. It was a very sagacious bit of business."

"A just correction, you mean, Mr. Cringar."

"A just correction, I should have said."

"And thus August 3d was properly transformed into August 23d, and $ 87,315, amount, into $ 97,315, with the more marked success, inasmuch as there happened to be ample space left between the *t* of August and the figure 3; and the 8 was more like a 9 than an 8 at the start. All this you have not forgotten."

"By no means, sir. It is a monument of your — r — justice."

"Of Mr. Baling's justice, you probably intended to say."

"I should have said, of Mr. Baling's justice."

"Thus, as you perceive, making an important difference between buying cotton on the 3d of August, at a dollar sixty-eight cents, to be sold on the 24th, at an advance of twenty cents to the pound, and buying it on the 23d of August, at a dollar eighty-seven cents, to be held and put on a sinking market, September 24th, at a loss of forty-eight cents to the pound."

"A very important difference."

"A difference so important, that instead of ten thousand dollars' profit appearing in favor of my deceased brother's estate, a loss of over twenty thousand is the just entry."

"It is quite true."

"A transaction, so consistent with the excitement of those days, is doubted by no one, who recollects the great whirl that caught up the brains of deeper men than Mr. Paige."

"No one can doubt it."

"They remember that cotton started in June from about a dollar, and went up like a pyrotechnic serpent, every now and then taking a downward twist, to mount upwards with a still fiercer rush, and dazzling the eyes of all beholders."

"Yes, all were dazzled. And when Allen went in at one sixty-eight, I feared — "

"At *one eighty-seven*, sir!" thundered the broker.

"Pardon my treacherous memory!" uttered the merchant, sinking back in a sort of cowering stupefaction.

"See to it that your treacherous memory does n't play its treachery with me elsewhere, sir!" returned the broker, at the same time slowly rubbing the outside of his breast-pocket, as if by an unconscious movement.

The merchant blanched.

"Yes, sir. You will recollect the excitement with which your partner hurried to Baling & Co., and bought one hundred and eleven bales of middling, at one dollar and eighty-seven cents, amid the hot predictions that the market would n't stop till cotton soared — the Heavens, toward which it was going, only knew where."

"I recollect it perfectly well," responded Cringar, reviving a little. "The Red River expedition started it up, — the fall of Atlanta sent it back. My partner was so unfortunate as to take it on the turn."

"Very true. I am glad to perceive your memory improving. Your partner — my lamented brother" (the merchant sickened at this heartless attempt at humor) — "was so unfortunate as to fall into the snare set by those predictions, and put in his money, and held on to his cotton when the market began to fall, convinced it was one of those twisting descents, preparatory to another grand upward flight; and down he went with it, scarcely giving him time to think, till, as he passed one forty, he threw the whole lot over to save himself; and not a day too soon, for you undoubtedly recollect that a blank appears in the quotations after this, till four days later it lights on one twenty to one twenty-five. There was wailing and gnashing of teeth in those days, was there not, sir?" asked the broker with a sardonic grin.

"A lamentable amount of it," responded the merchant.

"Your memory is now clear on all these points, and beyond the chance of slipping — or treachery?" continued Garvin, with a significant emphasis on the last word.

"Beyond all doubt, sir, — beyond all doubt, I assure you."

CHAPTER XXI.

THE broker now contemplated Cringar for a while in silence. He moved a little, that his own eyes might be relieved from the direct glare of the gas, as he threw into them all his reserved power of penetration, while he brought them to bear on the very soul of his victim. Instantly he made this change his pupils expanded with marvellous rapidity, and the rings increased with the intensity of their lurid light in proportion as this action of the pupils diminished their width. At the same time the upper lip drew slowly back, more slowly than we have yet seen it, and in a manner that gave to his glistening fangs their deadliest aspect.

Cringar, though he did not venture to look up, — having invariably dropped his eyes after each response to the foregoing recapitulation and admonitions of Daniel Garvin, — felt this deadly scrutiny of the broker, and trembled. He was not conscious of any overt act of treachery, but he *was* conscious of a state of rebellion within, which only the terrible power his tormentor held over him prevented from breaking forth with violence.

The most positively abject, under a crushing power, are those who, possessing a certain kind of strength themselves, have vainly contended against this power, their struggles only serving to exhaust them and leave their contending spirit demoralized and broken; which now and then, it is true, flashes up under its fearful trial, but in a manner that but too surely indicates its helpless condition.

Suddenly the broker spoke.

"Cringar," he said, "if I thought you were so much as turning the little finger of your hand, I would — " Here he tapped his breast-pocket with two or three strokes, made with such venomous rapidity that one is instantly reminded of the simile of the lizards, uttered by the excited Marland in his interview with the Veteran.

The merchant, whose spirit, under the reaction of the broker's sustained, imperious, and penetrating gaze, was preparing to make one of those rebellious, flickering efforts to which we have alluded, threw up his head with a frightened stare; and in a tremulous voice he ejaculated, —

"Ah, great God!" Then as Garvin continued his studious gaze, he uttered in a broken voice, "Mr. Garvin — give me a Bible — and I — will swear!"

The broker responded with another mocking laugh.

"Never mind your calf-bound paper!" he exclaimed. "I'll trust my eyes quicker than I will your God-packed oaths. You are innocent. That's my verdict. Now I'll tell you what has been done."

As the broker gave vent to this second blasphemous mockery, Jonas Cringar, who had been wrought up to a high pitch of terror by the former's significant, reptile-like action at his breast-pocket, could not withdraw his startled gaze from the blasphemer's face, and for a moment he fancied himself in the regions Infernal.

These fancies were not diminished by the action of the gas-light, which suddenly failed, ere Garvin had finished the last word of his sacrilegious speech, and after seeming for a moment to cling to the burner, went out.

Garvin uttered a curse, and rising from his chair, groped about the room for a match, which finding, he lit it and looked about him.

"There's water in the pipes," he muttered. "It's

played me the same trick before. It 's gone for this night, that 's certain."

Cringar, who was overcome with dread, now rose.

"I will come in at another time," he said in a quivering voice. "Don't trouble yourself on my account."

"Keep your seat, sir!" commanded the broker in a sharp, snarling voice. "I 'll furnish a light!"

Cringar fell back in his chair as though he had been shot.

The match in Garvin's fingers here burned out. Lighting another he went to an old stand in one corner of the room, and opening the drawer, took out a small piece of candle. He lit this, and then looked about for something that would serve as a candlestick.

"Ah, I have it!" he exclaimed; and he approached an odd-looking parcel, lying on the floor in another corner. "That boy of mine can do some good with his mud, which I think you and I will acknowledge in a moment, Mr. Cringar."

Undoing the thick brown paper, he brought to view a small mess of modelling clay, which William Garvin had left to take the next morning. Then he took an empty tin box from the shelf, and filling it with the damp clay, punched a hole with his ugly thumb, and inserting the bit of candle placed it on the table, and rubbed the clay from his hands with an almost comical air of triumph.

"No need of going home yet, Mr. Cringar," said he, thrusting his thumb into the armhole of his vest again. "Gas companies are not allowed to control Daniel Garvin's business. Now, sir, I 'll proceed to recount to you what has been done."

"I shall be happy to hear," responded Cringar, resigning himself.

"No doubt. Well, as I have told you, Baling's books have been examined, and with direct reference to that transaction of my worthy half-brother."

The merchant again looked frightened.

"Fear not," said the broker contemptuously; "but listen. Baling came the other day and informed me that a man had been to his office, while he was out, and under one plausible pretext and another had with great sagacity endeavored to work on his clerk to let him look at the accounts of sales for 1864. 'But,' says Baling, 'Bob 's got his eye teeth cut, and he would n't give him so much as a squint till he had seen me. So he told the stranger to call again.' In the mean time Baling had come to me to let me know what was up, for his suspicions pointed to this ill-advised purchase of your partner; which, you will bear in mind, though justly corrected on the books, he would naturally feel sensitive about, inasmuch as he is not often committed to such mistakes, and more especially to blunders where ten thousand dollars are made instead of twenty thousand lost. You can understand his feelings, Mr. Cringar?"

"Very well, sir, indeed. I understand them very well."

"Now, sir, what do you suppose I said to him?"

"To Mr. Baling?"

"Yes, sir, Mr. Baling."

"Really, sir, you must have told him not to allow it."

"The books not to be examined you mean?"

"Certainly, sir."

"Then certainly, sir, I have to inform you that I did no such thing."

"Great Heavens! you —"

"Told him by all means to open his whole safeful of

books to the inquisitive gentleman, if he wanted to look at them."

The merchant stared at Garvin in dismay.

The broker gave utterance to a guttural laugh of self-satisfaction, a tone of contempt for the terrified merchant being mingled with it.

"Well, do you take me for a fool that is not to be prepared for this sort of exigency? Know, sir, that I have made this cotton a bold point. I apprehended that it would be one of the first points attacked, if any one should ever be fool enough to assail us; and now, sir, let them examine. What do they find? They find a faultless entry. A daybook out of the reach of microscopes and chemicals. I paid money, sir, to have that daybook put in condition. Daniel Garvin leaves nothing to chance, — nothing, sir. The daybook being all right, the ledger was easily adjusted. Now, sir, the more boldly they are pushed under the eyes of curious persons the more thoroughly are these presumptuous meddlers repulsed, and beaten off from further attempts."

"I trust this will happen in the present instance."

"Depend upon it, sir, that such is the case."

"This man has visited Mr. Baling's office a second time?"

"He has, and went away with a flea in his ear. Do you not see the great point of this business, sir? Mr. Paige, who is declared by his admiring friends to have been a man of immaculate integrity and above all lies, is known to have reported that he cleared a large profit on his cotton speculation. The mining and oil-well business they confess they never heard him talk about, — and perhaps for a very good reason, Mr. Cringar," — here the broker indulged in a low ironical fit of laughter, and closed it by repeating, "and perhaps for a very good reason, Mr. Cringar." He continued: "Well, sir, these admirable friends became sagacious friends. 'Let us ascertain the name of the firm he bought the cotton of, and judge by the quotations,' they say to themselves. So with profound cunning they find out that he bought of Baling & Co. They go in, — ask to see his books with a depth of shrewd simplicity to be admired, — and find out for themselves that he bought on a market that must have inevitably let him down. They then find their eyes opened to the revelation, that their much-esteemed and lamented friend was no exception to the scores of deluded merchants of this inflammable city, who could tell a business lie as easily as they could eat their supper, provided they had the money left to pay for it. They will then give up the scent in disgust. Do you see it, sir?"

The merchant did see it, and his soul was seized with renewed pangs of remorse, as Garvin thus pictured the ruined reputation of the partner, whom he had loved, which was but an accompaniment to the ruin of his unfortunate family. These pangs refused him speech.

The broker divined his thoughts, and his own soul was filled with quivering rage.

This depraved schemer was not, as we have before intimated, free from the secret scourgings of his conscience. Could he have slain this conscience it would long ago have ceased to exist. This being beyond his power, all he could do was to throw about his heart the thick veil of wickedness, to make it, if possible, deaf to the voice of the ever-living and faithful monitor. But this veil would occasionally be rent; and then, in addition to the dull sounds that never ceased to be heard, and which placed him before the pure enjoyments of the world somewhat as one racked with inward pain is situated while he endeavors to listen to an entertainment, his exposed heart would be penetrated by a voice so quick, so sharp, so terrible, that he would inwardly tremble with a sort of desperate fury. Atheist that he was, there would in these moments sweep over him the overwhelming truth that there is a God that judgeth in the earth. The realization would be irresistibly forced upon his self-absorbing egotism, that over him was held the all-controlling power of a Supreme Master.

In the present instance he was subject to one of these secret dramas of the soul. He had, in the self-complacency of his criminal triumph, yielded somewhat to impulse; and his vanity, which with such men, in conjunction with their inordinate egotism, partakes of the spirit of monomania, had been allowed to lead in his recital to Jonas Cringar. While thus indulging this vanity, his mind had been more or less preoccupied with his self-exultant utterances, and he had consequently failed to observe those signs of the internal workings of his victim's soul which he usually so well understood. But when he closed his abominable dissertation with the abrupt question, "Do you see it, sir?" and received only silence in return, he suddenly bent his piercing gaze on the conscience-smitten merchant. Then it was that the reaction of his own indulged weakness, combined with the reaction, also, upon himself of his listener's terrible remorse, caused the veil about his heart to be rent as never before; and then followed his furious perturbation.

Cringar's first intimation of the existence of this rage was the grating sound of Garvin's teeth, as they gnashed together. Thus recalled to his senses he raised his eyes.

He had seen the broker many times with an aspect that struck him with terror, but never had he appeared to him so horrible as now. His eyes had broken from their intense gleam into a consuming blaze, which appeared to shoot forth, as it were, from two caverns; the beetling brows were bent into one continuous black ridge, and the prominent high cheekbones seemed to press outward and upward to oppose themselves to these ridges, while the sockets between them had the appearance of being drawn far back into the head. An unusual darkness seemed to gather on the skin, and the upper lip twitched with a spasmodic action, revealing the grinding teeth in contrast with this darkening flesh, and, to the merchant's agitated mind, in ghastly combination with the cavernous fires above.

As Jonas Cringar beheld this sombre and terrific visage, a cold sweat burst from the pores of his creeping skin, and for the third time during this interview he felt that horrid shuddering of the soul, which he had so often heard pictured as the disembodied spirit's first experience when ushered into the precincts of the damned.

"Wretch!" finally exclaimed this wrathful semblance of a madman, "do you sit there leading me on to gabble into your heedless ass's ears, while you are thinking how to betray me?"

"Before a just God! — "

The broker sprang to his feet.

"Fool! scoundrel! idiot! dare to speak that name here again, and I 'll show you that I am God in this place!"

"In God's name, hush!" cried the merchant, rising also to his feet, while a look of solemn terror took possession of his features; "hush! or He will strike you dead!"

At this instant a wild peal of laughter rose into the night air, which was immediately followed by a shrill voice, singing with a jumbling accent, —

"My gentle sirs, be very kind!
Your candle 's out,

My gentle sirs!
You 'll be found out,
My gentle sirs!
But gentle me you cannot find!"

As their ears were greeted by this laughter, the broker and merchant both started back, appalled by what seemed so unearthly an interruption. Their distended eyes were simultaneously directed toward the back window whence the laughter came, and there they beheld an impish face, pressed against the pane, while from its mouth issued the gibberish transcribed above.

The diabolical character of the scene was enhanced to these startled beholders by the candle's verification of the singer's words; for having burned to the bottom of the hole made by Garvin's thumb, it now sent up, preparatory to going slowly out, a ghastly, bluish light, which clung to the sides of the cavity as it ascended, as if the greasy substance of the clay lent itself to the flame.

"Ha! ha! ha!" burst from the throat of the broker, as the face swiftly disappeared on the utterance of the last word of the song. "It 's simple Sal, the janitor's daughter! You look frightened, sir," he said, turning to the trembling merchant, while he closed his jaws and compressed his lips in a powerful effort to control his own agitation.

The merchant was incapable of speech. The broker's awful blasphemy, the effort of his own solemn adjuration, the laugh, the song, with its idiotic, but to him its deadly prophecy, the dying, ghastly flame of the clay-entombed candle, and the broker's guttural, fear-fraught laugh, which penetrated his ears with an effect scarcely less horrid than the laugh of the idiot, all had left him utterly unstrung and speechless.

As Garvin was about again to speak, the blue flame ran

up the socket of clay, and, hanging for a moment in the air, went out like a vanishing spirit, leaving the room in utter darkness.

The broker grumbled out a strongly aspirated but suppressed curse.

"Take your hat, Cringar, and come along!" he grumbled. "No more talk to-night!"

Cringar obeyed with alacrity, and hurried from the office as if he sought to escape the awful curse that he felt was now brooding there.

Garvin scowled in the darkness as he followed him; and while he locked the door with his right hand, he brandished his left, clenched and unseen by the object of his malignant ire, and with the fourth line of the idiot's impish song still ringing in his ears, he muttered, —

"Craven! dare to fail me, and Daniel Garvin will teach you whose God can be depended upon!"

CHAPTER XXII.

IT is a warm and pleasant day. A train is passing over the track of the New Jersey Central, and as we shall find in the third car a spirit as bright, as buoyant, and warm as the sunlight, we will enter by touching this talisman which I hold in my hand, the author's pen.

It is Prescott Marland of whom I speak. He sits by the open window — for in New Jersey a warm April day is like a summer's day in a more Northern clime.

"Ice-cream candy!"

Prescott stops the boy who cries this, and takes from his vest-pocket a ten-cent scrip.

The boy hands him a paper of the candy.

As Prescott receives it he catches sight of a little fellow, who, sitting on the opposite side, has turned and now wistfully eyes the paper.

Prescott, on the instant, whipped out another piece of currency, which proved to be twenty-five cents, and taking a second parcel from the basket handed it to the longing boy, who blushed, stammered out a "Thank you, sir!" and then proceeded, without more ado, to tear away the paper and devour its contents.

As the young vender was preparing to give the fifteen cents change, Prescott asked him if he could afford to eat much of the candy himself.

"As much as my hide 'ld be worth, sir! Dad don't 'low it."

"Well, then, give me back five cents, and sit down beside me here (the boy was a neat-looking lad) and eat a paper at my expense, if you have time. I want to talk with you."

The little vender, with the characteristic freedom of a boy of his class, immediately responded to Prescott's invitation.

The young Lieutenant had seen at a glance that this boy was intelligent; and if there was anything he relished while travelling, it was to gather information from those sources which are passed unheeded by most travellers. As the lad ate his candy he led him into conversation, and gleaned much knowledge.

"I make a good deal of money for dad here some days," said the boy in the course of the conversation. "But it 's strange how it works! Some days everybody likes candy, and then some days they don't. I tell you what it is, I likes them days when the mammas bring in their little youngsters to see New York; then, whew! how it goes!"

"I suppose you have your ups and downs in this business, as they have in all others," rejoined Prescott with a smile.

"Yes, and no mistake. That 's what Joe Deering said when I took his place."

"Joe Deering!" exclaimed Prescott.

"Yes, Joe Deering. And a mighty fine chap he was, too. I liked that chum, I did; and if he should get well, and come back here for this place, I 'd be glad to give it to him."

"Is his father living?" inquired the Lieutenant, anxiously.

"His father, no! He was killed at the war!"

As the lad gave this answer, a man who sat in the next seat, front, turned his head half round to listen. He was about thirty, and had a look of energy.

"It is the same," uttered Prescott, in a ruminating voice.

The boy looked up at his interlocutor with an inquisitive air of surprise.

"Do you know what regiment his father went out in?"

"No, I don't," said the lad, scratching his head; "but I 'll tell you what I do know, and that is that he was killed under McClellan."

"It 's the same. Do you know where they live?"

"No, I don't. He did live on the Bowery; but I went up there one time to see him, and they were gone."

"Yes, the Bowery. That 's where they lived. What do you think has become of them?" asked Prescott, anxiously.

"I can't tell you. Are they acquaintances of yours, sir?"

"I have friends, my boy, that knew them," replied Prescott, at the same time that his mind flew off to her whom he first met while she was in search of Joseph Deering's family. He then thought of her anxiety for this family, who had disappeared from the old house on the Bowery, since he first met her, and for whose welfare she still experienced a deep solicitude.

The lad observed his emotion, but misunderstood his silence.

"Excuse me, sir," he said. "I don't want to be asking impudent questions; that ain't my business."

Prescott smiled in the midst of his anxiety.

"Your question was n't at all impudent, my boy. But I 'm sorry you can't tell me where he lives. Do you think they are in want?"

The listener in front here turned his head a little more.

"I 'm afraid they are badly off," said the boy. "He told me his mother was sick, and he 's got two little sisters, and he supported 'em all, — and when he had to give up sick himself, I tell you he felt bad, and I felt bad too, sir; for he was a fine fellow and no mistake. I wish I knew where they lived. You 'd help 'em, I reckon?"

"Yes, my boy, I would."

"I knowed you 'd say it, sir! You see, sir, it 's a soldier's family; and I 've heard a good many that rides in and out here say soldiers' families ought n't to be made beggars of, and allowed to starve after fighting for the stars and stripes."

"Good!" exclaimed the man in front.

"And I say amen to that," responded Prescott.

The boy looked up keenly at both men, and then muttered to himself, — "Soldiers!"

"Prescott at the same time fixed his eye on the stranger, and reaching forward his hand, said, —

"Comrade."

The other accepted the proffered hand, and said in response, —

"I thought you had seen service. Glad to see a soldier any time."

"That 's my mind exactly," returned Prescott.

The stranger now looked toward the boy's seat.

"Take it," said the lad, rising; and thanking Prescott he picked up his basket and went to the rear of the car, for his vending was through with for that trip.

Prescott's new acquaintance now came and sat by his side.

"I 've been listening to your talk with the lad about that soldier's family. It seems to me they must be seeing hard times, if that boy tells the truth."

"I don't doubt him."

"Neither do I."

"I 've known of this family before; and I know that if the mother is sick, and that boy Joseph too, they are starving unless they 've been helped," said Prescott.

His companion frowned.

"Promises! promises! promises! that was the song!" he muttered. "Do you think," he continued, "that this would have happened four years ago?"

"I do not."

"Or, say, when the Merrimack threw these Atlantic cities into a ferment, threatening them with destruction?"

"This family would not have then been forgotten."

"No."

"But, after all, it 's human nature."

"'T is true. It 's human nature."

"And therefore we must n't reflect too hard on the people at large, provided they 'll sustain others in doing what they have n't the time to think of doing themselves."

"That 's so! I 'm a little riled now and then when I hear of this soldier's family starving, and that soldier's family freezing, and no one seeming to look out for them, and when I call to mind the pledges the people who stayed at home made to the fathers of these families, before they were shot down by the Rebels; but, as you say, it 's human nature, and the best thing to do is for the soldiers, themselves, to go to work in such a way to make these pledges good that the citizens will take hold and help us."

"You have it. It 's the only sensible way. Look here, what 's the use of a man's crying out *broken pledges!* to a railroad train that 's left him behind, because they promised to take him on and did n't, and stand yelling to the winds, letting the next train pass by instead of hopping on!"

Prescott's new companion laughed.

"That 's the idea!" said he. "It's no use at all. If human nature 's human nature, I suppose we 've got to treat it as human nature. In short, we 've got to keep up with it."

"Yes, and if soldiers can't do it, who can?" rejoined Prescott, laughing in his turn. "Now let me tell you," he continued, "what is going to do it."

"Go on," said the other with a significant look.

"An association."

"Yes."

"An organization."

"Yes."

"An association of the soldiers themselves, — organized efforts."

"You have it!"

Prescott looked at his companion intently, and then uttered the three words,

"G. A. R."

The other looked in turn. "I take it you are a member of the G. A. R.," he said.

Prescott nodded.

"Glad to hear it, comrade," exclaimed the companion clasping him again by the hand in fraternal greeting. "We 've just organized in New York."

"You are engaged in this New York movement then?"

"Yes. If any city needs us it is New York."

"True. You will have cases enough to attend to."

"True again. And that is the reason we should be at it. We shall have enough to do. I presume I must look upon you as my senior as a comrade?"

"I joined in Illinois, in the first of it."

"Well, it 's wonderful how it 's going!"

"Yes, wonderful! And yet not so much to be wondered at. The men that went into this war are n't the kind, generally speaking, to stand, after the war's over, and see the families of their comrades suffer."

"That 's so, comrade, every word! And I 'm confident that every true-hearted soldier will take hold with us as soon as he knows what we are about."

"We shall have to contend against one thing."

"What 's that?"

"The outcries of our enemies."

"They can't hurt us."

"Excuse me, comrade; but I think they can."

"Not materially."

"For the time being, at least."

"How?"

"By their usual vituperative statements. You see we are necessarily a secret organization. Men have a good deal to say about secret societies, but I 'll tell you what it is, you 've got to put powder and ball pretty well out of sight to make them do the work when the priming sets them off. But here 's the chance for our enemies. They 'll have more stories to tell about us than there were colors in Joseph's coat."

"Bah! I've heard their stories; but who'll believe them?"

"A great many; for, do you see, we are compelled to confine ourselves to denials. What we may or may not do cannot be proved in all cases to outsiders, inasmuch as they are not admitted to our meetings to see for themselves."

"It is true. But I believe in the end their libels will do us good."

"I believe so, too. Libels, with but few exceptions, inevitably work that way."

"When I hear them talking about 'pandering to military ambition,' a 'political machine,' and the like, I think to myself that such venomous attacks will be sure to react on those that make them."

"All this, however, is an admonition."

"An admonition?"

"That we cannot be too strict in eschewing all these things. The very fact that we consider it important to refute the accusations of our enemies, should be sufficient warning that such indulgences would be inimical and disastrous to the Order."

"I agree with you there. I have understood that some of the soldiers' and sailors' clubs lent themselves to this outside business, and accordingly lost the confidence of the community."

"Yes, many of those clubs seem to have been formed rather for the purpose of making their voices heard in complaints than for good hard work in behalf of those who honestly stood in need of fraternal aid. And when men gather together to complain, they simply offer themselves to the first intriguer that happens along."

"That 's true. Still, we should give due credit to these clubs. They have undoubtedly done much good."

"Undoubtedly. But they did not form a responsible body, whereby the part is accountable to the whole. They have been valuable as forerunners of our present organization."

"I see that."

"From their very nature they were not calculated to resist the strong current that was bearing, and would always bear, against them, as it will bear against us, and which we are sure to withstand."

As Prescott uttered this remark, a booming sound announced that the train was advancing upon the long bridge that spans Newark Bay.

CHAPTER XXIII.

THE two soldiers gazed in silence for a moment over the calm, sunlit water, dotted here and there by small craft that lazily awaited any "cat's-paws" which might occasionally touch their sails as they swiftly passed, ruffling the water in their shifting course.

"This bridge offers a very good illustration of your remark," said Prescott's companion, who had withdrawn his gaze from the distance, and directed it to the powerful current immediately under them. "When the contractor undertook to build it there was a great cry that he would fail. The rush of water, as you see, is very powerful here, and it was predicted that his attempt would be his ruin; for this current would, before winter and spring had done with it, send it down the stream to be sold for old lumber."

"I have heard something about it," said Prescott, with interest; and he gazed on the rushing waters as they tore away from the bridge in their onward course, as if in rage at their impotent efforts to rend its foundations asunder. "Former experience lent force to these predictions; but the contractor put good hard sense against past failures and present predictions combined. This is how he did it. He sank a great mass of stone with every pile, all so fastened together that an earthquake would have to come along to undo the job."

"We are riding over a stone quarry then, I should think," said Prescott, laughing.

"That 's about what it amounts to. And if this current can lug off a stone quarry it can lug off this bridge. Now, comrade, the foundations of an Order like ours must be the same. As you say, there will ever be strong currents bearing upon it, and it must be founded in the granite of strict and consistent principles to stand against them."

"I like to hear you talk that way," rejoined Prescott, bringing a hand emphatically down on the other's knee. "Many entertain the idea that all that soldiers can have in mind, in gathering together, is to cut up their old camp shines, and keep their hands in so as to slaughter, one of these days, every unlucky dog who does n't happen to think as they do."

"Ha! ha! you are about right there. There 's a certain class of men that 's mighty afraid of soldiers!"

"Yes," returned Prescott with a significant glance at a hard-visaged old fellow, sitting just back, whom he had observed to scowl when the word *soldier*, uttered by them, had once met his ear; "and well they might be, seeing we have been so successful in putting down their friends."

"Of course," said the other, "they will stand ready to

denounce everything as politics, or dangerously military, that they can possibly get hold of."

"Certainly. It 's in their nature. But all we 've got to do is to be sure our base is right, and then push on, undisturbed by every little crack of a buckshot musket that we hear in the woods."

"There 's one thing about it. We shall often have to fight down unprincipled opposition in one form or another, and no doubt when we do so they 'll raise the hue and cry of '*Politics!*' as their last resource."

"O yes, there are men mean enough for anything; and if to carry out their petty spite they knew they were surely exposing a thousand families of the soldier to starvation, it would make no difference. They would probably say 'D—n the soldier, and his family too!' and let drive their venom with a louder hiss than ever."

The hard-faced old fellow behind heard this remark, and winced perceptibly, while Prescott, who had kept one eye on him, put his hand to his mouth and nudged his companion. At the same time he bent his head to the other's ear and whispered, —

"An old copperhead in the rear rank!"

"Let 's ask him to subscribe for the new Post!" returned the other with a grimace.

"He 's been posted as much as he 'll bear, I 'm thinking," rejoined Prescott.

His comrade laughed, and turning his head, took in, with an offhand glance, the features of the object of this sally.

He instantly turned back to Marland.

"I know the old fellow like a book. It 's Copperhead Snarling, — that 's what the boys all call him. He ought to have been hung. But General Dix did the next-best thing, — he put him into Fort Lafayette. Why, that old sinner would work night and day, if he thought he could do us an injury. A son of his was drafted, and the young scion had to go; and when he thinks it 's for his interest the hypocrite prates about his '*soldier boy!*' I should n't be at all astonished yet, if through this '*soldier boy*' he were to work away with malcontents to get up some kind of a flash opposition concern; and as he 's always yelled '*Constitution!*' when we 've shouted '*Republic!*' he 'd be sure and stick that into the name somewhere; and, again, as we should be powerful by that time he would undoubtedly advocate stealing all the thunder from us he could, and back it up by proposing to harness as much of our name on as they could trot under."

"Who knows?" returned Prescott, amused. "Of course they would give a wide berth to politics, seeing that is the cry with which they fill the air, when they denounce the Grand Army of the Republic."

"Lord, yes, sir! they would undoubtedly give politics a wide berth, — that is, in this way: They would probably come up from their sea of troubles groaning and sobbing, declaring to the world that, seeing no chance in the Grand Army of the Republic — rampant with its political demagoguism — they were going to have an organization so free from politics, so pure and immaculate, that as none but those of their own stripe could live in it, they should have it understood that here these harmonious spirits could find a political asylum, and none others."

"Well, well!" replied Prescott, still more amused. "I 'll note that down, and if it happens, I 'll call you a prophet.*

* Aside from the brusque language of Prescott's hearty comrade, especially that having direct reference to the man behind him, whom he called Copperhead Snarling, his implied prophecy seems in the main to have

But coming back to the G. A. R. in New York, I am greatly rejoiced to see the work going on. I have known of this movement, for, besides a slight influence I have been able to exert to this end, I have a friend who has been able to effect a good deal more.

"Is he from the West?"

"He is."

"I think I know whom you mean."

"Who?"

"General Hammond."

"You have it at the first guess."

"His soul seems done up in the Grand Army."

"It is. He would assist a deserving comrade at the risk of his life."

"I have no doubt of it, from what I 've heard of him."

"One such man giving his heart and soul to the cause, after having the time he has had to thoroughly understand it, does more to refute the slanders and libels of our enemies than could reams of foolscap."

"'T is true. But now tell me of the family you were talking about with the candy-boy. That seems to be one of the first cases for us to attend to."

"It is a family named Deering. The soldier's name was Joseph Deering. He went out in a New York regiment, and was killed in the Peninsular campaign, under McClellan," answered Prescott.

The other took out a memorandum-book, and proceeded to write this information down.

been fulfilled by individuals, who have recently taken preliminary steps toward organizing a society, to be called The Grand Army of the Constitution; the manifest absurdity of whose position is, that, while they make pretence of complaint, on the ground of politics, against the G. A. R., one of whose cardinal principles is the exclusion of politics, they themselves make politics the distinctive feature of their organization.

Prescott watched his companion's movements with intense satisfaction. Not only did he realize that a systematic effort would now be made to seek out and relieve this family, whose situation had so excited his sympathies, but he could bear the cheerful news to that other soldier's family; for even in the midst of their own trials they forgot not these suffering ones, whom they could not trace after they had left the old house in the Bowery.

"I trust you will find them," he said.

"If they are to be found in New York, we 'll find them," said the other with decision. At the same time he turned the leaf of his memorandum-book.

Prescott observed several names entered, with directions. Among these his eye detected one that looked familiar. As it was written very hastily he did not feel quite certain.

"Can I look over your list?" he asked.

"Certainly. They are all soldiers' families. They are to be looked up."

Prescott took the book, and examined it with an anxious eye.

"You have the name of Allen Paige here, I perceive," he said, slightly flushing.

"Yes. He was a true soldier. He was reported to be wealthy when he died, but it was found that speculation had ruined him; and I understand his family are in a state of destitution, and are really objects of relief."

Prescott reddened so suddenly that he was obliged to turn and gaze out of the opposite car-windows, with an air as if he had unexpectedly caught sight of an object of great curiosity.

It was a hard thing for an ardent lover to see the name of his loved one's family written down in a list of the destitute, to be aided from a Relief fund.

He recovered himself as quickly as possible, and turned to his comrade.

"I do not think this family will need your aid," he said. "I am quite well acquainted with them; and though they suffer privation, they go on the principle that everything they own, that seems in the least degree superfluous, must go toward their support before they will consent to receive aid from others."

"That 's the spirit I like!" exclaimed the other. "But look here," said he, thoughtfully; "sometimes these are the very kind — who have the true pride of a soldier's family — that allow themselves to suffer too much before accepting relief. Now I don't pretend to know much about this family, but I was told something by a comrade that looks as though they were in a hard situation."

"What was it?" inquired Prescott, whose emotions were growing every moment more painful.

"You see, he happened to be in a pawnbroker's shop the other day, and I will relate to you what occurred just as he gave it to me, dialect and all. The Jew was slightly acquainted with him, and it seems he had heard of the Grand Army; so he asked him if the soldiers were going to have Posts in New York. Comrade Walker told him 'Yes.' 'Vell den,' says he, 'I 'sh glad of it, for I likes der soldiers first-rate. I was always a goot Union man. Now look here,' and he took a box out of his safe, 'I show not der pawns to everypody that comes into mine establishment, boot you ish von good Union soldier, and I vill show you someding, and tell you der story. In der midst of der great storm, mit der sleet and wind and cold wedder, dat we have stronger than never were yet sence der month of January, dare come into mine shop a young lady mit der face so sweet and beautiful under der — what you call 'im

— vater-proof hood, all covered mit der sleet, and der sweet face looking so sad and worn mit der sorrow, that mine heart was very mooch touched. And then, ven she takes off der pin and tells me she vants to pawn it, and I see dat it must pe der portrait of her fader, and ish one vary fine-looking man, as you see, I felt mit mine eyes as if I must cry, and I advanced more than ever were yet py me, and I say to mineself — while she give von big sob when I takes der pin an' gives her der monish — if I was von soldier, I would go and work mit all my might and main, and make von big society of der soldiers; and mit der same I would help the family of der soldier — because, you tink of it, and you vill see dat der world ish vary apt to forget der big promises made to der brave soldier, ven he goes off to der wars. Their heads, and der houses, and der money-boxes, dey all pe safe and sound, and dey say to der poor soldier, 'Have a dundering jolly time at der war, you fine fellers, eh! An' mit der time you pe gone, I pay von hundred dollar to buy substitute for der town.' And then dey botton up their pokets, and mit der hands dey pat on der pocket-book jest so, and say, 'Der war, it tam near ruin me, an' I can give no more monish. Der soldier dat was killed was von tamned unlucky dog, and his family, dey must go to de authorities or to der tuyfel!' Well, den, mit mine eyes dey pe snapping ven I tink of dis, I say to der young lady, 'Vill you not take der seat and warm yourself?' but she was in von great haste, and mit der 'tank you,' she opens der door and flies away in der big storm."

"Well, all this while Comrade Walker was keeping his ear open to Isaac, and at the same time staring in amazement at the pin. 'You know der soldier?' said the Jew. 'Yes,' said Walker. You see it was Allen Paige, his Lieutenant-Colonel before Petersburg, but he did n't let on to the pawnbroker. He just asked what was to pay, and told him to please say nothing to any one, but to keep the pin safe, and if it was not called for he would redeem it; for you see he felt mighty sensitive about the matter; he thought a good deal of Colonel Paige, and had heard a great deal of his family. The Jew's figure was a high one, compared to what pawnbrokers usually advance on their pawned securities, which went to show that his talk was not all gab, but that he really felt for Colonel Paige's daughter, who undoubtedly was the one that called at his shop."

The speaker now stopped in surprise, and looked intently at his companion.

Prescott's face indicated the profound strength of his varied emotions.

His comrade's recital of the Jew's quaint but touching story had produced an effect, which the former little imagined as he rattled off the dialect of the kind-hearted pawnbroker. Prescott had observed the absence of that pin from Emma's beautiful throat, but he had said nothing. Now it was explained to him, and in a manner that wrung his heart again and again.

The Pawnbroker!

One usually hears this name in connection with the fortunes of a loved friend with dread. There are men who serve to redeem this business of the traditionary, hard-hearted avariciousness usually associated with it, one pawnbroker of our acquaintance being of unusually generous and open-hearted disposition, who has kept goods months after the expiration of the time allowed by law to redeem them, from pure kind-heartedness; but this does not render the knowledge that a dear and beloved friend has been driven to the pawn-shop in order to sustain existence the less significant of privation, and a consequent source of apprehensive dread.

But with Prescott Marland dread formed only a part of his present emotions. A sort of horror seized him; for he had good reason to remember the storm which the Jew had described; and the picture so vividly drawn of that devoted daughter and sister, flying in the driving, blinding sleet to a pawnbroker's shop to pledge her dear, sainted father's gift, that those she loved might live, was one well calculated to stir this generous and ardent lover's soul to its profoundest depths. He could scarcely repress a groan of anguish.

"What ails you, comrade?" asked his companion, somewhat startled.

"Nothing," replied Prescott, making a great effort to recover his self-composure. "I may tell you at some future time." He added, "I am well acquainted with this family, and I promise you the Post shall be notified if they need your assistance."

The train now entered the depot on North River, and the two soldiers, taking the boat, parted in New York City.

As they were about separating, Prescott said, with a half-laugh, —

"Comrade, I seem to have known you so well from the first, I 've not taken the pains to ask your name."

"The same with me. My name is Charles Roberts."

"And mine Prescott Marland."

"Good by, comrade."

"Good by."

CHAPTER XXIV.

THE reader has surmised that the examination of Baling & Co.'s books, as recounted by the broker to Jonas Cringar in Chapter XXI., was made at the instigation of the Veteran. We left him, at the time he parted with the book-keeper after the visit to the Surrogate's office, thinking of the cotton speculation in which Allen Paige was known to have been engaged, having expressed to Billings his judgment that here might, perchance, be found the weak point of the enemy's fortifications.

With this man of action, to think was to do. He accordingly determined at once to feel out the strength in this direction.

He again found in the book-keeper a ready assistant. Through his aid he ascertained that the cotton was bought of Baling & Co., cotton dealers. The next thing was to examine the books of this firm. The Veteran did not deem it policy to appear in person for the purpose of examining these books; Billings therefore undertook to perform this service. Disguising himself sufficiently to prevent recognition by any one who might have seen him in Cringar's store, he proceeded to the work with much sagacity; but, as Garvin had reported to the merchant, his sagacity did not succeed in hoodwinking Baling, who, having previously been warned by the broker, was on the alert for any movement of this kind.

We have also learned, through the broker, of the entire freedom given to the Veteran's assistant in his examination of the books.

Billings's report to the Veteran was in accordance with Daniel Garvin's statements to the merchant. He had found no evidence that the accounts had been tampered with; on the contrary, all appeared in regular order. When, therefore, they came to compare the report with the quotations of the cotton market of that day, they saw naught but very conclusive evidence that Allen Paige must have lost by his venture in cotton.

The book-keeper, who had looked with such dismay upon the array of statements in the inventories filed by Cringar and Garvin at the Surrogate's office, viewed with equal dismay the result of his visit to the house of Baling & Co.

The Veteran sat in deep thought.

Suddenly he seized the paper on which Billings had cautiously transcribed the entries from Baling & Co.'s books, and fixing his eye on a particular portion of it, he spoke with an energy which almost startled his companion.

"I can rely on every word, letter, and mark?"

"You can."

"These marks I can rely upon to go over the world with, if necessary?"

"I'll stake my life on them!" returned the book-keeper, surveying the Veteran with a puzzled air.

"Time is wasted in New York! Next week I go to Boston!"

The book-keeper looked amazed; but his brief aquaintance had taught him that the Veteran was, in a case like this, neither to be fathomed nor questioned.

On the same afternoon that comrades Marland and Roberts were entering New York by the New Jersey Central the Veteran took the Fall River boat for Boston.

This man of a former cosmopolitan life was always glad

to see his native town, with all its little foibles, and crooked streets. His experience in the wide world had, in his later years, taught him to hold in profound respect the character of a city whose voice could ever be depended upon in the cause of the great humanity. Like some stanch old uncle, who, while he occasionally entertains his neighbors with his innocent conceits and happy self-complacency, yet is held in profound respect by all lovers of their fellow-men, so seemed this good old city of Boston to its now famous Thorbolt.

But the Veteran had more important business on hand than the sentimental contemplation of this city of his birth.

At an early hour we find him in the Merchants' Exchange.

"Is Mr. Drammen in?" he inquired.

Drammen was a Norwegian, who had fought with a strong arm under the flag of his adopted country. He now had charge of the books of the Exchange.

The Veteran was informed that he was out, but would be in soon.

While waiting for him he looked over the gold quotations of the previous day, which had not yet been erased from the board. This gradually led him into a revery, in which the circumstances and incidents associated with his present mission to Boston passed one by one in review. These quotations brought before him with especial vividness the gloomy and satanic visage of Daniel Garvin, the Wall Street broker — who, perchance, had swindled some confiding customer by means of those very figures — as it had appeared before him in that home which, having driven from it his patriot brother's family, he now defiled with his own presence. He recalled the look of this heartless schemer while he questioned him on that stormy day, — a look in which ferocity seemed combined with an irrepressible fear; and a look also that had fastened itself deep in the mind of him who was now in revery, spurring him on in his self-imposed task for the sake of the plotter's victims. That distorted visage rose above the solid phalanx of statements and figures in the Surrogate's office; it peered over the entries transcribed from the books of Baling & Co., its ferocity rousing his soul in behalf of those suffering loved ones of his fallen comrade, — its fear fastening upon his mind the conviction that behind all statements, figures, and entries was that weakness of guilt which an unswerving energy might sooner or later reach and confound.

His meditations were interrupted by Drammen, who, having returned, was informed of the visitor's desire to see him.

The Norwegian did not require two glances to tell him that a soldier stood before him. The greeting, therefore, on the Veteran's introducing himself, was, though between strangers, as warm as if they had been friends for twenty years.

"How can I serve you?" inquired Drammen.

"By allowing me to see the reports of cotton shipments from New York for the summer and fall of 1864."

"That you shall see at once," replied Drammen; and in a few moments he brought the book which contained the reports of the arrival of merchandise during the period mentioned by the Veteran. He opened the book to the month of July, 1864, and then excusing himself for a few moments, left the Veteran to examine it at his leisure.

The latter instinctively turned several leaves at once,

which brought him into October. Then he turned slowly back.

Scarcely had he commenced doing so when his eye caught an entry of 111 bales of cotton, to O. U. Waite & Co. Even his strong heart sunk. If this was the lot of 111 bales bought and sold by Allen Paige, the date of the arrival, September 28th, corroborated Cringar's and Garvin's statements. At this time the market had been falling at a terrible pace, as had been described by Garvin in his interview with Cringar, the week previous, at his office in Wall Street.

Drammen was now returning, and the Veteran, raising his eyes awaited his approach with a calm, grave countenance, although his heart was secretly troubled.

"This is all the information to be obtained from your books?"

"It is."

The Veteran fingered a few of the leaves, and as he directed his eyes again to the book, he released them, one after another, in an abstracted manner.

He started. Great as was his self-command, a quick flush appeared on either cheek, and he sharply bent the falling leaf as he threw it back.

On the left-hand page, where he now held the book open, was another record of 111 bales, to F. Jaques & Co., and this date was August 25th!

"Comrade," he said, addressing Drammen, "I am here on an errand, — of which you will please say nothing, — that concerns the family of a soldier. I find recorded in this book the arrival of two lots. It is of the utmost importance that I obtain further information regarding them. Can I not obtain it of the parties to whom they were shipped?"

"I think you can," answered Drammen. "I am acquainted with both firms, and will call on them with you as soon as I am disengaged, if you desire."

"Thank you. It would be a great favor. How soon will you be at liberty?"

"In an hour."

"I will call on the minute."

"I will be ready for you."

At the end of an hour the Veteran promptly appeared, and they departed on their errand, which to the Veteran contained so much of import.

Waite & Co. were near at hand, on Kilby Street, and thither they first directed their steps.

Neither member of the firm was in, but both were expected every moment.

While waiting in the office, or rather room, of this enterprising house, the battle-scarred warrior had an opportunity of witnessing such a series of skirmishes as it had not before been his good fortune to behold.

In a long row of bins, situated on one side of the room, which extended from front to rear of the building, was thrown loose cotton that had once served as samples, together with old samples still rolled up in their papers, and having, to the Veteran's military eye, the appearance of dismantled guns. On a counter in the middle of the room was deposited a lot ready for present use, while the floor about him was white with others exposed to view like so many cotton dumplings, and so arranged as to receive the light to the best advantage. Each paper contained as many samples as there were bales to be sold, unless the number of the latter compelled the use of more than one paper, which was exceptional.

Presently a young man rushed in as if madness had seized him, and looking wildly about, shouted, —

"Where 's Waite? Where 's Lookum?"

"Will be in soon," answered the clerk.

"Can sell that lot of a hundred and fifty bales middling. Must have it right away!"

"Who to?"

The broker — for such was the excited visitor — put his forefinger quickly to the side of his nose in an inimitable manner, at the same time squinting toward the door.

This significant glance was explained by the entrance of a second broker on the scene. He was older than the first, but evidently quite as active, with a slight tendency to obesity, which indicated a happy possession of what was known in cotton circles, as well as in camp, as "cheek."

Without any ado he made for a large lot of the opened samples, and turned up the paper to read the marks.

"Right up to sample?" said he, picking a bit of cotton from one of the cotton dumplings, and drawing the staple rapidly between the thumb and forefinger of each hand, followed by a vigorous snap.

"Right straight up!" answered the clerk.

Without another word this second comer proceeded to roll the paper, and turn in the ends with a skill only attained by cotton-men.

"Hallo!" cried the first, reddening with anxiety and anger, "who told you you might have those samples?"

"Met Waite on the street a minute and a half ago, and *he* told me I might take 'em."

"Yes!" cried the younger broker, turning toward the clerk, "but Lookum promised 'em to me, and I can sell 'em too!"

"What time?" asked the clerk.

"He said I might have 'em at ten o'clock."

The second broker laughed, at the same time giving the

roll a swing as he held it by one end, and bringing it to bear like a small cannon upon his younger competitor; and then squinting along the top cried, "Bang!" with so loud and abrupt a tone that even the Veteran, whose ears had rang with thousands of cannon-peals, started in his chair.

"You 're a dead man!" exclaimed this facetious broker. "Don't you see you 're time 's up and ten minutes to spare?" And with this he disappeared, leaving this young competitor standing where he had been shot, red with disappointment, and chagrin that the other should have got the better of him.

"Curse that Bummeer's cheek!" he spluttered out, to the silent amusement of the Veteran. "Why did n't you stop him, Philbut? He 'll sell to my man! That 's what he 's after! O, hang his confounded cheek! P-s-h! I 'm done for on that job! He 'll sell him, if cheek 'll do it!"

The clerk laughed.

Just then in glided another broker, with a look as if he could ferret out a rat, though its hole ran zigzag through to China. Casting a look of contempt on his young brother of the craft, and a glance of suspicion at the Veteran, while he gave a slight nod to Drammen, he went straight up to the clerk and whispered in his ear.

The clerk whispered an answer, accompanying it by a nod at the young victim of another's "cheek," and then sweeping this nod around to the door.

The new-comer gnawed his lip, and glided from the room with a swiftness which evidently meant sharp competition with some other dealer's samples.

The disappointed applicant cried out, as this man slipped from the room, —

"By thunder! I bet he 'll settle Bummeer's hash for him yet! He 's on the soft with Evans, and 'll sell to him, I'll wager coat, hat, and boots!"

As he was speaking with his head turned to the clerk, in danced another young man with a sort of hungry, devouring look.

"Evans after cotton?" he exclaimed, rushing up, and catching the speaker by the arm. "By Jove! — say! — what does he want? I took supper with his agent's grandfather yesterday. I can sell him, you bet! What does he want?"

"O, you git!" cried the other. "Go 'nd find out what he wants! And then get the cotton if you can, — that 's what 's the matter!"

In their eagerness and excitement none of these competing brokers had paid any apparent attention to the presence of the Veteran and Drammen, except the third comer. This gave the Grand Army hero an opportunity of resting, by pleasant observation, a mind which had for several days been severely taxed in its efforts to unravel the dark and complicated plot which the subtle brain of Daniel Garvin had woven with such consummate art. To a man of his observation the scene he had just witnessed was as enjoyable and recreative as a comedy. And we have been led to delineate this little episode, from a sympathy with the state of tension to which the mind of this hard and indefatigable mental worker for the good of others had been brought. There was something, too, in the appearance of the white, fleecy cotton, flung about like foam on a surf-beaten shore, which captivated his eye, and lent its aid in soothing his mind.

Soon after the departure of the fourth broker Waite entered, and on recognizing the Veteran came forward and shook him heartily by the hand.

CHAPTER XXV.

"GENERAL," said the cotton-dealer, "I 'm very glad to see you!"

"Thank you."

"Is there anything I can do for you?"

"I 've called on you for a slight favor."

"I 'm sorry for that. I was in hopes it was an important favor. I am continually wishing something might turn up that would give me an opportunity of returning your kindness to me in Rebeldom."

"Say nothing about it, Mr. Waite. It was my duty to protect you, as a sound Union man. Nothing pleased me more, while in this Rebeldom you speak of, than to see an out-and-out cotton man that was an out-and-out Union man."

The Veteran, at one time in the Southwest, had rendered an important service to Mr. Waite, who was down there buying cotton under the protection of the government, and who, at the time of the service, was threatened with ruin through suspicion excited by a rival cotton-buyer, of being in treasonable intercourse with the enemy. It was only through the good judgment and decision of the Veteran that he escaped.

"Well, if you don't want anything said about it I won't say it; but make the favors I can do for you as large as possible."

"Thank you again. The fact is, though I remarked it was a slight favor I had to ask of you, I will do it the justice to say it is of great importance to me."

"Well, I 'm glad of that. Now please name it."

"It is that you let me look at your invoice book for September, 1864. A lot of one hundred and eleven bales of cotton arrived on the 28th of that month for you."

"Yes," returned the cotton-dealer, laughing, "I recollect it very well. I lost more money than it would take to buy a first-class farm by that lot of cotton. You see it came down reeling from a dollar ninety to a dollar eighty, and there it tumbled about awhile, and then took a long downward lurch to one fifty. The day it stood there I got a telegram from New York that a party who had one hundred and eleven bales was thoroughly demoralized, with a good many others, and would sell five cents less than market price to get rid of it. Well, I 'm willing to acknowledge that I was fool enough to think that the market would get sober again, stop its reeling and tumbling, and take another flight upward, so I telegraphed on to buy it, intending to hold it. And hold it I did, till it burned my fingers to the bone."

This rapid account by the cotton-dealer fell with the weight of lead on the ear of his listener. It was in striking accordance with the reports of Garvin which he had gathered, confirmed as they were by the copy Billings had made from the books of Baling & Co.

In the mean time Waite had obtained the invoice book the Veteran desired. The latter opened to the entry he sought, and then with a long-drawn breath proceeded to copy it into his memorandum-book.

The cotton-dealer was too well-bred to ask any questions on the strength of the privilege he was granting his former benefactor.

The Veteran, on his part, simply said,

"Mr. Waite, I am greatly obliged to you. At a future

time I may be free to make known to you my object for this — as it probably seems to you — rather strange visit. I wish to ask a similar favor of Messrs. Jaques & Co. Do you think they will grant it?"

"I at least will accompany you with pleasure, if you desire, and open the way," replied the cotton-dealer, with an air that indicated probable difficulty.

"Very good," said Drammen. "General, I should be glad to accompany you, but the truth is, Mr. Waite can do more for you than I, and I am therefore glad to resign you into his hands. If convenient to you, I shall be very much pleased to learn if you find all you desire."

"You shall know, comrade, and many thanks to you," responded the Veteran, shaking him warmly by the hand.

This large-hearted sailor then returned to his duties at the News Rooms, and the cotton-dealer departed with his charge for the house of Jaques & Co.

"Jaques is a little sore on the soldier business," said Waite, as he led the way to his brother dealer's rooms. "He 's lost money by them."

"How 's that?"

"Well, the fact is, he got bitten a good deal worse than I did, and all because he would n't believe the South could be subdued. He made money in the first of it because he judged more correctly than a good many others that the South would fight longer than ninety days, and would make downright war of it; so he laid in cotton, and sold at an immense profit. But you see he pinned his faith at the wrong end, when he went about declaring that Sherman would be destroyed, and Grant was a humbug, and Lee would whip them out yet. He lost money by it. Then, again, after Lee's surrender he fastened on the guerillas, and those kind of fellows who started the Ku Klux, and prophesied such a state of anarchy that cotton could n't be raised, which would bring the price up again. But his guerillas were soon disposed of; and I happened to be in the Southwest when this Grand Army of the Republic, that 's springing up over the land, settled the Ku Klux business in Mississippi, Tennessee, and thereabouts, as quick as lightning is quicker than a lame cow."

"Yes, the Grand Army did a good work there," responded the Veteran.

"It 's a fine institution, this Grand Army of the Republic; and for one I think it 's high time that the soldiers formed such an organization," continued the cotton-dealer. "I have done what I could for the families of fallen soldiers, because I promised to do so when these brave fellows left them in our charge. But the difficulty is to find them out. They are mostly people who are not given to begging any more than you or I; and it is a fact that many a family, in a most distressing condition, is unwilling to compete with forward beggars, who always stand ready to impose themselves upon the charitable whether they are needy or not. But, as I understand this Grand Army business, they are formed so as to bring organized work into the field, and act, so to speak, as responsible agents of the public, who through them can be sure of giving aid where it belongs, and thus intelligently keep their promises. Certain acquaintances of mine are down on this organization, but between you and me, they did n't do much for the Union; and I happen to know that the families of our fallen braves might go a long way toward starvation before they would get any help from them. This G. A. R., as you call it, has taken root in Boston, and my calculations are out if it does n't flourish like a green bay-tree."

"I 'm pleased to hear you speak, as a citizen, in such strong and just terms of our Order," said the Veteran.

"I take it you 're a member, General?"

"I am. I joined in the West."

"Glad to know it. Excuse me for saying that my experience with you on the Mississippi assures me that the Order and its objects will not suffer from your hands."

"I thank you. I shall endeavor to do all that lies in my power for an organization which I know every American, loyal at heart, will sustain when he comes to understand it."

"True!" responded the cotton-dealer. Then studying the Veteran for a moment, he said to himself, "One such man is enough to give the lie to a thousand vilifiers of the association which he so nobly represents."

They now arrived at the rooms of Jaques & Co.

Here the Veteran had another opportunity of observing the peculiar rush and scramble of the cotton brokerage business, which, as one of the results of the war, had been transformed from a business whereby a few strong and influential houses had been built up in the mercantile community, to an occupation in which vastly increased numbers contended, each separate day, for such morsels as might be offered them; though there still remained those old houses to remind one of what had been.

Jaques, who had been engaged in his private office, soon joined his visitors, and Waite made known the object of their call.

This speculator had, as Waite had said, lost much money through the courage and pertinacity of the Northern soldier, and the Veteran did not fail to detect an expression of annoyance as he was introduced by his military title.

"You would like to look at my books? Humph! an unusual request from a stranger, sir."

"I grant it, Mr. Jaques," said the Veteran with a dignified courtesy, which, in combination with the air of nature's royalty that sat upon his face, began at once to affect the somewhat irascible and very suspicious Jaques.

Jaques was also made to feel, by the presence and manner of this man, that he was likely to make a fool of himself by any useless attempt at "bluff," which speculators are apt to indulge in. He had seen enough of human nature to perceive that his strange visitor was not one to be easily baffled or trifled with; and though himself a strong man, he could not entirely suppress a feeling of admiration, conflicting with his annoyance at sight of a leader of Union soldiery, as he viewed this noble specimen of manhood.

The Veteran in the mean time contemplated the cotton speculator (such we entitle Jaques in contradistinction to the term *cotton dealer* as applied to Waite, the latter having always been engaged in cotton as a business, while the former simply took it up after the war opened as a speculation) with the solicitous attention of one who feels that much is at stake, in what he judged might appear to Jaques as an inquisitive and impertinent request, and of a character naturally repugnant to all speculators, especially one of Jaques's business predilections. He questioned to himself whether he should not make known to Jaques what he wished to transcribe from his books, and render his request more simple by asking him to do it for him; but his military experience at once gave the negative, until, at least, he had pushed the speculator to the utmost on the original request; for this experience had made him wary of plots, and all that appertained to them; and, working in the dark as he was, it was impossible for him to judge how far the ramifications of the subtle Garvin's schemes might have extended in the direction of this very speculator, who perhaps held in his books the identical secret, which, if the astute broker had been wise enough to foresee all the possible contingencies connected with his nefarious business (this, however, being where the profoundest scoundrels are weak), he might have provided against by enlisting the speculative Jaques in his interest, — though it is but justice to Jaques to remark, that it could have been done only by means of artful lies, as he was evidently not a man to knowingly assist Garvin in his damnable undertaking.

"I assure you, sir," he said after a pause, "I would not ask this favor, unusual as it must appear to you, if it did not have to do with important business which I am not at liberty to even hint at just now, but which I pledge you does not compromise nor in the least affect you."

"Mr. Jaques," interposed Waite, "my experience with General Hammond enables me to indorse, heart and hand, any assurance he may give you. It was he, if you will recollect, who saved me from ruin, down South, in sixty-four."

The cotton speculator's face relaxed.

"My friend does not allow himself to forget that," said the Veteran, while a smile flitted over his features. "Please consider it nothing but an officer's duty; who, if he had not been under the fear of a court-martial, might have demanded half the proceeds of that venture of Mr. Waite's as a condition of performing it."

Waite shook his head, and Jaques's face relaxed yet more.

"I believe," continued the Veteran, perceiving this to be the moment for the final charge, "that you will grant me the favor when I tell you that perhaps it may lead to as important results in behalf of others, whom I cannot now name, as was the result of my official action in behalf of our friend, Mr. Waite. Come to me, sir, and ask to look over my own books as an idle pastime, or from some private motive which I am not sure will not compromise me, and you may depend upon a positive denial; but assure me, as a man of honor, that much good to others may result, and that it shall not affect me in the least, and, sir, you shall be welcome to look from beginning to end."

The cotton speculator, whose eyes had been riveted on the Veteran's commanding features, which sent forth the influence of his strong will as he spoke, now gave vent to a quick, yielding laugh.

"General," he said, "I make no pretence of love for the Northern soldier; on the other hand, I owe him a grudge. But you have prevailed, and what no outsider has done yet I'll permit you to do. You can look at my books."

"Thank you. I simply desire to look at your invoices for the summer and fall of 1864."

"Look through the whole if you want to," laughed Jaques, who only offered another example of the effective power of the Veteran's magnetic will. Then ordering one of the book-keepers to furnish his visitor with what he desired, he entered into conversation with his friend, the cotton-dealer.

The Veteran being furnished with the entries of arrivals, turned to August 25th, 1864.

At the instant his eye fell upon the record Jaques happened to glance toward him.

"Waite!" he exclaimed under his breath; "look at your friend, the General!"

The cotton-dealer looked, and he with Jaques beheld the Veteran with his eye seeming to pour out his whole great soul upon the page before him, and then suddenly change to an expression which, to their astonished gaze, seemed fraught with impending retribution to some object of his thoughts; while his right hand, with which he had turned the leaves, was clenched as if he held a sabre in his grasp.

This was only for a moment. As suddenly as they had before changed, his features now assumed that air of settled sternness, so habitual to them when he contemplated the accomplishment of important work demanding powerful will and energy.

Then he took his memorandum-book, and they saw him copy the record with a motion of his pencil which seemed at each stroke as though it must leave a mark that could never be effaced.

When he had finished transcribing he scanned both original and copy with great care, as if each separate line were an object of his scrutiny, and then closed the book with an action as though he would securely shut the page from the curious eyes of men.

That evening, after notifying his comrade at the Exchange as he had promised, he took the express-train for New York.

CHAPTER XXVI.

WHILE plots and counter-plots are opposing each other under the direction of minds subtle, powerful, and persevering, we will visit the present abode of wretched unfortunates who have indirectly fallen victims to the machinations of one of these minds.

We enter Baxter Street, and ascend a dilapidated tenement, in front of which a crowd of ragged and dirty children are amusing themselves by hooting after a drunkard, every now and then one bolder than the rest running up and pelting him with handfuls of the filth and garbage which here reek with pestilential odors.

We mount flight after flight, the banisters here and there broken away, and threatening each moment to yield under our hands, while the rickety stairs shake beneath our weight at every step.

Finally after occasional halts, from an instinctive fear that the stairs are really about to give way beneath us, we reach the attic floor of the tenement, where we perceive two doors hanging so loosely to their hinges and fastenings that a child, if he should desire to enter as a burglar, could break them down with his slight weight.

We knock at the first door. There is no response. We glance through the cracks, and judging it is empty, we do not lift the latch, but proceed to the second door.

We knock at this also. Presently it is opened, and we step into the midst of one of those scenes of woe which in the great city of New York abound in such pitiable numbers, and yet of which comparatively so few are known to those who would reduce them.

In a low garret, not more than twelve feet square, the roof broken and gaping, and the shattered skylight scarcely admitting one dull ray through the mass of old rags and paper which bulge from the warped sashes, while a cold, drizzling rain imparts a penetrating chill to the noxious air, — in this fireless, exposed and almost sunless garret were huddled together the unfortunate family of the soldier Joseph Deering.

In one corner, on an old tattered mattress, lay an emaciated lad, hardly covered by the rags which served as a quilt, whom it would be difficult to recognize as that noble boy we have formerly seen to sustain the spirits of his mother with such exemplary fortitude, and on whom his little sisters had learned to look as a protector.

Bending over him is his mother, scarcely less emaciated than himself, giving him a drink from a stained earthen mug, while at the foot of the mattress sits Mary and the little crippled sister, shivering under their scanty clothes, their childish faces gaunt with want and starvation. The garments of mother and children seem in perfect keeping with the dreary garret, so worn, so thin, and tattered are they.

The soul yearns to fly to their rescue; and the heart bleeds in the contemplation of this harrowing scene. But we cannot help them, for it is only by our mental vision that we behold them. Solid feet of flesh and blood must ascend those shaking stairs; a real hand must raise the broken latch; a face that actually pales at sight of this group, and eyes that actually see them, and fill with pitying tears, must appear at the dilapidated door before aid can come to them.

Misfortune has driven these unhappy beings downward with a swift and relentless hand. Since we last beheld them their course to this appalling stage of destitution has been like a benighted traveller tumbling headlong down some rugged precipice.

Sickness had seized the mother while they lived on the Bowery, and, unable to pay the rent of even these dingy lodgings, they were compelled to take yet meaner quarters. Here they had just begun to eke out a miserable existence through the little that Joseph was able to earn by vending candy on the New Jersey Central Road, when this devoted boy was himself prostrated, and they were heartlessly driven forth, the mother wan, emaciated, broken-hearted, and poor Joseph stooping, tottering, and nearly blind with his fever, to find a refuge in this cold and gloomy garret, where starvation has caught them in its tightening gripe, and Death stands waiting with his grim and sombre presence.

When Mrs. Deering was taken sick Joseph went to West Twenty-Seventh Street to see Mrs. Paige, whom he had not visited for several weeks, but on whom he had promised to call at the time he announced to her his situation as candy-vender, if they should be threatened with new difficulties; for though Allen Paige's widow was then suffering from the effects of her interview with Cringar and Garvin, she did not forget the family of that other soldier who had fallen in the same cause which had claimed the life of her own husband.

This sensitive boy was met at the door, as was the Veteran, by the man, who had, in his youthful mind, seemed the incarnation of those diabolical fiends of which he had often read in his story-books.

"Boy!" cried Garvin, who, on opening the door, beheld the lad that had so penetrated his guilty conscience with his look on his former visit to this house, — "boy! what do you want here?"

Joseph was nigh staggering backward down the steps, as he was thus greeted by the voice and visage of this malevolent being, whose presence was so abhorrent to his sensitive mind. Steadying himself, however, he asked in a tone which, though determined, quivered with his emotions, —

"Is Mrs. Paige within?"

"Mrs. Paige, you young vagabond!" replied the broker, showing his teeth. "What do you mean by your impertinence? Mrs. Paige is poorer than you are — do you understand? — and is probably begging! — do you understand me, boy?" (Joseph stood staring with amazement and grief, but could utter no response.) "And be off with you and do likewise! but dare to come here again to do it and I'll shut you up in jail!"

"She don't live here, then?" stammered Joseph, who was determined to have an answer to his question, notwithstanding his injured pride, his grief and confusion.

"You young scapegrace!" exclaimed Garvin, showing a few more of his teeth, "this house is occupied by me! Did I not just tell you that she was poorer than you are? No, you impudent soldier's cub, she does not live here! She lodges as you do! — Be off!"

"Where —"

Before Joseph, who had wonderful persistence, could say any more, Garvin slammed the door in his face, and the confounded boy heard his vindictive footsteps receding through the hall.

When Mrs. Deering heard from the lips of her son the recital of what we have just related, her heart beat in sympathy and sorrow for those who had been in the past so kind to them, and her own trials were for the moment forgotten in the thought of their probable sufferings; and the first impulse was to urge her boy to try if he could not make enough at his candy-vending and occasional choring to enable them to offer some return to these friends, who in their prosperity had been so kind to them.

But, alas! Joseph's sickness forbade even the first effort toward carrying out so noble an impulse, and now, instead of proffering a testimonial of their gratitude to those who had so often aided them, they are presented to our eyes in a state of such deep despair that it would seem as if thoughts of the world around them had ceased to move their souls.

At the instant our gaze fell upon them the mother was moistening the parched lips of her boy with water from the earthen mug. She knelt by the side of the tattered mattress, which was stretched on the floor, there being no bed or other furniture except a single broken chair.

Joseph, whose head she slightly raised, took a little of the water, and then fell back exhausted and painfully gasping.

Mrs. Deering passed her thin, worn hand over his forehead.

He turned his eyes toward her, and even in his helpless condition his tender filial care and affection displayed itself.

"Mother," he murmured, scarcely able to speak above a whisper, while his voice was broken by his ominous gasps, "your poor — thin arm trembles — very much. Don't please trouble — yourself any — more for me."

This arm was the one on which she rested, as she bent over him.

The mother remained silent, her arm still trembling under its but too slight weight, while her hollow eyes looked as if tears had ceased to flow from their exhausted fountains.

Joseph again spoke.

"Thank you, — dear mother. — I — feel — better — now"; and then with an effort that sadly contradicted his words, he turned his head away, and lay like one dying.

She withdrew the hand, and letting it drop mechanically upon the mattress, raised her tearless eyes to heaven.

Her appearance at this moment would have excited in the breast of the beholder the deepest commiseration. Kneeling there on the floor of that desolate garret, with either hand resting on the torn mattress, her thin, gaunt form bent with suffering, while it perceptibly shivered with the cold, damp, penetrating air, and her sick boy lying before her wasted nigh unto death with both fever and starvation, — all this was of a character to awaken in the soul the profoundest pity, not unmingled with a feeling as if death in this group was making itself visible. But as the gaze rested on her upturned eyes, there was presented in the whole a picture in which was realized the appalling solemnity of the spirit, still confined within its earthly tabernacle, reaching out beyond the dark presence of impending death, and pouring forth the awful anguish of its tearless, almost emotionless despair into that invisible world, which seemed to have closed in upon her while the visible had receded from her presence.

The endless turmoil of the great metropolis, the struggles of ambition, the strife for wealth, all vain displays, and acts of hardened pride, pass in imagination by this silent figure of despair, and in the contrast appear an empty, mocking train, — shadows, as it were, before the dread reality.

A human being, driven by incessant blows of misfortune to the uttermost depths of poverty and desolation, in the midst of a great community, as hopeless of aid as the dying wanderer lost in some boundless desert, is an object that never fails to move the most hardened heart, — unless it be of some monster who may have worked for the accomplishment of this very end, — and the cry of sympathy and horror which goes up throughout the land, when such a case is discovered and made known, is the strongest evidence that the great public heart is equal to the prevention, through charity, of this suffering, if efficient means are but adopted to bring it before the public eye.

As this desolate and dying mother of sick and dying children thus remains without motion, her eyes cast toward heaven with the glassiness of that last terrible moment, when the soul prepares itself for insanity or death, the heart of one who looks upon this scene is torn with sympathetic grief.

By one of those coincidences which so often occur, and which seem to have assigned to them a special part in the great drama of humanity, we see the two mothers of the soldiers' families which occupy so prominent a place in our narration, each brought first to a state of privation by the death of the husband and father, and then plunged into the darkness of sorrow by the dangerous illness of her darling boy. But, oh! if Mrs. Paige, when her heart was wellnigh breaking with grief, could have had suddenly revealed to her by the hand of Heaven the appalling anguish of this other soldier's widow, her heart would have forgotten its own agony in pity for her sister's woe.

While this unhappy widow of the soldier — whose bones were mouldering near the spot where he fell in defence of the Union — was thus transfixed by her mute despair, her dying boy lay silent, as he had turned when she withdrew her hand from his head.

Presently he turned back sufficiently to cast his feeble glance upon his mother. As he did so his gaze became suddenly fastened on her uplifted face, and two tears commenced rolling down his emaciated cheeks.

"Mother!" he uttered in his weak, gasping tones, "dear mother! look on your boy Joseph!"

The mother continued for an instant fixed in the attitude in which Joseph had beheld her. Then a quiver shook her frame, and her glassy eyes were directed to her boy.

A divine smile rested on his worn and pallid countenance; and while the tears were slowly stealing down his cheeks, his eyes beamed with a light that seemed the reflection of heaven.

When she looked down upon him he turned his gaze upward, and in a voice which, though labored, was pervaded by an ineffable sweetness, he said, —

"Dear mother, God is near!"

The poor woman continued to look at him with tearless eyes, while her body bent gradually toward him.

He again turned his gaze upon her, and his heaven-full eye beamed into hers.

At that instant she thought she heard angels singing in the air above her. Through the broken roof the heavenly visitors seemed to come and go, — coming to behold, and going to bring others that they might see her boy Joseph, who was so much like them; who, ever being so near to God, could never know the chastisement of despair.

Her eyes were fastened upon his for a while, dry and with no motion of the lids, while all the time the presence of the angels seemed to her a beautiful reality.

"Mother," again said Joseph, "father is very near to us!"

On the utterance of these words the mother's lids began to relax, dampness suffused those eyes which had given such dread signs of an impending mortal wreck, and lifting her right hand from the mattress she placed it on Joseph's head. Then, as the tears slowly welled up from those fountains which had so long refused their blessed relief, she looked above, and in tones nearly as weak as her boy's, but strong in their fervor, she solemnly invoked upon him the blessings of an ever-watchful Heaven.

And then slowly her hand settled upon the roll that served the sick boy for a pillow, and her head bent gradually down, the tears now coming thick and fast, while the angelic company above seemed departing with songs of prophetic joy.

Yielding at length to the full sway of her long pent-up

emotions, the now profoundly agitated mother laid her head beside that of her boy, and gave vent to an outburst of weeping.

Suddenly Joseph, whose hearing was at the present time preternaturally acute, gave a quick start, and slightly raising his head bent it forward to listen.

"It inquires for us," he faintly exclaimed.

The mother looked up, and wiping the tears from her eyes, gazed upon her son with an expression of alarm, for she thought he heard those voices which presage death.

Mary and the little crippled Etta, who, overcome with cold and hunger, had been shivering and silent witnesses of the foregoing scene, also stared upon Joseph as he started up so suddenly and uttered words so wild.

"What do you hear, my son?" said the mother, soothingly.

"The voice. It inquires for *Mrs. Deering,* and — he is coming!"

As Joseph uttered these words his hollow eyes opened wide, and were directed with an intense gaze toward the door.

The mother cast one quick glance to heaven, and then directing her gaze also toward the door, she listened intently.

Soon she heard energetic footsteps ascending the stairs below.

They reached the second landing, and then stopped.

Then a female voice cried out, —

"You must go to the top!"

Again the steps were heard ascending, the frail stairs creaking as they mounted.

In another moment they resounded on the floor outside, and then the latch was raised, and a man with a kind, hearty face opened the door.

He started back, and his countenance assumed a look of horror.

"Great God!" he exclaimed. "*Is this a soldier's family?*"

CHAPTER XXVII.

WE will pass to another scene. About five o'clock on the afternoon of the second day following the visit of the Veteran to Boston, Daniel Garvin had just crossed from Brooklyn by the Fulton Ferry, and was going up the slip, when he felt himself plucked by the sleeve. He turned, and beheld the anxious features of Baling, the cotton speculator.

"A moment with you, if you can possibly spare it," he said in a low, hasty voice.

Garvin at once led the way to the waiting-room.

"What is it?" inquired Garvin in a tone indicating a mind ill at ease, as soon as they had seated themselves in a distant part of the room.

"Jaques & Co. have had a visitor this week."

"Jaques & Co.?"

"Cotton-dealers in Boston."

"What of them?" demanded Garvin, in a startled voice of apprehension.

"They bought Paige's cotton of Peeling & Co."

The broker's face grew dark.

"Who called on them?"

"Jaques, who was in my place this morning, and who, you are aware, knows nothing of this Paige affair —"

"The man who called is what I want."

"I am coming to it. Jaques was talking about business affairs in Boston, when presently he commenced telling me of this visitor — "

"Who? — who was the man?"

"He described him as a tall man, of imposing appearance, with a deep scar on his face, introduced to him by Waite, a brother dealer, as General Hammond," replied Baling, casting on Garvin a glance full of significance.

The broker audibly ground his teeth.

"He said," continued Baling, "that this General Hammond was very anxious to look at his cotton entries for the summer and fall of 1864, and that he was determined to refuse at first; but the man had such a commanding and seductive way with him, besides having saved his friend Waite from ruin in the South during the war — "

"That he let him look!" again interrupted Garvin with a malignant, yet apprehensive sneer.

"He did."

"No more! Not a moment is to be lost!" And the broker hastened from the waiting-room, that grinding step having now mingled with it evidences of nervousness and confusion.

"May every Union soldier, sound or crippled, be cursed, if there is a God to curse them!" muttered this inwardly quaking blasphemer, as he pursued his way up Fulton Street. "This presumptuous giant thinks, then, to crush me under his clumsy carcass! We will see!" Then rubbing his forehead with a rapid and savage-like motion for an instant, he said with fierce impatience, "His first move? Where does he strike?"

For a few moments he seemed in perplexed thought. Then suddenly increasing his already rapid step into a long stride, he exclaimed, —

"Cringar, you grovelling imbecile! if he has put on the screws and you have given in with your idiotic snivelling, woe be to you! I 'll soon put you under inspection!"

* * * * *

It is about an hour previous to the foregoing scene. The reader is introduced into the private office of Jonas Cringar.

The merchant is now given to long spells of lonely ruminations, if by such a term can be called the silent but terrible chastisements of remorse that hold him like one petrified with horror, and presents to his guilty soul those pictures which only remorse can summon to the inward eye.

But terrible as were these inflictions of a violated conscience, they did not alone operate to reduce this victim of another's wiles to his present wretched and miserable condition. Over him was continually held the lash of fear by the unrelenting Garvin.

In the hands of the ever-watchful broker was held the damning evidence of crime, by which his irretrievable ruin could be compassed at any moment. But besides the forgery Garvin always carried in his breast-pocket, to which pocket we have seen him direct the eyes of the cowering merchant at certain stages of their former interviews, this master of atrocious schemes held another source of power by which to govern his abject accomplice.

It will be recollected that among other criminal acts committed by Jonas Cringar, in that downward course in speculation which had been directed by the treacherous broker, was the defalcation of forty thousand dollars, as treasurer of the Bald Eagle Silver Mining Company. This defalcation, the reader will also remember, Garvin was to help Cringar provide against, in consideration of what, with a sort of grim humor, he termed unsuccessful ventures with him in Wall Street, and for the base work he was expected to perform in the future.

As will be readily seen, the broker's own interest demanded that this defalcation be shielded from discovery; for inasmuch as the merchant, as Allen Paige's partner, was the chief and most reliable instrument in his hands for the accomplishment of his infamous purpose, it was necessary that Cringar's credit, before the world, should remain untarnished. He had, therefore, purchased stock in the Bald Eagle Company, and, through his powerful influence, first been made a Director, and then by those means which all who have been intimately connected with joint-stock companies will readily comprehend, the payment of dividends was postponed, and time secured for such manipulations as were necessary to accomplish his object.

But this arch schemer was not so simple as to keep his promise made to the ruined merchant, that he would, by giving him credit for margins, put him on the up grade of speculative profits, and thus enable him to relieve himself of his terrible financial embarrassment. On the other hand, he continued to hold him over the same gulf above which he dangled in the opening of our story, while he compelled his tongue and hands to move like some wretched automaton, at the bidding of his own will.

As the reader is now ushered into his presence, Jonas Cringar sits lost to the existence of the outer world, and looks more than usually haggard and abstracted.

His mind has been more frequently buried than ever in the deep gloom of criminal darkness and remorse, since the fearful interview with Daniel Garvin, at the latter's office, which we last recorded.

In the midst of the appalling blasphemy of the broker,

combined as it was with expressions, threats, and an appearance, calculated to drive almost to frenzy his already shattered mind, the merchant now ever in his tormenting imagination heard the laughter peal, and saw the impish face of simple Sal, as it was horribly presented to his startled gaze, pressed against the window-pane; while from the mouth issued that song of idiotic gibberish, which to his guilty spirit seemed fraught with the prophecy of doom.

As he now sits before us, his torturing fancies revert again and again to this scene. The laughter, the face, the song are incessantly in his ears and before his eyes; and ever and anon he repeats those words, which, sung by a mischievous idiot, have power to haunt his guilty soul as if uttered by unearthly voices,—

> "*My gentle sirs, be very kind!*
> *Your candle 's out,*
> *My gentle sirs!*
> YOU 'LL BE FOUND OUT,
> MY GENTLE SIRS!
> *But gentle me you cannot find!*"

While an outraged conscience was thus lashing this unhappy merchant's soul, a visitor entered the outer counting-room who seemed to have come at this particular hour by command of the dread Nemesis.

It was the Veteran.

Billings, the book-keeper, was at that moment the only person in the counting-room.

He stepped forward, took the Veteran's hand, and in a low voice said,—

"He is within, and has given orders, as usual, not to be interrupted. He 's growing worse every day. I really think we have reason to pity him."

"Sinful as he has been, he has evidently been sinned

against," returned the Veteran, gravely. "I would see him at once."

"That you shall, orders or no orders. He has been particularly blue to-day, and I 'm inclined to think he 's in a good condition to come under your hands."

With this the book-keeper opened the door of the private office.

Cringar, who was at the instant repeating the idiot's prophecy for the fiftieth time, heard the turning of the door-knob, and gazed up with a startled frown. But instantly he beheld the grand and severe countenance of the Veteran he sank back in his chair, while an expression of abject terror displayed itself on his cadaverous visage.

A description of this stern, battle-scarred stranger had been given the now trembling merchant by Daniel Garvin, who, from the hour he was confronted by him in the house which he had robbed from the family of his half-brother, could not shake from his mind the profound conviction that in that visitor, whose glance had for the second time caused him to quail, he had found a dangerous and untiring foe, against whom it was necessary for his victimized and unskilled accomplice to be warned.

The Veteran closed the door, and stood contemplating the terrified wretch in silence.

The merchant could not remove his gaze from the deep, searching eye that was upon him, which he felt to be reading his guilty soul to its innermost depths; and as his visitor sustained his own gaze, his eye seeming each moment to increase in its penetrating power, this miserable man began to feel as if oppressed by some frightful nightmare, and his whole being seemed ready to give vent to one prolonged cry.

At length the Veteran seated himself, and still sternly

contemplating the terror-stricken merchant, he said in a low deep voice, which to his auditor's ears sounded like the voice of his inexorable judge, —

"Is this Jonas Cringar, executor of the estate of Allen Paige?"

The merchant appeared incapable of speaking, for his voice seemed lost in the gaze, which still remained riveted, as if frozen with nightmare, on his visitor's judge-like visage.

The Veteran repeated his inquiry, —

"Is this Jonas Cringar, executor of the estate of Allen Paige?"

On the repetition of this question Jonas Cringar aroused himself, and in a subdued, broken voice answered, —

"That is my name."

"You have associated with you one Daniel Garvin, broker?"

Instantly the sound of Daniel Garvin's name fell on his ears the merchant experienced, in an extraordinary manner, the effect of another power in opposition to that now exerted by his questioner. It was the power of him whose name had been pronounced.

It at once served to bring fear into opposition with fright. On the utterance of the name, Cringar instinctively withdrew his eye from the Veteran's, and cast a hasty, startled glance at the window. Then rising he went to this window and gave the curtain a twitch, though it was already drawn, and then with a sweeping stare around the room he resumed his seat, while the perspiration began to appear from the internal commotion into which the presence of the Veteran and the utterance of the broker's name had precipitated him.

The Veteran did not fail to observe closely this sudden

display of a conflicting fear; he surmised the cause of it, and immediately made up his mind how he should act.

"Mr. Cringar," he said, in a modulated and yet dignified tone, "am I not justly informed that yourself and Daniel Garvin are executors of the late Allen Paige's estate?"

"I must refer you, sir," answered Cringar, with a sort of desperate firmness, "to Mr. Garvin, if you wish information on this business."

"Indeed, Mr. Cringar, I had supposed, you having been Mr. Paige's partner, and I also having been given to understand that your relations with him were very intimate, that I could obtain certain information from you of all others."

As the Veteran uttered this speech, he had allowed his voice and manner to approach gradually that degree of depth and severity which he had momentarily relinquished.

The merchant felt this change, but the stormy visage of Daniel Garvin, together with that repulsive hand directed to the side-pocket in which he carried his large wallet, came up before him, and casting another glance toward the curtained window, he said with peevish impatience, —

"When Mr. Paige was living I knew more than any one else about his business; but now he is dead, you must go to another man."

"Jonas Cringar!" exclaimed the Veteran in a voice of vast but subdued power, "does not the dead Allen Paige sometimes engage your guilty thoughts?" And leaning his massive form slightly forward, his face assumed that appearance of overwhelming power we have formerly witnessed, while his stern gray eye was bent on the merchant with a look before which this gasping wretch shrank as from the eye of Heaven.

Blanching to a deadly pallidness, Jonas Cringar stared upon the Veteran with open mouth, his haggard features drawn, and slightly quivering. The avenging spirit of his former partner seemed to his frenzied imagination to be lending his supernatural aid to the power of that annihilating gaze. Mechanically reaching for the arms of the large chair in which he sat, he grasped them in his long bony fingers, which trembled as if stricken with palsy.

"Allen Paige!" he gasped, — "what do you know of the dead Allen Paige?"

The Veteran did not answer, but continued that terrible gaze, which seemed scorching the merchant's soul, and rolling it up like a heated parchment.

For an instant Jonas Cringar, by a sort of preternatural fascination, lost sight of the definite form and features of his terrible visitor; and in their place there appeared to his guilt-distorted fancy the image of Allen Paige, casting upon him that last expiring look, that mute appeal, which had haunted him by day and by night, until he were ready to cry from depths, compared to which the effort of the actor on the stage is but simple mouthing, —

"STILL IT CRIED, SLEEP NO MORE!"

At length his gaping mouth spasmodically closed itself, and then in a suppressed, but agonized voice, he shrieked, —

"Allen! before God, my heart was not guilty!"

This seemed to break the spell. Immediately those haunting, ghostly features vanished, and in their place still remained, confronting him, the silent, immovable, and sombre visage of his visitor.

His hands relaxed their hold of the arms of his chair, and then with a profound sigh, in which was mingled the ejaculation, "O my God!" he carried them to his face.

The Veteran still remained silent.

Suddenly the merchant sprang to his feet, and with another of those frightened glances at the window, he broke into a storm of invective, pouring out upon the Veteran a torrent of insane fury.

CHAPTER XXVIII.

THE Veteran sat beneath Jonas Cringar's sudden and unexpected attack with the same calmness with which he had, day after day, sat in his saddle in the midst of Rebel shot and shell. He was a profound student of the human soul, and accordingly did not fail to understand the symptoms of the merchant's insane fury; and we cannot better liken this remarkable scene than to the maddened waves dashing in foam and spray against some lofty rock-ribbed cliff.

Finally Cringar was on the verge of being overcome by his own foaming rage, which was lashed on by pictures of the impending vengeance of Daniel Garvin. He evidently realized this, and with one last effort he advanced upon his silent visitor with clenched fist, and in a voice to be compared only to the frenzied utterance of men, who, overcome in battle by rage and fright, will rush with gaping mouth and wide-stretched eyes upon the bayonet or sabre-point, he cried, —

"Liar! spy! insulter of a weak and broken man! begone! — begone I say! or I'll give you into the hands of the police!"

"Hush!" commanded the object of this outburst in a calm, admonitory voice, at the same time waving his hand toward the door, — "hush! or you will be heard!"

"I care not! Your black-mail game has failed here: so be gone! Be off, I say!"

The door at this moment was slightly opened, and Billings, the book-keeper, looked in.

The Veteran now rose, and drawing a paper from his pocket, he put his mouth to Cringar's ear and exclaimed in a voice of muttering thunder, —

"Shall I proclaim your guilt in the open ears of the entire city!" Then presenting the paper to his astounded gaze he said, "This is my evidence!"

The merchant dropped into his chair as from a stroke of electricity, and the book-keeper softly closed the door.

It seemed the fate of this miserable man to have some damning written evidence of his crimes thrust before his eyes, at the moment of arousing himself to the highest pitch of what, to his frenzied mind, might perchance have appeared annihilating fury. The reader will recollect that the destroying evidence in the hands of Daniel Garvin overwhelmed him under somewhat similar circumstances.

This was the paper which we have just seen produce so remarkable an effect on the astounded merchant: —

"*One hundred eleven* (111) *Bales of Cotton, bought by F. Jaques & Co., Boston, of A. M. Peerling & Co., Brokers, New York, August 23d*, 1864.

"MARKS, **A. N. Z.**"

The Veteran proceeded quietly to open another paper, and holding it before Cringar said in a calm voice, —

"Here is a list of quotations, dating from August 1st to October 1st."

The merchant looked at this list mechanically for a moment, and then falling back in a sort of stupor, scalding tears began to trickle down his haggard cheeks, and in a voice of unutterable despair he exclaimed, —

"My God! the idiot's song! Who can save me now!"

"Confide in me, and I will do my utmost for you," said the Veteran.

Cringar did not seem to hear at first; but continued in a half-conscious state, while the tears slowly forced themselves from his weary, bloodshot eyes.

The Veteran contemplated this human wreck with sentiments of sincere commiseration.

At length the merchant looked up in the midst of his tears, and, as if he had but just heard the assurance addressed to him, said, —

"You will help me, do you say?"

"Yes. I pledge you my word that if you will but confide in me, and reveal all you know of this business, I will spare no effort to shield you from such harm as it is in the power of man to prevent."

"Your name?"

This brief question was uttered in an indescribable voice.

"Julius Hammond."

"Julius Hammond?" repeated the merchant, who began to show signs of returning life. "General of Union cavalry?"

"The same."

"I have heard of you. Your honor and humanity I cannot doubt."

As Jonas Cringar uttered these words he dropped his head, closed his eyes, and drawing a long heavy sigh, seemed lost, for the time being, to all that surrounded him.

The Veteran had not miscalculated.

The striking appearance of his physiognomy, as observed by Jaques and Waite while he was copying the entry from the former's book, will be remembered by the reader. It presaged danger to those he was arrayed against. From that entry he bore away with him a weapon which in his hands was destined, as we have seen, to be formidable. Having, from the descriptions given him, formed a clear conception of the character and present moral and mental condition of Jonas Cringar, he did not deem it necessary to further risk exposing his plans to the enemy by an attempt to gain added information of Peeling & Co., whom he perceived by the entry to have been the New York brokers that sold to Jaques & Co., but determined to move at once upon the shattered merchant, calculating with a judgment that had often confounded the Rebels at the moment they saw victory perching on their banners, that he could by an opening charge so demoralize the object of his attack, as, at the right moment, to overwhelm him with the evidence he now possessed. We have witnessed the result.

The potent mental force which he brought to bear upon the weakened and distracted mind of Jonas Cringar was aided in a remarkable degree by the superstitious and guilty terror with which, as we have seen, his thoughts had almost incessantly reverted to the song of Simple Sal, and pictured it as the prophecy of an impending doom; so that when, at the height of his crazy reaction, his accuser with crushing power suddenly confronted him with the paper, whose contents we have transcribed, his diseased fancy instantaneously conjured up the hideous face of the singing idiot grinning from the midst of the writing before him, while into his soul seemed to thunder the judgment he had dreaded with such awful premonition. This state of frenzied commotion did not at first permit him to question whether his visitor could compass his and Garvin's downfall by means of this evidence; the picture of certain retribution and final ruin, as held in the hands of this strange man, was the only object presented to his mental vision.

But as he now sat with head dropped and eyes closed, he realized that this man pitied him, and his mind began confusedly to revolve the situation into which he found himself so suddenly and unexpectedly thrown.

At length the Veteran broke the silence.

"Mr. Cringar," he said, in a low, soothing voice, with a tenderness singularly characteristic of men of his physical and mental power, "the evidence I hold in my possession is for the purpose of saving a wronged family from the fate to which a heartless and unprincipled man would consign them. This man I propose to punish, but not you. You have done great wrong to this family, but you can atone for it."

These words penetrated to the depths of the merchant's heart. He was moved by an almost overpowering impulse to throw himself before the Veteran like a child, and utter aloud all that was passing within him.

But a remarkable revulsion took place.

Suddenly opening his eyes he rose to his feet, and with one more of those fearful glances at the curtained window, he exclaimed in a frenzied voice, at the same time smiting his breast, —

"O God! how that reckless act has bound me here!"

The Veteran gazed upon him in astonishment.

Cringar instantly reseated himself and sat for a while in silence, startled by his own outburst. Then after another internal struggle he addressed the Veteran.

"General Hammond," he said, "I am in the power of a

man who, so long as he holds that power, can and will destroy me the instant it is for his interest to do so. I pray you believe me, sir, when I say that I am ready to do everything I possibly can, even to the giving of my life if necessary — and God knows it would not be giving much now! — to atone for the part I have taken in wronging the family of my former partner, whom, sir, I esteemed and loved." His voice was here choked; controlling his emotions, he went on: "But, sir, this man, Daniel Garvin, of whom you have just spoken, carries constantly about him a paper by which he can crush me at any moment, and render useless any attempt you may make through me to restore to their rights those whom he, with my constrained assistance, has so wickedly defrauded."

"What is the nature of this paper?"

"A note."

"Only a note?"

"An indorsement."

"Simply an indorsement?"

"To you alone I tell it: an indorsement forged by my hand."

The Veteran did not speak.

"A reckless act; done, sir, in a moment of desperation, when threatened with ruin by speculation, as many another criminal act has been done by many another man in this city within these past few years. I realized not what I was doing, General Hammond, until it was done."

The merchant then confessed to the Veteran the manner in which he had been led on to his ruin, through the agency of speculation, by Daniel Garvin, and was then made use of to carry out the broker's long-contemplated plot against the name and family of Allen Paige.

In the course of this confession Cringar conveyed to his

listener a full idea of the position which Garvin then occupied, the power he wielded, the manner in which he held the Paige estate, and the instrumentalities he had at command in connection with it.

The Veteran, as will be readily imagined, lent to this recital an earnest attention. His comprehensive mind grasped the whole situation as Cringar unfolded the details that composed it. He perceived that, whatever might be the ultimate result of his other criminal acts, in the unfortunate forgery, of which Cringar had been so recklessly guilty, lay an insuperable barrier to his progress, so long as it remained in the hands of Daniel Garvin. He saw at a glance, that the subtle broker had so marshalled his other forces, that if Cringar, whom he evidently had never trusted, should finally threaten to be dangerous, he could instantly destroy him by means of the damning evidence of crime he possessed, and then hold his position against all "babbling" he might indulge in. This leader of cavalry had not been unobservant of the labyrinthian courses of the law. That possession was "nine points" of it he was very thoroughly convinced, especially when this possession was backed up by moneyed power and influence in New York City. He saw that if he were to undertake to use Cringar as evidence, and move directly against the broker with that forgery in his possession, he not only would himself give the signal for Cringar's immediate destruction, but would plunge the whole business into a contest where money in unlimited amounts must be supplied, or defeat inevitably result.

Strategy, not money, must do the work for him. Mind he could depend upon; money he had not for such a contest.

As he now sat in that office, while Cringar watched him

with intense anxiety, these things passed in swift review before his mind. He had accomplished much up to this moment, but he realized that work was before him, and a false step would ruin all.

His decision was taken; and Cringar experienced an indefinable hope as he witnessed the expression of that decision on those grand features, which, but a short time before, had so terrified him.

The Veteran rose to depart.

"Mr. Cringar," he said, "I must enjoin upon you, in this matter, absolute secrecy and silence."

The merchant bowed his head.

A pause ensued; and then Cringar, in a broken voice, said, —

"The boy, Albert, — I heard he was very ill." And with a smile of unspeakable sadness he added, "Mr. Cringar was a great favorite of his."

"The boy," answered the Veteran, feelingly, "is out of danger, and is doing well."

He moved toward the door as he spoke, while the merchant, having fallen back in his chair apparently exhausted by this interview, sat with his eyes cast to the floor, a prey to melancholy thoughts. The departing visitor had scarcely opened the door when a well-known voice was heard outside.

The instant this voice struck the ears of the exhausted and abstracted Cringar, he seemed to forget all else, and the old look of terror took possession of his countenance. His whole body trembled violently, and the cold sweat started out anew upon his forehead.

"Fear not," said the Veteran in a firm but soothing tone, as he turned and beheld the effect this voice had produced on the merchant. "It is not his interest at present to destroy your reputation."

He then passed out, closing the door behind him.

He was met by Daniel Garvin, who, having stopped to question the book-keeper, was now advancing toward the private office.

The broker's malevolent eye shot forth a gleam of defiant and revengeful rage, which the Veteran met with a glance fraught with what the book-keeper afterwards described as that deadly calmness which, in a voyage to the tropics, made a few years previous, he had observed to be ominous of an approaching tempest.

CHAPTER XXIX.

THE scene we have depicted occurred on Thursday. Friday the Veteran sat in his room, deeply engaged in revolving plans for the intricate work that was before him, when Prescott Marland was ushered in.

"General!" he exclaimed, "I have just seen two as precious scoundrels as walk the streets of New York!"

"Indeed! and who are they, pray?"

"Slaycut and Drorblude!"

"Slaycut and Drorblude!" repeated the Veteran.

"The same!" cried Prescott, snapping his fingers. "And if I don't draw blood out of both of 'em, then I'm no friend of the Paige family, that's all!"

The Veteran smiled. There was an irresistible tendency on the part of Prescott to make this grave man smile, no matter under what circumstances. If the latter had, like an old Roman consul, been in position where he must condemn this young friend to death, it were a question whether the condemned would not have compelled a significant relaxation of his judge's features, before he had done with him.

"I will tell you how it was," continued Marland. "You see I happened to be in Cringar's place to speak with Billings, when I heard the sound of voices in the private office. I recognized Garvin's and Cringar's; but I was more particularly struck with the others. There was something about them that sounded familiar, and I asked Billings who was in there.

"'Slaycut and Drorblude talking with Garvin and Cringar,' said he.

"'What, the men who held Allen Paige's notes for mining stock?' cried I, all of a sudden smelling a mighty big rat.

"'Hush!' whispered Billings. 'Not so loud! They are the gentlemen named in the inventory put in by Cringar and Garvin, and mighty attractive-looking men they are too.'

"Just then the door opened, and, by Jove! if there were n't two of the biggest rascals that ever cursed Montana, grinning and nodding like circus clowns. The moment their eyes fell on me, back they started, one of their boots coming down on Garvin's corns, I should judge by the growl, and there they stood staring at me. 'T was a rich sight!" exclaimed Prescott, laughing. "I did n't move a peg; but remained calm and majestic, like the ghost of Hamlet's father, and fancied I heard them mutter between their teeth,—

'Be thou a spirit of health or goblin damned,
Bring with thee airs from heaven or blasts from hell,
Be thy intents wicked or charitable,
Thou com'st in such a questionable shape,
That I will speak to thee.'

"But if that was their intention, that precious pirate of a Garvin did n't give 'em time to carry it out; for, drawing them back with that ugly hand of his, he slammed the door to, first sending a look at me that had more of the cut-throat in it than anything of the kind I 've seen for a good while."

"Well, you 've got them shut up with Garvin for the purpose of telling him who you are; now please tell me who *they* are," said the Veteran with interest.

"In about three words: they are by name, as I knew them West, Jim Fitch and Sam Ratter, two blacklegs and cut-throats who got jugged one day,—and the same night the miners went up to lynch 'em and found them gone. That 's the last I ever saw or heard of them till they burst upon me in the glory of Garvin's presence."

"So they never pre-empted out there?"

"Well, as to that I can't say. But if they did, it was to swindle the green ones with."

"A good many intelligent men have been swindled by those kind of fellows, here in New York," said the Veteran, seriously.

"Very true," returned Prescott, sobered by the Veteran's manner.

"'Even a scoundrel may pre-empt, and on the basis of real property get up a swindle here that it would be difficult to get behind, if there were plenty of money to stop one's progress."

"It is indeed so," said Prescott, in a meditative voice. "That Garvin seems to have things knotted up badly."

"As I will show you," responded the Veteran; and thereupon he proceeded to give Prescott a succinct account of his interview with Cringar on the previous day, and its results. "This discovery of yours," he said in conclusion, "is of the utmost importance in the future working of my plans, though it may not produce results so immediate as you had hoped."

"Yes," replied Prescott, "I see how it is. Law chastises scoundrels, and protects them too. That is to say, a rogue may swindle a victim, and then hop behind the technical meshes of the law for safety. And if he 's got money enough, Heaven only knows how long he will stay there! General, I think lynch-law is a capital thing sometimes."

"A desperate remedy, but effective in desperate cases."

They now parted.

On the evening immediately after the foregoing conversation between the Veteran and Prescott Marland, Daniel Garvin might have been seen, hat in hand, about taking his departure from the house of Dr. Pennell, who at that time had charge of a private madhouse in the upper part of the city.

"You understand everything clearly, Doctor?" said the broker, as he proceeded first to smooth his hat with his hand, and then to draw his handkerchief slowly around it, as if he would leave no stubborn ruffle unsubdued. "You will not forget that a nephew of such promise must receive from you a very special care."

The doctor, whose form was not unlike Garvin's, but whose visage, though partaking somewhat of the bony structure of his visitor's, was of a complexion light, sandy, and freckled, — this doctor gave vent to a subdued but sinister laugh, and said, —

"Do not fear, Mr. Garvin. If this nephew is the unfortunate victim of the hallucination you have described, he must necessarily receive from us more than usual care.

I know of no cases so dangerous as these patients whose mania consists in the fancy that all about them are thieves and assassins."

"You will have the carriage there at the hour?"

"Without fail."

* * * * *

A day passes by, when Prescott Marland on entering his boarding-house in the evening receives the following note, written in pencil:—

MR. MARLAND.

I have called to see you, but do not find you in. I have just discovered a little girl, dying from starvation, whom I have ascertained to be the unfortunate child of a soldier, named Joseph Deering, who was killed in the war of the Rebellion. I have sent temporary relief; but I am unexpectedly compelled to leave the city by the afternoon train, and therefore am prevented from doing all my heart dictates. I have been directed to you as one who belongs to an association that helps the suffering families of the fallen brave. In God's name, then, delay not in this case! To provide against all accidents I have ordered the same hackman that drove me to the place where this wretched little girl is now lying a skeleton to call for you at eight o'clock. Heaven pity the unfortunate!

Sincerely yours,

EDWARD SMALL,
A Friend of the Soldier.

Prescott called the landlady.

"How long ago was this left here?" he asked.

"About two hours ago," answered the landlady. "The gentleman who left it seemed much disappointed at not finding you in, and said he would like to write a line for you. So he came in and wrote the note I have given you, and begged me not to forget to deliver it the instant you returned, for life or death might hang on it."

"Strange!" muttered Prescott, after the landlady had left him. "Why did n't he inquire where I *could* be found? But all men are not born Solomons, and he must have been in a driving hurry. Well, he 's a good fellow, and has done what he could, that 's evident."

He now commenced pacing his room impatiently, at the same time re-reading the letter.

"Why did n't the man think to tell me where she was?" he again muttered. "The hackman be hanged! I should have been half-way there by this time, instead of making these boards creak under my boots! Poor child! Poor child! And what of the rest of this unhappy family? Dead, perhaps!" Then, after a silent pacing of several moments, he clenched his hand and exclaimed, "If that coachman is five minutes late I 'll strangle him!"

But the hack drove up to the door just on the hour.

"I had promised myself to strangle you if you were behind time," said Prescott, with a half-laugh, as he prepared to enter the coach.

"No danger of that on such an errand as this, sir, I assure you."

"That 's a good fellow! Don't spare the horses."

"Never fear, sir."

The clatter of the horses' hoofs and the rattling of the coach-wheels gave evidence to Prescott that the coachman was in earnest.

The drive seemed long and interminable to the anxious soldier. The coach whirled from street to street until he thought the whole city must have been travelled over.

Finally they stopped before a tenement in which Prescott, as he beheld it by the gas-light, judged poverty reigned in all its hideous deformity, and the coachman sprang to the sidewalk. He was instantly accosted by a man who had evidently been waiting, and who now spoke a few words to him in a low tone.

"All right," he returned loud enough for his passenger to hear.

Then opening the coach door, he said, —

"The girl has been carried to more comfortable quarters just above. Shall I drive you there?"

"Don't stop to ask, but drive ahead."

The coach again rattled over the pavements, and presently drew up before a substantial brick building.

"She has been brought here," said the driver, as he opened the door to let Prescott out.

The door of the house was opened as he ascended the steps.

He entered, and the hackman, with a meaning gesture, remounted his seat, and taking the reins in his hands prepared to drive off.

CHAPTER XXX

THE door closed on the young Lieutenant with an ominous sound that did not fail to strike ears rendered alert by service in the midst of an enemy's country. Impatient though he was to see the child he had been ostensibly driven hither to help, his soldierly intuitions caused him to take a glance about him.

He heard a distant howl, and at the same time a powerfully built man with a brutal face crossed the lower end of the hall, glancing toward him, as he passed, with a wolfish look.

He perceived, also, that the man who had admitted him was strongly built, with the same wolfish countenance.

All at once a terrible suspicion flashed across his mind. He would test it.

"A moment," he said, stepping back. "I wish to speak to the coachman."

He laid hold of the door, but he could not open it!

Turning to the man by his side he said in a low but commanding voice, —

"Will you be so kind as to open this door?"

"You had better see the child first," answered the man with an ill-concealed look of brutal triumph.

"Open this door!"

The young Lieutenant's eyes blazed as he uttered this command in a tone as short, quick, and distinct, as he would have given an order on the battle-field.

The man saw his game was up, and with a mocking laugh he said, —

"Them ain't the sort of orders we calculate to obey in this 'ere place, my young cove."

Prescott now shook the door violently.

"Open it!" he cried, "or I 'll batter it down with your skull!"

"Well!" exclaimed the fellow, sending a leering glance down the hall where the other man had crossed, "if 'ere ain't a mad un, an' no mistake!" Then, putting his hand to his mouth, he cried: "Say, Gryper! here 's a patient that 's crazy as a loon! Jest bear a hand!"

Prescott's terrible suspicion was confirmed. He was in a mad-house!

But this active and determined young soldier was not one to yield without a struggle to the fate prepared for him. With a spring as quick as the tiger's he planted a blow on the attendant's forehead that felled him like an ox. Then leaping to the door he hastily sought the fastenings.

Suddenly he felt himself clasped by two powerful arms around the body; and then he was dragged back from the door.

In another moment he heard the sound of many feet,— a cloth was thrown over his head,—and as numberless strong hands were laid on him he was tripped up by a skilful and vigorous stroke, and, after one tremendous struggle, lay at the mercy of his assailants.

He thought with a shudder of the strait-jacket, and expected every moment to feel its horrid embrace. This did not seem, however, to be the intention of his captors at present. They simply bound his hands, and then a rough voice commanded him to rise.

"I'll obey no orders here!" he exclaimed in muffled tones, but with determination.

"He's dangerous! secure him and put him in No. 7!" cried a shrill voice from the hall above.

"Tie his feet, and we'll obey the doctor's orders!" responded he who had bid him rise.

His feet were bound accordingly, and then he felt himself raised in two or three pairs of sturdy arms, and borne away, his head still covered by the cloth, while another of his captors, whom he recognized as the attendant he had knocked down, sang out with frightful cadence,—

"The dead! the dead! who'll bear the dead?
The coffin waits! who'll bear the dead?"

which was followed by a laugh of mocking merriment, accompanied by the scuffling of feet.

He heard door after door open, until at length he felt a current of cool air at the same time that he found himself being carried down a flight of stairs.

He now heard howls, and peals of insane laughter, and for an instant he thought himself in the confines of Pandemonium. He could not prevent a shudder as he wondered if those that bore him were about to fling him into the den of one of these howling wretches, as the Cæsars drove the doomed Christian martyrs into the jaws of roaring beasts of prey.

When the suspicion flashed across his mind in the hall above that he was in a mad-house, instantaneously with that suspicion had come before him the sinister and murderous visages of Garvin, Slaycut, *alias* Fitch, and Drorblude, *alias* Ratter. That this was a sequence of that unexpected meeting of the previous day he was fully convinced; and knowing well that no crime would be too great for them, and having already become aware of Garvin's diabolical method of accomplishing his aims, he had good cause to shudder as he now felt himself borne down into that chilly air, and heard the howls and laughter of the confined maniacs.

The voice that had bawled the sombre cadence above now sang again, this time the singer bringing his foot down with emphasis on the descending steps in time to his atrocious verse: —

"Sweet songsters of this stony deep,
We bring you merry company.
He 'll make ye laugh, he 'll make ye weep,
He will, I swear by Jemminy!"

The young Lieutenant felt the arms under him shake with the suppressed laughter that followed this essay. Then a voice at his head cried out, —

"Stop that, Mat! You 'll make me laugh till I drop 'im!"

"All right," responded the singer, closing a guttural

laugh in which he had himself indulged by repeating in a sort of double bass hum, —

> "The dead! the dead! who'll bear the dead?
> The coffin waits! who'll bear the dead?"

By this time they had reached the bottom of the stairway, and Prescott felt as if he would like just one leg free to kick the malicious songster, who was evidently affected by the crazy atmosphere about him, from basement to roof.

The next moment he was thrust into a cell, in which he heard the incoherent gibbering of a maniac, the cords were cut from his limbs, the thick door was closed with a dull slam, and the bolt turned upon him.

CHAPTER XXXI.

DANIEL GARVIN again waits in his office after the shades and silence of night have succeeded the din and confusion of the day's financial struggles. He has reckoned his gains, and, on this occasion, his losses, and now sits with one hand clenched upon the table, while the deep-wrinkling scowl, and the general look of bitterness, fierceness, and hatred that mark his unattractive features, tell of some unusual agitation.

That look of self-complacency and self-confidence, formerly so characteristic of him, has given place to an expression in which passionate and desperate determination predominates.

At a moment when he had congratulated himself on the success of his long-contemplated schemes, whereby avarice and revenge were to be satiated; when, with the air of some devastating monster of the fairy-books, he beheld before him nothing but impotence and fear, and had already begun to mock his unfortunate victims, who seemed beyond all chance of aid,—at this moment a champion had appeared upon the scene, whose puissant blows had already shattered the gateway of his infernal fortress, and now threatened to lop off his own abhorrent head.

Daniel Garvin prided himself on the power of his intellect to accomplish what he might undertake. He revelled, as we have seen, in the game in which living men should stand as the pieces on his chess-board. He had come to believe himself invincible in any such game, when sufficient inducements were offered for him to engage in it with the whole force of his will. But he now sits with his clenched hand upon the table, and his features distorted by desperate passion, because he has suddenly found himself in danger of utter defeat in the contest of intellectual forces, and is compelled to resort for safety to those means which, while he is capable of any deed that promises to save him from defeat and ruin, he has heretofore ascribed to the ignorant and brutal villains of a sensational romance.

At length a low series of taps on the outer door caused him to start with a sort of guilty terror that was undoubtedly new in his experience, and for a moment he stared toward the door without attempting to rise.

A renewal of the taps brought him to his feet, and going to the door with a creeping step which we have not before seen in him, he unfastened it, when the hag, Mammy Roone, walked in.

This man of inordinate egotism becomes almost an object of pity, as we behold him now compelled to lead this revolting old woman into his private office, there to make her a partner in the execution of his endangered schemes.

She remained with him an hour.

When they came forth two faces presented themselves that would have furnished studies not often obtained by even a Le Brun. Mammy Roone's horrible visage was lit up by a ferocious smile, while the dark face of the broker was made scarcely less horrible by an expression in which devilish malignancy was mingled with an irrepressible fear, and withal an air of fierce disgust and loathing, as he furtively glanced at the foul instrument of his designs.

An hour afterwards Mammy Roone was in secret conference with two characters whom we have also met with before, — Dick Smasher, and him whom that burly ruffian denominated the "Doctor."

"Well, me lads," said the hag, after having opened the business she had on hand, "how does ye like this swate job? for swate it must be to both of yez, I'm thinking."

"Yes, sweet and pretty," answered Dick Smasher. "I'd give that mighty fine soldier a few taps that'd put 'im to sleep according to regulation."

This witticism caused the "Doctor" to break out into a fit of thin, dyspeptic laughter.

"S-h!" commanded Mammy Roone, her own repulsive features relaxing into a responsive grin, which revealed in all their horrid array the broken fangs that she would have so relished to fasten in Emma's soft and rounded flesh; "do ye both mind that the walls about us have ears!"

"All right, mammy," returned the "Doctor"; "but that 'ere joke about the *taps* broke on me all of a sudden. You see the pictur' of Dick's tapping that 'ere big sheep's head for tallow was too funny. Why, dagger it! atween his taps and my lancet we 'll have 'im laid out on his bunk quick 'n regulation specifies. Won't we, Dick?"

"Don't ye go for being so confident, Doctor," said Dick, dubiously. "You were fast asleep, yerself, when this big fellow got his fives on me."

The "Doctor" did n't seem to relish this reminder.

"Niver ye mind," broke in the old woman, as she observed the scowl on his murderous-looking features. "The Smasher himself did n't come away from the young gintleman's fine fist without a beauty spot; that 's what ye 'll not be denying, me honey."

The powerful shoulder-hitter could bear twitting better than his weaker but more murderous companion.

"No, I 'll deny it not!" he exclaimed. "That young chicken 's got the true grit, and th' science to back it up. I 'd give 'im a shake of my hand any time he 'd ask for it."

"D—n him!" muttered the other, "I 'd give 'im a prick of my lancet!"

"Well, never mind about that, young man," returned Dick. "Give 'im a taste of yer blood-letter when you get the chance; but let me tell you that the man you 've got to deal with, if ye take hold of this 'ere job, ain't so sure of taking a lancet. Ye 'd better have a plenty of powder and ball, and the Devil take the 'peeler' that disturbs ye!"

"Yis, it 's betther to be prepared ag'inst accidents; an' that is what me owld man would always be afther saying, the Holy Virgin protict his blissed soul! and tin thousand curses descind on the heads of every mither's son of a Union sowldhier in Purgatory!"

As Mammy Roone commenced this sentence, she spoke in a low subdued voice; but ere she had ended her tones had risen — on memory of the deceased Patrick Roone's fate — to a pitch of savage frenzy.

"Easy!" uttered Dick Smasher, with a glance at the

walls of the room. "Don't be forgetting that ye told us a spell ago that walls have ears. Now, I guess the Doctor and myself will undertake this delicate job, for that leetle pile of greenbacks ye 've agreed to lay down. How is it with ye, Doctor?"

"Count me in, an' this ere professional instrument, too," returned the "Doctor," at the same time drawing a long, keen knife from his bosom, and laying it down with a smile of satisfaction on the table.

"Bah!" muttered Dick Smasher to himself. "I 'd bet ten to one I could knock the wind out of him every time afore he could scratch my waistcoat with his confounded skin-pricker!"

"Ye 'll say it 's a good bit of work Mammy Roone's secured for yez whin ye 'll be afther countin' thim same granebacks," hissed rather than spoke the beldam, who could not suppress a grin that made her auditors question whether they were not themselves in Purgatory.

* * * * *

Days had passed, and nothing had been heard from Prescott Marland. The Veteran had called repeatedly at his boarding-house, but his landlady, of whom Prescott was a favorite, and who was in a great state of alarm, could give only one answer, which was that she had heard nothing from him since the evening she had delivered him the note left by the stranger who had displayed such extraordinary anxiety.

The Veteran endeavored to assure her that she need feel no alarm; but she had learned to expect any form of crime in New York, and her fears could not be allayed. As for himself he had his own thoughts. Prescott's disappearance immediately followed his visit to him when he made known his rencounter with the Western impostors at Cringar's store, and his quick mind was not long left in doubt as to the man whose interests were involved in this disappearance, and whose scruples would not interfere with any action necessary to secure his own safety, or the safety of a scheme which the discovery made by Prescott would so seriously compromise.

It was about ten o'clock at night. He was returning to his rooms after a visit to Prescott's boarding-house, where he had been detained by an endless string of surmises from the landlady regarding her favorite boarder's extraordinary absence.

Suddenly he felt himself plucked by the sleeve, and on turning discovered a boy who seemed to be in great trepidation.

After looking cautiously around, this boy thrust a piece of folded paper into his hand, and then placing his finger to his lips he whispered, "I durn't risk being seen with you," and then with the words, "I 'll see you ag'in to-morrow," he disappeared.

Two thoughts instantly flashed through the Veteran's mind. One was the suspicion that here was some kind of trap set for him similar to that which he was assured had been set for Prescott; the other was the hope that it might possibly convey *bona fide* intelligence of the whereabouts of his missing young friend.

Approaching the nearest street-lamp, he opened the paper and read the following, written in a coarse hand: —

"General Hamond i am hired to watch a young man named Prescot marland. i carnt Stand it no longer and if You wil com and help me we can git him away. he told me to call you thorbolt and then you wood know that he is Realy here. come tonite or i am Affrade it wil be to late. i send my son with this meet me at haf parst ten at the corner of prince and Green streets."

The Veteran read this singular missive over two or three times. Was it indeed a trap for himself, or did it really open the way to the discovery of the trap into which Prescott had been inveigled? The question was, Would he risk forsaking his comrade by refusing to go to the place appointed by this note, or would he risk his own safety by going?

With a man of his character the time occupied by such a discussion was but short. He balanced a heavy walking-stick in his hand an instant, and then stepping up to a patrolman who, in a doorway near by, had been a silent observer of all that had passed, he inquired the way to the place designated in the note. The latter instructed him as desired, and he directed his steps accordingly.

But this patrolman, though a silent observer, had not been a disinterested one. He had recognized the boy by the street-lamp, and he instantly suspected foul play. He said nothing to the Veteran, however, but followed him at a distance just sufficient to keep him in sight.

At length the object of this watchful officer's attention passed out of his beat.

Another was soon notified, who continued on the track.

Finally, after one or two inquiries of passers-by, the Veteran found himself nearing the appointed spot.

He now began very ardently to hope that the missive was genuine, and that he might hear something of the young Lieutenant, whom he loved as a son; and especially was he anxious that something might result to clear the gloom which the ominous absence of this noble and generous friend had cast over that home in Vandam Street, where his presence had come to be depended upon as the sunlight.

But this hope did not cause him to relax his grasp on his heavy walking-stick.

Suddenly as he passed a small alley his meditations were aroused by what sounded to his ears as a cry of distress.

He stopped and listened. The cry again reached him, and this time it was surely a smothered appeal for help, and was accompanied by sounds of a murderous struggle.

Tightening the gripe upon his heavy cane, he hastened with his long stride down the alley.

This alley opened into a small yard piled with rubbish, in which the Veteran speedily found himself. Here he stopped and looked about him.

At the same instant a slung-shot descended obliquely from behind with tremendous force, and striking on the side of the hat, fell with great violence on his shoulder.

Simultaneously with this attack a man with a motion like a great rat sprang from behind a pile of old wood, with a long knife in his hand; and as he saw the gigantic figure before him reel under the blow of the slung-shot, he cried with a suppressed yell of uncontrollable exultation as he leaped for this figure while his deadly blade threw off a swift gleam in the starlight, —

"One for the Lancet and Mammy Roone!"

But he reckoned without his host. The unusual height of the intended victim had disconcerted his confederate's aim, and though reeling under the assault at his back, the Veteran instantly proved that he was not disabled; for raising his walking-stick with the instinct of a cavalryman, he made a rear *moulcaut*, and catching the glint of the murderous steel in the uplifted hand of his second assailant he brought his improvised but formidable weapon down with a front cut, delivering so fearful a blow that the skull upon which it descended was crushed in like a shell, — and the "Doctor" dropped to the ground, with the knife still grasped in his hand, but not again to be used with its owner's vaunted professional skill, for that owner was now dead.

With a curse Dick Smasher, whose aim with the slung-shot had been so faulty, now drew a pistol, levelled it at the head of the man, who through his prodigious strength threatened to become master of the situation, and fired.

The massive form of the Veteran swayed for a moment, and then fell extended at full length on the earth.

An alarm now pierced the air, and steps were heard hurrying along the street and up the alley, and the assassin, with a curse on all intermeddling "peelers," leaped the fence and disappeared just as the patrolman who had been following the Veteran entered the yard.

With a watchman's habit, the new-comer took a hasty survey of the field, and then listened. In the next instant he had sprung the fence in pursuit of footsteps which his quick ears detected as retreating steps of guilt.

As he disappeared a second patrolman entered on the scene, who proceeded to examine the two lifeless men who lay extended before him.

When he lifted the Veteran's head a stream of crimson blood flowed from a wound just above the ear.

"He 's gone! and a superb specimen of a man too," he muttered, as he let the head fall back.

Then he went to the other, and when his hand came in contact with the "Doctor's" broken skull he gave utterance to a loud "Whew!" and then, as he cast his eye from the glittering knife, still clasped by the dead ruffian, to the heavy cane also grasped in the muscular hand of its lifeless owner, he exclaimed, —

"This fellow might as well have had a tin sword!"

Rising, he looked around and muttered to himself, while he awaited the signal from the first patrolman.

In another moment that officer reappeared, his pursuit having been unsuccessful.

Men who had heard both pistol-shot and alarm now entered the yard and tendered their aid, while windows in the neighborhood were opened and utterances of horror followed as the startled gazers beheld two inanimate bodies carried away, leaving what their strained eyes detected in the bright starlight as dark stains on the gravel and rotten boards of the old yard beneath them.

As the sombre burdens were borne into the street, a small man of active movements arrived, and with pencil and memorandum-book in hand passed from one body to the other, making examinations and asking questions of the patrolmen, which they attentively answered, he being a newspaper reporter.

CHAPTER XXXII.

IN the old house on Vandam Street there was anxiety and sorrow. We have seen the Veteran almost forgetting any probable danger to himself, as he neared the place of rendezvous appointed in the note which the boy had given him, in the hope that something might really result to clear the gloom from the hearts of those who had so learned to love the noble and generous Prescott Marland.

The mother loved him as a son, and the young children as a brother; and both mother and children experienced a distress resulting from the mysterious disappearance of their favorite, which the sympathetic reader will readily comprehend.

We say a favorite; but while this word conveys an idea of the sentiments of welcome with which they were wont to receive him to their now humble home, it does by no means express the profound feelings of gratitude and affection which they entertained toward him. He was ever so thoughtful, so kind, so considerate; and, withal, he had such a way of raising them out of a consciousness of their present sad condition, and placing them for the time being in a bright sunlight, which had the effect of making their hearts lighter and their lives happier during the time that intervened between his visits.

And then he of all others had a power, peculiarly his own, of shedding a lustre over the memory of the patriot husband and father. While the world without had allowed itself to be led by a designing knave into a universal judgment, which was but little short of a denunciation of that husband and father for reckless and unscrupulous conduct in business, this feature in Prescott's character, this fidelity to the memory of one between whom and himself there had existed an affection so pure and noble, and so worthy the great cause the defence of which had brought them together wounded and disabled, this rare, unswerving fidelity was calculated, as the reader may readily imagine, to surround him in the midst of this home with a sort of halo, as if the unseen spirit of the patriot blessed him for his steadfast devotion to that sacred friendship.

We may readily surmise, then, what sorrow, what grief must have been theirs as they waited day after day with no word from this missing friend.

But what shall be said of the secret anguish of that heart which, under the formal relation of brother and sister, had suffered itself to become gradually so absorbed that its very life depended upon the responsive love of the heart of him over whose fate there hung such a terrible uncertainty?

Darkness seemed suddenly to have closed in upon her young life. As she looked back on her existence in that home of privation, as it was before this object of her supreme love had so strangely disappeared, she wondered how, with him so often by her side, she could have ever supposed it otherwise than a haven of unalloyed happiness; her heart offering an example of that great truth, that in life, as well as in art, the highest lights and deepest shades are relative, depending for their effect on those contrasts which the hand of Providence throws into the existence of men with all-wise and beneficent spirit.

In the midst of their gloomy anxiety this distressed family had indeed found one friend whose influence was strongly exerted toward buoying up their tried and dejected spirits. This friend was the Veteran. They knew that if Prescott was alive Thorbolt would never rest till he had been found. His self-sacrificing efforts for themselves they had almost forgotten in the contemplation of his untiring labors to solve the mystery that hung around his comrade's disappearance. Since the latter's abduction he had not failed to call on them every day, and though unable to report any definite progress in the direction which now interested all so deeply, yet his presence served to lighten the gloom, and inspire them with some of that spirit which in him seemed ever to ride the storm with an unwavering faith in the Almighty Disposer of events.

On the same evening that he was led into the snare of assassins through his anxiety for the fate of his comrade, he had made one of these welcome calls, and had, by more than ordinary effort, succeeded in planting in their hearts a feeling of hope such as they had not before experienced;

and when he left them the mother had turned to Emma and said, —

"This self-sacrificing soldier deserves the richest blessings which Heaven can vouchsafe! He seems a grand and noble guardian, and I feel myself to be a child in his presence!"

But not many hours were to pass ere another blow was to fall, which would wellnigh crush them to the earth.

On the morning following this last-mentioned visit of the Veteran, the family were seated around their humble breakfast-table, of whom Albert, who was now convalescent, formed one of the number, when a light nervous rap announced a visitor.

Alice opened the door, and William Garvin entered, looking pale and anxious.

This innocent son of a guilty father was an occasional visitor to the present home of his aunt and cousins, but never had he called before at this hour of the day. An event, therefore, so unusual, together with his agitation, filled Mrs. Paige and Emma with emotions of vague alarm.

William observed the effect produced by his unexpected visit, which tended to increase his agitation, and caused him to stammer somewhat in his speech as, unfolding a paper he held in his hand, he hurriedly said, —

"Happening this way this morning, and hearing the news-boys crying a murder in the city last night, I bought a paper; and I could not go home without first bringing it to you."

Then pointing to a flaming paragraph headed "HORRIBLE MURDER!" he handed the paper to his anxious auditors.

This is what they read: —

"HORRIBLE MURDER!!!

"A GENERAL OF THE UNION ARMY THE VICTIM!

"Last night one of the most horrible affairs that has ever cursed this city of horrible deeds occurred about half past ten o'clock, in the vicinity of Prince Street. At the time mentioned Patrolman McNeal was instructed by Patrolman Owen that a stranger who had just left his beat, and whom he pointed out ahead, was likely to be led on to some foul play, and suggested his keeping his eye on him. Officer McNeal accordingly followed and kept him in sight. Presently he observed the stranger, who was evidently a man of much more than ordinary size, turn suddenly into an alleyway. He now quickened his steps, and had nearly arrived at the passage when he heard the sharp report of a pistol. Hastening down the alley he discovered in a small back yard two bodies stretched on the earth. He instantly sounded an alarm, and thinking he heard the footsteps of the flying assassin in an adjoining yard he gave pursuit, but without success. Returning he found Patrolman Darley on the ground. Here was a fearful sight. In a pool of gore lay the victim, a man of immense size, with a fearful wound from a bullet in the side of his head, who was instantly identified by Patrolman McNeal, himself a returned soldier, as General Hammond, the celebrated cavalry leader. And even in death his terrible arm seems to have proved too formidable for at least one of his assailants. In his hand was still grasped a heavy cane, while near him lay the second body — which was instantly recognized as the body of a low and desperate character who has usually gone under the *sobriquet* of the *Doctor* — with his skull smashed in by what was evidently a powerful blow from this cane. Persons attracted to the spot by the report of the pistol and the watchman's alarm now lent their aid, and the bodies were conveyed to the station-house. Those who were on the ground immediately after the assassination pronounce the appearance of the murdered soldier to have been, with all its horror, singularly impressive. So great was his size that it required four strong men to carry him. His face was a grand one in that sleep of sudden death; and a deep, wide scar hollowed out his left cheekbone in a manner sufficient alone to identify him. To what a fate has this veteran of a hundred battles been doomed!"

Emma, who had borne up so bravely under circumstances that would try the strongest natures, turned deadly pale, and fell back fainting into the chair from which she had risen to read that terrible account.

Mrs. Paige, whose hopes, kindled by a knowledge of the labors of the Veteran in her behalf, were in this instant utterly extinguished, turned in alarm to her daughter, and dropping that fatal paper, hastened to her assistance, while Alice, also hastening to her aid, exclaimed,—

"O mother! what has happened? Is Prescott—?"

"No," interrupted the mother with a warning gesture. "A kind Heaven must have spared *him* to us."

In the mean time Albert had sprung for the paper, and his quick eye having caught the name of General Hammond in the account of the murder, he hastened to Alice, his eyes filled with grief and horror, and whispered the story in her ear.

Alice's face in turn expressed her startled emotions, as she continued her efforts to revive her fainting sister.

William Garvin on his part stood rooted to the floor, looking as if he felt himself to be guilty of the murder and all this sudden anguish.

When Emma fainted his first impulse was to spring to her support; but instantly he saw the mother hasten to perform this office a reaction occurred. Instead of flying to her assistance he felt like flying from her presence.

CHAPTER XXXIII.

MORE sensitive and more morbid even than when we parted with him on the evening of his adventure with the ruffians who attempted to abduct his cousin, the broker's son now presents a complete type of a young, sensitive, overwrought mind, scarcely more able to endure contact with the every-day world than are certain invalids to endure direct rays of the sun, who from a singular disease of the nervous system experience the most acute physical suffering if brought in contact with such a light.

But with this increased morbid sensitiveness has increased his secret adoration of his charming cousin. To the effect of her beauty has been added the influence of her misfortunes. With his idealizing and dreaming mind nothing could have happened more calculated to enhance his infatuation than the event by which she had been driven from the home where in early days he had been wont to join with her in the sports of childhood, and where as years advanced his love had taken root and grown to be almost his only life.

He had watched the progress of the intimacy between Emma and Prescott Marland with feelings that are well-nigh indescribable. Jealousy is scarcely the word to express these emotions. It does not comprehend that feeling in which wonderment and a profound incredulity are mingled with a deep, vague, tormenting anguish, as if one who has lived in the rapturous contemplation of a spirit whom he believes to be his guardian angel, should awake after a troublesome dream to find this spirit suddenly incarnated and borne away before his eyes by a man of the most undoubted flesh and blood of this material world.

When the news of Prescott's disappearance reached his ears he experienced sensations equally indescribable. The first impression was as if a dark shadow had quickly vanished from before him. Then in its place came another shadow caused by thoughts of the inevitable anguish of her whom he so adored. As we have formerly remarked, his love for her was not associated with ideas of possession; it was an adoration through which he saw her a being to be possessed by no mortal man, but who, exempt from the weaknesses of the common humanity, was created to live near the sky, on the ideal mount and in the ideal shades allotted her by his adoring fancies. Therefore thoughts of possible grief, whatever the cause, disturbing the happiness of this idealized queen of his secluded life would invariably throw a shadow across his heart.

As days passed and Prescott's fate seemed more and more certain, he began to experience a feeling which partook somewhat of superstition, as though no man could possibly presume to cast such glances as he had observed Prescott direct toward Emma, and live long enough to consummate his desires in possession. And that such a sentiment existed in this highly fanciful and morbid mind is not so much to be wondered at when we remember that even the strongest natures will yield to like feelings,— such as refusing with vague dread to give a child a name which has been borne successively by two or three generations of ancestors, all of whom have died young and under the same circumstances; and other innumerable displays of this sort, which those not concerned may smile at, but who, when the test shall come to them, will probably be found to govern their actions by similar motives.

But toward the Veteran this young artist entertained sentiments as exaggerated in their way as were his sentiments toward his fair cousin. As Prescott had informed Thorbolt in the interview that resulted in his introduction to Billings the book-keeper, he had affirmed that the picture of this man of immense stature, as he first appeared in the street when he was awakened to consciousness by Emma's shrieks, and saw her struggling in the arms of the desperate ruffian who was bearing her away, was before his eyes continually by day and in his dreams by night, — a vision that conveyed to his mind a realization of Homer's description of Jove in the midst of war.

Emma he associated with the angels; the Veteran with the gods. There was that in the majesty of the latter's mien and the lofty dignity of his mind which had the effect to overwhelm him. When in his presence he seemed to have no mind of his own nor individuality. All seemed absorbed in that grand character whose smile or frown caused the sun of his life, for the time being, either to shine with inspiring lustre or disappear behind dark and gloomy clouds.

The Veteran had met William at the house in which the Paiges now lived, and had requested the family to make known to him his desire that nothing of his own visits to their home should be mentioned outside to any person whatever; thus by this request including his father without specifying him. Emma had taken it upon herself to convey this request to William; and coming from such a source, and through such a channel, it was made ten times more binding than the law of the Medes and Persians.

So far as his father was concerned, however, there was not the slightest danger; for, though he did not in the least apprehend the foul business of which this parent had been guilty, his intuitions told him that relations existed between the broker and his half-brother's family which utterly forbade any reference to his visits there. We would here remark that the Paiges were careful never to express, in any way, their opinion of the father's actions in the presence of the son.

When William Garvin opened the paper in the street and read the dreadful news, he had nearly fallen to the pavement. The shock was tremendous. An unspeakable horror seized his senses as if the very sun had turned blood red, and then left the world in impenetrable darkness.

That man of sublime strength! of superhuman power! with the majesty of a god! — he dead! murdered! killed in an obscure back yard by a beastly ruffian, the bullet even tainted with the penitentiary that disgorged him!

This young idealist was stupefied, and for an instant everything around him was in a whirl. The earth itself seemed rolling from beneath his feet, and the passers-by appeared as unreal shadows luridly lit up by red letters which formed the word "MURDER!"

Immediately he had gathered his scattered senses, and was able to look at the reality with a degree of understanding, he hastened to Vandam Street, near which he often wandered in the early morning, and conveyed the dreadful news in the manner we have described.

As we have said, his first impulse when his cousin fainted was to spring to her support, and then as the mother hastened to her assistance the second impulse was to fly. He felt guilty of what was to him an inexcusable rashness in thus bursting in upon them with his startling and melancholy intelligence, and for a few moments he presented a picture of the most acute mental misery.

But now, as he stood gazing upon the anguish-stricken group before him, he suddenly experienced an emotion, vague but deep, which first caused within him a strange and ominous tremor, that was followed almost instantly by an overwhelming sensation as if the very soul were breaking up and losing its past identity.

This remarkable agitation was the result of a powerful reaction. Stupefied as he was by the perusal in the street of the account of the murder, he had, as we have seen, thought of nothing after but to rush to the family of his deceased uncle to break to them the news. But now as he contemplated his cousin rendered almost unconscious by the terrible blow this announcement had inflicted, the full realization of the Veteran's mortality, with all its dependences on the natural laws that governed him with the rest of our common humanity, swept in upon him. And then his ideal world seemed a chaos, without shape and void, and for a moment objects around him were in a sort of maze, as if the outer world were passing away from his vision.

But presently these objects began to reassume a definite aspect. His now reviving cousin especially stood out in strong relief to his vision like the central figure of an effective painting, and the object of his gaze happening at that moment to lift her sorrowful eyes to his face was startled by the new, strange look which appeared there; and confused, withal, for it was an unmistakable expression of the most intense and all-devouring love. That gaze which heretofore had beamed upon her with a timid adoration, and which she had ascribed to the natural ardency of a young artist, who would contemplate with the same expression everything in nature to which his soul might, in an ideal sense, be devoted,—this gaze had suddenly transformed itself, and now gave evidence of emotions which no heart of woman can mistake.

A blush instantly tinged the cheeks of this maiden, whose paleness, combined with her look of deep sorrow, only served to enhance in the eyes of the young artist that beauty which to him was so transcendent. Instead of falling to the ground, as but an hour before he would have expected, if, perchance, he should blindly permit himself to meet her eye with a glance of such fervid love, his gaze remained fixed, while it continued to increase in the intensity of its ardor until its object, no longer able to endure it, cast down her eyes with a look of deep pain.

A vague thought entered Emma's mind that this sudden and extraordinary display of passion was but a sequence of Prescott Marland's disappearance, and the assassination of the Veteran, and an exclamation that was on her lips, when she revived and encountered his gaze, was only uttered by her heart.

"O Heaven!" was the unspoken utterance, "this friend murdered! Then never shall we see dear Prescott again!"

The mother, who was bending over Emma, now rose, and seeing William still standing, requested him to be seated.

Her voice thus addressing him broke the spell; the hot blood rushed to the very roots of his hair, and stammering out an incoherent excuse, he hastily departed in the greatest confusion, leaving the family to indulge in sacred privacy a grief with which was mingled a feeling of utter loneliness and desolation.

CHAPTER XXXIV.

THE merchant and the broker both read that morning the news of the assassination.

On Jonas Cringar the blow descended with even more deadly force than was experienced by the family of his former partner Since the hour of the Veteran's visit to his office the broker had concentrated upon this unhappy man the entire reserve power of his malevolent will, and his eye seemed scarcely a moment to be elsewhere than upon his tormented victim. But while the merchant had nearly sunk under his renewed torments he did not utterly lose the hope which the Veteran at the close of his interview with him had inspired in his breast. He felt like a captive, who, being tortured at the stake, expects each instant to hear the rifle-shots of rescuing friends.

The reader may well imagine his emotions, then, when he opened the morning paper, after his now usual night of sleeplessness and horrid dreams, and read the account which we have transcribed on a former page.

With him the blow came with the more crushing weight, for he instantly recognized in this bloody deed the hand of Daniel Garvin; and to the mercy of a desperate assassin, as well as an infamous schemer and robber, he felt himself now given up beyond all hope.

As for Daniel Garvin, when he heard the cries of the news-boys he could not entirely conceal a look of fierce expectation as he bought a paper and opened it.

He read the story, and instantly the cries seemed directed toward him; and with the announcement of a

"*Horrible Murder*" his ears were pierced with what seemed to him the word "MURDERER" continually repeated. The gnashing of his teeth, the exultant yet fearful and guilty light in his eye, and the irrepressible shudder which seized him while he strode the street with the paper clutched convulsively in his quivering hand, told of the terrible commotion within, and the fierce efforts this hirer of assassins was making to control himself.

Arrived at his office, the first thing his eye fell upon was the same detailed account with its flaming heading confronting him on a table, where the paper containing it had been thrown by the clerk.

He seized it instantly and bore it from sight into his private office, as if he feared his guilt was there proclaimed.

After a while the fever into which his sudden sense of an enormous guilt had thrown him somewhat subsided, and this untiring plotter, having given orders not to be interrupted for an hour, began, like the spider that has beaten off his enemy, to take a survey of his broken web preparatory to making it whole again.

With his head buried in his hands he gathered his thoughts as best he could, and concentrated them on plans for future work.

* * * * *

Several days had passed, and the broker again sat in his rear office plunged in deep and troubled meditation. Suddenly he rose, and proceeding to the door ordered the messenger to go immediately for his son William.

In due course of time William arrived, and was immediately closeted with his father.

"William," said the broker, seating his son opposite him and then looking intently into his face, — "William, you are old enough to marry."

William reddened and slightly trembled, but made no answer.

"Would you not like to marry?"

The young artist blushed still deeper, but continued silent, while he gazed at his father with evident fear.

"Tell me, boy, would you not like to marry?" repeated the broker in a voice intended to be soothing, but in which the penetrating quality of an authoritative will predominated.

"I — I — can — can — not — say," stammered the son.

"Pshaw, my boy!" returned the father with a grim smile, "it would be the making of you. You would be a stronger and a happier man by marrying."

The young artist displayed great agitation, but answered not.

The broker now bent forward, and bringing his face close to William's, he said, —

"I would have you marry immediately, William."

The young artist now stared on his father with unmistakable consternation. This father was about to command, and he had never up to this time dared to disobey him.

"Don't be so frightened," said Daniel Garvin, with a light laugh. "She 's neither a stranger nor a bugbear, if your father is any judge of a beautiful young woman. I would have you marry your cousin Emma."

William's stare changed into a wild sort of gleam, and the hot blood rushed tumultuously through his veins, turning his face and neck to a bright scarlet.

"How does it please you, boy?"

Within the time which had passed since he hurried in such confusion from the presence of that adored cousin, whose lids had drooped beneath the look which had never before appeared in his timid glances, William Garvin's whole being had been, as it were, a scene of incessant and increasing tumult. The blow that had overthrown the ideal in which he had enshrined the grand Thorbolt had also disturbed the ideal world in which he had spiritualized his cousin, and suddenly, as we have formerly seen, passion revealed its ardent presence; and during those days there had been going on a strong conflict between the old ideal and this new passion, which, in violation of long-cherished sentiments, began to fill his heart with vague thoughts of possession. But the old ideal was tenacious in its hold on this young heart with its exquisite sensibilities, and its influence was strongly exerted toward subjugating what the timid and morbidly fearful lover felt to be a passion, which, if it should gain full possession of him, would drive him to despair; for while she had heretofore seemed an angel to be not even approached with words of earthly love, she now had to his mind all the beauty of an angel, with the addition of that terrible capacity for scorn and contempt which sensitive and timid young lovers so much fear in the beautiful object of their secret adoration.

Then, again, in the midst of this internal commotion appeared the dark presence of his father in a storm of fury, and commanding him to desist from desires so obnoxious to himself; and thoughts of disobedience to this imperious autocrat were calculated to make him turn pale at the very idea.

He was, in short, shaken like a reed in the wind, and his soul tossed about as a plaything by the contending emotions with which he was agitated.

Now it happened that while suffering the most unendurable pangs of heart and soul he had yet experienced, he received the commands of the broker to attend upon him at his office immediately. This message, breaking in upon him at this instant with such peremptory sternness, filled him with dismay. He was assured that his father, whom he looked upon as one able to read all men as if a glass were set in their bosoms, had scrutinized him for the past few days as if he were searching the most secret depths of his heart; and to be brought before his stern and penetrating eye, with his breast in such an extraordinary state of commotion, was to him a terrible ordeal.

Tremblingly, therefore, had this young artist entered into his dread father's presence, to be confronted by that gaze before which he had learned to shrink when it would read his hidden thoughts.

The strange and abrupt manner in which the broker had opened the interview did by no means tend to allay the fears with which the son had come before him. This idolizing worshipper, whose love had inflicted upon him such exquisite torments, felt certain that his father had discovered all, and in order to head off this love was about to command him to marry some young woman of his own selection; and the dismay with which he had received the command from the messenger to hasten hither was increased tenfold, and began speedily to display itself on his countenance in that look of consternation which we have observed.

His emotion then, when the inexorable father pronounced the name of his cousin, we must leave to the imagination of the reader, which can see so much more than our pen can delineate.

When the broker said, "How does it please you, boy?" the young artist could scarcely contain himself; but that natural cunning which love puts on to protect itself, even in the most innocent bosom, came to his aid in time to modify somewhat, at least, the impulse that threatened to overpower him; though, as it was, the display of his feelings partook of vehemence. Rising to his feet, he seized one of his father's hands in both of his, and in a voice of extreme agitation, he exclaimed, —

"My dear father, I do not think I have ever disobeyed you!"

"No, my son," said the broker graciously, "you have been an obedient child."

"Then great as is this command which you are pleased to give me, I will not even now venture to disobey you!"

"You are a good son, — a good son," responded the father, at the same time casting an admonitory look toward the door to indicate that his son must not speak so loud.

"But, father," stammered William in a lowered but not less agitated voice, "will — she — obey?"

"Who? — your cousin?"

"Yes — Emma."

The broker gave vent to a self-complacent laugh.

"Borrow no trouble in that direction, my boy," he said, purring his son's upper hand with his own disengaged palm. "Your own consent obtained, — and I trust you will not change your mind, — there will be no difficulty in that direction."

The implied deference to the young lover's will did not fail to produce its effect.

"Father!" exclaimed the youth, warmly, "your will is law in such a case as this, and it will be impossible for my mind to change!"

"A good son, a very good son," again said the father. "Your cousin is very beautiful," he added, while the slightest of smiles appeared, which an attentive observer would have pronounced grim, but which the infatuated young artist took to be a smile of kindly pleasure.

"Yes," answered William with an emotion he could not conceal, "she is — beautiful — very beautiful!" Then with a look of deep concern, in which the light of jealousy appeared, he said, "She has thought much of another."

"You mean the young soldier," returned Daniel Garvin, with an expression which, while it startled his son, the latter could not interpret, — "Phillip Mar —"

"Prescott Marland," interrupted the son, correcting the apparent mistake of his father, whose memory was not so bad as its owner would make it appear.

"Ah, yes! Prescott Marland!"

"He thought a great deal of Emma."

"And Emma of him, you say," rejoined the broker, with a satirical smile.

"I fear so, father," uttered the young artist; and his brow was bent into a scowl which for the first time indicated that, while he was a transcript of his mother in the common acceptation of the term, there was hidden away in his composition an infusion of his father's blood.

"You need fear him not!" said the broker, harshly. "This young man was an impostor!"

"They think him dead."

"Very likely he is," returned Daniel Garvin, with a twitch of his brows. "Now go, and say nothing. I will arrange for the bridal. So prepare yourself."

William obeyed his father's command, and departed without another word.

CHAPTER XXXV.

IT is necessary that we explain the strange move which we have just seen the broker initiate.

With the incarceration of Prescott Marland in the madhouse, followed by the startling yet fiercely welcome news of the Veteran's assassination, Daniel Garvin, as we have seen, proceeded to bend his thoughts as best he could to the consideration of the future.

The blow which his schemes had received from the hand of the Veteran had unsettled his inordinate egotism, and shaken him in his own estimation. He attempted with a sort of desperation to shut out such convictions as would naturally follow so severe a jar, but they came in forms too potent for his resistance. But now as he sat day after day in his private office, a conscious murderer, having been compelled by the power of another to resort to foul assassination as the only means left for that intellect of his which he had heretofore considered so all-powerful, he felt himself tossed on the waves of circumstance, and his thoughts were troubled by a distraction which was an unusual experience of his astute brain.

In the midst of these confused deliberations one thought leaped into his mind, and for the time being took entire possession of it. It was no more nor less than the marriage of Emma Paige to his son William. Here was a waist anchor to be thrown out in case of storms, which he now could but feel were likely to burst upon him at any moment,—for he had come to look with ill-suppressed fear on the existence of that organization from which had issued the two champions who had given him so hard a combat, and which, for aught he knew, might furnish a hundred more to do battle in the same cause.

Like a monarch who seeks to intermarry a member of his family into the royal family of another kingdom, that he may there have power, so did this scheming broker conceive that if his son were married into the family of his deceased half-brother, he would be provided with a base on which he could fall back if occasion demanded.

His hate for this family did not interfere with the plan, for his son was scarcely more to him than the son of an utter stranger. If the boy had taken after him, and as he grew up manifested an interest in his own hard money-getting business, he might, perchance, have entertained toward him a degree of paternal feeling. But he did not take after him; on the contrary, he had inherited his character from his mother, whom Daniel Garvin remembered as a weak, sickly, and, to him, complaining woman, who cost him a heavy doctor's bill; and, moreover, he stupidly took to making pictures like a girl, and whined sentiment like an idiot, instead, of making calculations and counting money like a man. Occasionally he had discovered lurking in his disposition a faint shadow, as it were, of his own, but so vague that only under extraordinary circumstances, when it would assume a more distinct form, could he perceive any semblance to himself.

There was, therefore, nothing in this direction to prevent him from using the young lover as a tool, for that he was a most enraptured lover, and that his cousin was the object of his love, he had long and silently been aware. A tool would this young artist be, to follow the beck of his hand as undeviatingly as the chisel follows the hand of the master mechanic, — not ready by calculation to do a base deed, but subservient to a will that would move him as by the hand of fate.

Regarding Emma, he understood her spirit of devotion to her mother and sisters, — he knew well their present condition, their poverty and privation; and he calculated on drawing those strings of a devoted daughter's heart, which every reader has undoubtedly seen worked by some wealthy villain in story or drama, from whom we might suspect he had taken his own cue, if it were possible to imagine him either reading a story or beholding a drama, which not being able thus to imagine, we must ascribe it to his own deep study of men and things around him.

On this morning, while in the midst of confused meditations, he came suddenly to a decision which resulted in the interview we have described.

When William Garvin was released from the presence of his father, he flew as on wings through the streets toward his studio. His feet seemed scarcely to touch the pavements, and all about him as he sped along had the appearance of a dream. Everything seemed beneath him and his head had nearly touched the clouds.

Arrived at the studio he locked the door and threw himself on the lounge, and clasped his throbbing forehead with his hand.

As the light streamed down from the upper portion of one window, which only remained uncurtained, it fell directly upon this fevered youth, and revealed him a figure suitable for a representation of the fabled lover whom the pangs of love drove mad.

As one gazes about this studio he is not impressed with the presence of a thorough and proficient genius, but perceives, instead, those crude, vague, ambitious efforts of a young man, who, with an all-absorbing yet baseless enthusiasm, is essentially lacking in the important requisites of a successful artist, here and there, it is true, displaying an exceptionally striking effect, or tolerably drawn figure, which, however, are rather the result of accident than performances that are sure to be repeated. A certain grace, innate in himself, pervades much that he has done, but it is the grace with which the child, if his motions be graceful, will draw his untutored pencil over the paper before he can read the print which he may, perchance, be defacing.

In short, the works we behold are a complete expression of the character which has conceived them, — one of those natures of extreme sensibility, with emotional temperament, and aspirations which never permit him to touch the solid earth; but leaping as he supposes the winged steed that is to bear him to the region where art only exists, he awakes after a comparatively fruitless life to find that he has been astride a wooden horse, the rocking of which has to his dazed imagination seemed the progress of flying.

Perhaps no difference exists in the world more marked than that which lies between the man of true artistic genius and him who, with a highly sensitive and morbid disposition, talks of art, and dreams a comparatively inactive life away in the midst of shifting clouds. The former is possessed of the most concentrated energies, and will, like Michael Angelo, hew a law-giving Moses, paint a Sistine ceiling, defy a Pope of Rome, or defend the fortifications of a native Florence; the latter has no self-made type in history, for he makes no history, passing through the world like a fleeting shadow, except that his emotional nature, with its morbid sensibility and impressibility, is ever a source of exquisite torment and unrest.

In the young man who has now thrown himself upon the lounge we see an example of the latter type. Artist we call him, for as such he has written his name on his cards and tacked it on his door; and so entrancing are his daily dreams in connection with art that we have not the heart to deny him a title in which he takes such infinite pride.

The subdued light and solitary silence of the studio by no means tended to diminish the burning fever which now seemed to threaten him with utter prostration. His body surged with the surging blood, and presently both hands were pressed hard upon his temples as if his senses were threatening to leave by these avenues.

At length he rose, and approached an easel on which was a painting covered with crimson cloth. He nervously snatched this covering from the picture, and stood gazing upon it with unutterable rapture. It was a portrait of his lovely cousin. Having drawn in the outlines from a photograph which Emma had given him with her own hand several months before, he had occupied himself day after day during those hours when he could lock his door against all intruding visitors, in giving vent with his pencil to the ecstasies which so completely mastered him.

Indifferent though it was as a work of art, it was yet characterized by an expression which only such sentiments and emotions as had directed this entranced lover's hand could have conveyed to the canvas.

He stood before it a moment as if spell-bound, and then dropping into a chair he shaded his eyes for an instant with his hand, while a look of the most incredulous joy overspread his delicate countenance.

Then again rising to his feet he quickly advanced to the painting and pressed his lips to it. Instantly on performing this act his entire face and neck were suffused with a deep blush, and a tremor took possession of his slight frame.

"O heavens!" he exclaimed in an uncontrollable transport, "can it be possible that my father has thus ordained my happiness!" And now giving rein to his emotions, as if madness had actually seized him, he covered the forehead, eyes, cheeks, lips, with kisses of rapture.

Just before this culmination of his ungovernable emotions two knocks had been given outside, the second after a moment's interval of waiting; but the infatuated young artist had not heard them. His senses seemed closed to all things except this picture of his idol. But now the door, which in his excitement he had left unlocked, was opened and closed with a hand so firm that but little noise was made, and then a stately form appeared beyond the screen and there stopped, as if he, whose presence was so unbeknown to the owner of the studio, were transfixed with amazement.

The portrait was partly turned toward him, while the face of the young artist was to the same degree turned away. He had entered upon the scene just as the broker's son was in the midst of his final rhapsodies.

Mingled with the wild display of his intoxicating love were the most impetuous and incoherent utterances.

"My father commanded this?—Dearest cousin! are you indeed mine?—Yes, you shall be happy, for my father says it!—You will be his daughter, and you shall no longer suffer!—No! No! I will make you happy with my kisses! Thus!—and thus!—and thus!" Then with a sudden vehemence he kissed the lips again and again, and exclaimed, with a voice in which the tones of his father's voice were perceptible, "Prescott Marland was a traitor! a despicable traitor! and not worthy so much as the faintest smile of these lips!"

This vehement denunciation of the bold and generous Lieutenant seemed to startle him into a realization of the outer world, and he cast his eye about him with a frightened glance of apprehension.

In the next instant he had staggered back against the wall, with his hands outstretched for support, while his effeminate features, recently so deeply suffused with his hot blood, turned to a livid white, as he gazed appalled on that silent visitor.

It was the Veteran, pale and worn with recent suffering, which served to enhance the expression of commanding sternness and severity with which he now contemplated the awe-stricken youth before him.

CHAPTER XXXVI.

AN hour subsequent to the incidents narrated in the last chapter the Veteran came forth from the studio of William Garvin, with a countenance in which an ineffable expression of pity was mingled with a look of inexorable resolution.

We will explain to the reader first, this apparent resurrection from the dead, and then the cause of this strange visit to the studio.

The wound inflicted by the bullet from Dick Smasher's pistol was severe, but not mortal. The ball struck the skull obliquely, and glanced off, tearing the scalp badly, and rendering the intended victim of the shot insensible. He awoke to consciousness at the station-house, not long after he had been conveyed thither, and on being informed by Officer McNeal, who was by when he revived, of all that had happened, including the appearance of the reporter on the scene, his unresting brain, alive to the situation even after this terrible shock, at once apprehended who was the instigator of the attempted assassination, and he took action accordingly. To his great satisfaction he found McNeal to be not only a soldier, as stated in the report of the attempted murder, but a comrade, and ready to assist him in the design he had in view, which was to let the report of his death remain uncontradicted in the papers, until he was ready to show himself in person, and the more effectually confound the schemer whose plans and actions would now be based on the supposition of his death.

McNeal not only securely provided against discovery by any who might come to the station-house, but he took the Veteran to his own home that night, and there kept him until he was convalescent.

The object of his strange visit to William Garvin's studio, which was the first made after his confinement, was nothing less than the employment of the young artist as an agent against the designs of his own father.

To a man of the Veteran's high principles of action it cost much profound consideration before he could decide to make this move, a circumstance the more marked as his decisions were usually made with clearness and rapidity after acquiring a careful knowledge of his ground. The reader will recall the earnest expression of a hope, made to Prescott Marland as recorded in a former chapter, that he might never find it necessary to set this young man at work against his own father, together with that utterance of prophetic fears in his concluding words: "Though

Heaven only knows, in such an affair as this, what instrumentalities will have to be used before we get through with it." But the necessity for immediate action was now imperative, and no other instrument was to him available for the accomplishment of that which was now all-important to his plans: namely, the recovery of Jonas Cringar's forgery.

When he entered the studio, as we have described, he was first amazed to behold a youth, who had always impressed him as singularly shy and timid, thus kissing a portrait in the frenzied madness of love; but the next moment, when he had recognized a resemblance to Emma Paige, and heard his wild utterances, closing with the vehement denunciation of Prescott Marland, his amazement was changed into a feeling of the sternest severity, for he saw in those utterances the motive spirit of the unprincipled and scheming father.

Nothing could have more effectually subserved his purpose than this remarkable manner of his introduction. Those sensations with which William Garvin had read of the Veteran's assassination, the morning succeeding the murderous attempt upon him, were not stronger than were the counter-sensations, so to speak, which he experienced when, in the midst of his frantic demonstrations of love and wild and vehement utterances, he turned and found himself as by supernatural agencies in the presence of him whom he had thought dead.

We have told the reader how the ideal image into which he had formed the Veteran, making him as one of the gods, was shattered by the announcement of his murder in an obscure yard by common ruffians. But how can we describe the emotions with which he now beheld that formerly idealized being standing thus unsummoned and unheralded in his studio, his lofty form almost lost in the dim shades there pervading, while the pale and slightly attenuated face which received the descending and concentrated rays from the upper portion of the curtained window was bent upon him, with its strong lights and deep shadows, in the full power of its impressive grandeur? As he staggered against the wall appalled by this sombre vision, which at that moment was as terrible to his conscience as it was sombre to his sight, his mind seemed swept up as by a whirlwind, and then sent dizzy and helpless into the grasp of him who now appeared vested with attributes far transcending those which his idealizing fancies had conjured up for him before the news of the assassination.

His heart was seized with a deadly sickness, for a voice seemed to thunder to his soul that the presence of this apparent vanquisher of death itself was the signal for the annihilation of those fevered hopes which, alas! had been so fiercely kindled to be extinguished in one short hour!

But even with all this endured, it were a question whether if that which was to come had been hurled in upon him unaccompanied by the sustaining will of his visitor, his distracted mind would not have yielded to the blow. As it was, the shock, when the full purpose of the Veteran's visit was in the course of that next hour revealed to him, had wellnigh left him utterly undone.

Subject though he was to the will of the Veteran, almost as the volition of the mesmeric subject has been affirmed to be under the absolute control of the mesmerizer, yet for a brief space there ensued a struggle which threatened to burst the bonds of that powerful influence, and render vain the purposes of this extraordinary visit. But the Veteran relied not alone on the power of his great will; he depended chiefly on the justice of his cause, his will acting as a necessary instrument by which to press home this justice so that the mind of William Garvin, while it might be subjugated by forces not to be resisted, would in this condition be made to realize the righteousness of the task allotted him in the *rôle* of the remarkable drama that was being enacted. Profoundly versed in the mysteries of the human heart, this man, with a comprehensiveness of mind equal to the strength of his will, proceeded to bring to the aid of his object that all-devouring love which the broker's son experienced for his cousin, in combination with those qualities he inherited from his mother.

Without revealing all the heinousness of the father's crime, he had made known sufficient to serve his purposes. At first, though told by one whom he looked upon as reflecting the virtues of Heaven itself, the spirit of the astounded son rose against the arraignment of that father who had but just now ordained so infinite a happiness for him; but his visitor soon compelled this spirit to yield to the truth, though the realization of it nearly drove him to despair.

But we will not occupy time and space in recounting the details of an interview the like of which, fortunately, the events of life do not compel often to be enacted. Suffice it to say, that when the Veteran went forth from the studio, with his inexorable resolution softened by the heart's unutterable pity, he left a soul, which he had found so full of wild ecstasy and joy, now crushed under what to the hapless youth seemed the iron hand of a relentless fate.

Night gradually advanced, and the studio grew dark while the light that descended through the curtained winnow came only from the stars; but still that slight form remained silent and motionless, as if it were wrought from the inanimate clay in which he himself had formerly endeavored to embody his impracticable dreams.

CHAPTER XXXVII.

WE will return to Prescott Marland, whom we left thrust into the cell of a mad-house, with the thongs which bound him severed and the door locked against him, while his ears were greeted by the gibbering of a maniac.

With the use of his limbs he instantly rose to his feet, and the gibbering ceased. He looked about him and found himself in a square cell, with walls of stone and a small, heavily grated window, which was dimly defined against the slightly illuminated atmosphere of night without. But what especially attracted his attention was the appearance of two lights, which he knew to be the eyes of a human being, glaring upon him from the darkness of one of the rear corners of the cell.

Suddenly this corner was lit up by dim, greenish rays from above, and Prescott beheld a maniac chained to the wall, his face long and haggard, with the beard and hair standing out like quills of the porcupine, sitting on a square stone fixed to the floor, while with his elbows on his knees he gnawed the finger-nails of either hand, and silently glared upon his new companion.

Prescott comprehended the situation in an instant. The cell, the maniac, and the light, which he perceived to issue from an aperture in which was set a bull's-eye of greenish hue, were all intended to carry out a diabolical object, such as he had read of in published accounts of places of this kind. He knew that abject submission, lunacy, or death, one of these three, was now the only end to be expected unless he could escape a prison so horrible.

Presently the maniac began again to mumble as he gnawed his nails, while his eyes remained fixed with their wild glare on the young Lieutenant.

Prescott, who had studied somewhat into the laws that govern the eccentric courses of insanity, began with a stout heart to consider how he should conduct himself toward his crazy fellow-prisoner. It occurred to him that, even with this raving maniac, he might so exert a strong will directed by an alert mind as to make himself, to a degree at least, master of the situation, and by this means enjoy perhaps some immunity from the terrible fate which it seemed probable had been prepared for him.

While this indomitable young soldier was busy with his thoughts the maniac continued to stare upon him, his mutterings increasing with a sort of guttural violence preparatory to an outburst.

Suddenly he leaped to his feet, and, brandishing his clenched hands before him, his countenance assumed a look of defiant rage.

"Vile shadow-legs!" he yelled in a screeching voice, "I saw it with these eyes! You shot him to get your furlough of sixty days! — He writhed! he writhed! he writhed! O, how he writhed!" screamed the madman, gnashing his teeth and raising his hands in the air. Then advancing on Prescott he exclaimed, "You lie, you Rebel dog! You shot him for a furlough! He fell on your accursed *dead line* when he dropped his crutch, and you shot him, and he writhed and kicked his one leg, and you mocked him and grinned at him! He was my brother, you infernal monster! and I'll tear your heart — no, no! I'll splinter it, for 't is made for the hammer!" And, rushing to the length of his chain, he beat the air with furious blows of his fist, while Prescott stood just out of reach calmly meeting the frenzied eye before him with a steady gaze.

The young Lieutenant at once apprehended that he was in the presence of a Union soldier, who had been driven mad by terrible suffering while in the hands of the Rebels as a prisoner, and whose raving recalled to his mind, with an inward horror that even surpassed the feeling aroused by his own present terrible situation, the atrocious order from Rebel head-quarters that "Any sentinel killing a Federal soldier, approaching the dead line, shall receive a furlough of sixty days; while for wounding one, he shall receive a furlough for thirty days."

All at once the maniac ceased smiting the air, and falling back a pace, stared at the object of his insane fury, and exclaimed, —

"Thou art no Rebel, to brave me with such a front as that!"

Prescott, whose eye still remained steadily fixed, now cried in a sharp military voice of command, —

"About — face!"

The mad soldier instantly brought his feet into position, and obeyed the order, the chains clanking with his movement.

"Forward — march!"

The left foot struck out with a prompt step, and a direct line of march was taken to the stone seat.

"Halt! — about — face!"

These orders were obeyed with the same alacrity, and the maniac stood with his left hand hanging by his side, and his right slightly raised, with the fingers bent as if he held a gun at shoulder arms.

Prescott now felt in his pockets for paper and pencil; but he found them empty, which recalled the action of hands about these pockets during the struggle in the hall. Without showing his momentary discomposure, he made a movement as if about to write on a tablet, and said, in the same voice of command, —

"Your full name and rank?"

"Charles Albertson Lenning, Third Corporal!"

"You are commended for your promptness and soldierly appearance, Corporal Lenning. Left face! — Arms — port! — Break ranks! — March!"

The mad soldier, whose wild and shrunken visage lit up with a gleam of pleasure at the compliment of his improvised commander, having "broken ranks," sat down on the stone, tore a shred from his tattered clothing, and picking up his chain commenced rubbing it as if it were a part of his accoutrements, which the compliment he had received had spurred him on to polish with unusual care.

Prescott now retired to another stone seat on the opposite side of the cell, and sitting down contemplated this miserable victim of Rebel cruelty with thoughts so absorbing that he forgot for a while that he himself was reserved for a fate perhaps equally as cruel. The maniac recalled to mind the reports that continually came into camp during the war of the horrible sufferings of Union prisoners; and he again experienced that feeling of bitter hatred of the savage and barbarous spirit displayed by the Southern leaders which myriads of his comrades felt who nervously grasped their weapons and strained their eyes in the direction of the scene of those Rebel atrocities.

This present bitterness was not diminished by the thought of the odious sentiments which had already found expression in the land by some who enjoyed the reputation of loyalty during the war, — by men who did not know the difference between magnanimity and the most abject toadyism, — men who with indecent haste were rushing to necks that an enlightened mercy had spared from the noose, and clasping them with eager arms, were crying with heart-sickening fervor: "Dear friends! we rejoice to see you once more in our fold! Utter not even a word of apology, but allow us to hang like penitents on these noble bosoms and we shall be happy! You displayed as much heroism, as much devotion to a principle, as we of the North, and your motives were as high and noble! Forgive you? We shall be but too happy if you forgive us!"

We say that the thought of the prevalence of sentiments such as these did not serve to allay the bitterness of the young Lieutenant's heart as he contemplated the human wreck before him. Here was a being driven mad through the terrible sufferings inflicted by the very objects of this disgraceful flunkyism, — a being doomed day after day to reproduce in his ravings the impression of the awful scenes in which he had been both actor and witness.

This young soldier represented the true magnanimity of the war, inasmuch as he represented the spirit of the Northern armies, — a magnanimity which can only belong to that high courage, that lofty devotion to principle, which causes him who possesses it to hazard his own life to preserve that of his country. The solemnity of the conflict is felt by him as by no other. Puerilities and mawkish sentiment are sloughed off. He comes to see things in the true reality of their bearing. He apprehends, with the profoundest philosopher, that, while thousands of men, through ignorance of those principles by which humanity alone can live, may have been deluded into a monstrous Rebellion, and their crime palliated accordingly; yet no intelligent leaders could have been guilty of the brutalities practised upon Union prisoners, and at the same time have believed themselves in the right. He realizes that such atrocities are the revelation of their consciousness of guilt, writing, as it were, in characters that flame with the fires of Hell, "*We fight against God and the powers of Heaven!*"

Our young hero represents the spirit which found such noble expression in the great commander of our armies, now the chief magistrate of that Union he did so much to preserve among the nations. General Grant fought the Rebellion with iron hand; but he stood ready to receive the truly repentant, as the father received the prodigal son. He did not demand that they should grovel before him as captives before a conqueror. All he required was that they practically acknowledge their error by submitting to the arbitrament of the sword, and henceforth conduct themselves like good citizens. While on the one hand he suppresses with unflinching resolution the outbreaks of a rampant rebellious spirit, on the other he nominates to an important office one who, though prominent and active in the war, is equally so in efforts that prove his enlightened repentance.

A desire for sleep finally terminated Prescott's thoughts in this direction. The maniac, now mumbling to himself, still continued polishing the links of his chain which in his insane fancy he had metamorphosed into his accoutrements, and the young Lieutenant began to cogitate some plan by which he could secure himself against an immediate interruption by his crazy cell-mate.

Presently an idea struck him. He possessed admirable powers of imitation; so putting his hand to his mouth he sounded the tattoo like a bugle a short distance off.

The instant it struck the ears of the maniac he stopped his rubbing, and with the remark, "Old Hiram 's prompt to-night!" he carefully put aside both rag and chain, and, extending himself on the stone floor, was soon fast asleep.

Prescott, who could not help smiling with amusement at

the success of his stratagem, though in the midst of circumstances so gloomy and depressing, now laid himself down for slumber, which after a while bore him away as he was in the midst of thoughts of her who was to suffer such anguish from his sudden and mysterious absence.

He slept with tolerable soundness for several hours, when he was awakened by the howling of the maniac, who was raving again on his prison life with the Rebels.

"O God!" he screamed, "don't shoot him! He 's my brother, I tell you! Don't you see he 's got but one leg? He 's a cripple, you hireling of the Devil! He 's starving and weak, and fell against it! O God o' mercy! he 's fired!" Here the maniac covered his eyes with his hands, and stood trembling. Suddenly uncovering them he glared in front of him, and staggering back cried, "He writhes! he writhes!" Then bursting into a fit of wild laughter he exclaimed, "Have a care, you lantern-jawed Reb! or he 'll kick your grinning teeth out! Ha, ha, ha! Have a care, I say! He kicks! he kicks! Tell Bob Lee he kicks!"

Prescott suspected that he had been put in this cell with his brother-soldier to carry out a grim jest of his persecutors, who expected to have him utterly broken of his sleep, which, with the terrible presence of the madman, and the damp, noxious air of the cell, would secure the result they aimed at. He therefore decided to act cautiously, and let them be confirmed in the idea that his rest and quiet were at the mercy of the maniac; so lying quietly, and making no noise, he allowed him to rave on with his screaming, howling, and laughter, to be heard by any one above who perchance might be awake.

The mad soldier abruptly changed the scene of his terrible fantasms. Suddenly beginning to rush about as far as his clanking chain would permit, he cried as he waved his hands toward the door, "Drive in the pickets! Drive 'em in! Drive 'em in! Now scamper!" he yelled with another wild laugh, — "scamper, you infernal Johnnies! Bang! Bang! Take that and be off! Hi, hi, there! Ha, ha, ha, ha, ha!" He was evidently, with his imaginary prisoners, hunting down the vermin of one of his prisons.

Thus he continued to rave, shifting from one horrible scene to another, and picturing some of them so vividly in his madness that Prescott shuddered as he listened.

Finally, when the latter judged his purpose in reference to those above had been sufficiently accomplished, he cried in suppressed but commanding tones, —

"Corporal Lenning, silence your men, and go to sleep!"

The mad corporal immediately responded by a loud "*Hist!*" as if to his men, and again lying down was soon once more asleep.

CHAPTER XXXVIII.

LONG, interminable days, and long and gloomy nights passed by. What with the incessant exertion of his will on the maniac, the cold, damp cell, and the meagre food, — which, with a wretched attempt at wit, the brutal attendant had once informed him "was such rations as was ruin to the government to furnish two such drones in the service," — these rations, as the reader will infer from the remark, being divided between him and his mad messmate, — the strong and robust Prescott Marland was growing thin, pale, and anxious.

Once he had sprung upon this attendant as he came to the door, but besides being powerful himself the fellow had called reinforcements, and the young soldier was tumbled about in his cell, promised short rations for a few days, and threatened with the "walking-over-him" performance,— which meant that a heavy, powerful attendant would break in his ribs with his knees,— if he tried it again.

But just as even the elastic and buoyant spirit of Prescott Marland was about to settle into a sort of dull despair an event occurred on which the watchful doctor and his wolf-like, vigilant attendants had not calculated.

One night, when all was still throughout the mad-house, Prescott, who was awake, heard a peculiar clicking sound at his door; in another moment the hinges slightly creaked, and some one whispered,—

"Is Marland here?"

Prescott instantly returned the answer, also in a whisper,—

"I am here."

"I am a friend,— come!"

Prescott went to the door.

"Who are you?" he asked.

"A friend who will open every door between ourselves and freedom in an hour."

Prescott thought a moment.

"I understand you," said the other, while the young Lieutenant was made aware that this strange and unexpected friend was silently laughing. "But I am no more crazy than you are. I'm an unfortunate inventor, that is all. But I can't stop here to talk! Come with me into the open air, or stay here, as you choose. I have that here"— and he showed two pieces of bent wire— "which will pass us along without tickets."

The maniac, who had also been asleep, now stirred, and Prescott, startled for fear his voice would expose the open door, darted out, and in another moment the inventor had silently closed it, and, taking his companion by the sleeve, began ascending a stairway.

The young Lieutenant looked back and mentally uttered a "good-by," and sighed as he thought of the unfortunate being whom he had learned to regard, with all his raving madness, with the sympathy of a messmate.

"If I succeed in getting out of here, my poor comrade, you shall have better quarters than this nest of devils furnishes you!" he exclaimed to himself as he cautiously mounted the stairs.

As each succeeding door was reached his guide proved as good as his word. To Prescott's astonishment, bolt after bolt of the heavy locks, which fastened insane patients and sane prisoners alike in this abominable and falsely named asylum, yielded to the pressure of his simple implements, and flew back to let them pass.

Once they stopped in suspense, startled by a noise above. It was only the voice of a harmless lunatic. They heard nothing else and went on.

They neared the hall which led to the front door.

"Here," whispered the inventor, "is the doctor's private office."

A thought struck Prescott.

"If I but had a light," said he, "I would like to take a survey of this same office."

"It shall be done," said his companion with another of those silent laughs. Opening the door with his magic wires he bade Prescott enter, and following him took a match from some cotton-padding which he got at through a rent in his vest, and lit it, at the same time saying with a grin, "When these stupid fellows prove a match for Jacob Easter then Jacob Easter 'll give up the match."

Prescott's eyes now fell upon a small nursery-lamp, which had evidently been left there that night by Dr. Pennell in somewhat of a hurry, inasmuch as the cap was left carelessly hanging. After a little effort the lamp was lighted, and the young Lieutenant, with the assistance of the inventor, quickly proceeded to business.

With the aid of smaller instruments than he had been using, which he improvised from the wire of the doctor's gas-shade, the inventor rapidly opened desk, drawers, and safe, the lock of which was not complicated, and all papers that Prescott could lay hands on were confiscated as contraband of war. Tying them into a bundle quicker even than he had ever packed his knapsack on a ten minutes' notice to march, he gave the word to his companion to put out the light, and left the office with a look of supreme satisfaction.

When they arrived at the front door Prescott's heart beat with quickened pulse as in anticipation he breathed the free air of heaven into those lungs that had for so many days inhaled the pestiferous vapors of his cell.

This lock gave the inventor more trouble than had any of the others.

While he was working away at the obstinate bolts they heard a loud yawn; and then a rough voice, which Prescott recognized as the one that sung his funeral dirge when he was borne to his gloomy quarters, called out, —

"Betty! have done with that scratching! You know what I told ye if ye did n't stop that kind of night work!"

The inventor reached out his hand, and placed it over the young Lieutenant's mouth as a warning for perfect silence; but the latter was already as motionless as were he and the scouts whom he often commanded, when in the night they would suddenly find themselves in the vicinity of Rebel pickets, though as he listened a light would have revealed a face in which the determination to die rather than again be incarcerated was strongly apparent.

But nothing more was heard. Silence again reigned throughout the mad-house, broken only by a faint howl, which Prescott shudderingly fancied to be the wail of the mad corporal on finding his commander gone, and once more the inventor essayed to pick the last lock, his very fingers seeming conscious of the necessity for the most extreme caution.

Presently one or two sounds, so slight that they could hardly be called clicks, were heard, and then the door was silently swung on its hinges, and in another instant the two captives stood in the open air.

Closing the door as quickly and silently as he had opened it, the inventor exclaimed in a whisper, —

"Now the sooner our legs carry us out of this the better!"

And thereupon they sped away, keeping a lookout for patrolmen, who might take them to be thieves.

When they felt confident that they had put themselves beyond all attempts at pursuit, they slackened their pace and fell into conversation.

Prescott expressed his astonishment at what had just been done by his companion.

"If I had been told all this I should scarcely have believed the story," he said.

The inventor laughed. "With the exception of taking along a companion as I have to-night, all this has been done before in a much larger place than this den of iniquity, and under more extraordinary circumstances. The freedom given me enabled me, with eyes and ears made alert by a speedy knowledge of the character of the place, to post myself in regard to your sanity and the number of your cell; and as for my performance with my wires, if you would like to hear it, I will tell you what happened in Massachusetts several years ago, which really suggested to me what you have just seen me do."

"Now is the very time to hear it," answered Prescott. "After my incarceration in that terrible cell with the ravings of a madman forever in my ears, nothing would please me more than a narrative of more wonderful exploits than yours has been to-night."

"It happened several years ago in Boston and vicinity, and the actor was an inventor like myself," said the other. "He had been quite sick, his illness threatening to settle on the lungs. One day he was attacked with a paroxysm, as near as I could ascertain, and he cried out for air. Those about him would give him none. He was suffocating, and again demanded air, telling the servant to let down the window; but he was again refused, and interference combined with the refusal in a manner which tended to excite his already fevered brain, and a will naturally intense and calculated to repel such interference. His chest was now terribly oppressed, and leaping from his bed he opened the window himself. It was immediately closed by one whom he considered had no authority to do so. This treatment, together with his condition, which those about him should have seen required that his wish be granted, increased his paroxysm to such a degree that he rushed out of the room and through the entry crying, "Air! air!" and reaching the front door he kicked out the side-lights and commenced breathing the fresh air into his laboring lungs.

"The cry now arose, 'He's mad! he's mad!' and strong

men for whom he entertained an intense personal dislike were sent for, and forthwith everything was done to increase a temporary paroxysm — started by congestion and aggravated by unwise treatment — into the symptoms of madness. While the men whom he so intensely disliked were hastening to ignorantly do all in their power to increase these symptoms, he was making his way to the yard for "air! more air!"

"The end of it was, he was driven an hour or so afterwards to the Somerville Asylum, and there treated as insane. He had a high spirit, and would not brook being treated as a madman. He did not choose to lie and cringe, nor did he wish to adopt the policy of enduring his treatment with pretended patience. He behaved as you or I would, if any one should come to our houses and undertake to treat us as if we were crazy. If you have studied the history of insanity to any extent, you will readily apprehend that if once a sane man gets into an asylum as an insane man, any display of that high spirit with which sanity will repel insulting and unjust treatment will be set down, with perhaps rare exceptions, as the evidence of insanity!

"'I am going to leave your place,' said my fellow-craftsman one day to Dr. ——, 'and you can't prevent me.' The doctor smiled. But his smiling did n't prevent his so-called patient from keeping his word; for being allowed to walk in the garden, one day he secured an apple-twig, and that night with this and a piece of wire he picked every lock that stood in his way, and went home."

"It seems incredible!" exclaimed Prescott.

"Hold on," said the inventor. "I have n't finished yet. You see this going directly home was to me the only really insane act he seems to have committed. The doctor sent right over there as soon as he found him gone, and his wife, whom I understand to have been a woman of rare excellence, was induced by the ill-considered warnings that were poured into her ears, to give her consent that he be again incarcerated. He was accordingly seized and taken back to the asylum, where he complained he was treated worse than he was before, — and he declared that his former treatment was bad enough. He told Dr. —— a second time that he should leave. I don't recollect distinctly what he reported the doctor's answer to be, but I think it was a threat of severe punishment if he should attempt it. But go he did, in spite of an extra watch that was set on him, this time picking his way out with a wire and bent nail, if I remember aright."

"And did they catch him again?" asked Prescott, deeply interested in this remarkable account.

"They did not. He hid in a cornfield the rest of the night, and then contrived to send a message to his wife through relations in Charlestown, informing her of his escape, and telling her that if she would send word that he could return home and remain in peace, he would come; but if not, he should leave the place, I think forever."

"And she sent the promise?" said Prescott.

"Yes. And the striking part is, that this man who had been twice incarcerated in an asylum, escaping the first time and then the second, in spite of the doctor who pronounced him insane, and treated him as such, and, according to his statements, in a manner to be condemned, — this man to-day is exactly the man, as to sanity, that he was when he picked his way out of the asylum; and yet since that time he not only has borne a sound reputation as a worthy and useful citizen, but has produced an invention the value of which may be judged from innumerable infringements, and has fought his way back in some degree to the pecuniary position which he enjoyed before his sickness, but which he lost during this illness through the dishonesty of others; moreover, having lost his first wife, he has again married, — which is the only evidence of insanity, I presume, that even Dr. —— would venture to adduce." *

Prescott, who had continued beyond the corner where he was to turn, that he might not interrupt his companion's interesting narration, now stopped, and after a moment's thought he said, —

"This seems to me an impressive lesson in reference to private asylums. If such a case could happen in a public asylum under the direction of a State which is known to devote so much attention to the subject of insanity, what may we not expect of those private mad-houses where it is for the interest of the proprietors to have their establishments well filled, and which, say what men please, are to a degree irresponsible? Of course this villain, from whose clutches we have just escaped, is an exception. He evidently is a monster who, like the wolves that put on the preacher's garb as a covering for their crimes, institutes a private mad-house as a means for his own infamous ends, — and if I have that here," he said tapping the bundle of papers taken from Dr. Pennell's office, "that will in any way enable me to break up his den, I shall account my sojourn under his roof as well recompensed. But aside from this fellow, I think there is something about private mad-houses which requires that they be looked into."

"You speak my thought," responded the inventor, shaking hands with the young Lieutenant. "I know myself to be the intended victim of designing men, and I suppose

* This account is literally true, the authors being personally cognizant of the facts.

you know equally as well from whence your madness springs!"

"I presume I do," returned Prescott, compressing his lips in a manner that boded ill to those whom the inventor's words called up to his mind. Then with another shake of the hand they parted, promising to see each other again.

CHAPTER XXXIX.

PRESCOTT had scarcely passed a dozen blocks when a man suddenly appeared from a side street, and met him on the corner under a street-lamp.

"Hallo!" exclaimed this man. "Why, comrade! what in the name of these short hours brings you here?"

Prescott saw to his surprise that it was Charles Roberts.

Grasping his hand he in turn exclaimed,—

"Comrade Roberts! You here this time of night!"

"Well," said Roberts, laughing, "my presence answers your question, but my question remains unanswered.".

"True," returned Prescott, with a change of countenance. "I promise to tell you at some other time, and also why I am looking a little strange and sickly, which I perceive you are wondering at."

"All right." And as the countenance of the other also changed he said, "I am just returning from a comrade who will tell no more of his adventures here. I watched with him. He died two hours ago, and I remained to help attend to the body."

"Does he leave a family?"

"Yes, but they shall be cared for."

"They are poor, then?"

"Yes; but, thank God! we are now so organized that we can get at many of our comrades' families and relieve them, from the funds with which so many of our generous citizens respond to our call. Fortunately one or two of these children are nearly old enough to help the whole family, and all they need is a little bridging over."

The Deering family was continually in Prescott's mind. He now asked Roberts if he had yet heard from them.

"Heard from them! Heavens, comrade! Save me from another sight like that!"

"My worst fears were realized, then!"

"Realized, comrade! You could not have pictured it! Up, up, up I went, the broken and rickety stairs threatening to crush in at every step, and then I opened a door that was ready to fall at a touch, and there was a sight that beggars my tongue to describe to you! My first exclamation was, '*Great God! is this a soldier's family?*' I 've read of such scenes, but I never saw one before. They were dying of starvation, comrade, in a wretched, dilapidated attic, the roof broken in, and no fire! Another day of such sickness and starvation would have finished the boy, and two days would have seen the sad work completed! Scarcely was there flesh enough on the whole four from which to draw a single drop of blood. Their eyes were as sunken as the eyes of the dead, and their faces looked like masks of parchment! And the cold was raw enough to make me shiver even in my warm garments!"

"And they but meagrely dressed?" uttered Prescott, forgetting his own recent trials in the contemplation of this suffering family.

"'Dressed!' Comrade, if I could but have marched that wife and those three children of a fallen soldier through these streets as they then looked, with their pinched and sickly visages, and their attenuated forms draggling with their scant and tattered garments, and placed a banner over them with the motto, 'BEHOLD A FAMILY OF THE COUNTRY'S DEFENDERS!' I fear me more than one heart would have bled that does not often move with emotion, and eyes that rarely weep would have viewed the passing train through tears they could not hold back!"

"But, thank God, you have found them!" exclaimed Prescott, deeply affected.

"Yes. It was a long, close search, but I persevered and traced them at last. My first move was to obtain nourishing food. Ah, comrade! you should have seen the two little girls eat! The crippled one would have killed herself if I had not stood by to watch her. Then I had them removed to comfortable quarters, and they are all doing well. It won't be long before Joseph will be able to go to work for their support."

"From all accounts this Joseph is a noble boy, and deserves a better position than vending candy on the cars."

"The Grand Army will attend to that. As soon as he is sufficiently recovered he shall not want for a good situation that will pay him enough to make them comfortable, with what the mother may be able to earn; and the G. A. R. will see that she has plenty to do, at a price that will pay for her labor."

"Comrade!" exclaimed Prescott, clasping the other's hand, "may Heaven bless the soldier who conceived and initiated the Grand Army of the Republic! This one family preserved from so terrible a death is sufficient to repay our Order in this city for years of labor!"

"True, comrade! every word true! But this is only one of many cases — though the others may not be so bad —

which we have already taken in hand, and which would probably not have been reached by any but ourselves. The idea of the soldier taking care of the family of the soldier has been tested to the satisfaction of every one who desires that the vows made to the Union volunteer when he enlisted shall be sacredly fulfilled. And I tell you, comrade, I think every day of the talk we had on the train about the principles of our Order. As one case after another comes up where we find soldiers' families in want and are able to relieve them, they each add emphasis to that principle whereby we are to eschew all acts which demoralize, and which are sure in the end to prove disastrous.

"I knew your experience here would confirm in your mind all we then said."

"My observation has also shown me that care must be taken not to tire our friends by incessant cries dinned into their ears. Let us be bold, but circumspect; not backward in pressing the just claims of the soldier, but judicious in so doing. If Justice herself bawls with a loud voice she is repelled, — you know that, comrade, — and the soldier cannot expect to fare better. Let us rather imitate our own victorious commanders, whose heads and arms did the work, the tongue wagging sufficiently for the purpose, but no more."

"You are right, comrade. The soldier should make it a point to teach rather than be taught that practical common sense which it is believed service in the field imparts. Of course it is the impulse of the soldier to fight; but it is also his training to see that he fights to some purpose."

"That 's so every time! As regards politics, I by no means would advise silence where citizens as represented by their local governments manifestly fail year after year to keep their pledges to the soldiers, as in the case of monuments to the memory of the fallen, and other forms in which the promises of a nation can only be fulfilled through such governments. Here it may become absolutely necessary that the soldiers rise in their united strength and enforce the fulfilment of these pledges. But not as politicians, — simply as the executors of justice."

"And executors of the loyal and patriotic spirit of the country too."

"Yes. But this once accomplished, let the soldier not display weakness, and become demoralized by the smell of the political blood which may have been necessarily spilt in the operation. Let him fall back to his proper base, and attend to the work that belongs to him; and if he wishes to engage in politics simply as a politician, let him not advance his claims in this business as a member of the Grand Army of the Republic, nor in any way attempt to involve the G. A. R. in political schemes. My sentiments on this subject have been made if possible the more decided by a letter which I received last week from a soldier, where no Post has yet been organized, who writes that a soldiers' club to which he belongs, though flourishing a short time since, is now threatened with dissolution from tampering with politics, having not only lost the respect and sympathy of the citizens, but created dissension in their own ranks. The difficulty was, they were made use of by an ambitious member, under the specious plea that if he got into office he should look out for the soldier at every turn."

"A good warning," replied Prescott. "In view of all these things, it is gratifying to know that the national officers of the Order are so strict and emphatic in their injunctions to shun all such causes of disaffection in organized bodies."

"And no Order should be kept more pure than ours," responded Roberts. "Besides its beneficent work, the Grand Army of the Republic is to stand as the representative of that loyalty and patriotism which has in so sublime a manner been displayed in the recent conflict of liberty and freedom against slavery and servitude,—which in a day transformed the American citizen into a soldier with rifle on his shoulder and knapsack at his back, and sustained him through the horrors of one of the most terrible of wars, with a spirit which only a great cause can inspire! Comrade, I think you will agree with me that the principles which govern our Order are the only principles that can insure a thorough and enduring harmony between the North and South. No reconciliation can endure which is not founded in justice; and especially is no reconciliation sure to abide between the North and South that is not founded in that justice which is the result of single-minded devotion to the highest and best interests of the whole country as a country of freedom. And who so likely to appreciate the sacred institutions of liberty as those who have fought to maintain them? They had too solemn a duty to perform easily to forget that for which they offered up their lives. No; let our principles of Fraternity, Charity, and Loyalty abide and perform their high mission, uncontaminated by those influences which, emanating from private ambition and political aspirations, can only touch to destroy."

"Nobly uttered, comrade!" exclaimed Prescott. "There 's not a true member of the G. A. R. that will not indorse that! While outside issues can only tend to diminish the efficiency in respect to charity, a proper consideration of these great principles of which you speak can but enhance that efficiency by inspiring within us yet higher and more enduring motives of action. I do not understand you to oppose the sentiment," he continued, "which demands that the soldier, other things being equal, shall have the preference in all offices of trust and emolument at the disposal of the government they fought to preserve; and that the promises of citizens, to the effect that the deserving soldier should not lack for employment if their efforts could secure it for him, and other assurances of this kind, be fulfilled in the spirit with which they were made."

"No, indeed! On the contrary, I stand ready to pronounce any other line of conduct, by either government or citizens, as ingratitude and a violation of their pledges. I regret to say that there have been too many instances in connection with government employ where the just claims of the soldier have been ignored. It is well known, for example, that at the navy-yards such cases have occurred with reprehensible frequency, and demand the rebuke of the loyal public!"

"You express my own mind. I am convinced these are the sentiments of all just and candid citizens, and to your last words they would give an outspoken response, were they knowing to the facts."

Prescott and Roberts were now about to part.

"Tell me, comrade," said the young Lieutenant, "where the Deering family may be found. There are those who will not let many hours pass before visiting them in their new quarters."

Roberts, taking out the memorandum-book in which Prescott had with such painful emotions seen the name of Allen Paige's family entered, stopped by a street-lamp and wrote the desired direction on a leaf, and tearing it out, gave it to him.

"Thank you," said Prescott, reading it: "*Joseph Deering's*

family, No. — Eighth Avenue." And the noble fellow actually forgot for the moment the anticipated delight of once more being in Emma's presence, in thinking of the happiness of the whole family when he should give them this direction, and tell them what the Grand Army had done for the poor sufferers to whom it would guide them.

"You promised to tell me if the family of Allen Paige should need aid from us," said Roberts. "Have you heard from them lately?"

"I shall probably see them to-morrow," replied Prescott, while a shadow passed over his face; "and if they need assistance, I'll not fail to inform you. Good night."

"Good night."

CHAPTER XL.

OUR present chapter opens not far from the Bowery, in Chatham Street. We enter a building which seems nodding to its neighbor over the way; and, mounting three flights of stairs, pass into a kind of loft, now occupied by one of those characters which only New York and California combined can produce.

As the occupant is out for a few moments, we will take a survey of this singular chamber. One would think, at first sight, that he was inside a menagerie. Bear and buffalo skins form the bed; a panther-skin covers one wooden chair and the hide of a wolf another. A skin so worn that it would be difficult to name it is spread upon the floor as a mat; and the boards which form the walls of the room are covered with a variety of unique California relics, such as an eccentric adventurer would be likely to bring East as trophies of his exploits in that famous region. The effect of these embellishments was enhanced by two fantastic suits, such as are worn by circus clowns.

A lasso coiled over a nail, one end carried in a picturesque way over two or three adjoining nails, tells of exploits on the prairies with the national weapon of the Mexicans, which perchance brought down the poor buffalo whose hide now serves for a couch.

Several cannon-balls of various sizes appear in one corner of the loft, not far from which lies a small pile of hides that bear evidence of long and rough usage; while in different parts of the room are heavy weights, clubs, and other implements suggestive of athletic amusement.

Presently the proprietor of this grotesque apartment enters, and we behold a man of powerful frame, with a face combining simplicity and shrewdness. His gait has that peculiar rolling motion characteristic of the powerful gymnast, whereby is indicated the perfect "floating" of the hips, which seems to be the very foundation of that statuesque grace, yet unrivalled, that characterizes the works of the ancient Greeks.

Preparing his dress for exercise, he takes a couple of the largest clubs and flourishes them about his head as though they were made of bamboo. Then he picks up two of the heaviest weights, and gives them such a handling as indicates prodigious strength.

After practising awhile with these weights, he puts them down, and approaches that part of the loft where lie the cannon-balls and worn hides. Drawing the latter a little farther into the room he spreads them so as to cover a circular space about four feet in diameter, and then grasping a large ball he proceeds to the performance of the remarkable feats of the circus arena, that causes the spectator to hold his breath as he follows the round mass of iron running about the arms and chest of the performer, and thrown high in the air to fall heavily upon his massive neck.

The use of the skins is now apparent, for as he allows the ball to come to the floor after each performance, it falls on them with so deadened a sound that those below cannot be disturbed in the least.

We will give a brief sketch of this extraordinary character.

His real name we never learned. He went by two *aliases*, Wrenchy and Saxey; as the former is the name by which he was more generally known, we will use it ourselves. During the Mexican war he went out in Stephenson's notorious New York regiment, which was ordered to California. After it was disbanded there, Wrenchy fell into the ranks of that lawless faction known as the *Hounds*, which was composed of the most reckless characters who gathered so rapidly in California when the gold-fever spread through the country. Deserters from merchant-vessels and men-of-war helped fill their ranks, in which Stephenson's discharged volunteers were the master spirits. These *Hounds* were led by such men as Sam Roberts and Jack Powers, the latter of whom is reported to have once hired ten men, at $25 a day, to take three wagon-loads of specie, won by gambling, from the mines down to Stockton. Men like Billy Mulligan and Wrenchy associated with him as special aids. There was a certain picturesqueness about this band, their hats being adorned with strings of beads and a handkerchief, to distinguish them from the *Coyotes*, the opposing faction, which was composed of those determined to sustain the laws, and protect the *foreigners*, who were chiefly Chilians and Senorians, and whom the *Hounds* made the special objects of their persecution.

The term *Coyotes* was applied by the *Hounds* to their opponents because the latter were industrious miners, always burrowing in the ground like the small prairie-wolf of that name. It acquired additional significance from the fact that often the lawless miner and the law-abiding miner would stake out claims that joined on the same lead, and then while the former would rest on his pickaxe the other would dig down to the gold, and when there would occasionally burrow into his lazy neighbor's claim, replacing ore with dirt. On the other hand, the lawless fellows would often wait till these industrious miners had struck gold, and then leap in and drive them off, sending the contents of their pistols after them as they fled through the camp. Hence the term *Hounds,* the chief occupation of the dog for which they were thus named being to hunt down the coyote on the prairies when crossing with the trains.

An idea of the state of society in California at this period may be formed from the fact that in Tuolumne County, with a population of 15,000, there were 1,700 murders in one year, and the only man hanged was a man that stole a mule!

While engaged in his lawless proceedings as a *Hound,* Wrenchy would have lost his life on one occasion, had it not been for the interposition, under circumstances of rare magnanimity, of Julius Hammond, who was then acting as sheriff, and who appreciated what was really good in the man.

After running a course of this kind of life he travelled with Winde & Provost's circus as the "Strong Man," and was famous as a "cannon-ball tosser," besides being a first-rate acrobat and clown.

The Rebellion brought him East; he having enlisted in the California Battalion which was attached to the Second Massachusetts Cavalry; and he is now back again in New

York, the practice in which we see him at present engaged indicating that he still catches cannon-balls on his neck to put bread into his stomach, which occupation his remarkable constitution has enabled him to continue beyond the age usually attained by such men.

After changing awhile to two smaller balls, the gymnast returned to the large one, and with the cry, "Come, my little mouse! run! run! run!" he commenced rolling it about on his person until it seemed alive. Presently grasping it in both hands he gave it a more than ordinarily strong toss, and bent his head to receive it as usual on his neck.

Just as it was reaching its highest altitude the door opened, and a man with a strong, bear-like form, full black beard, and green spectacles entered.

He started back in alarm as his eye fell on the heavy sphere of iron just beginning to descend upon the bended neck of the athlete; and when it struck with its terrible weight he could not suppress an ejaculation.

The clown turned, and on seeing his alarmed visitor cried out with a laugh, — "*Hyer*,* stranger! coming into the show as a deadhead? Ye look scared, old hoss! Conscience bad, eh? Then I 'll set one of my mice after ye!"

His mice were, as we have seen, his cannon-balls.

As Wrenchy thus addressed him, the visitor started in alarm, for his conscience instinctively made that in earnest which the athlete only meant in play.

That his conscience is bad the reader will at once apprehend when we inform him that this bearded stranger with the green spectacles is none other than the redoubtable Daniel Garvin, who as we now look at him recalls a statement we heard some time ago, that insanity ran in this

* Pronounced Hi-yar'.

family of bilious temperament and intense passions. His present errand, undertaken in so questionable a guise, has certainly an insane tinge to it.

He has found himself driven into a corner, and he rushes hither and thither like a wild animal who is irresistibly driven into an enclosure by converging fires.

This deep-dyed sinner realizes that the wicked have no place to stand upon, and when the desperate clutch which they have fastened on the object of their criminal cupidity is threatened, they move their feet to find no firm and solid earth, — nothing but miry and slippery places.

The disconcerted broker, the forces of whose intellect have become to a degree demoralized, has received news of the failure of the attempt to assassinate the Veteran, and like the worst class of Southern Rebels, who, after their power had been broken in a fair fight, savagely resorted to the most brutal means to continue their flagrant work, so this unprincipled man of schemes can see no way through his own iniquitous business except by a continuance of such atrocious instrumentalities as he has already found himself compelled to use.

It did not take the athlete long to learn the object of his visitor. He had met such men before, but he inwardly pronounced the broker the greatest scoundrel of them all, and resolved to repay him for so complimentary a call, which was made under the supposition that he was a cold-blooded hireling. As a man of quaint humor, also, he perceived that game for a little entertainment was here offered him.

This singular being therefore met his would-be employer in the performance of a dastardly deed full half-way, and put on such an air that Satan himself, with all his reputed shrewdness, would have been taken in were he in Garvin's place. As his visitor opened his business in a manner as cautiously as one would cut a bit of steel from the cornea of a machinist's eye, the clown lit up his face with a gleam of savage intelligence, mingled with fear and apprehension. He fixed upon the broker a look of the most intense suspicion, and cast his glance with subdued fierceness well assumed on one of the heavy clubs near by. In short, he ogled his tempter into the self-complacent idea that his never-failing sagacity had discovered in the returned Californian a criminal, on whose secret consciousness of guilt he could work with his usual subtlety and mastery of the manipulative art. The result was, that in the course of an hour this clown of the strong muscle, with a face so simple, and yet so shrewd, was in possession of the whole plot.

He also had the name of the intended victim; and this was where he felt as if he had nearly exposed himself. When the broker first uttered it, the old-time *Hound* and recent soldier gave a start which caused a shade of suspicion to pass over the ever-wary face of the schemer. Wrenchy perceived this, and hastened to remove it. Frowning and gnashing his teeth, he exclaimed in a suppressed but intensely vindictive voice, —

"Was this Hammond in California in 1849 as a sheriff?"

"He was," returned the broker with triumphant emphasis.

"Then may the Devil take him, when I've done with him! You perhaps have heard of the *Hounds*, a fine set of fellows in California at that time?"

"I have."

"Well!" cried the "cannon-ball tosser," in a voice like the rolling of distant thunder, "I was a *Hound*, and this Hammond was a sheriff!" And he fixed on the broker a diabolical look which brought to the face of the latter a gleam of secret exultation. In another moment the latter was nodding with a look of the most infusive and sympathetic villany.

"I see! I see!" he said, showing his own white teeth under his false mustache, in a manner which suggested to the athlete a charnel-house lit up by the moonlight. "Those rascally sheriffs! They were the ones that ought to have been hung!"

Wrenchy continued to chew his self-generated rage, and looked with a furtive scowl toward a heavy horse-pistol which helped adorn the side of the loft.

At that moment the clock struck seven, and this well-assumed villain sprang to his feet, and turning slightly away, as if, with the instinct of guilt, to conceal his watch, — a gold one which he had carried as a keepsake for fifteen years, — he exclaimed, —

"Too many irons in the fire spoils the whole! If I have n't slipped up on this other engagement I 'm a lucky dog!" Then suddenly lowering his voice almost to a whisper, he said, "Be here to-morrow at this time, and" — with a knowing and ferocious leer — "we 'll start this job to our mutual satisfaction."

The broker departed, saying to himself with an intelligent nod, —

"That watch had the snuff of blood about it. This is verily a most unconscionable villain!"

CHAPTER XLI.

ABOUT the time the foregoing visit was made by the broker to the fantastic apartment of the athlete, the object of his conspiracy was closeted with Jonas Cringar.

The pen would fail to convey an idea of the emotions experienced by the desolate merchant when he received information from Billings, the book-keeper, that the Veteran was not dead as reported, but was actually at that moment moving with the old indomitable will in the working of his plans to confound the now desperate Garvin. It seemed to his reacting spirit as if the very hand of Heaven had reached down to direct the battle against his Satanic tempter.

The interveiw in question was of a very different character from the one we have formerly described, as the reader will readily imagine. Jonas Cringar greeted the Veteran, not with the stare of consternation which was then his welcome, but his haggard face bore a look of joy unutterable. And this joy was not for himself alone, but for those whom he had so deeply wronged; for since his heart had been opened to the Veteran on that first visit he had continually prayed to God that the promise regarding the family of Allen Paige, which the presence of his visitor then awakened in his soul, might in some providential manner be fulfilled.

The Veteran gave an account of the attempted assassination, and the manner in which he had secluded himself during his recovery; and then after speaking of the Paige family (whose rejoicing on once more seeing their friend alive was one of those scenes which brightened a life that had seen many shadows), and the ominous disappearance of Prescott Marland, he came to the subject of the forgery. He told Cringar of the visit to the studio of William Garvin for the purpose we have previously mentioned.

"It is very sad!" uttered the merchant, while the look of wearing pain on his features increased in such a manner as to indicate the direction of his thoughts. "How much does one reckless act cost! A son against a father! General, if this unhappy young man accomplishes the object you have assigned him he secures his own father's downfall!"

"It is not pleasant to think of," said the Veteran with deep feeling. "More especially has it become painful since his interview with me last evening. He came to me and wept as he told me of the trial which his heart had experienced, since he consented to undertake the recovery of that forgery. I could see that it was in danger of driving him mad, and I am informed that madness runs somewhat in that blood."

"My God!" ejaculated the merchant under his breath as he recalled the broker's appearance that night when Simple Sal's laugh burst upon them, "I think it does!"

"He told me," continued the Veteran, "that he had wrought himself up to an attempt night before last, but the Laocoön so distracted his mind that he was utterly unfitted for the work."

"The Laocoön!" exclaimed Cringar in astonishment.

"Yes. He said that with his mind strung to the working-point, but still in despair at the very thought that he must do it, he was passing down Broadway, and thinking to find a little relief from a distraction which was little short of craziness, he entered an art store to view the works there on exhibition. Nothing could fix his attention.

All seemed in a whirl. Presently he came to a small copy of the Laocoön in alabaster. This commanded more of his attention, for the agony which the ancient sculptor has depicted with such power was to him a reflex of his own internal state. He said it held him as by fascination, and he seemed to exult in measuring his own torments with theirs. But erelong the group was changed, to him, into a terrible vision. The two sons became as mist before his eyes, and the father alone riveted his gaze. The awful agony and anguish which is expressed in the face and throughout the entire body held him in a trance of stupefied horror, for he had suddenly seen that struggling priest of Neptune transformed into his own father, and himself he saw in the dread serpent whose fangs, charged to his frenzied mind with venom, were fastened in the palpitating side! He felt himself rooted to the floor, and his soul cried out to him, as if it were another being separate from himself, '*The fangs of the son are prepared for the father! Let him strike and see his father die!*' Then he said the statue and the serpent seemed to live, and he witnessed as a reality the dying struggles of the one, while the skin of the other swelled and quivered, and its eyes shot forth flames, as the folds tightened about its victim, and its jaws, with their deadly fangs, closed deeper and deeper into the purpling flesh. Then everything swam, and he knew no more till he found himself lying on a couch with a group of persons around him, from whom he learned that he had fainted."

"This is indeed terrible!" exclaimed the merchant, through whom there shot a pang of remorse wellnigh as overwhelming as the anguish described by the wretched young artist.

"So terrible," said the Veteran, "that I could not do

otherwise than tell him that he should be released from the unnatural office, — for the present, at least, — and I would, if possible, study up some other means of accomplishing the object."

"And this made him happy!"

"I cannot say so much as that," returned the Veteran, thoughtfully. "He seemed distressed by an internal conflict. He knows that those whom he deeply esteems are in their turn suffering from the fangs of their unnatural relative, and will continue to suffer till the power which he obtained by treachery shall have been taken from him."

The merchant now became absorbed in the most gloomy thoughts, and the Veteran took his leave, after a few kindly words, which the former responded to without seeming to understand.

That evening the Veteran sat in his room, meditating on the interview with William Garvin which he had described to the merchant, and turning over in his mind one expedient after another by which he might attain his end without the aid of this miserable son of the guilty broker.

While in the midst of these meditations a rap sounded on his door. He opened it and Wrenchy stood before him!

They recognized each other at once, and their greeting was a hearty one. Especially was this the case with the gymnast, who ever remembered the Veteran with gratitude for saving his life.

After a little introductory talk about the old times, Wrenchy entered at once on the business for which he had called, with an account of the extraordinary visit made him that evening by the man with the black beard and green spectacles. His description was close, and the ready mind of the Veteran found no difficulty in identifying this strange and sinister visitor.

"When he came to your name I was pretty nigh spoiling the whole thing," said the clown. "But I caught my balance, and gave him such a taste of the diabolical that he saw you pinned right there before his black devil's eyes!"

"You are to meet him again to-morrow?"

"Yes."

The Veteran's brows were for a moment contracted in thought, and then a smile that was scarcely perceptible stole over his face.

"Wrenchy," said he, "do you think you could handle your fingers with your former skill?"

By one of those apparent anomalies of nature this "strong man," who tossed cannon-balls so easily that he called them his "mice," was wonderfully expert in the manipulation of minute objects.

"*Quien sabe?*" he laughed, mixing his dialect as he and the Veteran were wont to do in California,—"Who know?" Then he added, "If you will stand up a moment, I will show you."

The Veteran stood up.

"Now," said the ex-*Hound*, "the day was when I could engage a man's attention and then show him this."

The Veteran looked casually down at the other's extended palm, and to his astonishment he saw his watch therein.

"I'll put it back," said Wrenchy; and he proceeded to attach it to the chain and replace it in the fob. "*Hyer!*" he exclaimed, and making a pretence of stooping for it, he presented the Veteran with his memorandum-book.

"A truce!" cried the latter, laughing. "If my eyes ever trouble me I'll get you to take them out! But for the time being I'll keep them to look upon a document which

I believe, with your skill, you can obtain as readily as you just now obtained my memorandum-book." And thereupon he proceeded to enlighten the athlete as to the object of the question which caused his remarkable display of the sleight-of-hand talent. This object was to engage him in a plan for the recovery of the forgery and the release of William Garvin.

The gymnast gave emphatic approval. It was a work that pleased him. His honest course of life for several years past had afforded him no opportunity for the actual use of his accomplishments in this direction, though he had from habit and taste kept up his skill, occasionally delighting a circle of friends by tricks of magic, in which he excelled, and which to see this Hercules perform was like witnessing the exquisitely finished boxing of the grizzly bear.

"For once we can give the 'cly-faker' profession a touch of honesty," he said with a broad grin.

The Veteran experienced a deep feeling of relief when he thought of the load that would be taken from the suffering heart of William Garvin, if his object could thus be accomplished through the very instrumentality which the broker would make use of for his own heinous ends, thus doing his work through the laws of retribution.

CHAPTER XLII.

ON the following day the disguised broker again appeared at the apartment of the gymnast, according to appointment. He was received by that odd genius in the fantastic suit of a clown. The latter did not take up much time in preliminaries on this occasion, but at once proceeded to call the attention of his would-be employer to the lasso which hung festooned upon the wall.

The eyes of the latter glistened under his green spectacles. This thong of raw-hide in the hands of the "cannon-ball tosser" and around the neck of the man who stood so stubbornly in his way would be absolutely certain to give that man his quietus without noise or confusion. His power would avail him nothing with this about his throat.

Wrenchy watched him with an expression of grim humor, which the broker mistook for suppressed exultation at the thought of this opportunity for vengeance.

"Are you dead sure of your mark?" asked the spectacled Garvin, while his mouth seemed to water as his teeth slightly appeared through his false mustache.

The clown, who at one time was known in California as a *vaquero* (herdsman), silently took the lasso from the wall.

"*Esta 'paso,*" * he said; and with a smile which the broker still interpreted as the smile of anticipated triumph over his old enemy, he put the coil on his left arm and proceeded to unwind it to a sufficient length for present use. Then with a quick movement the noose flew in the air and a large empty box, that was standing upright in one corner of the loft, was drawn toward him.

"Bravo!" cried the bearded spectator. "Are you as sure of a man?"

"*Hyer! vm corrajo vejez estafado!*" † returned the clown; and having released the box, the lasso was the next instant flying through the room toward the broker's head, and before he could so much as move his tongue he found himself bound to his chair a helpless prisoner.

"Ha, ha! *Hyer!*" laughed the acrobatic clown turning

* This way. † "Here! you cussed old sharper!"

a double somersault, while the simple expression on his countenance, of which we have before spoken, assumed a look of the most innocent glee. "How is that for man, beast, or devil? I care not for the word!"

The broker neither enjoyed the fun of being lassoed, nor did he relish the sportive language which the eccentric gymnast seemed to apply to him in English, taking aside the Mexican dialect, which was Greek to him. He tried to put a good face on the matter, however.

"A very good illustration," he said with a forced laugh, while he bit his lips with vexation; "a very convincing illustration indeed!" At the same time he winced under the tightening lasso.

With another laugh of what seemed simple and mischievous glee, Wrenchy cried, "Now for it!" and with a sudden pull down came broker and chair with a crash. "Heigh-ho! master!" he exclaimed, rushing to the aid of his sprawling victim; "this old clown has carried the joke too far! He forgot himself, and mistook you for a 'greaser'!" and grasping the prostrate Garvin he tumbled him about in rude apparent efforts to right him, until the discomforted plotter cursed the clumsy fellow from the bottom of his soul. Then seizing the hat which rolled off on the floor when its owner fell, Wrenchy put it on the broker's head and, with a stroke he had learned years before on the Bowery, he knocked it over his eyes, sending the green spectacles down over the end of his nose.

"Ha, ha, ha!" once more laughed the irreverant acrobat. "You must be the Evil One himself to put this clumsiness into old Wrenchy! His skilful hands are turned to the paws of a lout!"

Finally he succeeded in raising his dupe, who ventured only to mutter his curses between his teeth, while he readjusted his spectacles and clothing.

"You perceive, master," said the clown with a grin, that this bit of raw-hide is sure. I will explain its peculiarities. You will see that it is plaited, and rendered elastic by greasing, which makes it as soft and pliable as silk. 'T is a very remarkable piece of ingenuity, sir, if you will please examine it."

"I 've tested it very well, my good fellow, very well indeed," replied the broker with a painfully responsive grin, still inwardly boiling with rage at the treatment he had endured. "I have n't time for a particular examination. You can let your old California friend attend to that, and assist him by starting his eyes out a little."

The gymnast could scarcely refrain from compelling this murderous broker's own eyes to start out by a compression of his windpipe in his powerful fingers, as he uttered this fiendish remark. But he carried out the part he had assigned himself, and his designing visitor at length departed, rubbing his ugly hands with self-congratulation, though mingled with this self-congratulation was an inward trembling, arising from a consciousness of guilt which one attempt at assassination had not been quite able to harden him to.

* * * * *

On the night of the second interview between the broker and his fancied hireling, which we have just transcribed, William Garvin sat in his room, hour after hour, a victim of the most conflicting and disturbing thoughts. It was, in fact, a state of mind but little short of frenzy.

The reader has already been informed, in the account given by the Veteran to Jonas Cringar, of the terrible experience through which the distracted young artist had passed since his visit to his studio. After the interview referred to by the former, which resulted in his releasing the broker's son for the time being, the sufferings of this miserable youth rather increased than diminished. He felt himself compelled to act upon his own responsibility; and the very claims of justice which had compelled the Veteran to assign him a part so repugnant to his feelings now appealed with direct force to his heart.

He saw the family to which for so many years he had seemed but little less than a son suffering from wrongs perpetrated by his own father. He saw her by whom his life had been so absorbed living in penury and want. He saw them all, in his mind's eye, in the attitude of pleading, and he heard them in imagination praying him to perform that act which the man, whose word he dreamed not of doubting, had told him would secure the restoration of their property, and relief from their present state of destitution.

So his mind surged from side to side till it was nearly prostrated by its tumultuous unrest. If he performed the act, his father would be given by his hands into the power of his foes, and probably over to destruction. If he did not do it, the family in which was the object of his wild idolatry might remain in misery forever. With the insight we have given the reader into the mental character and morbid condition of this young man, he can readily comprehend the state in which we now find him, after two days and nights of such internal conflict.

In the afternoon his mind had surged toward the execution of the deed, the ever-present vision of Emma and her family, in which the majestic but to him now sorrowful figure of the Veteran appeared, proving a stronger influence than the picture of a guilty father's retribution; and not far from the very hour in which that parent was engaged in hiring a supposed assassin to do murder, this struggling son had finally resolved to secure the forgery.

His plan was to abstract the forged paper from the broker's pocket-book while he was asleep. To insure that sleep, — for he paled and trembled at the thought of the slumberer awaking while he was engaged in the contemplated act, — he determined to administer a sleeping-potion by means of the tea which his father was sure to drink in the evening. Having often been obliged to take somnific drugs to secure sleep himself, he had carried out this part of his design with but little difficulty.

But now as he sat in his room after the father had retired, he was again compelled to undergo an internal conflict; for the strain on his overwrought mind, from the effort already made toward the accomplishment of his object, had been followed by a reaction; and for a while he was again threatened with prostration and utter inability to carry out what he had now begun. Again his mind surged to and fro, and in his mental anguish he was ready to cry out, —

"Great Power of Heaven! take me hence!"

It was considerably after midnight when once more that desperate resolve took possession of his spirit, and with a wild start he hastened to his door, opened it convulsively, and stole swiftly toward his father's chamber, carrying in his left hand a small metal lamp.

He reached forth his right hand to turn the knob, when to his dismay quick, heavy footsteps were heard within, and the door opened.

Confronting him was the livid, furious face of the broker.

Seizing his son by the throat he bent this face down to his, and exclaimed in a hissing voice, —

"Vile thief and burglar! what have you stolen from my pocket-book?"

"Nothing! before God, nothing!" shrieked the son, overcome with mortal terror.

"Nothing! you dauber of canvas! You lie!" cried the foaming broker, shaking the young artist till the lamp fell extinguished from his hand, and it seemed as though with this rough usage and his own terror he must drop lifeless to the floor.

"O no, no!" again shrieked the gasping youth. "I swear! I swear! O father! I swear!"

"As that damnable Cringar swore, you chattering cat-bird!" And at thoughts of Cringar and the Veteran Daniel Garvin shook his son still more violently. "Swear, you young imp! I 'll teach you to utter oaths that 'll burst your windpipe!" William's throat now began to gurgle. "The paper!" yelled the broker like a madman. "If you don't give it up right here on this spot, and instantly, I 'll kill you!"

At that moment the commotion of alarmed servants above served to bring the furious man to a consciousness of what he was doing. Relaxing his hold from his son's throat, he grasped him by the collar and, dragging him into the chamber, he slammed to the door.

The young artist now fell on his knees and declared in the most piteous and heart-rending tones that he had not taken the paper.

"Why were you at my door at this time of night?" demanded the father in a voice that was still filled with rage.

"You — you looked sick and wretched at supper, and I could not go to bed for thinking of you, and I came to see if you slept!" uttered the trembling youth with a readiness which fright often imparts.

William Garvin was not given to uttering lies, and this one caused a blush of shame to tinge the deadly pallor of his cheeks.

For an instant the broker continued to fix his blazing eye on his son, and then suddenly his features, which had begun slightly to relax, once more grew black, contorted by an expression in which impotent fury and startled fear were darkly mingled. Opening the door he flung the youth from the room, and then again closing it with a loud slam he turned the key, and commenced pacing the floor with strides that even surpassed those with which he started for Jonas Cringar, after the information given him by Baling at the Fulton Ferry.

"The cannon-ball clown!" he hissed between his grinding teeth. "Duped! Daniel Garvin duped! Duped by a clown! Lassoed like a mule, and robbed like a fool!—A rhyme, Daniel Garvin! You 've made a rhyme! Go to work and write poetry for monuments, and first see to it that your own epitaph is written!"

The last of this speech was uttered with a bitter laugh, and one is startled by its strangeness.

The furious schemer's large pocket-book lying open on the stand by the bed suggests the cause of this remarkable demonstration.

The sleeping-potion which William had prepared for his father might have proved sufficienly strong for himself, but its effect on an organization so powerful as the broker's, more than usually excited as it was by his recent interview with the athlete, was of short duration.

Not long before the young artist grasped his lamp in the desperate resolution to finish the work he had begun, Daniel Garvin, who had thrown himself undressed on his bed, awoke with a violent headache, and troublesome thoughts began to sweep through his mind, as was now usual with him at the dead of night.

He thought of the Veteran, and his face lit up with exultation as he ruminated on the sure vengeance which would now be visited on his enemy through the athlete and his lasso. Then he passed to the merchant, and his heart gloated over the retribution he intended for this man, whom he hated with all the intensity of his brooding nature for the traitorous part he felt certain he had acted against him.

While in the midst of his revengeful pictures he rose and sat on the side of his bed. His lamp still burned, and he drew forth his pocket-book — now a frequent habit with him — to feast his eyes on the evidence by which at any moment he could tumble the merchant into the abyss of irretrievable ruin.

"Strange!" he muttered, as he opened the wallet, to find the forgery missing from the place in which he usually carried it. "It is not easy for Daniel Garvin to confess it, even to Daniel Garvin, but truly his head is not so clear of late. I like not this confusion," he added, tapping his forehead. "The time was when Daniel Garvin could put his papers away twenty years running, if necessary, and never in the wrong place; but there seems to be a little trouble here."

With this he commenced nervously searching for the missing forgery among his other papers. But it was nowhere to be found!

"I've been plundered!" he exclaimed in a suppressed voice of rage and consternation, and throwing the pocket-book upon the stand he leaped to his feet.

At that instant his ears caught the sound of creeping feet outside; in another moment he was at the door, and then ensued the scene we have described.

Throughout the remainder of that night sleep visited neither the lids of the father nor son.

CHAPTER XLIII.

ONCE more to the old house on Vandam Street.

We have spoken of the joy with which the sorrowing family of Allen Paige had greeted that noble friend, whom they supposed had been murdered. On the evening following the night of Prescott Marland's escape from the mad-house they sat talking of this friend with a gratitude and an affection which only such devotion as he, a comparative stranger, had displayed in their behalf could command.

"Do you observe, mother," said Emma with much feeling, "how pale he is? I fear his anxiety for us has led him to forget himself in so soon recommencing his arduous labors for us."

"I have observed it," responded the mother, sadly. "And it grieves me. I spoke to him yesterday, and admonished him to think more of his own welfare, but he answered me in such a manner that I could say nothing more. One feels in his presence as if he knew what was best, and so must needs leave him to act according to a judgment which seems beyond questioning. He appears very anxious about Prescott, whom he evidently loves as we all do."

A blush tinged Emma's cheek; and then tears filled her eyes. Mrs. Paige observed this emotion, and with a mother's sympathy was about to change the subject of conversation, when a well-known knock at the door announced a visit from the one of whom they had been speaking.

With the words we have heard uttered by Mrs. Paige and her daughter regarding the appearance of this soldier so fraternally devoted to the interests of a comrade's family, one is struck by the paleness of his massive face. It is evident that anxiety for others has caused him, after the confinement from his wound, to venture prematurely on those labors which demand so great an exertion of the mind and will.

But the observer almost immediately forgets this appearance of illness in an expression of suppressed joy, which beams from his deep gray eye, and pervades his strong, benignant features. He himself sees that this expression has attracted the attention of those who now greet him, and he hastens to say, —

"My friends, I have to inform you that one great source of power held heretofore by Daniel Garvin has been taken from him; and I am now able to tell you that the prospect of the restitution of your rights is very favorable."

This did not seem to explain that emotion which still lit up his countenance.

His gaze now fell on Emma's face, and he observed the tears still standing in her saddened eyes. A look of inexpressible tenderness overspread his features.

"Perhaps we shall have a visitor soon," he said in a gentle voice.

Through Emma's tears there instantly appeared a light which brought to the countenance of the Veteran a smile so kind and yet so grave, that, while a blush again heightened the color of the fair girl's cheek, she was strangely moved, as if the presence of her father accompanied this apparently Heaven-appointed friend.

At that moment another knock was heard at the door.

Emma partly started from her chair to answer it, but as Albert hastened to do this she gave a quick glance at the Veteran, and sank back trembling in her seat while the tell-tale crimson mounted to her cheeks.

Albert opened the door, and Prescott Marland crossed the threshold, and stood before them, that handsome, generous face, though pale and thin by his incarceration, still beaming with the old hope-inspiring smile.

The greeting which now followed caused the young Lieutenant to declare to himself that for a repetition of it he would willingly endure another imprisonment like that from which he had just escaped.

That day the Veteran had told him of the success which had attended the mission of the gymnast, — who, it is needless to inform the reader, had abstracted the forgery when he gave the broker such a rude handling, and knocked his hat over his eyes, while he was sprawled on the floor, — and as he took Emma's hand he experienced in his hope a thrill of delight which he did not care entirely to suppress, as he looked into her eyes and thought of the possibility of being permitted erelong to throw off the bonds which for so many months had restrained him, and declare with all the fervor he then felt the deep, strong love which trial had but served to render even tenfold more ardent than it was the day he was surprised gazing on the sunset picture.

Mingled with Emma's joy was a feeling of pain, as she beheld his features so thin and pale; and the indignation of both herself and the rest of the family may well be imagined, as they listened to the story of the manner in which he had been entrapped and held in worse than solitary confinement. When, however, he came to the description of his escape through the ingenuity of the inventor, and told them of his adventure in Dr. Pennell's private office, their countenances were expressive of lively enjoyment.

Their sympathies were strongly excited toward the poor mad corporal with whom he had been incarcerated.

"It is the height of cruelty to confine even the most dangerous victim of insanity in such a cell as that!" exclaimed Mrs. Paige.

"Do not fear but that the cruelty and the rascality, in New York at least, of that sweet villain of a mad-house doctor will come to a speedy termination," said Prescott, with a voice of decision. "My raid on his private office was a very successful one, as both he and Garvin will find out to their cost, besides a few others who have used this mad-house for their infamous purposes!"

But he had another pleasant surprise in store for them, in the report he had to render of the Deering family.

Nothing could have more effectually served to call forth a display of the goodness of this family of Allen Paige than the young Lieutenant's recital of what had been told him by Charles Roberts. They forgot the hopes for themselves, which the Veteran and Prescott had inspired, in listening to the story of those unfortunate ones, compared to whose sufferings their own seemed to them as naught. The account of their discovery, after a long and seemingly hopeless search, by a comrade of the Grand Army of the Republic, and of their immediate relief by the Post, called forth such expressions as would have made the heart of the comrade who reads this thrill with pleasure, had he been there to hear them.

The two members of the G. A. R. who were then in their presence forgot all else for the moment, as they listened to the words of blessing poured out on their Order by those who in their prosperity had undertaken the same office which had devolved on the Grand Army.

"I have never felt so proud of our organization as I do at this moment!" said the Veteran. "I would that all loyal citizens might hear you!"

"We are not worthy such attention from all loyal citizens," replied Mrs. Paige. "But there is one I have recently heard of who is."

"Who is that?" asked Prescott, with interest.

"A lady in Salem, Massachusetts, who, when suffering so much from disease that she was obliged to lie day after day in one position without being moved, held up her hands and knit stockings for the soldiers who were fighting for her country."

"And does she still live?" asked the Veteran.

"She does; and is the same devoted friend of the soldier."

"Then let the united prayers of the Grand Army of the Republic ascend for her to that God who blesses the good!"

The Veteran uttered these words in a voice so fraught with the deep emotions which this brief story had awakened, that we opine the angels who heard it bore the benediction to her who has proved so worthy of it.

That was a happy evening for the family of Allen Paige, happier than any evening they had seen for many months; and as the Veteran and Prescott took their leave, the latter clasped Emma's hand closer than had formerly been his wont, which she returned with a look that attended him in his dreams.

Yes, that family was happy; for though the resources and pertinacity of their wily persecutor had taught them that the morrow might not realize the hope of to-day, yet that "son and brother" whom they loved so much was not dead, but living.

CHAPTER XLIV.

JONAS CRINGAR sat alone in his private office, after all but Billings had departed from the store. He held in his hand a letter which had just been given him by the book-keeper. It was from the Veteran, informing him that he had had an interview with the President and four of the most influential Directors of the Bald Eagle Silver Mining Company, to whom he had stated all that was necessary for his purpose, and who, though shocked and confounded on learning of the merchant's defalcation, had under the circumstances decided to waive immediate action, and await the development of the movement which the Veteran had initiated. The President, he wrote, freely told him in the course of the interview he had with him before seeing the Directors, that both he and some of his associates on the board had for some time past viewed the broker with suspicion, who, as the reader will recollect, had purchased stock and managed to become an officer of this company that he might, through his influence and manipulative skill, cover Cringar's defalcation till such time as its exposure would not endanger his own criminal operations.

As the merchant now sat with this letter in his left hand, which hung over the arm of his chair, he gave evidence of a marked change for the better. Though still bearing that worn and haggard look, there was apparent on his countenance an indescribable expression of relief, which told of a realization that the clutch on his throat by his hell-inspired tormentor had been loosened by a friendly hand.

The Veteran, to whom the gymnast had brought the forgery immediately after the departure from the loft of his guilty dupe, chose, for judicious reasons, to retain the document till he had seen all his plans safely carried out. This the merchant expected; but it gave him very little uneasiness, for he knew he had nothing to fear in that direction if he proved himself as good as his word, in endeavoring with all his power to atone for the wrong he had done the family of his former partner. He knew, also, that in the Veteran he had a friend who looked kindly upon him; who, while he did not fail to condemn his guilty acts, yet realized that with a heart not naturally bad he had through his weaknesses been made the victim of a strong and designing man; and he felt that if there were any hope of rising left, this magnanimous soldier would be disposed to do his utmost to assist him.

"Satan is always near when you 're thinking about him," is a saying which is often confirmed; and in Jonas Cringar's case it now held good; for just as he was absorbed in thoughts of that relentless tormentor, from whose clutch he congratulated himself he was about to escape, Garvin's well-known voice was heard questioning the book-keeper, who was preparing to leave the store for the night.

Its tone was hoarse and unusually vindictive, and for the instant the merchant shrank cowering in his chair.

The door opened and the broker's visage was thrust in, distorted with an absolute grin of baffled rage.

On sight of this diabolical visage Jonas Cringar trembled with his old terror, and the sweat began as in former times to appear on his forehead. But as the broker continued to stand at the threshold, bending upon him his lurid eye, in which unsteadiness was now perceptible, he brought to his aid his native strength, and with the realization that the dark-browed man before him had lost that by which he had formerly held such terrible power over him, speedily subdued much of his agitation, and fastened his gaze on the other's countenance with a firm and determined air.

Garvin could not endure this. Closing the door and striding into the room, he brandished his fist, and cried in a voice that was choked with rage,—

"Jonas Cringar! do you think you are to escape me?" Then as he compressed his beetling brows still farther over his eyes, he almost whispered as he hissed these three words, leaving a marked interval between each one, and increasing his vindictive emphasis as he uttered them, "Traitor!—*defaulter!*—FORGER!"

The merchant quailed under this attack, and as his paling countenance gave evidence of his fear the broker laughed derisively.

"Let me tell you, Jonas Cringar," he exclaimed with fierce sarcasm, "by breaking faith with Daniel Garvin you have incurred his terrible vengeance, and thrown yourself into the jaws of destruction!"

Cringar recovered himself sufficiently to look with a steadier eye on this baffled but still threatening plotter. It was impossible, however, for him to suppress an agitation which resulted both from the influence of his unwelcome visitor's presence, and the consciousness of guilt which still haunted him with the fear of retribution.

"Mr. Garvin," he said conciliatingly, "I do not understand this language. You are very hasty."

This attempt at conciliation, instead of sinking to the very floor under Daniel Garvin's threatening words, was so significant of the change wrought in their relative positions, that the broker could scarcely contain himself. Approaching nearer the merchant, he assumed such an aspect as caused his former victim to tremble for his life, and instinctively to push back his chair with his foot.

"Clown!"

As Daniel Garvin uttered this epithet the word recalled the clown who had made such a dupe of him, and his passion, which seemed to have overleaped all bounds, verged on the ravings of insanity.

"Clown!" he reiterated. "That is the word for such a traitor and swindler!"

Jonas Cringar was stung to the quick.

"Have a care, sir!" he exclaimed.

If the conciliatory words before used by the merchant had the effect to stir the depths of Garvin's wrath, this admonition of one whom he had so long and exultingly held in the most abject mental slavery now served to destroy any self-control he might have had remaining. Seizing Cringar by the throat, as he had his son when he discovered him at his chamber door, he shook him violently, growling savagely through his clenched teeth, —

"'Have a care!' — do you tell *me* to have a care? Say, dog of a forger! do you tell me to have a care? I will teach you who is master! Give me back that paper you hired an accursed monkey to steal from me!"

"I did not!" uttered Cringar in a stifled voice, as he strove in vain with his shattered strength against the powerful and infuriated broker.

"Liar!" returned the latter, closing his hand still tighter about the throat of the strangling merchant. "I knew you the night that Simple Sal gave us a bit of her jargon! Damn you! you crept out of the door like a skulking traitor! and I determined then that if you dared to fail me I'd teach you whose God was to be depended upon! and I will, you sanctimonious hound!" This word *hound* again recalled the California clown, and with a renewed burst of fury he shook Jonas Cringar against the wall, crying, "Hound! fox! wolf! cat! and —"

The raging broker released his grasp as he observed a sudden expression of joy appear in the eyes of the merchant; and while his teeth still remained apart to let the interrupted epithet pass between them, a heavy hand was laid upon him and he was dragged back with irresistible power.

"Mr. Garvin," said a deep, stern voice, "you are fond of violent deeds."

Garvin turned, and found himself confronted by the Veteran. The expression of his face was for an instant hideous. The entire strength of his diabolical nature seemed to concentrate itself in his dark visage. Hatred, spite, fury, desperation, each contributed to the seething caldron within, as foul as the caldron of Hecate's witches. His eyes, whose unsteadiness was noticeable as he appeared to Cringar, rolled under the black and lowering brows, sending out shifting and lightning-like gleams; the cheeks became mottled like a reptile; while the upper lip played with spasmodic jerks, showing his teeth in a manner that imparted unwonted fierceness to all the features.

The Veteran instinctively stepped back as if a poisonous thing had suddenly sprung into his path. Then bending upon this repulsive visage a look of grave severity, he said in a calm voice of still greater depth, —

"Daniel Garvin, neither the assassin nor the strangler will now avail."

For a moment the broker seemed about to spring like a foaming beast upon this calm and intrepid soldier; then suddenly turning he went to a chair, leisurely took his seat, and with a ferocious grin similar to the one with which he had greeted Cringar, but kindled by a still intenser passion, he cast his glittering glance from the Veteran to the merchant.

"Fools!" he exclaimed in a tone of the bitterest scorn, "do you think you have a child to play with?—This is Jonas Cringar, I believe?" he said with mock gravity, grinning at the merchant, while his eye blazed upon him with a look which startled his former slave into a responsive nod. Then directing his glance to the Veteran he said, "And this is General Hammond, *alias* Thorbolt, if I mistake not?"

The response in this case was such a look of the firm gray eye, whose power seemed enhanced by the pallor caused by his own guilty act, that he was for a moment discomfited, and his eye rolled toward the door, and then back to the merchant, at sight of whom he regained his voice.

"Well, Mr. Jonas Cringar and General Thorbolt Hammond," uttered he with a sarcastic snarl, "you think you have—let 's see—you called it the right bower, the left bower, ace, king, and queen in California, I believe, Mr. ex-*Coyote?*—ha, ha! you perceive I 'm good-natured and in excellent spirits! Well—that is a word I repeat—*well,* thinking you have these cards, you propose to sweep the stakes without so much as asking me to show my hand."

Then taking pencil and blank-book from his pocket, he wrote down several items in silence, while the Veteran as silently observed him, both puzzled and startled by the strange conduct and appearance of this thwarted schemer.

"There," said the latter, tearing out the leaf on which he had been writing, and holding it up in view of his auditors; "you will perceive that one or two tricks can be made in an humble way, even with such a bad hand as has been dealt to me. Here," he said, laying the point of his pencil on the item specified, "is a card which calls to mind one Richard Slaycut, and here another that reminds one of Slaycut and Drorblude, and others that you can examine after the game is played. A certain card has been spirited away from my deal, on which, gentlemen, you congratulate yourselves as leaving me with no alternative but to throw up the game. But really, my worthy gamesters, you expose a greenness much to be wondered at. — Jonas Cringar!" he cried with an unexpected and startling fierceness, "so you think because my pocket-book has been rifled that you can go with this sheriff Thorbolt, and perjure yourself with lies about certain documentary statements, and be believed, do you?" Then waiting till he had given vent to a sneering laugh, he said, "The Bald Eagle Silver Mining Company will make excellent judges in this case. Do you suppose," he added with an appearance of his old concentrated power, "that Daniel Garvin is a verdant fool to attempt the game with only one trump card?"

"Make no calculations in that direction," said the Veteran, gravely, "the majority of the officers of the company to which you refer have been informed of everything."

"A pleasant deception, sir, for passing amusement," uttered the broker, who could not entirely conceal a look of dismay.

"They understand the part their unhappy treasurer has enacted, and the part you have performed so skilfully."

Daniel Garvin first showed his teeth, and then bit his under lip till it bled.

"I care not!" he exclaimed, rising from his chair. "Bury forgeries, defalcations, and all the rest, beneath the crust of the earth, and I tell you in the name of Daniel Garvin's power, that that which my hand is on cannot be taken from me!"

"You refer to the property of Allen Paige's estate, I presume?" said the Veteran, his countenance beginning to assume that air which indicated the massing of his mental forces.

"*My* property, is what I mean!" returned the broker in a voice now loud and harsh. "My property, and none other!"

"You mean by this, that the property which belongs to the widow and orphan children of your patriot half-brother you do not presume to keep longer from them?"

"Patriot!" cried Daniel Garvin with a look of the most intense hatred. "*Patriot!* A curse to all such patriots, who went down to slay their Southern brethren! As for the dam and cubs of this particular patriot, let the maledictions of the South light on their heads, but no property do you wring out of me for them!"

The broker now took a stride toward the door.

"Hold!" cried the Veteran in commanding tones. "Daniel Garvin, I have not done with you yet!"

CHAPTER XLV.

GARVIN stopped in his tracks, as his eye encountered the Veteran's commanding look, which corresponded with his voice.

"Daniel Garvin," repeated the Veteran, who was determined if possible to bring the plotter to terms at this interview, "know you aught of such a man as Dr. Pennell?"

The broker retreated before both the look and the question, while a startled expression he could not control took possession of his features.

The Veteran again spoke:—

"You have heard of a soldier named Prescott Marland?"

The conspirator stared at his questioner an instant, and then making a powerful effort, controlled to a degree his agitated features and sat down.

"A lieutenant, whom Mr. Paige met at the hospital?" he said in his craftiest voice.

"The same."

"You perceive by my answer that I have heard of him, —that is all."

"Your name has travelled an equal distance, for he also has heard of you."

"Indeed!"

"If I mistake not he had the pleasure of meeting you once in this office."

"You alarm me! My memory, which has always served me well, has seriously failed if this be so."

"It matters not. We will suppose an incident.

"I will not take your time."

"I will be brief. A young soldier is in a counting-room. A door to the inner office is opened, and he sees before him two desperate criminals who escaped merited punishment by breaking jail. These men, under *aliases*, are serving another criminal, who, being present, eyes this young soldier with a look that means mischief. The next day the young man receives a note, begging him to attend to a case of charity, and is decoyed into a mad-house. After days and nights of treatment that plainly meant murder, he escapes with a fellow-sufferer."

"Bah! what care I for this old woman's story?"

"A moment. On their way out they stop at the Doctor's private office; the companion opens the door, and all valuable papers are secured."

The broker started, but instantly controlled himself. "Your story, sir, is too long and broad," he said, and was again about to rise.

"I will close," returned the Veteran, waving him, with a powerful look, back to his seat. "Among these papers are documents which furnish irrefutable evidence against the party through whose machinations this young soldier was incarcerated."

Daniel Garvin's face suddenly grew black, and losing his self-control he muttered as he ground his teeth, —

"Has the doctor, too, betrayed me? He pledged himself to burn everything! Why have I not heard of this?"

At the same instant the door opened with a quick movement, and Prescott Marland entered.

"Ah, General!" he exclaimed, "I have been looking for you!" Then with a side-glance of scorn at Garvin, he whispered, "Those rascals have fled the city!"

"Slaycut and Drorblude?" said the Veteran aloud, who desired that Daniel Garvin should understand.

"Yes," returned Prescott, who, perceiving the intention of his friend, turned with a mock bow toward the broker, "Slaycut, *alias* Fitch, and Drorblude, *alias* Ratter, have disappeared as speedily as they did from the mines; and one Augoring, oil-merchant, has kept them company."

Garvin, who had started almost from his chair on seeing the young Lieutenant, now returned his sarcastic bow with a look which caused the object of it to exclaim, —

"By Jove! you ought to have been jailer at Andersonville!"

The Veteran gave Prescott an admonitory glance; but the latter did not see it, for his eyes were fastened in wonderment on the broker.

This baffled and penned-up master of plots and men, as he had deemed himself, now bore an aspect absolutely frightful. As we have seen, both Cringar and the Veteran had wrought him up to a fury which threatened to pass the bounds of sanity; but now with his full situation before him, — his plots and crimes gathering like messengers of vengeance about his own head, — the words and manner of the young Lieutenant seemed to have inflicted the final blow. The combined expression of a. wild beast and a venomous reptile at bay could alone give an idea of the looks of this infuriated man.

Catching the Vetetan's arm, the young Lieutenant pointed at the hideous head as if it were a mask without sight or hearing, and cried, —

"By Heavens! General, he 's mad!"

Billings, the book-keeper, who, observing Garvin's appearance as he came in, had remained to be ready for any emergency, now appeared at the door.

The instant the broker's eye lit on this young man he sprang to his feet, and pointing at him with a quivering finger he drew a poniard from his breast, and leaping toward the merchant with his finger still extended toward the book-keeper, he cried in a voice that vied with the unearthly noise of a flying shell, —

"The tool of your perfidious treachery is there! Here the instrument of my vengeance!"

Jonas Cringar raised his hands with a half-articulated cry for mercy. The broker responded with a horrible laugh, and clove the air with his dagger.

In the next instant he was hurled with tremendous force to the other end of the office, and the Veteran, now fully aroused, turned upon him with a face the passionate power of which passes all description.

"Assassin!" he exclaimed in tones that rolled like the heavy artillery with which he had so often mingled his voice, — "assassin! and hirer of assassins! are you not satisfied with your attempts at human life? Do not beldams, ruffians, mad-house doctors, and desperados serve to satiate your wolfish appetite?"

"*Beldams!*" cried the would-be assassin, half-stunned by the treatment he had received from the Veteran. "And has that toothless hag also blown the deed I paid her for?"

"Your deeds are all made known," returned the Veteran, now advancing toward the broker, who still held the poniard in his hand.

Garvin perceived the object of this man whose strength he had just felt, and drawing slightly back he raised his weapon.

The Veteran's eyes now began to blaze with internal fires such as Prescott had often seen preparatory to battle. But his demeanor was calm, and his gaze as steady as the sun.

"Give me the dagger!" he said, in a low, commanding voice.

The broker glared upon him with rolling eye, and then drawing back his upper lip he revealed in all their threatening array his white, glistening teeth.

The Veteran understood this look. Bending his gaze with still greater force of will upon those unsteady glaring eyes, he advanced with a firm step, while his pale face assumed an air which was absolutely solemn in the grandeur of its concentrated strength.

He came within the length of his own arm of Garvin's uplifted wrist. The latter continued to return his gaze with his own fierce glare, but he did not move his threatening hand.

Prescott and the book-keeper remained silent witnesses of this scene, while the merchant sat half stupefied by his impending death, and unexpected escape. Prescott's first impulse had been to spring to the unarmed Thorbolt's assistance, for the broker with his thick heavy frame was not to be despised, even without his weapon. But there was that in the air of the Veteran as his towering form confronted the muscular, but now somewhat shrinking figure before him, which forbade interference, and the young soldier held back.

One more step was taken. The broker made a movement of his arm; but it was too late. The Veteran's iron grip was on his wrist. He prepared for a furious struggle; but his antagonist tightened his grasp, and with a yell of rage rather than of pain the dagger dropped from his rigid fingers.

"Attempt no more murders!" said the Veteran, relaxing his hold. "The arm of an Almighty God is against you, and your own crimes have confounded you!"

The broker burst into a laugh, which chilled the blood of those who listened.

"'An Almighty God!'" he sneered, "that was what Cringar talked about one night. You remember it, don't you, my boy?" he cried, looking at the shrinking merchant across the office, — "the night Simple Sal gave us the anthem! She was a pretty young wench, was Sal, with her flattened face framed by the window-sash! eh, Cringar! You looked scared that night, poor dotard! — You see," he continued, addressing the Veteran, with a profound bow, "this same Simple Sal sang words which to a weak, superstitious mind were not agreeable. I'm no singer, but my old friend there, who has fought the bold battle of life, and robbed his beloved partner's family of everything they possessed, he has a very fine voice, full and sonorous; and by the will of Daniel Garvin! I swear he could ring the chorus right well with the sweet songstress of that memorable night. Let's see, Cringar," and he again looked at the merchant; "it ran somewhat in this way, if I recollect aright, —

'My gentle sirs, be very kind!
Your candle 's out,
My gentle sirs!
You 'll be found out,
My gentle sirs!
But gentle me you cannot find!'

Ha, ha! she withdrew with great alacrity, and left my friend gaping as if he'd spied the Devil! You see there was something in that song, General Thorbolt, that shocked his guilty soul —

'You 'll be found out,
My gentle sirs!'

I remember it all very well, for I've hummed it a good

many times since. It struck me, sir, it struck me very ridiculously, — the whole thing, — Cringar and all!" Then with another burst of laughter he exclaimed, "An Almighty God! The arm of an Almighty God is against me!" And now straightening himself, and smiting his chest, he cried: "Daniel Garvin is sufficient unto himself! If there is an Almighty God, let him take care of the imbeciles! Drop the curtain and pick up the swords! — the play is over! ha, ha, ha! Good evening, gentlemen, a right pleasant good evening"; and being near the open door he stepped off with a quick movement, similar to the action of a man intoxicated, who with unsteady head starts briskly away in a straight line to convince himself and others that he is sober.

The Veteran gazed after him with a perplexed countenance, while Prescott and Billings exchanged meaning glances. The latter tapped his forehead with his finger, and Jonas Cringar looked toward the door, muttering to himself, —

"His soul was haunted by that song as well as mine."

Suddenly, as the wind whistled through the store, the Veteran started forward.

"This is wrong!" he exclaimed. "If I mistake not, that man has lost his wits, and may be even now doing violence as a madman!" and hastening to the outer door, which Garvin had left open, he looked in every direction. But the retreating broker had disappeared.

The sky was overcast with heavy clouds, and the wind that had been rising for the past half-hour now blew violently through the street, slamming unfastened blinds and shutters to and fro with a loud noise, the creaking signs joining in the dismal concert.

Presently the sound of rain was heard swiftly advancing, and in another moment it swept by the store in a flooding torrent.

*   *   *   *   *

Toward midnight two sailors were leaning over the taff-rail of a brig that lay at anchor in East River.

"If this continues," said one of these men, "Hell Gate will have to wait for the Betsey Jane."

"I am afraid it will," returned the other, impatiently, as he watched the scudding white-caps fly before the wind that whistled loudly in the rigging.

The rain, which had held up for a space, now poured down in sheets, and began to run in streams through the scuppers.

"By the shades of old Nep!" cried the second speaker, "I think I'll turn in out of this!" and he moved toward the gangway.

"Hist!" cried the other in a loud whisper, pointing to the pier near which they were anchored. "Yonder comes a man who is either drunk or crazy! His head is bare, and, by my own bald pate! as near as I can make out through the rain and darkness with this dim light, his hair is but a poor covering."

His companion turned; but not having the sharp sight of the other, he could only discern an outline of a man striding from side to side at the end of the pier.

As he was about to speak a shrill, harsh, mocking voice pierced the storm, and the sailors both listened intently.

"Blow your rain!" cried the apparition on the wharf, brandishing his arms wildly in the air. "Whistle, ye noisy winds! You 're dark enough to whistle well! Ha, ha! Ye are negroes all, and whistle the hallelujah of your freedom, eh!" A shrieking gust now tore through the storm. "Ay, join in with your sweet voices, you black and devilish imps! join in, I say! That ape that set you free, let him direct you! Hear ye not my command? Hear and tremble when I proclaim myself! My name is Daniel Garvin! Ha, ha! shriek with terror, for if ye cross him in one single note of your dinning concert he 'll be quick with vengeance!"

"He 's mad!" exclaimed the sailor who first discovered him.

"As a March hare!"

"Hush! He 's at it again!"

"Vengeance! vengeance!" screamed the voice. "Pour down your vengeance on this bald head! Let it receive thy vengeance without stint, thou frowning Heaven! 'T is a traitorous crown! a perfidious crown!" And he beat his bared head with fury. "Burst it, ye elements! Crack the skull with your hammer, old Scandinavian Thor!"

The madman suddenly dropped his hands, and coming to the edge of the pier, looked straight toward the spell-bound mariners, and with a low bow he broke into a fit of wild, ironical laughter.

"Your servant!" he cried. "General Thorbolt, your servant, — your most humble servant! — What! you give return with an air so patronizing that methinks you take me for a portrait-painter! Ah, you hypocrite! I understand it! Folded in that tail which I see coiled beneath your skirts is the writ! The writ, do you hear! — Cease your nocturnal din!" he yelled, with a commanding gesture toward the heavens. "Cease! for Daniel Garvin would be heard! — The writ, I say! You have the writ! but where 's your man? Uncoil your harpoon tail and hang by it to the yard-arm! Grin like the clown who entertained me with his gambols! Laugh! laugh! I 'll count you as you laugh! Jonas Cringar, lead the file, and as you pass by split your sides with merriment! And you, you foul denizen 'twixt heaven and hell!—you smiling she-wolf, end off the train, and crack your laughter through your broken fangs! Come haste your steps, for I 'm choleric, and feel my temper rising!"

"Let us go to him," said the sailor who had spoken first before, "or he will drown himself."

"Ay, ay! but we must do it carefully. A man like that is dangerous."

Without more ado, they proceeded as quietly as possible to lower the stern boat, which was out of sight of the madman, who continued to rave.

"Heigh-ho! heigh-ho!" he now cried with an exultant laugh. "How well the heavens tune their strains to the music here!" and he beat his breast. "'T is a secret! Blow it not, O sympathizing Boreas, and I 'll tell you what it is! I 've built an organ here, and the imps of hell pump in the wind, while the facile fingers of their master play the keys!—the pedals? ha, ha, ha! With his cloven foot he has a knack that beats them all!" Then smiting his breast with blows that resounded through the storm, he howled: "Pump in the wind, you lazy imps! The organ groans! Satan, you defy the very laws of sound! The temple shakes to its foundation with your pealing tones! Now let the choir sing the glory of Daniel Garvin, victorious! Sing! rend your lungs, but you must sing! Ay, All-ruling God! Satan's music vies with thine! Cringar prated, in his fear, of thee! and in spite of thee I 've crushed him! Ay, Daniel Garvin is a god unto himself! Sing with a louder strain, ye voices! Satan drowns you with his roof-cracking notes!"

As the mad broker recommenced the furious blows on his breast, his eye caught sight of the boat which at that instant appeared shooting out from behind the stern of the brig, and with a renewed burst of laughter, he yelled, —

"Too late! Erie 's gone! — Down with your hands and cease your clamor!" turning his eyes to the storm. "You 'll break in the walls with your loud-mouthed bids. The bulls have it! — do you hear? The bulls, I say! Go home, ye bears, and lap your chops for honey!" He then bowed low to the sailors. "What! gone short, and want Daniel Garvin to help you out? Go to my namesake, — Uncle Dan! He 'll give you a lift, if your hair and claws are long enough!"

The sailors, who for a moment had rested on their oars, now renewed their strokes with vigor.

"What!" howled the maniac, straightening himself. "Are ye all traitors! Tell me you come for stock! I see your irons! Your fetters are not for me! Melt them into Union grape, and pepper well that thin-shanked Jonas, and the fangless she-wolf!" Then with a final peal of laughter that curdled the blood of the laboring oarsmen he screamed: "So ye think to cage the strong-horned bull! You 're mad! These bawling winds are mad! The heavens are mad! Ay, the whole world is mad! and I 'll be mad unless I go hence, quickly! — *One!* — Avast, you bailiff water-bugs! — *Two!* — If I rise from the immersion, slip your fingers o'er my watered scalp! — *Three!* — I 'm gone!" And leaping to the opposite side of the pier he plunged into the river.

With a cry of horror the sailors pulled to the spot where he disappeared; but even the eddies which his body created as it went down were mingled with the waves, and they watched in vain for his reappearance.

CHAPTER XLVI.

A MONTH has passed since the incidents occurred which have just been narrated. We are in that drawing-room in which we have witnessed scenes described in former chapters. All is as it was then,—the same paintings hang in their old places, the same pieces of statuary stand on the accustomed pedestals and brackets, the same piano awaits the familiar touch in its own corner, and the same furniture with its rich carvings invites one to sit and ruminate like Joseph Deering over the comforts of competency.

But now steps approach the door which, in a manner still more pleasing than all we have just surveyed, tells us of the change this past month has brought about.

The door is opened, and a face appears in lovely contrast to the forbidding visage which greeted the Veteran on that stormy day when he came to this house and found the family of Allen Paige turned from beneath its roof. It is the face of Emma Paige, radiant with happiness; for she has just left her mother sitting in that room where the patriot husband was tended in his illness, and contemplating the dear objects sacredly associated with his memory, which bring tears of mingled joy and sadness to her eyes.

A brief statement of the circumstances which have led to this happy result is all that is necessary.

Directed by the information given by the sailors, the authorities searched for the body of the mad suicide, and after two days' grappling found it at a considerable distance below the pier from which he made his fatal leap. The body was instantly identified as that of Daniel Garvin, and was buried with feelings of grief and desolation by his son William.

With the broker dead, the young artist hastened to make all the restitution in his power for the wrongs committed by his father. He was assisted in this work by Jonas Cringar, who was well acquainted with the details of the operation by which Daniel Garvin had defrauded the family of his half-brother, and who worked day and night in this labor, with a sort of happiness which seemed to him more like a dream than the reality.

William, whose conscience, as the reader is aware, was naturally tender, and whose few days' experience before and after his father's tragical death had done the work of twenty years, was not content with an exact restitution of actual property taken by the broker; he also desired to mend as far as possible the harm which he had done for which the law could claim no compensation. In such work he had a wise counsellor in the Veteran, whom he looked up to with perhaps greater reverence than ever before.

Among other things to be accomplished in this direction was such judicious assistance for Cringar as would enable him to repair, in a degree, his broken life, which had been shattered through the machinations of his tempter; the guilt for which he himself was responsible having been expiated in the terrible sufferings he had experienced. Through the influence of the Veteran an arrangement was made with the Bald Eagle Silver Mining Company, by which the merchant was to return the money he was responsible for by semiannual instalments with interest, William Garvin guaranteeing the same. To enable him to do this, as well as re-establish himself in business, William, under the advice of the Veteran, advanced sufficient to clear pressing liabilities, and set him well on his feet. All this the son was amply able to perform, the father having left property amounting in value to nearly two hundred and fifty thousand dollars.

The Paiges found their old home comparatively undisturbed, one of the great sources of enjoyment on the part of the broker while he occupied it having been to gaze around on the evidences of former comforts experienced by his half-brother, and that family to whom, then, it was apparently lost forever.

The past few months seemed to them like a shadowy dream, from which sometimes they could hardly believe themselves yet awakened. There was a feeling of strangeness when they first passed from room to room, as though they had been absent for years. Their recent experience had been so crowded with events and trials that it seemed a separate life, not to be measured by the ordinary divisions of time. This served rather to enhance the unspeakable happiness with which they moved in the midst of those sacred associations from which they had so nearly been for all time excluded.

Emma had enjoyed a communion with her mother in the room which had been sanctified by the impressive death of the husband and father, and in which Daniel Garvin had not obtruded his unholy presence after the first day he moved in; for here his conscience disturbed his gloating vengeance to a degree which, while he with characteristic pride refused to acknowledge it, compelled him nevertheless to retire, no more to cross its threshold. Mother and daughter had wept together as they talked of the loved one who there passed away; and in the interchange of their hearts' grateful sentiments they had not failed to bless the comrade of this loved one, through whose labors they were returned to these cherished scenes. And now the heroine of our story, radiant with that happiness which reflected the tearful yet soul-awakening joy of her whom she had left alone, entered the drawing-room and gazed around with beaming eye. Then approaching the piano she opened it and touched the keys.

Ah! the heaven-inspired notes which the spirit that deeply feels may bring from this responsive instrument! Under the delicate hand of that fair girl, from whose heart welled emotions she would express in music, the chords swept forth and filled the room, giving her feelings an utterance that words could never yield; and intermingled with them was an air gently yet sadly floating, telling of a soul whose bliss soared to those ideal realms where joy and sadness dwell inseparably together.

One now came to the door and listened. He had entered the hall without ringing, for he had been affectionately forbidden to pull the bell when he came to visit this home. He listened with his head slightly bowed as if his heart would unite with hers in the utterance of those prayerful and blissful emotions.

The harmony grew deeper, and the melody more tender, until the instrument seemed voluntarily pouring out its notes from a living spirit. Then suddenly from these strains a simple accompaniment stole tremblingly forth, and Emma with heaving breast and glistening eye commenced to sing.

He who stood without now wiped the tear from his cheek as he listened, for she was singing "HOME, SWEET HOME!"

Her voice trembled as she sang, but the heart sustained it, and it hovered in the air with touching sweetness: —

"Mid pleasures and palaces though we may roam,
Be it ever so humble, there 's no place like home;
A charm from the skies seems to hallow us there,
Which, seek through the world, is ne'er met with elsewhere.
Home, home, sweet, sweet home,
Be it ever so humble, there 's no place like home.

"An exile from home, splendor dazzles in vain,
O, give me my lowly thatched cottage again,
The birds singing gayly, that come at my call;
O, give me that sweet peace of mind, dearer than all.
Home, home, sweet, sweet home,
Be it ever so humble, there 's no place like home."

As the last note died tremulously away, Prescott opened the door. Emma rose to meet him, a smile lighting up her tearful eyes.

As he took her hand he said, —

"Emma, I have been a listener for several moments. If I have thus stolen rare happiness I must beg you to forgive me."

The blush that suffused her cheek when he entered deepened.

"You must not turn flatterer now," she answered, dropping her eye before his ardent gaze.

"I cannot flatter you," he returned with a smile, but in a voice not free from agitation. "Such music is beyond even my powers of flattery."

Then bending over the piano he began looking in a searching manner along the sounding-board and under the wires.

Emma, who anticipated some quaint turn of Prescott's humor, followed him with her eyes in pleased silence.

"I do not find them," he said, at length, raising his head.

"What do you seek there?"

"Angels."

"Prescott — "

"You must not scold me, dear sister," exclaimed the young Lieutenant, "for I mean no harm!"

"You have surely turned to a giddy-headed flatterer," rejoined Emma, who, while rebuking him with a severity which does not often so partake of tenderness, did not fail to observe traces of the feelings with which he had listened to her song. "When one begins flattering a friend 't is a warning that the esteem between them needs the aid of a ready tongue."

"It may be so, — it must be so if you say 't is so — "

"Fy, Prescott! you are in strong mood for flattery to-day."

"Dear sister," said the young Lieutenant, a look now appearing on his handsome face to which, with maidenly intuition, Emma responded with a fluttering heart, "I cannot satisfy you with my speech-making. I pray you, therefore, let me sit and listen to more of the music which you would have me call so poor."

Emma concealed a slight confusion which began to manifest itself by hastily seating herself at the piano in response to this request.

"I did not ask you to call it poor, but I fear you 'll have reason to do so," she said as she swept the keys. "You know I am out of practice."

This reference to the recent past touched Prescott deeply, and he gazed on Emma with an expression which told how deeply his heart was moved.

Sheet after sheet was played, the fair performer now throwing a sentiment into her instrument which caused the heart of her listener to thrill with the magnetism with which the notes were charged. In that improvisation to which Prescott had given such rapt attention at the door, the spirit had found its utterance; in these performances the heart was plainly speaking, — and time stole swiftly on.

At length Emma ceased playing, and rose from the piano. Prescott's head was slightly inclined forward, and his eyes raised in the same degree as their gaze was fixed upon her with all-absorbing love.

Involuntarily from her own eyes there beamed a responsive look, and then the lids drooped as if to conceal what the maidenly heart would not prematurely make known.

The enamored lover was entranced by the picture now presented by this charming girl. With an irresistible impulse he rose and took her hand.

"Emma," he said softly, "will you walk with me? There is a beautiful sunset I have longed for many a day to gaze upon with you."

She cast upon him a quick glance, and then suffered herself to be led to the painting, which had been enshrined in the memory of both.

"Emma," he said yet more tenderly, "when I first stood before this picture my heart formed it into a reality. My fancies gave a name to those two figures whose souls seem so united in the midst of that western glory."

As he thus spoke he pressed her hand more closely.

"Do you not see, dear Emma, that a halo surrounds them? Their lives are to be happy, for they love one another — "

Her hand trembled in his.

"— And their hands are clasped as they behold together the glowing scene; for each knows the love which burns in the heart of the other."

Deep blushes came and went as Emma gazed on the picture, which seemed all of a golden haze.

"Darling!" whispered the lover, suddenly raising her hand to his lips, "shall not the picture I formed when I first stood here be made reality? I called those figures You and I!"

In another moment that lovely head was nestled on his bosom, while his arm gently stole around her waist; and then as her face turned up to his, that first lingering kiss was given through which two yearning hearts pour the sweet current of their souls.

An hour flew by, and the mother entered the room. The lovers were sitting side by side; their faces, covered with gentle confusion, told the tale. She smiled with a happiness which only the mother can experience who realizes that her daughter is beloved by a man she can herself love and trust as a son.

Prescott came forward, and said,—

"Mother, will you not give me a pledge that will insure my right to call you 'mother' for all time?"

Mrs. Paige led the young soldier to her daughter, and placed his hand in hers.

"My dear children," she said, "I bless you! It is the blessing of a happy mother's heart. And," she uttered, raising her eyes above, while she held their hands clasped in hers, "there is one that has gone before us, whose blessing I believe is joined with mine."

Tears filled Emma's eyes, and she felt Prescott's hand press hers, as if he said, "In memory of that dear parent, I consecrate my soul to your happiness!"

Then she thought of another.

"Ah!" she uttered to herself. "My happiness would be complete if *he* were here."

The wishes of her heart were unexpectedly answered;

for scarcely had she uttered them when the Veteran was ushered into their presence.

In the countenances of the happy group before him he read all that had taken place.

"They await your blessing," said Mrs. Paige.

The Veteran advanced, and placing a hand on either head, he uttered a benediction so fervent and impressive that the tears trembled on Emma's lids, and Prescott's eyes glistened with sympathetic feeling.

There was that in the appearance of the grand and ma-majestic warrior which added solemnity to this touching scene. The pallor of his countenance had increased, and there was a look in his eye that seemed to come from depths, which, when observed in any person, convey an impression that the spirit is already gazing into that land where it is to find its eternal home. To Emma, who had from the first ever associated the Veteran with her father in a manner she could scarcely explain, this appearance was especially affecting. At the same time that she felt as if the benediction insured the kindly care of Heaven for the years of wedded life that might be hers, there was also an impression as though he who gave it was about being separated from them by the space that divides the visible from the invisible world.

But the object of these thoughts soon restored cheerfulness to the hearts of all; and Alice, having now joined them, the two sisters entertained the company with duets which were enchanting to the soul of the happy Prescott, and to which the Veteran seemed to listen with an inward ear as he gave attention with an air of deep meditation.

CHAPTER XLVII.

"THIS story, Comrade Roberts, sounds like the creation of a novelist's brain. And has it really occurred right around us here in New York?"

"All right here among us."

"Allen Paige's family have certainly given it a tone of reality I'll confess. Their donations to the Grand Army surpass anything I have yet heard of."

"Yes indeed! In these donations you see the expressions of benevolence and gratitude combined. It is a remarkable shifting of the scenes in this every-day life of ours. It seems scarcely yesterday since I enjoined it on Comrade Marland to notify us if this family should need aid; and now here we are almost staggering under the load of contributions sent in by them."

"'T is a marvellous change, truly. You know I have followed them in one way with unusual interest."

"Through the breastpin?"

"Yes. I shall not soon forget my feelings when I went into old Meinshon's pawn-shop and saw that pin with the likeness of our brave Colonel, and heard the Jew's story about his daughter coming in that stormy day and pawning it."

Roberts smiled.

"I can understand much better now," he said to his companion, in whom the reader will recognize the comrade he had spoken of to Prescott on the cars as the one who gave him the quaint but touching story told by the kind-hearted pawnbroker, and with whom he was now returning from a Post meeting, — "I can understand much better now, Comrade Walker, why the Lieutenant was so deeply affected when he saw Allen Paige's family entered on my relief-list, and heard the story of the breastpin." He thereupon gave Walker an account of his first meeting with Prescott on the New Jersey Central train.

"That must have been hard," returned the latter. "But he is well repaid now, for of all beautiful girls I have had the good fortune to meet, I think she is the most beautiful."

"There is soul there, as well as a handsome face."

"That is the secret. She has the true beauty; and I observe that while every one gazes at her with admiration, she wins all by her goodness. Comrade Marland is a lucky fellow."

"He deserves to be a lucky fellow."

"That 's so. There 's not a soldier but is ready to congratulate him. He has a grand start in life as partner in that store."

"Yes. But the benefits will not be on one side, let me tell you. The Lieutenant goes in to take charge of the Paige interest, and he 'll double it in a short time, or I 'm no judge of men."

"He 'll be sure to succeed, or I 'm no judge of women."

"What do you mean by that," asked Roberts, laughingly.

"I mean that, with such a wife as he is to have, he cannot fail. I have remarked that good wives are a strong guaranty of a man's success in life."

"I agree to that."

"My friend the pawnbroker has an exalted opinion of Miss Paige. It was only the day after she had been to redeem the pin in person, that I called to learn if it was still there. He gave me an account in his graphic broken English of this second visit of hers. She must have appreciated his goodness of heart, for he being a pretty deep student of human nature, besides entertaining a sincere admiration for her, was desirous of engaging her in conversation; and she indulged him with a courtesy and good sense which so delighted him that he lost a customer, who came, waited, and went, in his enthusiasm to recount to me his interview with her."

"Have you heard how Comrade Marland first met her?"

"I have not."

Roberts narrated the circumstances as Prescott himself had related them to him.

"That diabolical old woman ought to have been hung!" exclaimed Walker when his companion had finished.

"You hit nearer than you suppose. It was this old hag that Garvin hired to put Thorbolt out of the way. She it was that set those assassins on him."

"Who found that out?"

"The General himself. You see, when he was struck with the slung-shot by one of the scoundrels, the other thought he was done for, and he was so full of exultation that when he sprang at him with his knife he was fool enough to cry out, 'One for the Lancet and Mammy Roone!' This, together with the identification of the scamp, who was called *Doctor*, — whose skull, you will recollect, was broken in by a front cut of Thorbolt's cane, — put the police on the track. But she was too wary for them, and made off with the fellow who they say fired the pistol, — Dick Smasher they call him, — and neither of them are likely to be seen in these parts for one while. It is a bit of consolation to know, however, that if this precious beldam and her hireling have n't got their deserts, the little Irishwoman who warned General Hammond of Mammy Roone's plot against Miss Paige has; for the family employ her continually, and give her enough to keep her from want for a score of years."

"Good! That's what I call gratitude to the humble!" exclaimed Walker. "So Billings was in that adventure," he added. "I'm slightly acquainted with him. He's book-keeper at Cringar's, and seems to be a pretty smart fellow."

"That he is," returned Roberts. "He has been of great service in the Paige and Garvin affairs; and Marland tells me he will eventually enter the concern. And from what the Lieutenant has dropped, I judge that he is going to take his chances and wait for Emma Paige's younger sister, Alice, a girl who promises in a few years to be as charming a young woman as her elder sister, and who seems to have a high opinion of him."

"Marland must have looked as though he had just broke a Rebel prison when you met him the night he escaped from the mad-house," said Walker after a moment's silence.

"He did, indeed! He saw my surprise, and promised at a future time to tell me about what had happened, which he did. 'T was a thrilling story, as you can imagine. It was a marvellous piece of business, — that inventor's picking their way out."

"I should say so. But the best part of that story is the raid on the Doctor's private office.

"I agree with you there, Comrade," replied Roberts, laughing. "And what is still better, Prescott captured enough to break up the den, and drive the Doctor and his whole pack from the city. I shall not soon forget the way he told me that his cell-mate, the mad Corporal, had got into comfortable quarters. You would have thought he was talking about a comrade that had gone all through the war with him."

"Comrade Marland has a warm heart."

"Yes, as warm as it is bold. I like him. I 've yet to see the man that does n't. I venture to say he 'll not soon forget the inventor."

"No, I guess not! Judging from his knowledge of curious inventions, I 'm inclined to think they 've seen much of each other since their escape."

"Well, I must leave you here," said Walker, parting from his comrade. After proceeding a few paces, he turned quickly and said,—

"Comrade Roberts, write that tale out and read it to the Post."

CHAPTER XLVIII.

MAY had departed. June had come, with its fresh, green verdure, its wild-flowers, its feathered songsters, and its balmy days.

In a chamber overlooking the placid Hudson lay one whose great strength would have seemed sufficient to hold back for years to come that mighty Conqueror of all that is earthly in mortal man.

It was the Veteran. He was repaying with his life the efforts it had been his privilege to make in behalf of a comrade's wronged and outraged family. Those premonitory signs which had filled with sadness the hearts of this family were being realized as prophetic. In his anxiety for them he rose too soon from a sick-bed, which, with the arduous mental as well as the physical labor he at once engaged in, had completed the work a life of exposure and numerous wounds had done much to accelerate.

His iron will had sustained him till all was done for which he had labored; then a fatal relapse set in, and the final breaking up came with that suddenness which often marks the end of powerful men; and now at the close of a June day that had been unusually calm and tranquil, he lay serenely awaiting the orders from Head-quarters to join that great army on whose banners are inscribed celestial mottoes.

The windows were open, and the joyous songs of birds filled the air, harmonizing with the divine beauty of this scene, in which Death was clothed in bright garments, making ready to give the final summons with beatific smiles.

The dying Veteran had fallen into a brief sleep. When he awoke he turned to the nurse who was attending him in this his last illness, and asked in a voice which, though weak, indicated its former depth and richness, "Have they not come?"

At this moment sounds of an approaching carriage were heard, and presently Mrs. Paige, Prescott, Emma, and Albert entered the room.

The Veteran greeted them cheerfully, and took each by the hand.

"You are not all here," he said, after Albert had come to the bedside.

Mrs. Paige looked at Emma. "You need not fear," said the Veteran with a smile; "I want you all around me. You know the sick are whimsical at times."

Emma went out, and returned with Alice and Little Dorrit. As the latter was led to him she exclaimed,—

"O Uncle Thorbolt, I 'm sorry you are sick! You are so good, I know God will get you well!"

He again smiled, and reaching forth his hand, which

his strength still permitted, he placed it gently on her head, saying, —

"My little pet, God has been very kind to Uncle Thorbolt, and he will take him soon where he cannot be sick again."

The child evidently understood these words; for tears came into her eyes, and hiding her face in the folds of her mother's dress, she gave vent to her childish grief.

The dying soldier followed her with his eye, and then turned an imploring glance on Mrs. Paige.

"I pray you," he said, "teach this little one to look on Death as an angel of brightness; not the enemy, but the friend of mankind. Teach her so that she shall visit the tomb without dread, without sorrow. He who is called to a distant land to enjoy extraordinary good fortune is not mourned; neither is the family which bids him a temporary farewell bereaved beyond the first pangs of parting. Rather are they rejoiced at the good fortune of the one they love. So is it with what we term death. Those who are called above go to a land in which is insured a happiness surpassing our conception. Were it not that this last chill to my mortal frame is on me, I fear my self-control would not avail against the manifestations of my joy, as I think of that world for which I shall so soon depart."

The little group about him listened with a kind of awe to words like these, spoken by one who felt himself passing away from this life. Mrs. Paige, especially, who in her Samaritan labors had witnessed many death scenes in the course of her experience, never before beheld one so impressive as this. Here indeed was the type of a Christian soldier; one who, before that stage was reached when the dying so often gaze with ecstasy into the world which they are about to enter, lay calmly on his pillow, and with a clear knowledge of his approaching end, discoursed with the faith and clearness of a Christian philosopher. And how beautiful his views of death! As she listened, Mrs. Paige vowed silently to Heaven that her little girl should never know, if her efforts could avail, the fear which makes a dread visitant of that Presence which is truly a seraphic angel come to welcome home the Heaven-bound spirit.

The Veteran continued.

"The 'City of the Dead' is calm and peaceful. And forgive an old comrade," he added, turning his gaze with a smile upon Prescott, "for presuming to preach to you; but I would say, so live that this 'City' shall ever be pleasant to you. Not simply a place of curious epitaphs, or tasty works of art, but a spot in which the very mounds shall speak to you of Heaven, and hold you in elevating meditation; making your heart pure, and inspiring you with higher resolutions to perform the duty which God has assigned you as your share of work before he takes you hence. Prescott, it is a state of mind to be thankful for, when one can say, 'This is a beautiful world, and I continually experience a happiness I cannot express; but nevertheless I blissfully contemplate that moment when the Lord shall say, "Thy work is done. Come up hither."'"

Prescott, whose eyes had filled when the Veteran commenced addressing him, now bowed his head; and taking his dying comrade's hand in his, he inwardly prayed that sentiments like these might actuate his life, and that in death the Lord might find him so well prepared as he who thus addressed him.

The Veteran now lay silent for a while, a slight compression of his mouth indicating temporary pain.

When Emma saw this, she was obliged to turn away to conceal her emotion.

"Are they not coming also?" he said at length, raising his eyes.

"Who?" asked Prescott.

"Mr. Cringar, and his book-keeper, — or rather his and your book-keeper," he added, smilingly correcting himself in a manner which, recalling as it did the labors he had undergone for their sakes, touched them all to the heart.

"They will be here soon," answered the young Lieutenant.

"Jonas Cringar has suffered deeply," continued the Veteran as if to himself. "Think you," he said, again looking up, "that he could have been happy in the 'City of the Dead,' when he was so sorely oppressed with his guilt?"

Prescott shook his head.

Albert now went to the window, and looking out, exclaimed, —

"They are coming, General Hammond, — Mr. Cringar and Mr. Billings."

"Thank you, my dear boy," returned the Veteran in a gracious way that reminded those about him of the times that had passed. "You would make me a good aid, were I in the service just now."

Albert, who was an impressible lad, drew back and silently wept.

The merchant and book-keeper entered the room directly after, and were received by their dying friend in the same cheerful way he had greeted the others. His reception of the former was accompanied by a look which caused this man, so recently broken and wretched, to join his left hand with his right; and he thus stood for several moments clasping in both of his the hand that had greeted him, and gazing with an expression of veneration and gratitude on the face of the magnanimous Thorbolt.

"My friend," he said at length; but his voice faltered, and he could not go on.

The Veteran regarded him from his pillow with so kind an air that he exclaimed from an irresistible impulse, —

"Dear General! If the Lord would but take my life for yours, I would gladly give it!"

"Ah, no," responded the Veteran, "you are to be of great service to them all." And he looked around affectionately on those who stood witnessing this scene.

"Ever thinking of others!" murmured the book-keeper, whose countenance was expressive of deep reverence.

The merchant unclasped his hands, and forgetting for the moment all else around him, raised them imploringly to Heaven.

"O God!" he exclaimed, "take me, — a poor, shattered, broken-down man, — and restore him who has done so much good!"

All were deeply affected; and so earnest was the prayer, it seemed for an instant as though it must be answered; as if he, so shattered by his past sufferings, would be taken as the offering for him who was lately so strong and efficient a worker among his fellow-men.

Jonas Cringar continued his upward gaze, while his hands folded themselves as they slowly fell, like one awaiting a response to his soul-uttered petition.

The tranquil object of this prayer remained silent until the suppliant lowered his tearful eyes. Then he said, —

"To you, my friend, is reserved a noble work. In that great city which has recently witnessed so much that is eventful to you, destitution and misery hold multitudes of victims. Relieve them as you shall have the means to do so. No happier life is passed than in constant works of benevolence. No happier death is there than that which is attended by the blessings of those whom he that is passing away has aided in life."

"Such shall be my work!" uttered the merchant in a fervent voice. "God has been very kind to me who was so guilty, and I will repay it by acts of kindness to his suffering children. May my death-bed be like this!"

"Ah! you can make it far happier in that respect," said the Veteran, with a sad smile. "I have done little. You can do much; for keep to your good resolutions, and Heaven will prosper you."

Jonas Cringar bowed his head in silence.

The soldier now cast his eyes toward the open window through which he could gaze off to the southwest. As he did so his face lit up with a gleam of pleasure, and he exclaimed in a stronger voice than he had yet used,—

"How grandly those rugged clouds are piled one upon the other! They catch the beams of the setting sun! How warm, how radiant are the last rays of day!—My friends, so may it be with the last hours of human life. They should be the happiest and most glorious of all."

He gazed awhile in silence with an expression of solemn admiration. "They marshal for the thunder," he continued. "How obediently do they array themselves at the beck of Heaven! They make ready to hurl their fear-inspiring bolts; but as we behold their Great Commander with the eye of childish faith, directing them with an all-wise hand, they teach humility; for with their towering grandeur, their threatening fronts, and their dread artillery, they yield unquestioning obedience to his orders. Oh! how strong is man, when with humble heart he listens to the word of God, and believing all things well, fights the good fight in the panoply of Heaven! He then surpasses these cloudy Titans with their thunderbolts, as the spirit, made in the image of its Creator, surpasses all inanimate matter!"

The listening group which had gathered in sorrow around his death-bed gazed on this departing warrior with amazement and awe. The term "comfort the dying" was reversed. He was their comforter; and in these last moments their impressive teacher also.

He now closed his eyes, and his breathing indicated that he had sunk into a gentle sleep.

Presently the rumbling of distant thunder broke the pervading stillness. The sleeper moved, but did not awake. Another distant peal rolled over the earth. As its reverberations entered the chamber, the Veteran partly raised his closed lids, and said, —

"Well, boys, the ball 's opened! What regiment has the advance to-day?"

Then suddenly he looked up.

"What!" he said smilingly as his glance fell on Prescott, "is old Thorbolt sleeping on his post?"

At that moment the deepening thunder again re-echoed through the sky. The soldier's eye gleamed for an instant, lit by the old martial fire, and then he spoke: —

"Prescott, I would have given much to see that charge of Zagonyi's Body-Guard in Missouri, when the four Philadelphia brothers went in together for the Union."

"The brothers Newhall?" returned the young Lieutenant, desirous of preventing pain to the Veteran's mind by a silence which would imply grief.

"Yes, the brothers Newhall. It must have been a noble picture! The East and West were joined hand in hand in that charge."

"Yes," responded Prescott, "and through the war too, General."

"Ah, yes! to the end. They were hand in hand to the end. The Army of the Potomac grasped the Rebellion by the throat, and the Army of the Cumberland crushed in its trunk. May they ever work together. God be praised that erelong there will be no sectional North and South! The dividing line is vanishing, and soon fraternal feelings will extend to the Gulf; and then will there be the great East and West to behold the rising and setting of the sun."

The heavy rumbling of the distant thunder continued, and while listening to its reverberations the Veteran's eye again revealed the old fire.

Presently he said, as if speaking to himself: —

"The Union-loving States! sisters, bound by common bonds of pride and grief, — pride that each like a Spartan mother had sent out its myriads of children to fight for liberty, — grief when thousands were laid low amid the thunders of war which vied with these that echo through the sky, — and pride again that each fallen son had found a patriot's grave! Every State sent forth its heroes, whose record enriches its archives." Then suddenly turning his gaze on the young Lieutenant he exclaimed with unwonted energy: "The dead shall not be forgotten! The States shall not forget them! Neither shall the Republic! Their memory shall be held even more sacred in the next generation than in this! Neither shall the living whom the dead have left pass from the minds of this nation! — Prescott, I feel that the moment is not far distant when my tongue is to fail me. I would therefore adjure you as a Comrade to ever hold high the standard of that Order which, like this voice of Heaven that succeeds the thunder-clap, shall sustain the tones with which Liberty made the whole earth tremble!"

Prescott bent his head, while his face, reflecting the solemn inspiration of the dying Thorbolt, glowed with the soul's deep and holy resolve. The heavens seemed cognizant of this scene; for at that moment the lightning darted for the first time from the clouds upon which the Veteran had gazed, and was followed by a peal much nearer than those that had preceded it, which thundered over the now darkening world with a sound that impressed the silent group as if the Eternal Voice were speaking to them.

Soon these clouds were lit up by almost incessant flashes; and as the twilight pervading the room was illuminated by the lurid glare, those who still listened in awed silence to the nearing thunder gazed steadfastly on the upturned face. As the mighty concussions shook the earth beneath them, that face, so grand in health, now assumed an aspect of sublimity. It seemed to partake of the character of those white, rugged cloud-tops, which so often present colossal semblances of men, with marked features and swelling muscles, the effect increased by the infinite sky beyond, against which they stand out in surpassing relief. The spirit was evidently moved by scenes of war, which the thunder-storm with its vivid flashes called up before the great cavalry leader's fading sight; while immediately beyond, the eternal heaven appeared to enhance the power of this last manifestation of enkindled mortality.

Erelong this expression gave way to a look of ineffable tranquillity, which the resounding heavens served but to increase. It was a look that gave those who gazed a realization of the tranquillity to come, when with the mortal body laid off, the spirit may labor on, if such be the will of God, rendered infinitely more efficient by the heavenly peace, which even on the earth so signally adds to the powers of him who is blessed with its divine presence.

Silence still pervaded the room, except that occasionally

an awed whisper might have been heard, as the eye was directed toward the Veteran, who lay as if contemplating scenes beyond their power to conceive. In the midst of this silence the door was gently opened, and a slight form stood trembling at the threshold. It was William Garvin.

As he thus stands hesitating to come forward, one is reminded of the time he stood by the door of Allen Paige's chamber, when that patriot was passing to the higher life; except that now he is much thinner even than he was then, and there are plainly perceptible the marks of wearing anguish.

The Veteran seemed at once to realize the presence of this new-comer. Looking toward him he smiled, and beckoned him to his bedside.

The young artist, his face quivering with emotion, hastened to obey, and falling on his knees, clasped the Veteran's hand. Breaking into loud sobs, he covered it with his tears.

"O my friend!" he uttered between his sobs, — "my friend! — my friend! Do not leave me now! Ah! if I too could die!"

"William," said the Veteran, gently, while a slight dampness suffused those eyes whose fountains were now gradually drying up, "your turn will come in due time. If I am your friend, what do you think He can be, who in his providence is taking me home?" He stopped a moment, for he could not sustain his speech as he had previously, and then continued in a voice in which was mingled deep solemnity and touching pathos: "Look, William, to that dear Father who, as I lie here awaiting the final call, I tell you is kinder than you can ever realize in your present existence. And you have a Guide, who has made known this Father. Learn of Him, follow His counsels, and tell me when you shall join me in Heaven if happiness has not been yours."

William, with a renewed outburst of grief, kissed the Veteran's hand, and sobbed, —

"I 'll try! yes! yes! I 'll stay and try! — Alone! alone! I shall be indeed alone!"

"HE will ever be near you."

"Ever near me," repeated the desolate youth. Rising then to his feet, he leaned over the bed with an irresistible impulse and kissed the broad, pale forehead, exclaiming, "Farewell, my best of friends! farewell!" Then turning, he approached Emma and Prescott, and convulsively seizing the hand of each, he placed one in the other. He tried to speak; but his voice failed him, and with one silent, pleading look for forgiveness which Emma returned with tearful eyes, he hastened from the room to spend his brief remaining life in travelling over the world, and doing good with the money the broker had left, deriving from his acts of benevolence and a prayerful spirit the comfort the dying warrior had promised him.

* * * * *

It was nigh unto midnight. The storm had passed, and the thunder had hushed its voice. Hushed, too, was the voice of the Veteran, for he had slept his last sleep. He commenced sinking rapidly immediately after the storm had ceased, as if the grand commotion of the elements had lent the spirit strength to stay for a space the progress of dissolution. For several hours he had in his unconscious intervals re-enacted, as did the patriot merchant, the scenes of battle through which he had passed, and now the windows of that mortal casement were needed no more, for the soul had left the mortal to put on immortality.

CONCLUSION.

IT is the 30th of May, 1868. The bells toll throughout the land, the booming minute-gun mingles its tones with their brazen notes, and columns of marching men, with votive garlands in their hands, move to the graves of their fallen comrades to the measure of the solemn dirge.

It is MEMORIAL DAY, — the day instituted by the Grand Army of the Republic for decorating the graves of the Union dead.

It is a day ordained for the expression of a nation's grateful heart. The bells, the guns, the dirge, the solemn tread, the draped flag, — all speak the nation's sorrow. But the garlands, — they speak the love which ennobles and sanctifies all grief. As the angels look down upon our land this day, they see these floral offerings wet with many tears.

Nothing connected with the history of the Rebellion will command the respect of future generations in a more marked degree than this national memorial service. It derives no part of its impressiveness from ambition, love of strife, or taste for adventure; but as a bereaved family gather around the last resting-places of their dear ones, and strew the graves with flowers, and consecrate them with prayer and affection's silent tear, so on this day does a grateful nation gather about the mounds where sleep the patriot dead, with floral offerings to their memory.

As the future reader of history shall look back on this sublime observance, he will exclaim, "*The nation had a living soul!*"

It has been objected to this service that it will serve to perpetuate ill-feeling between the two sections of the country. Such fears are groundless. No complete harmony is possible without sincere contrition on the part of those who took up arms against their country, and no sincere contrition is possible, unless they perceive their wrong, and stand ready to thank those who saved them from accomplishing their own ruin. When they once stand in this position, they will express in stronger terms their gratitude to the memory of their country's defenders than it is possible for them to do who took no part in the fratricidal strife.

Those who are continually uttering their fears, as one form of permanent memorial to the Union dead follows another, that all these things will keep alive the bitterness of the South, represent no spirit of magnanimity, but rather that disposition which in private life is forever expressing apprehensions of ceaseless troubles between one party and another, thereby aggravating difficulties which but for their folly would be speedily adjusted. Reconciliation is not secured by timid fears, but by boldness in doing what is right.

We turn and gaze upon the lineaments of a martyred soldier, a general of the Union armies who loved his country, who fought for it in the highest spirit of patriotism, and died a sacrifice on its holy altar. Shall his countrymen, who revere his memory, abstain from a public expression of their sentiments for fear of injuring the feelings of those who slew him while fighting to uphold the Stars and Stripes? If he could speak to us, would he not say that they who advocate a course so pernicious are but inviting a future repetition of the great crime of the recent Rebellion? If all the patriot dead could rise and speak to us from the spirit which actuated their going forth to offer up their lives for freedom, would they not tell us that these baneful utterances should serve to make all loyal men the more strenuous in their determination to perpetuate those memories that make the love of country and its liberty to be prized and held in the highest honor? For such unwise deference to the feelings of pardoned Rebels offers a premium to their crime; and future generations will look back to see nothing but a duel in that which was the most momentous war that the world had witnessed, — a duel where the opposing parties met to fight, and then shake hands, with a tacit understanding that when their honor is again wounded they will fight it out, and again shake hands.

Let us not be in haste. So deep a wound as this country has just received cannot be healed in a day; and the future welfare of the whole body politic must not be endangered through anxiety to secure so factitious a result. Let the healing process go on through the healthy co-operation of natural laws, and then it will be lasting. And among the manifestations of these laws is the country's testimonial to the memory of its defenders.

On this first Memorial Day a group were gathered about two grassy mounds rising side by side, and strewn with garlands of flowers. Of those who composed the group there was one who could not fail to attract attention by the loveliness of her inspired countenance. Taking in each hand a wreath, she advanced between these graves, and lifting her eyes to heaven she for a moment moved her lips in silence, and then kneeling, kissed the wreaths and placed them on the mounds. Then a young man went gently forward and raised her.

"Prescott," she said, "their comrades have strewn their graves with these precious garlands, and your dear hand was with them. O, bless you all! I weep, dear husband, but I am not unhappy." And she whom we have known as Emma Paige leaned her head on the bosom of Prescott Marland, her husband, while tears she could not restrain flowed like a silent river down her cheeks.

The graves, on which she had placed her heart's offering with such holy affection, were the last resting-places of all that was mortal of Allen Paige and the Veteran.

The relatives of the latter, who was unmarried, notwithstanding a pleasant jest uttered to the young Lieutenant which the reader may possibly remember, had, on learning the circumstances, cheerfully consented that he should be thus buried beside that comrade whose widowed wife and fatherless children had found in him so noble a benefactor.

The mother, Alice, Albert, and Little Dorrit also, all were there; and with them were the merchant, and he who, formerly a book-keeper, is now a partner.

Mrs. Paige, whose own memorial offerings had been given, approached those two whom wedlock had made her own, and looking upon the mounds with eyes that bore the signs of recent weeping she said with ineffable tenderness,—

"Our hearts are indeed made both sad and happy this day. Sadness we feel; but ah! it is a blessed privilege to have them here, side by side, to receive these tokens of our love and gratitude. And O, how happy the assurance, that by the hands of those who call them comrades these precious mounds shall in the years to come be strewn with love's garlands, like these sweet flowers they have placed here to-day with such fraternal tenderness!" For a moment she gazed upon the graves in silence; then she said, "It was indeed a Heaven-inspired thought, to bind the army here remaining with that army gone before with these memorials of the heart's deep affection."

When she ceased, a faint strain of music floated through

the air from a distant cemetery. As it reached the widow's ears she looked above, and with the eye of faith beheld the myriads of transfigured comrades gathered together, and chanting to the Lord God, while in sacred accompaniment the pealing notes of the celestial organ rose with their swelling voices through the archways of Eternal Heaven. And she saw hosts of angels bearing in their hands immortal wreaths, with which to crown each comrade as he shall pass from earth to join in responsive anthems to the annual utterance of a nation's prayer, — till the last surviving Soldier of the Union shall have performed the sacred office of Memorial Day, and then ascended to receive upon his brow the final wreath, and answer to the heavenly roll-call, "HERE!"

THE END.

Cambridge: Electrotyped and Printed by Welch, Bigelow, & Co.

www.ingramcontent.com/pod-product-compliance
Lightning Source LLC
Chambersburg PA
CBHW021537110726
47902CB00004B/923
* 9 7 8 3 3 3 7 0 6 4 9 9 0 *